This book is a work of fiction. Names, characters, places, and incidents are either the product of the author's imagination or are used fictitiously, and any resemblance to actual persons, living or dead, events or locales is entirely coincidental.

No part of this book may be reproduced or transmitted in any form or by any means, electronic or mechanical, including photocopying, recording or by any information storage and retrieval system without the written permission of the author, except for the use of brief quotations in a book review.

Copyright © 2018 by Andrea Long.
This version © 2022 by Andrea Long.
All rights reserved.

Cover design and formatting by Tammy.

THE VAMPIRE WANTS A WIFE

SUPERNATURAL DATING AGENCY
– BOOK ONE

Chapter 1

Shelley

Another freaking troll.

After a year in business running a dating agency, I still got frustrated by pranksters who wrote out ridiculous application forms. This loser obviously had nothing better to do as he had filled out the entire questionnaire extensively. Most morons put a stupid name like Superman and then followed it up with swear words as the answer to every question. Seeing as this one had made an effort, and it was Monday morning and my coffee hadn't sunk in yet, I decided to sit back and read it. Perhaps I'd print it off for when I wrote my book at the end of my dating agency career, *Confessions of a Matchmaker*.

Name: *Theodore Robert Landry*
 Date of birth: *1 January 1891*
 Age: *126*
 Hair: *Black*
 Skin colour: *Alabaster*
 Height: *Six feet two inches*
 Weight: *Perfect*
 Any distinguishing features? *I'm a vampyre, so fangs?*
 Place of Birth: *Goodacres Farm, Withernsea, East Yorkshire*
 Current address: *The Basement, 27 Sea View Road, Withernsea. (I was thrown out of my place of birth on becoming a vampire. I'm on a quest to win my home back, but currently my duel has not been accepted. They keep sending a policeman around asking me to desist).*

Any family history of note: *All deceased. I was the only family member to survive. The rest of my family were drained of their blood. It was difficult at first but it's true time is a healer. I think fondly of them now. It's quite usual for a newly turned vampire to kill their family members by accident.*

Favourite food:*A classic O-neg, preferably drunk straight from the source. I note you don't ask blood type on your application. That may be something for you to consider for future.*

Ideal dating venue: *Can only be after 8pm, up until 4am, to be on the safe side. A nice, dark environment such as a park, graveyard, nightclub, restaurant (I can eat human food, but it has no calorific value for me) would be ideal.*

Reason for Application

I have been trying to find a wife now for several years. I am extremely good looking and have a vast intellect due to my many years on this earth. Unfortunately, when I discuss the fact my girlfriend would have to be turned into a vampire and be my wife long into the eternal night, they leave. Usually rather rapidly. I am therefore reaching out in these modern times to your dating agency. Your tagline promises to find 'your ideal partner'. My ideal partner preferably would be a vampire like myself, complete with no heartbeat, but should you not have such members on your books, a beautiful human lady who is willing to be turned would suffice.

Jesus! I clicked on the attached photograph, fully expecting to see a dick pic, but instead there was a picture of a pale-faced sex-god-like creature. He couldn't be real because he was far too fucking hot. It would be a model shot. I quickly did a Google image search of the photo, but nothing came back. Hmm, interesting.

At that point the door burst open, making me upend my still hot coffee down my front. I jumped up and down doing the dance of the scalded, wafting my top and holding it away from my skin. "Oh, God. Oh fucking God. That's hot. That is fucking hot."

"Oh my, he is fucking hot," said my assistant and best friend,

Kim, looking at my screen. "You fanning yourself for a coffee burn or for this stud muffin?"

"Want to share why you're an hour late?" I'd long ago learned to expect Kim when I saw her. She never missed an appointment or meeting but believed her hours were completely flexible.

"I got the chance for a penis power hour, so I took it," she said, unfazed. "Anyway, go dry your top while I read this application."

"I'm going to pop to Ebony's downstairs and buy a new one. Screw it." Our office was situated above a boutique, on a block that housed a café and a pet grooming salon. It was a great mix of female business owners, and we had a collective that met monthly, *Female Entrepreneurs do it with their Colleagues.* I'd not had the heart to tell Jax from the café that it sounded all kinds of wrong. She was a sensitive soul and likely to close the café for a few days if upset, and no one needed a lack of coffee and cake. No one.

I walked down the back stairs, out to the rear of the property and through the front entrance of the shop. Ebony took one look at me and shook her head.

"I know. Kim made me spill my coffee down myself."

"Oh, honey," Ebony said in her cut-glass accent. "Kim did you a huge favour. That top needs a cremation. RIP to the shapeless v-neck."

I groaned. Ebony was always trying to give me a makeover, and I just liked to keep things simple. Truthfully, I wasn't a power suit kind of girl. I preferred to meet clients looking like someone they felt comfortable to chat with intimately. It was through getting to know them that I knew who to match them up with. I was amazing at my job and had one of the most successful dating agencies in England. The irony being that the only person I couldn't find an ideal date for was myself. Running through my own application there had so far been no one who had measured up as a fit for me. I was awkward and picky and destined to be on my own forever.

"Here we go. This is what we need you in, darling. It will highlight that red hair and pale skin." Ebony held up a black tight tank top with a red rose on the front. It had an overlay of black netting. It would go with the skinny jeans I was wearing, but goth girl really wasn't me. I was a jeans and plain tee wearing girl who on the rare occasion she got dressed up would wear floral tea dresses.

"Have you got something else, a little lighter in colour?" I asked.

"No, sorry, I have nothing else in your size."

I looked around the rest of the well-stocked boutique and raised an eyebrow.

Ebony exuded calm. "All of this stock is pre-ordered. You can only have the top you're holding."

I sighed and handed over my credit card and went into the changing rooms to change it over. Looking in the dressing room mirror I saw that Ebony was totally right. It really did suit my complexion. Maybe I should adopt a goth girl persona and start watching *The Corpse Bride* and wear black lipstick?

Ebony clapped her manicured hands complete with red talons when I emerged from the changing rooms. "Look at you. A vision. Can I curl your hair up a little before you leave?"

"No," I snapped. "Leave me alone, you're giving me a complex."

"Darling, you keep wondering why you're single and I'm trying to help you. He's coming you see. The one for you. We need you ready for him."

I raised an eyebrow again. "Ebony, are you pissed from last night still? How many voddies did you have? Or do you have a bottle behind the counter again, because I've told you, it will put customers off if you dance with them. How many times have we had this conversation now?"

Ebony's gaze darted towards the door, then she lowered her voice. "Look, I will confess all. I drink vodka at times because the thoughts become too much, too intense. If I'm a little mellow, I can cope and they dissipate. Otherwise, I get bad migraines. Anyway, I've not had any alcohol today, but I'm receiving strong thoughts when you are around. That you must be prepared because your 'one' is coming."

I rubbed at my eyes. This day was clearly sent to test my patience. But I needed to tread carefully with Ebony, and to chat to Kim and Jax about keeping a close eye on her. It was a struggle to run a business on your own, and I was concerned she might be drinking a little too much. I decided to give in, purchase the top, and let her do my hair.

She sat me on a stool at the counter and wound my long hair around tongs until I had the most beautiful spiral curls. I would never have taken the time to do this for myself. Ebony reached for some cosmetics that she had displayed under the counter. I was about to protest when her mouth set in a pout. I sighed and let her put makeup on me. I could always call down the corner shop on the next block for some baby wipes to take it off if I found it too much. In the meantime, three customers had come in and were watching Ebony at work. It turned into a makeup class. I felt like I was on freaking QVC.

"Voila. Go back to the changing rooms and see!"

I hopped off the stool and looked at myself in the mirror. I hardly recognised the person looking back. She'd put bronzer on my face and used the cosmetics to give me a healthy glow instead of my usual wan look.

"Okay." I came back out. "I admit defeat. You're amazing."

"I know." She smiled as she wrapped up makeup sets for the three women who were watching. "You need this." She held up a fourth set. "So altogether that's fifty-three pounds eighty pence with your staff discount." She waved the credit card I'd handed over earlier and I nodded and watched as she rang me up. I was going to kill Kim. That coffee spill had set me back a small fortune.

I went back upstairs and stood in the doorway. Kim was still sitting in front of my computer.

"So, what do you need me to do…?" She paused. "Holy fuck, where's Shelley? Seriously, where's she gone? Who is this beautiful creature in front of me? I'm straight as they come, but hell, I reckon I could be persuaded."

I crossed my arms. "Ebony decided I needed a makeover, and it's cost me the best part of sixty quid so don't expect a bonus this month."

"Hey." Kim waved her hands in the air. "I wasn't the one who got so flustered looking at Mr Hot Vampire that I spilled my drink down myself."

"Oh yes. That reminds me, can you contact him and send him a decline email?"

Kim looked down at the floor. "Oh, where's my earing gone?"

I gave her a pinched stare. "You don't have pierced ears, Kim. Sit up straight and look me in the eyes. What have you done?"

"Welllll…" She bit on her lip. "His photo is reaalllly hot, and I thought we didn't get too many sexy men coming in, so I sent him an appointment for the next stage."

"You did what?" I screamed. "He's just a troll. Or maybe he actually believes he's a vampire and is struggling with his mental health. What if he tries to bite one of us?"

She shrugged. "I don't think he would because he's an old

vampyre, spelled the old-fashioned way. He must have got past that fledgling stage long ago."

"He's *not* a real vampire."

"I know, but since *True Blood* finished, I'm desperately missing Eric. Also, Ian Somerhalder got all married and loved up. Let's interview the hottie. And if he has got delusions we could direct him to a mental health service couldn't we? I really don't think he'll try to bite us. Not if he wants us to find him a wife."

"Kim, could you, as my assistant, please get me another coffee, and a chocolate doughnut. Things are stressful today. Now, what time have you arranged for Mr Landry to come for an interview?"

"I said eight pm, at Hanif's."

"Hanif's? The Indian restaurant?"

"Yes, it's dark. Mr Landry can't come out before then."

"Go get me my coffee. Do not forget the doughnut. In fact, make it two doughnuts. Go now."

"God, you're in a mood. Are you jealous cos I got some this morning?"

"Make that a box of doughnuts. A box of twelve," I shouted after her swinging backside.

Chapter 2

Shelley

"So..." Kim tried to look innocent, gazing up through her dark fringe.

"Why aren't you looking ready?" I asked her. We'd been working up until we needed to set off for the date. She owed the hours due to her 'flexitime' working.

"So, I can't make it," she said. "I totally forgot I had a doctor's appointment booked for eight. Sorry I double-booked, but I'm sure you'll be okay with the vamp."

I sighed heavily. "Firstly, he is *not* a real vampire. Secondly, there are no doctor's appointments happening after five pm at our practice. What the hell are you talking about?"

"I do have a doctor's appointment." She pouted. "With Dr Francis Love. In his bedroom, at eight pm."

"Go." I made shooing motions at her with my hands. "I've heard enough of your nonsense today. I will deal with Mr Landry myself."

"That's hurtful you know? Saying I talk nonsense. You're mean. A mean boss. I'll need to come in late tomorrow, so I have time to work through my hurt feelings."

With that she gave me a wink and walked through the door, leaving me to grab my fake leather jacket and head to Hanif's.

~

"Hey, Rav. I'm meeting a Mr Landry."

Rav, one of the waiters at Hanif's, had rushed over to greet me on my arrival.

"Yes, yes. He is here. He asked to be seated in the back corner. I will take you through to him."

I followed Rav to the back of the restaurant. The smell of delicious spices wafted up my nose and made my stomach rumble. I'd not had any lunch, having been stuffed full of chocolate doughnuts, and now my body was reminding me it needed sustenance. As Theodore turned to face me, another part of my body made its feelings known. Yeah, my vag definitely needed sustenance. It had been a *long* time.

He was even more striking in the flesh. That dark hair and his dark, almost black looking irises contrasted against the paleness of his skin. I thought I was pale, but I think he even outdid me. I wondered if he was anaemic. He had a slight rosy glow to his cheeks, which might have been a little show of embarrassment or nervousness. Oh, bless him. He stood up and held out his hand, towering over my five-foot-seven frame.

"Miss Linley?"

I held out my hand. "Mr Landry."

His hands were cold to the touch, rather like my feet when I got in bed at night. I felt myself tremble slightly, but that might have been due to him being majorly hot, rather than cold.

"Call me Theo, please."

"Okay, well, I'm Shelley." Like I said, I preferred being down to earth with my clients. Now I just had to wait for this one to admit to pranking me and we could get on with finding him a match.

Rav came over to us. "Can I get you any drinks?"

"Erm, a glass of white wine for me, Rav, please." I rarely drank on the job, but then again, I rarely interviewed someone who thought he was a vampire.

"Small, or large?"

"The biggest you have."

"Two glasses and you get the bottle free?"

I sucked on my top lip and nodded. "Sold. Bring the bottle, my man."

"And for you, sir?"

"A glass of red please. Do you have a Merlot?"

"Yes, sir." He handed us a menu each. "I shall get your drinks and will be back to take your food order."

We nodded.

"So," Theo said. "What happens at this follow up interview?"

I placed a napkin over my lap, feeling edgy and like I needed to do something. "I go through the questionnaire with you. Ask any additional questions I may have, and then if everything is in order, I run it through the computer programme back at the agency and see if we have some matches for you."

"And if you don't?"

"You can either stay on our books as new people join all the time, or you are of course free to try another agency."

"But there are no other agencies in Withernsea."

"Yes, but there are agencies around the country, the world even, and the internet is a big place. I'm sure you could find someone."

"I have more chance of finding a mate in Withernsea. This is where my kind live."

Here it was.

"Your kind, as in vampire?"

"Of course. What else could I mean?" He looked at me with a furrowed brow.

"Er, nothing. Let me get my paperwork out of my bag."

"After dinner," he said. "Let's enjoy the meal first and you can get to know me better."

Great. I had planned to go through the questionnaire, declare him unsuitable, and hot tail it out of here. Although looking at the menu I could see they had prawn puri, my absolute favourite. Hey, hang on, vampires couldn't be near garlic, could they? That's what Kim said. Hmm, what would happen if I ordered a garlic and coriander naan bread? I decided to go along with his prank and turn it against him.

Our drinks arrived and Rav got his notebook and pen ready.

"And for you, sir?"

I hated that. Why did they ask the guy what they wanted first? Totally sexist. Bastard.

"I will have a chicken balti, with a plain naan bread. Thank you."

"No starter for you, sir?"

"No, thank you. I'm afraid I already ate a little before I came."

I pulled a face. Who did that? Arranged a dinner and then ate already. Wanker.

"And for you, madam?"

I wanted a starter. I wanted prawn puri, but now dickwad wasn't having one, I wouldn't either. Otherwise, I'd be here even longer than I needed to be.

I studied the menu while sucking on my bottom lip. "I will have... let's see... I'd like your Chef's special: the garlic chicken, and garlic and coriander naan bread."

Rav leaned over and whispered in my ear. "This is why you're single."

I gave him a dirty look. "This is a business dinner."

"Okay then. Food coming right up." Rav scurried away.

"You say you ate already?" I asked him. "You might not want to arrange dinner with a woman if you've already eaten beforehand."

"It was just my regular O-neg," he said. "Obviously without it, I'd die." He showed me his teeth. "Are they a little red stained? That's why I ordered a glass of red, it disguises the blood stains."

I sighed.

"Look, Theo, can we just drop this whole 'you're a vampire' thing?"

"But I am a vampire."

"No, you're not. Vampires aren't real."

"I am." He sat up straight. "How old are you?"

I folded my arms across my chest. "Not that it's any of your business, but I'm twenty-six."

"Well, I'm one hundred years your senior, so in this circumstance, I'm afraid you need to have some respect and believe me when I tell you that I am a vampire."

I was about to get up and leave, but Rav brought over a pickle tray and some poppadoms and I was weak.

"Fine, you're a vampire."

Theo breathed out a sigh of relief. "Usually at this point the woman leaves. Admit it. If you were a date, you would have left by now."

"If I wasn't hungry, I would have left." I bit into a poppadom and decided to humour him a little. "You might have to not tell people at first, maybe? So that they get to know you as a person before you confess your secret?"

"Hmmm. I don't know."

I met his cool gaze. "Look, let's practice tonight. While we eat dinner, pretend you're not a vampire, but a regular human guy." I pointed. "Like Rav, a regular guy like Rav."

"Rav is not a regular guy. Rav is a demon," Theo replied. A

crease appeared between his eyebrows. "How long have you lived in Withernsea? You are not very aware of your surroundings. I was told the people of Withernsea were like the undead. That's why I stayed here."

It was one thing to insult me. It was quite another to insult my hometown.

"Hey. Just because we're a quiet seaside town does not mean you get to diss the people that live here."

Theo turned to me and started to chuckle.

"Do you know I have to take regular classes to keep up to date with modern technology and language? I only learned 'diss' in 2015. By the way, I very much like your outfit. You look dazzling, simply sensational."

"Pardon?" I was still trying to catch up with the 'classes to keep up-to-date' conversation.

"I'm pretending to be a human male, so I'm complimenting your outfit."

My jaw set. "Oh. You don't actually like it then? You're saying that because it's expected of a human male?"

"Well, I preferred the attire of my day, when you could catch a glimpse of a lady's bare ankle and think all your birthdays had come at once. Your outfit is quite acceptable though. The trousers are a little tight, but this is compensated by the flow of the top over your bottom. It clings over your breasts a little. Always remember, less is more. It creates lust in a man."

"Are you quite finished?" I was gripping my knife so hard my knuckles had turned white.

"I've already said I'm not eating until my main course."

Would it have been considered rude if I punched a potential client in the throat?

"Why do you think you haven't already found the woman of your dreams? Do you think it might be your way with words?" I huffed.

His eyes dropped to the floor and his mouth downturned. "I don't know how to approach a woman anymore. Once upon a time they wanted you to take charge. Now they want to be equal. My head's all over the place with how to approach a date. I've had over one thousand girlfriends. I'm very jaded about the whole thing."

One thousand girlfriends? He needed to be on *The Bachelor,* not the books of my dating agency. Okay, if he'd not found a wife in over one thousand girlfriends there was definitely something wrong with him; something more than him believing he was a vampire. Surely, there'd be at least one Withernsea woman who'd take one look at Theo, and let him play vampire in bed every night?

The smell of garlic permeated the air as our main courses were brought to the table. Theo didn't flinch. I waited until Rav had left and tore off a piece of garlic naan. I threw it at Theo's face to see if he had a reaction.

He reared back in his seat. "What are you doing?"

Hmmm, a little reaction. Not sure the garlic touched him though. I took my fork and flicked some of my garlic chicken sauce at his hands. Once again, he leapt back, shaking his fingers. He picked up the water jug from our table and poured some over his hand.

Rav ran over. "Is everything okay?"

"Is it Indian culture to throw food at your friend while they eat?" Theo asked.

Rav turned to me, and I looked away.

"Shelley?"

"I'm sorry, I have a small twitch." I punched out my arm and wiggled it around. "Must have been a trapped nerve. It seems to be okay now."

Rav leaned over again "This is why you're sin—"

"I get it," I snapped. "Tomorrow, I'll book in for *The Undateables* and appear on TV, okay?"

"What is this *Undateables*?" Theo asked. "I don't watch much TV. Just the news and *Celebs Go Dancing*."

We took our seats again. Theo wiped his hands on his table napkin.

"*Celebs Go Dancing?*"

"Yes, I love watching the old-style dances and of course you have to support your own."

I took a deep breath. "Go on."

"Sophia is one of us. Can you not tell, with all that dark hair and eyeliner, plus the fact she never appears to age?"

"Sophia Coleman is a vampire?" I clarified.

"Yes. She bit Ken. That's the real reason he retired as head judge last year."

Help me, God. Help me now. If the chicken hadn't tasted so damn fine, I would have run for the hills. That and the fact that

Theo was *so* pleasing on the eye. I made a note to pick up an *Undateables* application form. They'd probably snap my hand off. A dating agency owner who could find love for everyone else but herself.

I began to feel guilty about the garlic incident. "Sorry about the food. Pass me your hand. Let me check I didn't harm you."

Theo wiggled his wrist at me. "No harm done."

"Ha. I knew you weren't a vampire," I spat.

"Pardon?"

"Garlic. It was a test. I touched you with garlic. You should have burned or something."

Theo sat back in his seat; his eyes wide.

"That is folklore. Vampires do not react to garlic. But it concerns me that in order to check this fact you threw not one, but two items of garlic containing foodstuffs at me, knowing that the potential was there for me to burn. You would wish me harm? I have done nothing to deserve it."

Theo pushed his chair further back. "I made a mistake coming here. I'm not sure I'm altogether safe in your company. You're making me feel uncomfortable and apprehensive." He took his wallet out of his jacket pocket.

I was making the vampire dude feel apprehensive? Well, there was an outcome I wasn't expecting.

"Theo, I'm sorry. I didn't really think it would do anything."

"Then why try?"

"I just wanted to show you that you weren't a vampire."

Theo stared at me. "I see."

"Please would you let me get in touch with a doctor on your behalf? Maybe ring MIND?"

"I think I'll get the bill now," he said, shutting down the conversation.

He insisted on paying the bill, and we sat in an uncomfortable silence, until Rav had dealt with us.

"How are you getting home?" Theo asked.

"On the bus." The number 46 bus was due on the half hour, so I intended to make my way to the bus stop around the corner.

"Would you like a lift home?" he offered. "You would have to make a vow to not try to cause me harm."

"No, it's fine. I'm sorry about the food throwing thing. It wasn't very professional of me. Maybe you could call into the office tomorrow afternoon, and I'll go through your application with you then?"

"Do you have an appointment around five?"

Of course. He needed vampire hours. What was it about him that prevented me from telling him to get lost? It was like he had an allure. Yeah, Shelley. More like you have horny hormones. I was due on at any moment and always felt like I could mount my bedposts when I was like this.

We'd just got outside when I felt a tell-tale trickle. Well, that was a fitting end to this awkward evening. Time to go to bed with a hot water bottle.

"Aaarrrgh."

I turned to see what was up with Theo now. Perhaps he had a weak stomach for Indian spices? I froze in place—stunned—as right in front of me two fangs descended, and his eyes went red.

"Aaarghhhhhhhhhh. You're a vampire," I screamed, turning on my heel and running as fast as I could towards the bus stop where I could see the number 46 in the distance.

Theo ran after me, catching up to me with lightning, unnatural speed. Before I knew it, he put me in his arms and ran with me. In what seemed like five seconds I was outside my door, trying my best to not vomit up my garlic chicken.

"Wh-what, th-the...? Wh-what the...?" I repeated.

But when I turned around Theo was gone.

Chapter 3

Shelley

I unlocked the door of my two-bedroomed semi-detached home and staggered through to the sofa where I sprawled out. What the hell had just happened?

It was the wine; I had drunk most of a bottle. Or... *Theo had spiked it!*

But that made little sense because he'd brought me home and left me. Surely the point of spiking my drink would be to take advantage of me?

Hey, how did he know where I lived? *OMG. Theo was a stalker!*

But that made no sense either because if he was a stalker, he would have been hanging around here and work, wouldn't he? Not meeting me in restaurants where everyone could see him.

There was no way he had fangs and red eyes.

I decided I must have fallen asleep on the sofa after getting home and I must have just woken up. That would be it. I went out, had too much wine, Theo brought me to the door and then I'd had a bad dream.

I rolled onto my back and stared at the ceiling. Right now, I didn't feel the slightest bit drunk. In fact, I felt perfectly okay, except for thoughts of the weirdness of the evening. I replayed what I'd seen in my mind.

Canines descending.

Eyes going red.

No fucking way. He must have put something in my drink. He'd got to have.

I got his questionnaire out of my bag. It was only a quarter to eleven and in any case, if he was a vampire, he'd be up all night, right?

Finding his number from the papers, I called him from my mobile.

"Hello?"

"Theo. It's Shelley."

"Shelley. Oh thank goodness you called. I thought it best I leave you, but I wasn't sure if I was doing the right thing. Are you okay? Are you in shock? Perhaps you could get yourself a cup of tea with a few sugars?"

"Theo, I'm going to come right out and say it. Did you spike my drink? Because I've had some weird thoughts tonight."

"Ah."

"Ah...? Do you mean you did?"

"No." He sighed. "I mean ah, you've done what everyone else does—enter into the stages of supernatural denial. 'Oh, there must be some logical explanation. I didn't really see his fangs and a flash of a red eye or two'. No, far more reasonable to suggest to the nice gentleman who took me for dinner that he drugged me."

I sighed. "There's no other explanation."

"Other than the fact I'm a vampire."

"I don't think I can help you find a date or a wife, Theo. Your behaviour is... unusual."

"You threw naan bread and curry at me to see if the garlic burned, yet you say I sound unusual."

Damn. The guy had a point.

"The problem is that I've never met a supernatural person before, and well, I just don't believe in it. There has to be a logical explanation; like for instance your family have dental issues and there's some weird genetic defect that makes your eyes look a funny colour, probably in a certain light."

"Or it could be that my vampire nose detected the sweet smell of blood coming from between your thighs and because it took me by surprise and my guard was down, your sweet perfume made my fangs descend."

"Ugh. That's the sickest thing I ever heard. Menstruation is not sexy."

"I didn't say it was. What I said was the smell appealed to my vampire nature. I don't and won't ever drink that. It's not pure."

"And that's the end of that conversation. I don't know why I called. Why I expected anything you said to make any sense."

"Yet you did call. Because one small part of you, Shelley... one small part deep inside you, wonders if I am telling the truth."

I sat back against the sofa. Did I want this to be the truth? Maybe so. Maybe it would provide some excitement in my boring life. Yes, I had good friends here, but I didn't have family around. I was adopted and had never gotten along with my adoptive parents. Not after they had a child naturally ten months later and made sure I knew that I wouldn't have been adopted had that pregnancy test showed positive earlier than it did. Oh well, I was a career woman, I decided. I didn't need a social life, or a man. Instead, I'd carry on matchmaking for everyone else.

"Are you still there?"

Shit. I'd gone off into one of my 'fuck you all, I don't need anyone' daydreams. Actually, if it was at night, shouldn't it be called a nightdream?

"Look, Shelley, I'm going to Facetime you, and slowly show you my fangs again, and this time you have to try not to freak out. Although you probably will. It usually takes a person three viewings before they believe they're real. The third time they always want to touch them, like I'd want someone's dirty fingers in my mouth."

"A vampire who sucks people's blood can't deal with dirty fingers?" I scoffed.

"Hygiene is everything. For years now my blood has been delivered. It's a long time since I had a woman who let me partake directly from the source."

"You don't grab people from the street and drain them dry?"

"No, and I don't sparkle either. Any more stereotypical questions in that head of yours?"

"You'd better Facetime me first."

The call came through. I accepted and there he was on the screen. My core went slick at the sight of him. Traitorous hussy.

"Are you ready?" he asked.

Oh God, yeeeaaass, came from the inner workings of my mind which was no doubt colluding with said traitorous hussy core. Instead, I went with a simple, "Yes."

He looked into the camera and opened his mouth to show a row of perfectly normal teeth.

I was disappointed.

He caught my expression. "Hold on there a second, Shelley. I can't just perform like that. I'm not a circus animal. Now let me get a drink." He held a glass of what looked like tomato juice up to the camera, but I got a feeling it wasn't tomato juice at all. I watched with morbid fascination as his fangs descended.

"Oh my god."

I slapped my hand over my mouth, careful not to drop the phone. "I'm sorry, blaspheming affects you, doesn't it?"

"Here we go again. Let's go over everything you think about vampires."

"Okay. So, you can hear the word God, etc?"

"Yes, and I can say 'holy crap' or anything like that."

"Can you go into a church?"

"I hope so, because I want to get married, remember? Although I'd have to use a fake ID as they never believe I'm 126. I do look fantastic for my age."

"Can a stake kill you?"

"Clarify. What sort? Steak meat or stake, stabby thing?"

"A stabby thing."

"No, another piece of misinformation. It's steak that can kill us. We have sensitive throats. It often gets stuck there and chokes my kind to death."

"And garlic has no effect?"

"No, unless it's in a fresh from the oven sauce and burns your skin."

I bit my lip. "Uhhmm, sorry about that."

"Just promise not to throw food at me again. Going forward."

"Going forward?"

"I'm seeing you again at five tomorrow. Do I need to wear protective armour?"

I laughed. "No. You'll be safe. From me at least."

He frowned. "Who might I not be safe from?"

"All the other women near where I work. You're not exactly ugly."

"I used to model you know?"

"You did?"

"Yeah, kept getting mobbed everywhere I went so had to fake my own death. That was Los Angeles in the 1950's."

"I can't get my head one hundred percent around you being a

vampire. Never mind that you would have lived a massively long life and have done and know so many things."

"I have lots of experience," he said, and he goddamn smirked.

Down girl, I told my pussy, and no I didn't have a cat. *Don't let your mind go there. Don't let your mind go there.*

How many women has he slept with?

Can he have normal sex?

Does he only have one penis? What if vampires had two? Oh my word, the possibilities...

"You've gone into a daydream again. I guess I'd better let you get some sleep," he said.

"Yes, sleep. So, you won't be sleeping yet?"

"No. I go to my room around six am and then I'll get up around four pm. The whole sunlight thing is a crock of shit too. I don't get badly burned. It's just that our body clocks are set for that time and to go against it can make us feel very ill."

"So, dating wise, you can only see a woman from four pm to six am?"

"Unless they come to my room. Although it wouldn't be much fun for them as I'm dead to the world then. Or of course, if they're a vampire themselves they could sleep with me, but that would only happen if things got serious."

"And do you sleep in a coffin?"

At this he guffawed. "No, I don't sleep in a coffin. I sleep in a perfectly normal, though King-sized bed, given my height. It has a lovely memory foam mattress. I do, however, have top security in the room and lock myself in with windows and shutters. I'm vulnerable when I'm asleep."

"What, someone might break in and stuff some pieces of steak down your throat?"

"Stranger things have happened to try to kill us in the past." His expression became subdued.

"So, how can you die?"

"There's a place we can go. You're counselled and then if they agree with your decision to end your life, you say a secret incantation and you crumble to dust."

"But can people kill you?"

"Why, was throwing naan bread not entertaining enough for you?" I laughed.

"We can be killed, but I'm not going to say how. The less people that know the better. No disrespect, but I barely know you."

"I understand."

"Time for bed now, Shelley."

Jesus, would he stop saying things like that? He had a low, growly voice that made it sound like a command.

I yawned. "Yes, time to call it a night. Thank you for showing me your fangs."

"Do you believe me?" he asked, looking at me with a hint of vulnerability in his eyes.

"Right now, I believe you. In the morning when the wine has left my system and my rational mind has had time to dissuade me from the evidence, then I'll probably need to put my filthy hands in your mouth."

"Well, seeing as it's you." He winked.

I ended the call and made my way up to my room. My lovely double bed, just for me. An advantage of living alone. My mind conjured up an image of a six-foot-two-inch hunk laid there with his feet hanging off the edge. I shook my head to make the vision go away.

"Enough already," I whispered. "We somehow have to find him a wife."

I visited the bathroom then quickly undressed, put on my pyjamas and then dived under the duvet. Sleep claimed me in minutes.

∽

"Shelley."

I sat up in bed. Who shouted?

A woman with long dark hair with a white streak running through it sat in a golden chair at the end of my bed.

But I didn't have a golden chair. And it was like, glowing.

"Shelley. Can you hear me?"

"Who are you?"

The woman clapped her hands. "Whoa! Can you hear and see me? At last! The curse is broken. You believe!"

"Who are you? What the hell are you talking about?"

"Sssh. Don't say hell. She doesn't like people using it to curse."

"Who doesn't?"

"Lucy."

"This is the strangest dream I've ever had. Now if you'll excuse me, I've had a mindfuck of a night already having potentially met a vampire, and so if my mind could let me have a restful night's sleep it would be much appreciated."

"This isn't a dream. I'm in *your dream because I'm not on your plane, but I'm really here."*

"Yeah? And who are you?"

She looked sad. "I'm your mother."

I bolted upright, sweat pouring from my forehead. Stupid dream. Meeting Theo had messed with my head. I picked up my phone to see what time it was and noticed I had a new message, sent thirty minutes before.

Theo: Just in case you wake up and wonder if it was all a dream...

Underneath was a photo of his fangs.

I was too tired to give it any more thought. I fell back to sleep and this time I didn't have strange dreams about the supernatural or my parents.

Chapter 4

Shelley

A miracle had occurred. When I'd got to work, Kim was already there, waiting, with a paper cup full of dark, delicious coffee on my desk and one in her hand.

"All messages taken care of. All you have to do is take a seat and tell me about Mr Dark and Delicious."

Ah, she had an agenda. Figured. Couldn't usually rouse her out of bed before nine thirty.

I slumped into the seat behind my desk and yawned.

Kim gasped. "Did you stay out all night? Was it love at first bite?"

I rolled my eyes. "Can you lower your voice, just a teeny tiny bit, only it's too early for diva operatics."

"God, what bit your arse, or rather did he not and you're disappointed this morning?"

I rubbed at my face. "I didn't sleep well. I had nightmares. Now, let me have a drink of my coffee and I'll update you."

Kim clapped her hands.

"I want deets. Every single detail of the evening." She winked.

I sighed and took several large gulps of my drink.

"Okay, so write this down." I indicated for Kim to pick up her pen and notepad.

"I. Am. A. Nosy. Bitch."

"Hahahaha." Kim tilted her head. "So, meal last night. What happened?"

"Well, basically it would appear that he is a vampire, but he has no aversion to garlic, which I found out when I threw some naan bread at him."

I recounted the details of the meal and Kim shook her head. "*Shelley*! I'm surprised we don't have a lawsuit on our hands this morning. You attacked a potential customer."

I stared at her. "That's all you have to say on the matter? Nothing about the fact he's a vampire?"

"Oh, if he wants to think he's one of the undead, as long as it doesn't hurt anyone, what's the harm? Might be a nice little kink for a boyfriend to have actually. My neck's quite an erogenous zone, a few little nips would be nice."

"No. He *is* a vampire. He showed me his fangs."

Kim huffed. "You're being very silly this morning, Shelley. So, are we taking him on our books?"

"He's coming in at five. I didn't get a chance to go through the questionnaire."

"Why not?"

"Because I was too busy trying to get him to admit to not being a vampire."

"Oh, Shelley." Kim tutted and once again shook her head. "We do very well at this agency, but there's always room for growth. He wants to live his life as a vampire. Where's the harm as long as he doesn't try to drain someone of their blood? There were three people living their lives as mermaids the other day on *This Morning*. They'd even done a course. One was a merman."

"Well, prepare to be here until six, because we're going through the questionnaire together. I want you to meet him and see what you think. I want a second opinion."

"Stay behind to stare at a hottie for an hour. Gee, I'm not sure I can fit that in. What time's he coming again? Phwoar o'clock?"

"Five."

"I couldn't think of anything that went with five." Kim pouted, her dark fringe falling in her eyes.

"So, how was your evening, anyway? With the love doctor."

A dreamy look settled on her face. "It was amazing. You see, he has a kink. He likes me to pretend I'm dead. I lay on the bed all corpse like, and he reanimates me with his magic wand." She winked.

I made a retching noise and pretended to heave. "Jesus Christ, Kim. That's weird."

"You need to get laid. I bet you've only ever done the missionary position. You'd have to lie really flat on your back with that stick stuck up your arse."

"I'm not going to respond to that."

"Because it's true. I'm going to quiz old True Blood to see if he'd like to take a bite out of you."

"You'll stick to the questionnaire and behave yourself. I'm not part of the system as you well know. How unprofessional would it be to put myself in the algorithm?"

"Shut up. Put yourself in when you get a spare five minutes. I do. It's just I have so many dates I don't need to use the info. Who matches up with you? Show me. We've got time."

"No."

"God, you're no fun today at all."

I looked at the floor.

Kim's mouth dropped open. "Does *no one* match up with you? Is that it? You're far too choosy, Shelley. If you don't change, you're going to be alone forever, and your fanny is going to heal up."

I placed my hands over my ears. "You can go to your office now. Go deal with the new clients. My ears are bleeding."

She left and I welcomed the silence. I fired up my laptop. Four new applications had come in since Kim had been in here.

I heard her door bang, and she rushed into my office. "Have you seen the new applications?"

"I've only just put my laptop on, Kim. You've only been out of the office for a few minutes."

"Well, it seems that True Blood is recommending you to his mates," she said, her eyes going wide as she smiled.

"You need to stop calling him that. His name is Theo."

"Anyway, open the first email." She beckoned for me to get a move on.

Name: *Darius Wild*

Supporting information: *Wolf shifter (also known as werewolf)*

Name: *Dominic Moore*

Supporting information: *Demon*

. . .

Name: *Isaac Renshaw*
Supporting information:*shifter (bear)*

I didn't bother to open the last one, scared of what I would find. Either someone was having a rather large laugh at my expense, or Withernsea, and indeed the world around me, wasn't what I thought it was.

"See, True Blood's obviously told his kinky friends about us. He's good for business," Kim said. "We just need to hope the women of Withernsea are up for some role play!"

∽

I immersed myself in work and debated whether I believed Theo to be a vampire. I went back to thinking he was a magician or a theatre prop person. The fang trick was obviously very clever make-up. Fancy me believing he was a real-life vampire! I really needed to quit watching *Twilight* repeats just to ogle Jasper.

Kim brought the post through. On the top lay a bright red envelope with my name written in a swirly font. "I've not opened that one as it looks like a personal invitation."

"Thank you," I told her and put the post on my desk.

"Aren't you going to open it?"

I folded my arms across my chest. "So you've not opened it for my privacy, but you want me to open it while you're here so you can see what it is?"

"Well, duh." She took a seat.

Give me strength.

I opened the envelope and took out the card within. A large, dead spider fell out, and I screamed and pushed my chair back.

"Oh my fucking god. Who would do that?"

Kim shook her head. "It's almost Halloween. It's obviously a fake spider and a Halloween party invite. For God's sake, I'll read it, you're hopeless," she said, grabbing the card.

As she read it, the blood drained from her face.

"What is it?" I asked.

She passed the card to me. Inside it read:

Stay away from things that don't concern you in Withernsea. We were all okay as we were. Refuse to help Theo or you may find yourself dead either way.

"It's a death threat! You need to call the police," yelled Kim.

"Don't be stupid. It's obviously a prank. Or an ex-girlfriend of his. I'll be extra vigilant, but I'm sure it's nothing. I'm not going to take Theo on the books anyway, so no harm done."

"Well, I'm bringing a rounders bat into the office from now on and we all know the only sports I do are water ones." Kim huffed and turned to leave. "Just so you know, if we get any more threats, I'm phoning the police, and that's the end of it."

"Fine." I held my hands up. "If there are any more, we'll phone the cops. Jeez."

Theo arrived promptly at five pm and Kim introduced herself and indicated he should take a seat opposite me. I remained behind my desk, but Kim decided to seat herself next to him. He moved his chair about a foot away from her and she scowled.

"Sorry," he said. "You smell a little of magic and I find it overpowering. It gives me a headache."

"Oh, I'm wearing Miss Dior, actually," Kim said haughtily. "Magic must be a knock-off version. I'm not into copies; I like originals."

He shrugged and sat back in his chair.

"Okay. Before we get started, would you like a drink?" I asked him.

"No, I had some refreshment before I came here," he said, and I noted the slight pink tinge to his cheek. Oh-kay then.

"You smell as well," Kim said. "Like you've been around pigs or something." She turned her nose up.

"I called at a local farm for my refreshment today. My apologies," he said to her.

"Right, if we could get on with going over these questions." I tapped into my screen. "Okay, so I might have to change a few of these answers, with your consent, of course, just to make the algorithm work better."

"Whatever you feel necessary. As long as ultimately, I find a wife, I have no objections."

I began. "Your full name is Theodore Robert Landry and your date of birth 1 January 1891, making you 126."

"That is correct."

"Well, my system won't work with anyone over the age of a hundred, so I'll change that to 1 January 1981, making you 36, which is an optimum age.

"There's nothing I need to change about your appearance." I looked over the section.

Kim snorted.

"What is it, Kim?" I asked, starting to wish I'd not asked her to sit in.

"No disrespect, Theo, but you look like you've not seen sunlight in decades."

"I haven't."

"Look, it might go with the whole, 'I'm a vampire' thing, but it's going to put women off. You need a nice glow. Shelley, give me that make-up palette you bought."

"No!"

Theo raised his hand. "Actually, if it can make me look healthier, I wouldn't mind trying it."

I ran my hands through my hair while Kim helped herself to the palette from my handbag. Maybe I should pop downstairs and ask to share Ebony's vodka, because it did appear that my assistant was giving a vampire a makeover in front of me.

She held the mirror part of the palette up to him and he moved his head from side to side as he stared in it. "Wow, this is amazing. Where can I get one of these? I need to purchase one immediately I leave here."

"I thought vampires didn't have reflections?" I asked.

"Stereotyping still?" he shot back.

"The palettes are from Ebony's downstairs. Have you got thirty quid? I'll go fetch you one."

He took the money from his wallet, gave it to her and sat back in his chair. "This is going to transform my life," he said. "Could I just put this palette on my Instagram while we wait for Kim to come back?"

I shrugged my shoulders. "Sure, why not? Maybe tweet it too."

"Oh, my kind don't do Twitter. We're far too wordy. Can't possibly say everything we want to divulge in less than 140 characters. Entirely impossible." He held up the palette. "Take this for example. I need to describe the feel, the tones, the wonderful packaging, where it's from, how best to apply."

"Okay, I get the picture," I said, just as Kim returned to the room.

"Okay, boss. Carry on," she quipped.

"You mention in your application that you used to live on a farm, but now live on Sea View Road. However, you mention some trouble with the police calling round to see you?"

Theo sighed. "I want my birthplace back. I was happy there, and it's possible that the spirits of my family might hang around there, what with them having had such traumatic deaths."

"When you drained them of their blood?" I clarified.

"It happens a lot with the first thirst. My sire should have protected me, but my father had been eating a juicy rare steak when he broke in."

"Let me guess, your sire choked?"

"He did. Leaving me alone and unfortunately meaning my family were no more. I didn't know then that I could have fed from at least one of them and brought them back to life."

"Wow, you are really great at this vamp shit." Kim pushed his arm. "You ever thought about being an actor? I reckon you'd win awards."

"I did that from 1926 to 1930," Theo replied. "Learning lines gets boring after a while."

"You are such a hoot. Isn't he a laugh, Shelley?"

I raised my eyebrows. "He's something."

Theo looked at me and smirked.

"Okay, Theo. My suggestion while we try to find you a wife is for you to step back from your ongoing pursuit of the farm." Theo looked ready to protest, so I raised my hand. "Just until we get you a wife and then you could tell her about the farm. I mean, she might not want to live on one, and then all your efforts would be for nothing. She might like a simple two-up, two-down with central heating and a patio."

"Fine. I suppose I could desist for a few weeks." Theo huffed.

"Now, Kim is going to go through our additional questionnaire which is all about your ideal woman and your dating habits."

"Okay," Kim said, crossing one leg over the other and trying to look official. "Do you have any preference for an age range, hair colour, any other personal details?"

"A fellow vampire would be excellent, or a woman willing to be changed." He looked at me. "I noted this on my first application."

"You could have changed your mind between then and now. Carry on, Kim."

"So someone who likes your vampire kink thing or who is willing to join in. Noted. Next question, when was the last date you went on? Describe it for us a little."

"It was a month ago. I met a nice lady in a bookshop and arranged to take her out for dinner. She ran out of the restaurant about a minute after we sat down."

"Why was that?" asked Kim.

"Well, I've been looking for a wife for a long time now and the whole dating, getting to know someone thing gets very tedious when after a month or two you tell them you're a vampire and they run away. I decided to get it out there at the beginning. Save wasting both of our time."

"And have you had dates with others of your kind? Surely there are places to meet other 'vampire' women."

"Yes. I've done that. But most vampire women are very jaded. If they're my age, they tend to have been married several times and for some reason prefer to spend the rest of the time single. They hang around university gyms in an evening, or student nights out where they take advantage of young men who are inebriated and don't remember anything the next day. Of course, the bite marks heal quickly, and the men put their tiredness down to an amazing night out, not a lack of iron."

Kim pulled a face at me, clearly now alarmed by Theo's statements.

"We'll just go to my office now to discuss your application, Theo, and then we'll be back to give you our decision," she informed him, smiling afterwards, though it didn't reach her eyes.

He nodded.

As soon as we were out of the door, she beckoned me to her office, moving quickly. "Beautiful guy. *If* you can find a woman who doesn't mind dating someone who truly believes he's a vampire. I think we're going to have to let him down."

"It's okay. I have a default in the programme that can come up with no matches. I've not had to use it before, but it means we can put him 'on hold', let him down without destroying his confidence.

Essentially, we'll lead him to believe it's our fault we can't find any matches."

"Oh, what a great idea."

The truth was I couldn't match him up with any of my clients because for one, they'd assume he needed the help of a psychiatrist, and secondly, I didn't know him well enough to know he wouldn't kill one of them. What if he got this thirst again that had made him drain his family members?

"Let's go back," I told her, and we retook our places in my office.

"Right, Theo. If you'd just give me a moment. I'll input the rest of your information and we'll see if we have any matches for you. If we do, then Kim can take your first month's membership payment, and we can get your first date arranged."

"That would be wonderful," he said. "May I watch it do its thing?"

"Of course. Just a minute."

I keyed in the information so it looked genuine and then pressed the button that would give him no matches before turning it around showing the 'search' procedure. Theo clapped. "Oh my goodness. I didn't for a moment think this would be possible. I thought it might go against some ethics, but I'm very happy with this. Yes, I think your computer is amazing."

Wow, Theo was one satisfied customer. Yet that didn't make sense because it should be showing no matches. I span the screen back around to myself and then gasped, my mouth hanging open. I went through what I'd keyed in, running the process through my mind. I'd done everything right? So why was it showing Theo that his ideal partner was me?

Chapter 5

Theo

Some things were best left unsaid. I'd given away some vampire secrets, but I didn't get to live to 126 without keeping a lot of them to myself. For instance, the stake. It could absolutely kill me and reduce me to dust if it went through my heart. That was entirely true. Choking on steak? Well, it had happened to an old vampire friend on a night out. It hadn't killed him but did put him off eating human food. I'd found my sire in a pile of ashes, killed by my father's farmhand.

Also, I had above average hearing, meaning that I could hear every word of the conversation between Shelley and Kim when they went to the other office.

But my best kept secret? I adored all things computers. At home I developed programmes for other vampires on how to keep track of our mortal enemies. I'd also developed a kind of Facebook for vampires called Faceblood. Years of experience and time on my hands allowed me to hack the weak to me security (quite adequate for others without my skills) and change Shelley's system to show her as my ideal date.

Because I wanted her.

Since the minute I'd set eyes on her in that restaurant I'd decided no other woman would do.

She had hidden depths and secrets either she was unaware of or didn't wish to divulge. I could smell them on her.

More than that, she was beautiful inside and out.

Setting up a dating agency, and finding love for others when she didn't have it herself, was such a self-sacrificing thing to do. I'd looked up her history, seen that she'd been raised by adoptive parents, and as far as I could see she had no idea of her family background. Interesting.

Research into her agency showed that it was one of the best in England. I thought she deserved it to be *the* best, so I'd advertised her service on Faceblood. Hopefully, she'd get some extra business. Dating a supernatural guy or girl was difficult, and there were a lot of us that remained single. We needed someone like Shelley on our side.

Shelley was still staring at the screen, but her colleague found the entire thing hilarious and couldn't stop laughing. "Well, Shelley, looks like you have a date. About time," she said. "Hey." She poked me in the arm. "I just thought, you coming here, we had an 'Interview with the Vampire', get it?"

I smiled at her. "Very witty. Do you know the whereabouts of all your main clients? Don't have any 'Lost Boys'?"

"I can't go on a date with you," Shelley insisted. "It's against my ethics."

"I won't tell if you won't," said Kim.

"Not helping," Shelley replied.

"Well, technically, as you stated earlier, until I pay for a month's membership, I'm not actually a client. So, my apologies but I won't be joining your dating agency." I looked at Kim who beamed and gave me a thumbs up. I was warming to her even if she did smell. At some point, I'd have to warn her about sleeping with wizards. It could get messy.

"So, what say you, Shelley Linley? Would you like to go out with me? Preferably somewhere where there's no food you can throw?"

Shelley closed her eyes for a good thirty seconds. Then she opened them and nodded. "Why not? If nothing else, I can teach you how to date a woman without scaring them away, and Christ knows I've nothing better to do with my evenings."

It wasn't a no, but I couldn't say her acceptance did a lot for my diminished ego.

"Excellent. I'll pick you up from your house at eight pm tomorrow evening.

"I'll see you then, Theo," she replied.

I bowed to her and Kim and left the agency with a twinkle in my eye and a spring in my step. Things were looking up.

As I walked through the park on my way home, a stray firework hit a tree branch above me. It broke off, narrowly missing my head and landed on the ground in front of me, its broken point sticking up. Wow, if that had fallen a couple of seconds earlier and I'd tripped, that would have been the end of me. It really was my lucky day. I started singing Kylie's 'I should be so lucky'. God, I missed Scott and Charlene, they had the most epic romance. I'd really like to find that for myself.

∼

Thursday night was cards night at mine. I arranged some dips, crisps, and beer around the table and awaited my guests. Before long Rav, Darius, and my best friend Reuben—another vampire—were seated, and the cards had been dealt.

"It's going to be a lot better without Frankie here," said Darius.

"Yes. Despite his assurances that he wouldn't bewitch the cards, he won every hand until I threatened to drain him," Reuben commented with a glint in his eyes.

I looked at my friends in turn. "I couldn't have him in the house again. He smelled terrible. There isn't an odour remover that deals with removing the smell of magic."

"It has a smell?" said Rav. "I didn't smell anything."

"I've a very sensitive nose. He smells like rotten vegetables." I turned up my lip. "Anyway, we need to keep an eye on him. He's sleeping with the assistant at the dating agency. I smell a rat."

"That's not a nice way to describe him, even if he does stink like refuse to you," added Darius.

"I don't trust him. He's up to something, and if I can manage to get near enough without wanting to hurl, I'm going to find out what it is."

"I applied to the agency myself today," said Darius. "How are you getting on?"

I smiled. "I have my first date, and I'm very confident that eventually, she shall become my betrothed."

"Really?" Darius said. "That fast. Wow, I hope Shelley can set me up that quickly."

"Alas, I think you may have to wait for her to accept that our kind really exist. She's currently on the fence—one moment she believes me and the next she's back to thinking it's parlour tricks."

"Well, it's not as difficult for me to disguise myself. As long as I don't have a date on the night of a full moon, I just come across as ripped and hairy. I hear human women are all about the man bun and beard at the moment," Darius added.

"Indeed, if their current book covers are anything to go by. There's quite a bit of shifter paranormal romance out there too, so you could be making dreams come true by dating human women."

"God, that would be epic."

"No." I shook my head. "It's not epic these days, it's sick. That's the current word for it."

"You just said 'alas'," Darius protested.

"So who's the date with?" Rav asked. "By the way, you owe me for calling you sir all night at Hanif's and pretending not to know you. At least you don't have to repeat the crazy that is a meal with Shelley. She runs that agency and is brilliant at matching others, but she has no clue about love. None." He turned to the others. "She threw hot food at Theodore yesterday. I don't know what her problem is. She's fit." Rav mimed a decent rack and patting a tush with his hands. "But strange."

He turned back to me. "So, who did she set you up with?"

"My date is with Shelley."

"What? How? She's not in her own system, surely?"

"I rigged it when they went out of the room. I didn't have to pay either because it's not ethical to date the owner so win-win."

"And she agreed to go out with you? A vampire? I told you she was strange."

"There's something about her. A connection between us. She's mine, meant to be. I just know it," I mused.

"So you got a date without even paying?" Darius sulked. "We need to get rid of that wizard so I can have a crack at the assistant."

"Maybe you'd get further with women if you didn't use language like 'having a crack' at them," Reuben answered, looking down his nose at Darius.

"Don't start acting superior with me, vampire. I'll kick your arse."

"Hang on, let me look when the next full moon is so I can book you in to do that." Reuben picked up his phone. "Oh look, you can't kick my arse for another few weeks. In the meantime, I'll keep you in my basement like a pet and drain your blood every evening, keeping you half alive. I quite like wolf blood."

"Stop antagonizing him," I berated Reuben. "Take no notice,

Darius. You know as well as we do vampires can't drink much wereblood. It makes us volatile."

There had been quite a few twelve-step programmes set up for vampires before the truce had been called in Withernsea between vampires and weres. Reuben had been one of those who had to attend.

"So, when's your date?" asked Rav. "Please don't bring her back to Hanif's."

"Tomorrow evening, and about that." I looked at the others. "Any suggestions of where I could take her?"

Suggestions were made and then the game began in earnest. All thoughts of women and interspecies fighting were forgotten while us four men enjoyed a few simple games of cards.

Chapter 6

Shelley

It was time for our monthly meeting of *Female Entrepreneurs do it with their Colleagues* and we'd closed the agency for an hour while we headed down to Jax's café.

She already had pots of tea and coffee on the large central table along with a selection of buns and cakes. The aromas were magnificent.

As we took our seats, she nodded towards a woman with ginger bobbed hair. The woman sat behind us, drinking what looked like a strawberry milkshake.

"I told her we were closing at two for business, but she's not getting the idea." Jax scowled. "I hate that 'customer is always right' mantra. Why can't we accept that some customers are a pain in the arse?"

"She's wearing Louboutins," Ebony spoke, making all our heads turn to check out the woman's feet.

"If you don't do what I've asked you'll be fired," the woman spat down the phone.

We passed looks between ourselves.

"You think my temper is bad? Wait until you meet the big boss," she yelled. "Now do what I've asked you to do, and don't disturb me again. I'm busy."

She ended the call, threw her phone in her quilted Chanel handbag and then slowly sucked milkshake up a straw.

She broke off when she caught us looking at her. "Sorry, I'm a devil at being naughty. I realise you're waiting for me to finish. Just carry on, I won't listen. I'm almost done." She smiled, revealing perfect white Hollywood style teeth.

"It's fine. You enjoy your drink," said Jax, turning back to us and rolling her eyes. "Ow." Jax gripped her forehead, yelling in pain.

"What's the matter?" I asked placing a hand on Jax's shoulder.

"Stabbing pain in my eyes. I bet I'm coming down with a tension headache. It's the stress of running this business."

"Here," Ebony said, going in her handbag and taking out a small bottle of vodka. "This helps."

"Will you stop encouraging everyone to drink in the middle of the afternoon," I told her. "Seriously, Ebony. Do you need AA?"

"I don't drive," she said looking down at me.

"You know full well I'm referring to Alcoholics Anonymous, though I do worry you're having a breakdown."

"I don't get the voices when I drink vodka. I told you. It blocks them."

I looked across at Kim with a raised eyebrow.

"Well, enjoy your afternoon, ladies. I must be going," the customer said, scraping back her chair and rising from her seat. "It's a shame I'm not able to open a café at my place of work, but it's too hot with the furnaces. Could have asked you to open a franchise of Jax's there. Oh well, maybe in the future I can corrupt you into it." She laughed. "In the meantime, I'll have to call in here more often. It's good to check out the local businesses, see if I have any competition." She looked at me as she said that. She couldn't own a dating agency, could she? Not if she had furnaces. She must own a smelting company or something.

"Well, ciao," she said before walking out of the door.

"Fricking bitch. No doubt from the café in the new development near the Aldi," said Kim. "Scoping out the competition."

"Or someone thinking of opening a rival dating agency," I said. "God, I hope not." I looked at Ebony. "You're looking paler. Are you okay?"

"I'm getting one of my migraines. Something's trying to come through, but my vodka consumption won't let it. We best hurry with this meeting before I have to go to lie down."

"Right, well, first order of business," said Jax. "Are we all still okay with the open day in the café on Halloween? I'm going to do the obligatory buns with cobwebs and spiders and serve pumpkin spice lattes."

I made a gagging noise.

"Customers like them." Jax pouted.

"That's fine with us," Kim said. "I've ordered some new business cards to bring with us. Are we getting dressed up for the event?"

I groaned.

"Yes, we *all* have to get into the spirit of the event. Spirit, get it?" Jax clapped her hands at her own joke. "I'm dressing as a zombie from *The Walking Dead*. What about you, Kim?"

"I think I'd look hot as a ghost. I have an idea for it already. Shelley can be a vampire in practice for when she becomes a real one. What about you, Ebony?"

"I'll come as an undead fortune teller."

"What about Samara? Could she not get away from the grooming salon?"

"She took the week off. Said last week was really busy after the full moon," Jax replied. "She's going to come as a pumpkin though. I've told her if she knocks my cups and plates off, she's paying for any breakages."

"Oh, and are we going to the fireworks this year on the beach? Apparently, there's going to be a really good display and a bonfire," Kim said.

"I suppose so." I looked at the others and they shook their heads in agreement. There weren't many events in Withernsea so we felt we should make the most of the ones that came along.

"Anyway, what's this about you becoming a vampire?" Jax asked.

"She's got a date with one. Tonight." Kim winked.

"I don't understand," Jax added.

"Theodore Landry. Total sex god but he thinks he's a vamp. The computer picked our Shelley as his ideal match. So she's off out on a hot date.

"Burning. Fire," drawled Ebony who was staring into space.

"I really need to get Frankie over here to take a look at her off the record," Kim said, nodding in Ebony's direction.

"Do you know, that's a good idea. Get him to drop by tomorrow morning if he can. I'm getting worried about her."

Ebony's eyes rolled, and the whites flashed. "Your one is here, but the path to true love is paved with danger."

"She really ought to sit with a crystal ball in the café, instead of behind that boutique counter." Jax shook her arm. "Ebony. EBONY. Get this coffee down you."

Ebony came to and swigged down the coffee, quickly following it with another one. "Thank you." Her shoulders loosened, then she pointed at Kim "You have a date with a police officer."

Kim pouted. "I do not. It wasn't me who had sex in the graveyard. There was no proof."

"Other than you left your panties there, which had your name sewn in them." I laughed.

"I can't help it if I like to go down the gym knowing which clothing is definitely mine. Someone must have nicked my clothes off the washing line."

Jax looked out of the window, making me realise that there was some kind of disturbance outside. It sounded like arguing. "What's going on out there?" Jax queried.

"I'll find out," Kim said. "Hold up." She pushed the door open and went outside.

"Should we let her go out on her own?" I bit my lip wondering whether I should see if Kim was okay when the lady herself stuck her body back halfway through the café door.

"Wow. Ebony, you better open your shop." She looked at me. "It looks like me and you better go help. That makeup set we showed Theo? There are about forty people outside wanting one. I told them you'd not hold that many in stock and they're willing to order, *and* I told them it was sixty quid, not thirty. Your day's looking up, Ebony."

Ebony brightened. "I knew that would be a winner."

"Saw it in the tea leaves, did you?" I joked.

"No, last month's *InStyle*." She gave me a weird look.

"Well, we'd better go assist," I told Jax. "Thank you for the hospitality and for bringing us together as a business community."

"It's my pleasure," she said. "Now, enjoy your date tonight, and just in case, wear a big scarf around your neck so he can't bite you."

"Yeah, okay."

"Where's he taking you, anyway?" she asked.

"No idea, but he seems a gentleman, so I'm sure it'll be somewhere nice."

I should have kept my mouth shut.

Chapter 7

Shelley

"A walk around a cemetery. Very original idea for a date," I told Theo as he guided me around.

"I read in a dating guide that you should take your girlfriend to meet your family. It shows your intentions are serious."

"That means living family, Theo. Ones you can be introduced to, you know? Get to know. They show you embarrassing pictures of you as a kid in your underwear."

"There are no such pictures of me. I could have some taken if that is acceptable?"

Fucking hell, yeah.

"So, Theo. Why don't you tell me a little about yourself? That's kind of a date thing, getting to know each other."

"But is it?" He pulled a face. "In these times of social media, I can consult Facebook and know what your life has been like for the last six years, and without being too insulting, might I say, your life has been extremely dull. Just constant selfies where you puff your lips out. I don't understand women at all, especially modern ones."

"Why do you want a wife anyway?" I had to admit I was intrigued.

He straightened. "I want a family. My fertile time is coming around again very soon. I think 126 years is old enough to not have experienced fatherhood."

I took a step back, taking care not to fall in a newly dug grave. "You want a family soon? Don't you think you should slow down a little?"

He ignored my remark. "My kind can procreate every 101 years. I was turned at 26, so my time will be in the New Year. Then it will be over for another 101 years."

I rubbed at my forehead. I didn't even know where to start with this guy.

"Theo. Have you consulted a doctor lately?"

"Yes, I'm in perfect health. My fake documents say I'm thirty and of course I can use the power of suggestion on my general practitioner if he gets suspicious."

"The power of suggestion?"

"I guess you'd call it a kind of hypnotism. Basically, if humans get suspicious of my true nature, I can look into their eyes and make alternative suggestions."

"Really?" I scoffed.

"Yes, really. Shall I do it on you?"

"Okay. Make me believe that tree is a Celine handbag."

Theo stood still, got hold of my face and looked down into my eyes. He started chanting and then turned to the tree.

"Tell me what you see."

"The most beautiful handbag."

"See?"

"No, I don't. I'm lying. I see a fucking tree. Theo, I don't know why I like you, but I do. However, you're full of shit."

"That's totally incorrect. Vampires are not made of faecal matter, and I need to try again because you should definitely think that tree is a bag."

He held my face again and looked deeply into my eyes. I had to admit that it gave me goosebumps. He was so gorgeous. Once again, he chanted.

"Okay, look at the tree."

My face twitched. "It's still a tree, Theo."

"Well, that explains it then." He clapped his hands and did a little skip which looked ridiculous on a six-foot-two man. "The only person a vampire is unable to coerce, according to our archives, is their one true love. You, my dearest Shelley, must be my one true love."

He got down on bended knee.

"Please would you do the honour of becoming my wife?"

"Easy, tiger," I told him, though I had to admit my goosebumps had goosebumps and I was feeling a little giddy. "Still on the first date here, getting to know each other, remember?"

"Ah, yes, my apologies. We have to do this the human way. How long does that normally take by the way, approximately?"

"People can take as long as they like. I think the average is probably like two years."

He placed a hand on his chest. "Two years? I can't wait that long. I'll miss my fertile window. My body clock is ticking."

"Well, it certainly needs to be longer than one date." I smiled. "Come on, I'm getting cold out here. Let's go for a burger. I'll meet your family another time."

We went to a local burger bar, and I told him this was my treat. He gave me some cock and bull story about how he could enjoy food, but it had no nutritional value—again. As I sat across from him, I had to admit that something about him amused me. He wasn't boring that was for sure.

"So, tell me about your family, Shelley."

I felt myself tense up. "There's not a lot to tell you about my real family. I was placed up for adoption when I was a baby. I was finally adopted when I was two years old. I don't remember anything about my parents. My adoptive parents got pregnant with a natural baby a month or so after they adopted me, and they made my life a misery."

"Because you weren't their natural born?"

"They said I was cruel to my younger sister. I was no doubt jealous. I was almost three years old by the time they had Polly. Adoption takes time. All of a sudden there was another child there. I wasn't good enough anymore. They pushed me aside."

"I should like to visit them and kick their arse."

I burst out laughing. "You sound so weird saying that. You look so gentlemanly. Do you always wear a suit and shirt? I especially like your tie."

He looked down at his purple and black striped tie. My mind imagined it bound around my wrists. *OMG, stop it!*

"I enjoy being smart. But I can wear other clothing if that should please you. I have some jeans the shop assistant said hugged my arse and made it look like a peach. By the way, is it a recent thing that shop assistants feel your derriere in clothes? This one did. He said it was how he ensured the jeans were a good fit."

"Oh, Theo, no. He made a pass at you." I started laughing. "What are we going to do with you? Were you kept in solitary confinement from birth? You know so much about some things and are so innocent with others."

"I grew up on the farm."

"Ah, yes, the farm. What's this about you trying to get it back?"

"My sire would have inherited the farm once my family was killed. But then he was killed by the farmhand, so it went to his sire. I never met him, but apparently, he sold it on Rightmove. I want it back, but the head of the household won't give it to me. He says if I want it, I'll have to pay for it. He keeps ringing the police and having me removed from the property."

"What does he mean, pay for it? Is he blackmailing you?"

"No, it's back on Rightmove. He says he's had enough of me. It's been up for sale for a couple of years now. Every time someone goes to visit, I do my suggestion thing on them on the way out, so they think it's a wreck and the owner a pervert. I've hacked into the estate agency website, so I know when the visits are."

"Why not just buy it?"

"It's a matter of principle. It was stolen from me. I shouldn't have to buy it."

"But the man who owns it wasn't your, erm, sire's sire."

"No, but he gave money to the sire. Money that should have been mine. I didn't ask to be bitten by a vampire and turned."

Theo went into a sulk and turned his head to look out of the window.

"Okay, then," I said. "Erm, fancy another coke?"

"I think I'd like to go home now."

I sat back in my chair surprised. "Theo, have I said something wrong?"

"It's talking about the farm. I get emotional about it."

"Look." I placed my hand on his. "I'm sure there's a way of getting it back. I'll help you, okay? We'll have to find this sire's sire."

His mouth dropped open. "You'd do that? You'd help me get my farm back?"

"Wellll, I'll help you look into it further. See if there's a way of you owning it again. Do you have savings? Just in case we have to do a deal."

"I will not pay a penny for that property. Although yes, I have several million at my disposal."

Coke shot out of my nostrils.

"Pardon?"

Theo sighed. "Shelley, I've been around a long time. I've been a film star, a model. I've made a lot of money in that time. It's invested though, so don't think you can visit my place and find thirty grand under the sofa," he huffed.

"I think we will call it a night. You've gone really moody. I've just got rid of my own PMT without encountering a male version."

"Males don't get PMT. We have no womb."

"It stands for Petty Male Tantrum, and you own it tonight, pal." I felt my body tensing up.

"I do not." He looked out of the window again. What a mardy prick.

"Yes, you do."

As my frustration mounted, Theo's glass slid across the table, gaining momentum before it upended straight down his shirt and the front of his trousers.

"*Shit. Jesus*, that's cold." He grabbed a handful of napkins from the table and began dabbing at himself. "Well, would you look here. I said no food to be thrown at me, so you got me on a technicality, throwing a drink at me instead."

"I didn't do it," I protested, looking at the table legs to see if there was a wonky one.

"I suppose it just shot across the table and tipped over me," Theo said with dramatic hand gestures.

"Yes. Yes, it did. It was weird."

This date was going to hell in a handbasket. If I didn't rescue the situation, I was going to put poor Theo off females for life.

"Stand up," I ordered him. I grabbed a few more napkins from the condiment table and started to dry his shirt, feeling his rock-hard abs beneath the napkin.

Oh my.

"Erm. I think I'm dry now," he said just as a man in a suit approached us. The badge on his lapel identified him as the manager.

"I'm going to have to ask you to leave before I call the police. This is a family-friendly establishment, although thankfully there are currently no children present." The man's face was puce and his chin taut.

"What bug crawled up your arse? I'm only drying this man's—"

And then I realised, and I almost died. Without fully concentrating, I'd moved downwards. My hand was currently rubbing napkins over Theo's wet lap, and over his now rather erect cock.

"Oh my god." I reared back, at which point the help yourself drinks machines spurted juice everywhere. Fountains of black, orange, and clear liquids rained over the restaurant floor.

"What is happening? What have you done, William?" The manager scurried off, shouting at the poor lad at the front who was innocently wrapping up a value meal.

"Something strange is going on," said Theo. "Only I find myself unable to concentrate as you are still rubbing my penis."

What the fuck was wrong with me? I'd started again. But it felt glorious beneath the napkins, and it had been so long since I'd felt a man. I wanted him.

I took Theo's hand and dragged him outside of the restaurant.

"Can you try that suggestion thing on me again?"

"Yes, I'll suggest you never throw food or drink at me again." He leaned over me. The minute he was near enough, I reached up and pressed my mouth to his. My warm lips met his cool ones. He really was going to have to see a doctor about his extremities. Maybe he had poor circulation?

Theo wrapped his arms around me and pulled me against him, against those hard abs I'd felt through the paper napkins. Now I was feeling them through my chest. There were too many clothes involved here.

And then I felt a little nip at my lip and a small wetness that Theo licked away. As he licked, a heat seared up my groin. *Whoa. Calm down there. Pussy gone wild.* I placed my finger to my lip and looked at it. A small tinge of blood smeared my fingertip. "You bit me," I said, staring up at him and seeing his descended fangs.

"How do you make those come down?" I said, reaching up and touching them. Then I pulled at them and realised that they weren't fake at all.

"You really are... you really are..." My breath came faster than I could process it and I went increasingly dizzy.

"Told you it always takes a third time," he said as he swept me up and away. That was the last I knew as everything went black.

Chapter 8

Shelley

When I came around, I was in my house laid on the sofa, with Theo sat at the other end looking at me with concern.

"Oh, thank goodness. Any longer and I would have called for a doctor," he said, stroking my forehead.

"How long was I out?"

He lifted his arm to look at his watch. "Oh, around a minute-and-a-half."

I stuck my head forward. "Theo, my house is thirteen minutes away from the burger place—by car."

"We didn't travel by car," Theo answered. "Now, how are you feeling?"

I scrunched up my forehead. Why was I back here, anyway? What had happened? Oh yeah, I'd been kissing Theo and... and... he'd grown fucking fangs.

I scooted to the edge of the sofa, tucking my arms around my knees.

"You're a vampire!"

"Yes. I think I told you that in my application, and again at dinner—where I thought you'd begun to believe me—then again at the second interview, and once more earlier, where you felt my fangs and fainted."

"But it's not possible."

"Why isn't it?"

"Because you're made up. You don't exist."

"It's very conceited to believe that you, as a human female, can exist, but I, as a vampire male, must be some kind of an illusion. I've just as much right to be around here as you have. Anyway, you weren't complaining when I was kissing you."

"When you bit me slightly."

"I got excited. I don't have to do that, but it is quite enjoyable, for both of us."

I remembered the feeling I'd had, fire down below.

"And what about sex? Do you do anything different from a human male?"

"No, other than to say I lost my virginity at 16 years old, which means I have 110 years of sexual experience. I've picked up a trick or two in that time." He winked.

My stomach fluttered.

My heart beat faster.

My vagina went *cooommmeeee oonnnnn*.

And I launched myself at him.

He pushed me away and held me at arm's length with what I felt to be considerable strength from arm-porn arms that made Captain America's look like shoelaces. "Are you sure you're feeling up to this?"

"Hell yeah," I announced, and that was it. He brought me back to him and crushed his lips to mine.

His mouth trailed down my neck, eliciting goosebumps as his cool touch felt like the tickle of a feather upon my skin. Theo stripped off his jacket, and I undid his tie, throwing it aside and then unbuttoning his shirt. There were so many buttons. By the time I got to about four away from the bottom, Theo helped me by ripping it straight off, buttons pinging everywhere.

I raised my arms as he lifted my top over my head, leaving me in a white lacy bra.

The sound of my heavy breathing filled the room. I realised Theo's didn't. I wrapped my hands around the back of his neck and pulled him closer, kissing him again and then I rested my head in the crook of his neck, waiting for the tell-tale rise and fall of his chest. It didn't come.

He wasn't breathing.

Ah well. Some of my dates acted more brain dead than Theo. I'd worry about it after I'd had my wicked way with him.

I unfastened the button at the top of his jeans, and he lifted his hips up as I pulled them off his legs. Then I took his socks off. That left just his boxer briefs, and I prayed to God that the bulge in his pants wasn't a hot dog he'd stolen from the burger bar and saved for later.

Placing my fingers at the edge of his pants, I pulled them down.

His dick sprang up—it was *huge*. It almost took out my eye.

Holy mother of God, not all of him was dead.

I was still in my skirt, and I quickly slipped it off, leaving me in my bra and lacy thong. Then I pushed Theo back against the sofa and took him in my mouth, and yes, I had to open wide.

He groaned.

"Your mouth. It's so warm against my skin. Vampire women's mouths are cold."

I let him slip back out. "If you mention other women again while I'm doing this, you'll find you're not the only one who can bite," I told him.

"Fair point," he said. "As I was saying, your mouth is so warm. It feels amazing. Best ever."

Now he was talking. I was the best ever giver of head. You betcha, mate. I swirled my tongue around that baby and sucked on him like I was in a top porn movie until I heard his groans increase.

Theo moved away from me, then lifted me and carried me upstairs. He pushed open my bedroom door after I pointed to it, taking me inside where he placed me on the bed. There, he removed my bra and thong and positioned himself over me, moving down and catching a breast in his mouth. He bit on my nipple and that same sensation flooded through me. There must be something in his saliva. Holy guacamole, what was it going to do to me when he went *down there*?

I was about to find out. Theo lowered himself so he was between my thighs and then his cool tongue licked up my seam. It was like he'd been sucking on an ice cube. The sensations were exquisite. He nipped on my bud and my thighs came off the bed with such force that if he hadn't reared back, I might have knocked him unconscious. Then I wondered, could you make an undead person unconscious? *I don't care* screamed my brain as Theo went back to town on my clit, licking and sucking until I felt the pressure build and I exploded into his mouth.

Dear Lord, I apologise for all the cursing and blaspheming but I've never experienced anything like it.

Then he was back above me and lining himself up at my core. He pushed inside. I was about to remind him about a condom, but then I remembered he wasn't fertile until January.

"Hey," I interrupted, and he stopped, staring into my eyes. *God, he was fucking gorgeous.*

"Thanks," he said, and I realised I'd said it out loud. Crap! "Can I carry on now?"

I shook my head. "That wasn't it. Do you have health checks? Are you free from diseases; you know, like STDs?"

"I don't have any diseases, Shelley. I'm technically dead and disease free." His mouth turned up at the corners in a smirk. "Anything else?"

"Nope." I shook my head. "We're good to goooooooo."

He'd pushed inside me before I'd finished my sentence and filled me to the brim with that magnificent cock of his. I seriously wanted to ask him to pause and withdraw so I could get up and do a little dance of smugness. His head moved to the side of my neck as he thrust inside me and once again goosebumps rose across my skin. The sensations across my skin and between my legs were so good it was beyond explanation. He worked us into a frenzy, my hips meeting every thrust until I felt him stiffen and my own climax build. And then he bit my neck.

He bit my neck as he came inside me, and it was like stars floated and unicorns danced. Rainbows must have surrounded me, and angels must have sung as I came, and came, and came. Yes, three times with aftershocks like no earthquake could ever hope to produce.

I think he killed me.

And I was happy to have died.

Theo gathered me into his arms and snuggled us under the covers. I felt sleep overtake me. He kissed my forehead and whispered, "I'll stay until you're sound asleep and then I'll have to leave. I need to go back to where I'm safe while I slumber."

"Okay," I said, and I drifted off thinking that if he'd proposed again right now, the sated me would have said yes.

∾

"Shelley!"

Oh God, not this again. I opened my eyes and looked around. Theo wasn't there in bed with me anymore. I was totally alone. Well, apart from the weird woman sitting on a black chaise longue this time. Where did I make this dream shit up?

"You're not dreaming, Shelley. We need you to realise that you're in danger. Also, you're getting your powers back and you need to be aware of this."

I sat up and stared the woman down. "What are you talking about?"

"Shelley, I'm your mother. Now whether you believe me or not right now—and if you could, that would really help—I need you to listen. I'm a witch. You are part-witch. Your father made a deal with her to secure your safety."

"A deal with who?"

"Lucy. She agreed not to look for you if your father went with her. It was a trick. She just wanted him. Wanted to split us up. I warned the Linleys that you might exhibit some signs of magic, and if you did they needed to get a witch or wizard to put a binding spell on you. I gave them the number of a friend. They must have done this as I've not detected you until this past week. But this week you've done something. Something that's disturbed her. The warnings are that she's about to leave her chambers and come looking for the cause of the disturbance."

I slapped myself in the face a few times. It was bad enough I had slept with a vampire and had the whole undead thing to deal with. I couldn't process this dream shit too. Fantasy needed to stay away right now; real life was enough.

"Shelley."

How was she still there?

"Shelley, I'm not a dream. I'm IN your dream. I've told you this already. Look, go see the Linleys. Let them tell you the truth and then we can talk again. But please be careful. She doesn't want people to be happy. Withernsea has been her pet for years. She didn't care while you were matchmaking humans, said it gave her the chance of extra recruits, but she wants you to leave the supernaturals alone. They're her toys. And she doesn't know who you are yet. That you're our daughter."

"Who is this goddamn Lucy bitch?" *I asked.* "She sounds like she has a right attitude."

My dream mother looked at me with a great deal of anxiety on her face.

"I told you. Lucy. Lucy Fir. The head of Hell."

. . .

I woke up.

What the fuck was that dream? I hoped all sex sessions with Theo wouldn't give me nightmares, although truth be told he hadn't boffed me when I'd had the first one. Recurrent dreams, hey? I must have things on my mind. Well, the first thing on my mind was to make myself a massive cup of coffee because last night's shenanigans had worked up quite a thirst.

I headed down to the kitchen, feeling a satisfying ache within my thighs. I'd had sex! Extremely amazing sex! Whoo hoo! I made a fresh pot of coffee and then wandered into the living room with a mug before jumping and tipping half the thing down my front. For fuck's sake, this was becoming quite the habit.

I stared at what had made me jump. In the middle of my room was a flame. Just hanging there in mid-air. As I moved closer to it, the flame turned into smoke, black wisps forming the words:

You were warned

The words dissipated and then it was like none of it had ever been there. Was I sleep deprived and had imagined it? Maybe having sex with a vampire had drained some of my life energy or something. I couldn't even talk about it with anyone, could I? Who'd believe me?

I went upstairs to change. At least I didn't have to spend money on a new top at Ebony's this time.

Oh. That was it. I needed to talk to Ebony. Maybe my thoughts that Ebony might be a little crazy were wrong.

Chapter 9

Ebony

I'd wondered when Shelley was going to realise I wasn't batshit and on the verge of alcoholism. Being a seer was draining, especially if warnings and messages about someone very close to you were coming. Vodka wasn't my drug of choice; it was a necessity to get through the day if I didn't want to be pestered by the voices.

I'd started having messages about Shelley a couple of weeks ago. First it was just the odd sweeping of words into my mind.

Her one is coming.

She's awakening.

This was followed by feelings of edginess when she was close. Like the balance of something was out of kilter.

But as she walked into my boutique this morning, the blast into my mind almost knocked me to the ground. I held my head until the pain ebbed away.

"Ebony, are you okay?"

"Give me a moment," I said, taking a seat behind my counter. "It's the thoughts and visions. They come too fast sometimes."

"Do you need your vodka?" Shelley asked, and I stared at her.

Do you need your vodka? Not berating me for drinking. Something had changed.

It was time for me to do my thing.

I got another seat and placed it next to me and indicated for Shelley to sit. "Could you pass me your hand?" I asked. "And no matter what you see happen to me, do not let go of it. Understand me? If you want answers, that's how we get them."

"Okay," she said, biting on her lip before holding out her hand.

I took it and centred myself, asking for protection before I opened myself up. The messages and visions kicked in and I knew that to Shelley my face would have taken on a grey pallor.

Finished, I closed myself down and thanked the angels for their protection. Then I opened my eyes.

"Jeez. I'm glad your colour is returning. I thought you were dying on me," Shelley said, concern etched in her features.

"I have to straddle the line between life and death. It's draining," I explained. "Now. You and Theo. He is your one. You can take your time. You can deny it. But they scream it at me."

"Who's they?" Shelley leaned forward, sliding her chair even closer.

"I don't know. Beings so high they don't have a face, just a presence. They tell me you are in danger though. That you are at risk of death."

"Well, duh. Theo will want to make me a vampire, won't he, if I stay with him?"

I shook my head. "No, that is not who intends to harm you. Your agency is causing a change in Withernsea. There are those who oppose it."

"I've been having weird dreams, Ebony," Shelley confessed. "This woman says she's my real mum and that I'm half a witch and that the head of Hell is after me. That's not real, right? That's me having a bad dream."

My eyes widened in shock. "You upset the devil?"

"I guess so, but only in my dreams. Apparently, she's called Lucy, and she's pissed with me."

I tried to gain traction on my thoughts but couldn't hold onto anything. "I don't know if it's her. I feel like there's more to this. Another presence. Tell me more about these dreams."

Shelley explained about seeing her mum twice and that she'd been told to visit her adoptive parents. That her powers were emerging now she'd embraced the supernatural world.

"And then there was the flame this morning."

"Flame?"

"Yeah, one flame hanging in the middle of the room, then it puffed out, and a message said, 'You were warned'."

I gripped the edge of the table. "That is one of Hell's calling cards."

"What am I going to do?" she panicked. "I upset the devil. Who does that? I'll be burned alive!" Shelley started pacing around the shop picking up different clothes. "I might as well max my credit cards if I'm not going to survive the night."

"Look, let's say these dreams are real and not dreams at all. Your mum said you should visit your adoptive parents. That's a start. Go see what they have to say to you. Why not tell Theo? Maybe you could take him along with you for support? If you're getting threats, you need the police."

"Oh yeah, 'Dear policeman, I've seen a flame hanging in mid-air. Can you check it out?' I'll be sectioned."

"There's a secret branch of the force," I told her. "I'll make some calls. Now, if it's true you're part-witch, you'll need to ask someone, a witch or wizard for guidance. Maybe your mum could help? You need to learn some simple protection spells. I have ones for opening and closing myself to spirits, but they aren't going to help you."

"Thank you, Ebony." Shelley touched my arm. "I'm sorry for doubting your abilities. I misjudged you. You've been so very kind. Now, I've just found out I might be part-witch, I'm shagging a vampire, and the devil is after me, so could I please have a vodka?"

"You shagged Theo?"

"I did." A massive smile broke out on Shelley's face. "And it was heavenly." She sighed. "Bloody hell, Ebony. What am I going to do?"

Bloody hell indeed.

Chapter 10

Shelley

It was ten am before I made it into the office. Yes, we worked Saturdays, but only until lunchtime. Arriving late was so unlike me but hey ho. The sound of muffled laughter came from Kim's office, and I walked towards it and knocked on her door.

"Come in," she shouted.

I walked in to see her lipstick smudged across her face and her cheeks pink. In front of her was a good-looking, blonde-haired guy. I presumed this was the good doctor.

"I'm Shelley, the owner of Withernsea Dating, and you are?"

"Dr Francis Love. My friends call me Frankie." His green eyes flashed with a touch of mischief. "I'm sorry to come here causing mayhem. Your assistant left something at mine. I wanted to return them to her." He went into his pocket and pulled out a pair of panties.

"How did they get there?" Kim looked astounded and looked down the top of her trousers. "I could swear I put those on this morning."

He threw them at her and gave me a wink. I rolled my eyes. The man was a moron.

"Well. Nice to meet you, Dr Love," I said, making sure he knew exactly how friendly I felt towards him. "Kim, could you go get us some coffee and a couple of doughnuts from Jax's? I'll see you in my office in fifteen?"

"Yes, boss." She was still looking down her trousers.

"And you might want to put some knickers on," I told her before stomping out of the room.

～

A knock came at my door not a minute later. "Come in," I sighed. I really needed that coffee.

Frankie strolled in, the door closing behind him as he walked in front of me. "Oh, Shelley, it seems we got off on rather the wrong foot."

I rubbed my forehead. I did not need this tosser this morning when I was trying to work out how to get the devil off my back.

"We're fine. You can go now." I pointed at the door.

He pointed at my head and a wispy tendril of what looked like white smoke unfurled into the air from my temple, not dissimilar to what had happened with the flame earlier. The words revealed themselves one by one before disappearing into thin air.

Tosspot.
Knobhead.
Get out.

"Oh dear. I really haven't made a good first impression, have I?" A comfy cushion appeared on the seat in front of me, along with a matching footstool and he sat down. "I can smell you, you know? It's delicious."

"Fuck off, you sleaze," I shouted, and the footstool whipped across the room, smashing into the door.

"Ooh, yes, we need to get a handle on that. I can smell your magic, darling, not your pussy. No, you've sullied that thing by poking the vampire."

"How do you know I've been with a vampire?" I snapped. Then I felt myself flush for yelling it.

He smirked at me. "I'm not giving away all my secrets, we've only just met. Tell me, have you had any more episodes of things flying around with your temper? You could hurt someone if you don't get it under control."

I cleared my throat. "Are you saying I did that?" I pointed to the footstool.

"Yes, and untrained magic is dangerous. But not to worry because I can help you."

"You mean you're a supe too? Is there anyone here who isn't?" I pursed my lips together.

"Kim isn't. The coffee shop woman, Jax, she's not. Ebony's a seer. You're a witch. I'm a wizard. It was so funny seeing Kim's face when I magicked her panties off her body into my hand."

My mouth dropped open, and I rubbed my eyebrow. "I'm really part-supe?"

"Yes. It's very faint, but there's definitely a smell of magic emanating from your pores. Now, it's in my best interests to teach you how to handle it. Otherwise, you're going to out us all and some of us like to fly under the radar—and no, you don't get a broomstick. That's just stereotyping."

"Did you read my thoughts then? Because that's not okay?" I pouted.

He sighed, looking weary. "I'm a wizard not a psychic. I said the word fly. The natural association of that word to a new witch is broomstick. It's so predictable."

I folded my arms across myself. "You're annoying."

"I am, and yet I'm going to help you. Be at mine at six pm this evening for your first lesson."

"I'm making plans for this evening. I have a date and might be seeing family."

"Not tonight you're not. Do you want to cause people harm?"

I shook my head.

"I thought not." He walked over to my desk and flicked his fingers near my notepad. His address appeared on it.

"Hey, can you teach me a protection spell?" I asked him.

"Hmm, you pissed someone off already? Can't imagine that with your uber-friendly demeanour."

"Bite me," I spat.

"Getting me confused with the boyfriend again. Yes, I can teach you a simple protection spell."

"Will it protect me from evil?"

He tilted his head at me. "How evil?"

I held my hand out in front of me. "If this is evil, then," I indicated before raising my arm as high as it would go, "then way, way, way, up here evil."

"Demonic?"

"Like the head of Hell."

He exhaled loudly and grabbed my hand. "Then you mean way,

way, way down here." He pulled my hand to the floor, almost toppling me over. "Mine at six pm. You can't afford not to make it."

The door opened and as Kim walk inside, he vanished into thin air.

Holy fuck.

"Sorry about that," Kim said. "Frankie turned up first thing. We did have a snog, but I wouldn't shag in the office. I could swear I put my knickers on this morning. We're really going to have to try sleeping when I see him. It's messing with my head."

"Don't worry about it. I'm not sleeping well either," I said and then I winked.

Kim placed the coffees and doughnuts on the table. "You dirty mare. Tell me all about it," she demanded. So, I did.

∞

The problem with a vampire lover was that I couldn't phone him in the morning. I had to wait until after four pm. I called his mobile and a lazy, sexy arsed drawl came from the other side. "Shelley." I swear to God if my name had been a chocolate fondant that gooey centre had just dripped out and my tongue was licking that bitch.

"Hey, Theo. Good sleep?"

"Hmm, wicked dreams," he said and my core pulsed. "So, what are you doing tonight? I think I need more dating help."

"Nice try," I told him. "That's why I'm calling. I can't do tonight. Some things have happened." I filled him in on recent events.

"Ah, that explains how I ended up doused in coke."

"Yeah, I'm sorry about that. Looks like I have anger management issues that need addressing."

"Are you really sorry, Shelley? It led to the most pleasant evening I've spent in a long time. And when I say a long time..."

"Yeah, maybe tens of years. I get it. You're really old. Good point though. No, I'm not the slightest bit sorry. It does mean that I need to have a little lesson in managing my temper though."

"Oh, now magic. It smells like turnips or sprouts to me. Thinking back, there was an odour. I thought you or one of the other patrons had flatulence," he said. "So, who is giving you this lesson about magic?"

"Kim's boyfriend, Frankie."

"Oh, Dr Love."

"You know Frankie?"

"Yes, his odour is most unsavoury. I'd suggest a name change to Frank Lee Hestinks if I was his mother.

"Theo! Are you being bitchy?"

"It's the stench. It's unbecoming."

"Well, I hope I don't start to smell like that. It'll put a blot on our date nights."

"We're having date nights?"

"Oh, I should think so."

He laughed. "You're falling in love with me."

"Steady on, we've only had one date."

"Yes, but you need to admit it. You love my mouth, my fingers and my cock, so we're getting there body part by body part."

"Theodore Landry! I thought you were a gentleman. Where's this naughty streak come from?"

A deep hearty chuckle came down the line. "Listen, I'll definitely escort you to your parents' house tomorrow. Would you do me a favour and make an appointment to view the farm next week? I'd like to show you where we're going to raise our children."

"Theo!"

"Yes, I know. I'm doing it again. That's how I scare women away. But I can't help myself with you, Shelley. There's something about you, like we're meant to be."

"I'm meant to be at Frankie's at six and I want to grab a bite to eat first. I'd better get a move on."

"You might want to have to have a bath in some extra-strong scented bath soak before I see you tomorrow," Theo said. "If all else fails, expect to be Febreezed as soon as I see you."

"You're just so romantic, Theo. See you tomorrow."

I realised I had a stupid grin on my face as I ended the call.

∾

I rang the bell as I stood outside the front door of Frankie's self-detached bungalow. I'd thought being a wizard he'd have a dark mansion with turrets and cobwebs everywhere.

He answered the door, took one look at my face, and huffed. "I have bad knees, can't do with stairs, and you're stereotyping again."

"Me thinks I need to learn how to have a game face before spells," I told him before following him into his living room.

A black cat walked up to me and weaved around my legs. "Aww, you're so pretty."

"Scoot, Maisie," he said, and the cat showed Frank her butthole, gave a hiss and scurried out of the room.

I raised an eyebrow. "Wizard with a black cat?"

"Coincidence," he told me. "So, I made a fresh pot of coffee and I bought some of your favourite chocolate doughnuts. Let me just bring them through."

He was starting to grow on me. Well, his bribes were. I helped myself to a doughnut.

"So, how much of your magic are you aware of?"

"That'll be, well, how to put it, shit bugger all," I told him. "I may have upended a drink on someone, may have caused drinks to spurt out of a machine, may have thrown a footstool. Or…" I paused. "The table wobbled, and the drink fell over; the drinks machine had a fault; and you kicked the stool."

"Only one thing for it then. Let me get a ball."

He placed a ball on a small coffee table in front of me. "Keep your mind on this, not on the coffee or doughnuts. I have expensive carpets."

I focused my eyes on the ball. It was a small, orange-coloured, light plastic and more than likely belonged to Maisie.

"Okay. Relax your mind and move the ball."

I stared at it and willed it to shift. Nothing.

"Keep trying."

Nothing.

"Hmmm. Maybe it only surfaces when you have heightened emotions. Like when I annoyed you earlier, and the footstool went out. That means your powers are quite weak. Pathetically weak." He looked at me with deep disdain.

"Who do you think you're talking to and looking at like that?"

The ball flew off the chair, sailed around Frankie's head and hit him on the nose.

Frankie chuckled. "Okay, I think we established it's tied to your emotions. Fact."

I stared at my shoes until I felt I could make eye contact again. "Sorry for snapping."

"I'm getting used to it." He winked. "Right, I'm going to teach you a spell that will keep you protected from outside harm. Say it every morning and every evening."

"How will I remember it?"

"I'll write it down," he said. "But practice it until you know it off by heart."

"Thank you. I'm sorry we got off on the wrong foot, Frankie. I have a lot to process at the moment after realising the world isn't what I thought it was. *I'm* not what I thought I was."

"Not to worry. I have a feeling we're going to be spending a lot more time together as your powers grow. Now, just one thing. I know you have no reason to believe me, but the vampire. Please tread carefully. Don't ever forget he's a killer."

I looked at him with narrowed eyes. "Thanks for the advice, but I can handle my own love life, and while we're on the subject let's talk about yours. Let me tell you, if you hurt my friend, you'll have me to contend with, and with that level of untrained anger who knows what I'd do to you." I realised I'd snapped at him again. At least nothing had launched at him this time.

Frankie flinched at my words. "I only thought it prudent to remind you. The vampire killed his own family, his own kin whom he must have loved dearly, so don't be so complacent as to think you're safe."

I sighed. "Sorry. I do understand what you're saying, Frankie. I'll ensure to say my spells to keep myself from danger."

He nodded. "Just be aware that some beings are too strong for the spells, Shelley. You'll need to harness your magic to free yourself of them. But more on that another time."

I finished my coffee and stood up. "Thank you for this," I said. "I do appreciate your offer of help."

He smiled. "It's no problem at all. Let Kim know that I missed seeing her tonight."

"I will."

"Did she say what she was doing? I had a bad feeling, like she might have another date." He looked at the floor.

"She didn't say so."

"Okay, well night then."

I walked out of his house and caught the bus back home. I couldn't work out what I thought about him, so instead, I got out the expensive bottle of Jo Malone bath soak I'd purchased before I went to Frankie's and soaked in the tub for two hours. There was no way I wanted Theo thinking I smelled like turnips.

～

I slept without dream interruptions from family members. After getting ready for the day ahead, I called in for coffee at Jax's before heading to the office. Kim had sent me a text saying she'd had an emergency and would be in as soon as she could.

About ten minutes after I got there, she arrived. I went through to her office with the still quite hot drink.

"Thought you might need this? Oh, what's happened to your neck?"

She touched the piece of gauze and tape on her neck. "I've been bitten by something, and the damn thing won't stop itching. I got some insect bite cream from the pharmacy but it's not doing anything. It's so annoying."

"Let me see," I said.

She removed the gauze and my mouth gaped open. The puncture wounds on her neck looked exactly like a vampire bite. The skin around it was raised and red, and she was definitely having a reaction to it.

"Let me get the first aid kit and clean it up."

I went into my office for the kit. Shit, how had she got bitten? She clearly remembered none of it. I would have to ask Theo if there were any rogue vampires on the loose. But first, I'd have to question Kim to see if she'd had a secret date last night.

I wandered back into her office with some salt water in a bowl and some cotton wool. I dipped the cotton wool in the salty solution then squeezed it and applied it to her neck.

"Christ, it won't stop itching. I'm going to scratch my own neck off."

"Hold still."

For some reason, I felt the need to bathe the bites with the salt solution and say some words. It was like an inner suggestion to do so. I held the cotton wool over the wounds and whispered, so quietly Kim couldn't make out the words, "Please wound, hear my spell, take in the salt and make all well." When I took the cotton wool away, the bites were almost closed.

"What did you do? The itching has stopped. Oh, thank fuck."

Kim moved her head from side to side and then stretched. "God, that is so much better. I could kiss you. What were you mumbling about?"

"Just saying I hoped the salt water did the trick," I lied. "I'm going to put a plaster over it now and then we'll do the same again after lunch to make sure it stays okay."

"I can't thank you enough. It was torture."

Things were getting serious. The threats were one thing, but some vampire had toyed with my friend. I needed answers, and I needed them quickly. "Did you go out last night? I thought you were having a lazy evening."

"That's exactly what I did. I didn't go anywhere. Sat watching TV until ten and then I had an early night." She lifted a large bag from behind her. "Right, I'm just going to pop out to the launderette. There's obviously something in my sheets that bit me. I'm never leaving it a month between washing my bedding again." She opened the bag and pulled out a tie. "Do you have to handwash designer ties?"

My mouth gaped open for a second time.

"Where did you get that?"

"It was on the floor by my bed. Frankie must have dropped it during one of our sessions. I thought I'd get it laundered."

"Can I look at it?" I asked her.

"Sure." She passed it to me.

I held the purple and black striped tie in my hand and turned it over. It had splashes of a dark liquid on it and I held it to my nose. Coke.

"I'll sort this out for you. You have to be really careful with designer stuff. Might take me a couple of days," I said. "You go now while it's quiet."

"Okay." She hopped off her chair. "See you in ten."

She left the office, and I sat back on her desk. Bite marks and Theo's tie? What was going on? Had my vampire boyfriend really attacked my friend?

Chapter 11

Shelley

Theo arrived to pick me up from my house at six. I'd done a protection spell on myself to ward off any evil spirits, so if he reacted to me, I'd know he was a suspect.

I opened the door and leaned towards him to give him a kiss and he hissed and jumped away from me.

"God, I knew it. Why did you bite my friend? You utter *bastard*." I was so enraged, Theo whipped into the air as if taken by a sudden gust of wind. He hit his car with a loud thud.

"Ouch. Fuck that hurt." He stood up, clutching his back. "It's a good job I'm already dead. What did you do that for?"

"You bit my friend," I yelled. "Were you trying to kill her? Turn her? Or were you just hungry?"

He tilted his head and stared at me with narrowed eyes. "I'm sorry about my reaction. You've done magic haven't you, because you smell like refuse; like soiled nappies to be precise. I'm not sure how to proceed with our outing. Do you have a peg for my nose? I don't need to breathe. I just need to stop the smell going up it. It's not really a look I want to continue going forwards though. I kind of like my dapper, designer clothed, and smooth self."

"Ah yes, talking about designer clothing, excuse me a moment." I disappeared into the house. When I came back out, I dangled his tie in front of him.

"I wondered where that went. You're distracting me with your beautiful face and body. At least I only left my tie behind, not my trousers, hey? That would have got me some strange looks."

"You left it at Kim's," I told him. "Along with another souvenir of your visit."

"Kim's? I don't even know where she lives."

"Well, she found your tie next to her bed, and she had two puncture wounds on the side of her neck that I had to heal this morning."

Theo crossed his arms. "I can assure you that I have not bitten your friend and left my tie at her house, if that's what you are trying to insinuate?"

I threw my hands up. "What other explanation is there?"

"How about if I was set up?" He looked at me and disappointment crossed his features. "You are so quick to judge me as guilty. I can see in your face that you don't believe me."

I glared at him. "You'll have to excuse me, Theo. It's the whole you're a vampire, I'm a witch, Frankie's a wizard shit that's going on. Ebony's a seer, my mother comes to me in dreams. I can't handle all this right now. I don't know what's going on and I feel like I'm going crazy." Feeling tears threaten, I looked down at the floor and then back up.

"Look, I'm going to visit my parents on my own, Theo. Thanks for the offer to come and to drive, but I'll get the train. I think it's better that I don't see you for a couple of days. Just until I get my head together."

Theo stared at me. Anger flared in his eyes; a quick flash of red appeared and then left. "I'm disappointed in today's events but as you wish. I'm not sure I could have shared a confined space with you, anyway. The fact remains that we have a problem because I'm not sure I can date someone who smells like they have terrible flatulence. Go to see your family. I hope they provide some of the answers you're looking for. You know where I am if you wish to speak to me again." He turned around and walked away.

There was a lump in my throat. I had been quick to judge him, but what other explanation could there be? I pushed the thought to the back of my mind. Right now, I needed to focus on information gathering. Train timetables needed to be consulted as the Linley family were expecting me at eight.

∽

Mark and Debbie Linley lived in a three-bedroomed semi in Hull. As I arrived at the entrance to the driveway, I spotted cobwebs surrounding the house. It was covered in them. What the fuck was going on? I stood at the front door and pulled strings of the web away, pressing on the doorbell.

My adopted dad answered the door. He shone with an orange glow. If they turned out to be supernatural too, I would scream.

"Why is your house covered in cobwebs?" I asked, clearing some away to enter the house.

"You can see them?" he asked, his eyes wide.

"It's be hard not to. Ever thought of getting the place cleaned up? You might need to employ someone if you have a spider infestation."

He sighed. "Come through, Shelley. We need to talk."

I followed him through to the living room. It had been decorated since I was last there and looked really nice. Brown leather sofas, a cream carpet, and some rose gold ornaments gave it a modern feel.

"The place is looking good, Mum," I told the woman sitting on the sofa. She'd had her hair cut since I'd seen her last, with it now in a short brown bob. She looked at me, a smile hovering on her lips, like she wanted to welcome me but couldn't bring herself to do so.

"She can see the webs," my dad told her.

"Oh shit," said my mum.

"Er, language?" I hadn't been allowed to swear when I was home. In fact, I hadn't been allowed to do most things. Largely, I'd been confined to my bedroom and lived my life out of their way.

"Anyway, you're being so welcoming, folks. It's a pleasure as always."

My dad rubbed his forehead. "Yes, well, sometimes you decide to adopt a kid, and you don't get what you were expecting."

My heart sank in my chest. They didn't even try to hide their disappointment.

"I'm sorry I'm not the daughter you wanted me to be. I'm not sure what I did wrong, but I guess that's why I'm here. Shall we skip past the bullshit politeness and get down to what I need to know about my childhood?" I looked from one to the other. My eyes resting on my mother's. "Do you know about my real parents? Only I'm having a few problems right now and need some answers."

My parents looked at each other. "Take a seat, Shelley," my mother said. "We have quite a bit to tell you."

I sat down on a chair opposite them. "You'll have to excuse us a minute," my mum said, and they closed their eyes before launching into an incantation. They spoke in unison and the glow around them grew brighter still. They stopped and looked at me.

"Who are you protecting yourself from?" I asked.

"You," they replied.

"Excuse me?" My eyes widened. "Why would you need to protect yourself from me?"

My mother sighed. "When we decided we wanted to adopt, we found it was rather more difficult than we thought. The adoption agency told us it would take years to be accepted. We'd made our peace with this, and then our keyworker phoned to say she had a child for us. You." She pointed to me as if I didn't know who I was. "We came to visit you and you looked so adorable, with your red hair. We fell in love and after visiting with you a few times we agreed to adopt you."

"Okay, this all sounds perfectly normal."

"Before your adoption went through, we went to the agency and were escorted through to a room where we met your real mother. It was apparent, more or less straightaway, why you were being adopted. They'd told us your father had left her, and she was struggling. She was babbling about a devil taking her husband and that we were to protect her child."

I swallowed. "What did she look like?"

"She had long dark black hair with a white streak through it. Of course, we thought she was crazy at the time. The meeting was brought to a halt because of her distress, and we didn't see her again."

I closed my eyes for a moment. Was this because she'd been taken to another realm?

My mother continued. "As your adoption progressed, you asked me why you had a new mummy. I told you that yours was poorly and that you'd been sent to be my special daughter as I couldn't have a baby of my own. That my tummy was broken." A tear came to my mum's eye. "You placed your hands on my stomach and closed your eyes and you said, 'Please mend my new mummy's tummy'. A couple of months later my pregnancy with Polly was confirmed. We'd heard that this happened a lot, you adopted and got naturally pregnant. They put it down to us relaxing about conception."

"But?"

"You kept singing. About the baby sister who was coming. In time, we found out that we were expecting a girl. You told me she'd be born a month early, but I wasn't to worry, to just take you to the hospital and you'd make sure she was okay. That your magic was strong. I started to feel a little edgy as your mum had talked about you having magic. We'd put it down to stress.

"Polly arrived prematurely, and she struggled to breathe. Things were touch and go, and I begged your father to bring you. You looked through the incubator, closed your eyes, and said, 'she's okay now', and she was." My mum was openly crying now. "I felt like I had been given two miracles. You, and Polly."

"So, what went wrong?"

My mother sobbed, incapable of talking, so my dad took over.

"Babies need a lot of attention, and I guess because Polly was our natural born, she got even more. We're not proud of that, but of course, we'd see the family resemblance in her, something that couldn't happen with you. We saw her first smile, her first teeth. You were young and became very jealous." He took a deep breath. "We walked into Polly's bedroom one day and she was hovering above the cot. You'd opened a window, and said she was keeping you awake. That she needed quietening down. We felt you were at risk of harming her. Dropping her out of the window. We got you to lower her back into the cot and while your mum hugged you, I phoned the number your biological mother had handed me before she'd been taken away. A man answered the phone and said he'd been expecting my call. He came straight round, and he placed a ward of protection around us. To those with magic, it looks like cobwebs. We can't see it."

"Oh," I said. "And it didn't occur to you that maybe I was trying to settle Polly back to sleep and get some fresh air in the room?"

"We couldn't risk it being the worst-case scenario. The man waited until you slept and then he bound you with a spell that suppressed your magic. He reassured us that it likely wouldn't appear again although there were no guarantees."

"So we kept you away from us and Polly," my mum said between sobs. "We weren't proud of what we did, but we needed to keep her safe. To keep ourselves safe."

"You ignored me!" A vase wobbled precariously on the sideboard while the webs flashed with silver sparks and glowed brighter. They looked at each other and anxiety etched across their faces.

And then I understood, and everything calmed.

"I can't excuse what you did. You turned your love away from me and only gave it to Polly. You distanced yourself from me. But I understand now why you did it. You were afraid. I wouldn't have harmed Polly; I love her dearly. Thank you for explaining everything to me. You can have your wards put back up or not, but please don't be afraid of me. I would never cause you harm. You provided for me and kept me clean, fed, and safe. For that I thank you, but I won't visit again." I stood up.

"No," my mum protested. "We want to see you. Now you know and we can openly protect ourselves."

My dad interrupted. "You need time to process everything. Maybe we can talk it over some other time. When did your magic return?"

I sat back down for a moment. "This last week. I didn't know what was happening to me. I started having dreams in which someone who said she was my real mum appeared. She looks like you described, but as you can imagine, I'm having a hard time processing that any of this is real."

My dad shot my mother a look fraught with anxiety. Mum said she still wanted to see me, but my father's body language told a different story.

"Well, thank you for meeting with me," I said, ready to leave now, to go and think everything over. "Oh, just one thing. Do you still have the number my biological mum gave you?"

My dad nodded and went in his pocket. "I thought you'd ask for it."

We said our goodbyes. My leaving was awkward. I didn't want to hug them. With everything they'd said, I didn't know what I thought about my relationship with them. I needed time. But first, I wanted to know if this man could meet me and provide me with further answers.

Once I was enroute to the train station I called the landline number I'd been given.

A woman's computerised voice announced, "This number is no longer available. Connecting you to an alternative number unless you say cancel."

I waited.

"Frankie Love speaking."

It took me a few seconds to find my voice. "*You!* You knew I had magic, and you stopped it. Oh, you certainly have some explaining to do," I told him. "Get ready, I'm on my way back to my house. I'll be there at eleven. Meet me."

"I'm already there. Wizards have no problems with locks. By the way, you need to get some beers in. I've magicked some up, but that doesn't help local businesses."

Ending the call, I walked towards the train station. I'd come looking for answers and ended up with more questions than ever.

Chapter 12

Theo

Great. I was finally dating a woman I felt could be 'the one' and she thought I'd attacked her best friend, showing a complete and utter lack of trust. Okay, she'd only known me for a week, and I had confessed in writing to draining my family of their blood, but I'd been a fledgling then. It wasn't my fault my sire was killed. If he'd have survived, I'd have been prevented from the thirst. He would have taken me to a blood bank. I called Reuben and Darius and asked if they fancied a drink at mine. Reuben and myself were enjoying a nice vintage of blood, and Darius loved scotch, so I'd given him a bottle. Rav was working so he couldn't join us.

"So, what's this all about? We don't usually see you more than once a week. What's happened to your elusive vampire side?" asked Reuben.

"Women," I said.

Darius spluttered scotch down his cream cashmere jumper. "Fuck. That'll have to go in the bin. Cashmere doesn't clean well."

"I'll buy you a new one," I grumbled. "What's another fuck up today?"

"You are down in the dumps," declared Reuben, looking at Darius' jumper. "Bloody hell, Darius, what a mess. You weres are so uncouth. You need a bib."

"Hilarious. Don't go for a career in stand-up any time soon," Darius snarled.

Reuben flashed his eyes red at him.

"Yeah, yeah, yeah. Vamp party trick. They don't look as good as mine," Darius said, before flashing his wolf eyes with their hint of yellow.

"You two. Real problems here." I called their attention back to me. "Shelley thinks I took a bite out of her friend."

"What?" Reuben laughed. "Nice one. How did she come to that conclusion? Her friend's dating that dodgy magician, right? Whatever happened to her, you can bet he'll be responsible."

"My tie was left at the scene."

"Couldn't the magician have conjured one up?" said Darius.

I sat back. That made a lot of sense. "Yes. Yes, you're right, he could. It'll be Mr Turnip trying to cause trouble. He's started giving Shelley lessons in magic. He's trying to drive a wedge between us. I know it."

"Magic?" said Reuben. "Why would Shelley be having lessons in magic? She's mortal, isn't she?"

"It appears not. She's apparently half-witch on her mother's side."

"Really? How interesting. How did she find that out?"

"Every time she's been losing her temper, some object has gone flying, apparently. She coated me in Coke on our date. I just thought she'd spilled something."

Reuben guffawed. "Her magical powers are spilling Coke? Oooh, let's all hide."

"Yeah, well, she was going to visit her adoptive parents tonight to try to get some answers on her background. I don't know if this is the extent of her powers or if they'll get stronger. I might not get to find out if she bins me off thinking I've had a drink of her best friend."

"Bin you off? What sort of language is that?" asked Reuben.

"Modern language, you old bastard," replied Darius. "It means to terminate the relationship."

"I'll terminate you if you don't show some respect to your superior."

"Stop it, you two. For goodness' sake," I told them. "Can we have one night without your sparring?"

Darius looked at Reuben. "He really is a misery guts, isn't he? Put it there, bro." They bumped fists.

"So, what do I do?" I asked them both.

"Take her out on a nice date. Go into the country or something with a picnic. Women like that kind of thing, and suggest she avoids

Frankie. He's up to something. I will keep an eye on him, see what he does while you're both out," Reuben said.

"You'd do that for me? Thank you."

"You're my best friend, and seeing as how Darius is a cop, he can help me."

"Yeah, I can cover the day shift, you mean." Darius rolled his eyes.

"Are you making fun of my disability? Sleep impairment is no laughing matter."

"You're not sleep impaired, you're undead, you cretin."

They proceeded to carry on bickering, and I sat back, enjoying my drink and left them to it. I felt better now we had a plan.

Now to convince Shelley that the only person I wanted to bite was her.

Chapter 13

Shelley

"Why didn't you tell me the whole truth?" I asked Frankie, frustratedly.

"Because it was your adoptive parents place to tell you, not mine. Now we can move forward because you can know the rest of the story."

"There's more?"

"Of course. Don't you wonder why your real mother can only appear to you in a dream?"

"She told me. Because of Lucy."

"Ah, yes, Lucy." He sat back on my sofa. "Go get us a bottle of wine to share, dear. I think we'll need it."

I stood up to head to the kitchen. "I thought you brought beer?"

"I've already drunk those."

"How old are you, anyway?"

"Thirty-seven. Why?"

I shrugged. "I wondered if wizards lived for hundreds of years like vampires."

"I'm afraid not, though you can anti-age your wrinkles and give yourself a different look entirely. He waved a hand over his face, so it looked like Prince William was sitting on my sofa. It faded off. "It doesn't stay very long though, a day at the most, so I don't tend to bother with it."

"You were only young then when my parents asked for your help?"

"Yes, but I'm a very strong wizard. Always have been."

"Oh, right. By the way, do you really like my friend?" I asked him. "Or have you been dating her to keep an eye on me?"

"I do like her, but Kim and I are frankly what you call fuck buddies. Neither of us sees a future in it and there'll be no hard feelings when we're done. In fact, the minute I stop going hard, I'll call it quits."

I made a vomiting noise. "You're gross."

"What can I say, she loves the wand." He sighed. "Now, what do you have to do to get a drink around here?"

"Okay." Frankie took a drink of wine. "So, before she became a demon, Lucy dated your father—your real father."

He gazed out of the window. "They were engaged to be married. The church was booked, and then... your mother moved to Withernsea."

"She stole him?" I gasped.

"It was more of a case of love at first sight. Your father was torn. He visited the boutique, which at that time was run by Ebony's mother, who was also a seer. She told him that he was meant to be with your mother. That they would have a child. He ended his relationship with Lucy and called off the wedding."

I put a hand over my mouth while I considered what he'd just said. "Lucy must have been devastated. To lose someone she loved and for it to happen in the place where she lived."

"She was furious. Swore to get revenge against them. Ebony's mother, Yolanda, allowed them to stay in the apartment over the boutique."

"My business premises?" I queried.

"Yes. One night a fire started. Your parents escaped. Yolanda wasn't so lucky, and neither was Lucy."

"She killed Yolanda? And then what, got trapped or died of smoke inhalation?"

"She denied having set the fire as she was taken out on the stretcher, but the next we knew, Lucy appeared in Hell, having become a devil and taking the post of head of Hell."

"A devil, not *the* Devil?"

"No, you are thinking of Satan himself. He oversees Hell and has his subjects to guard his empire. Lucy became one of them, and she took your father with her. We don't know how she did it. It has never been known for someone to cross the planes without death, and indeed, to go to Hell without committing an evil deed. Your mum went into hiding until you were born, but eventually went to the astral plane, meaning she had no earthly body for Lucy to capture or torture. It meant she could still communicate and try to find a way to rescue your father. She has yet to be successful, but that is why she is able to communicate with you via your dreams."

I drank down a whole glass of wine. "Huh, if I didn't think things were complicated before. Now I discover I have Hell and an astral plane to deal with."

"There are many planes of existence, but for now we need to talk about those that are currently relevant."

"Well, Lucy is angry with me because I'm trying to make Withernsea happy and in love. She doesn't know who I am yet. There'd have been more than a hanging flame warning, I'm sure, if she knew who I really was."

"It won't be long before she works out the truth. Now, we need to develop your magic as we don't know what her next move will be. You are powerful, Shelley, more powerful than a half-witch is supposed to be, and I have no explanation for that. However, I have been letting your magic out a little at a time so you can embrace it rather than be overwhelmed. I believe you are much more powerful than I am, and that is why we must tread carefully."

"You've been putting the brakes on my magic?"

"Yes."

"I healed bite wounds on Kim this morning."

"Bite wounds? She didn't mention this to me?" Frankie looked concerned.

"Because she didn't know what they were. She thought they were insect bites and once I'd healed them, she probably thought no more about it. She also found Theo's tie at her bedside."

"Hmm." Frankie scratched his chin. "And what do you make of that?"

"I asked Theo outright. He wasn't very impressed."

"I should imagine not."

"You don't think he did it?"

"I can't say whether he did or didn't. I don't know him that well, which is why I told you to be careful. But he's 126 years old, surely leaving a tie by a bedside would be a little careless?"

I placed my hand over my eyes and took a deep breath before letting my hand fall back to my lap. "I accused him. Shit. No wonder he was mad at me. What am I going to do next?"

"I'm going to teach you two things tonight. Firstly, how to see through glamour, so you'll be able to recognise that things like the hanging flame aren't real. Then I'm going to teach you how to make your own glamour. They can come in very useful. Tomorrow, as its plain to see how desperate you are to see that vampire again, why don't you spend the day with him, give him the benefit of the doubt and practice your glamour on him? It could be fun."

"Thanks, Frankie, for everything." I hugged him. "A day out where I can try to figure things through sounds like a good idea."

⁓

I called Theo and apologised for my earlier behaviour. He still wanted to visit the farm, so I agreed we'd go there the next day. Next, I called Kim and told her I was taking the day off and that she'd better do some work if she was there alone. I was busy working on my glamour, to see if it was possible to make Theo look like someone else for a short while and get him past the doorway of the farmhouse. All I had to do was contact the estate agents in the morning. I couldn't see it being a problem since the farm had been on the market for years.

Then I settled myself down to sleep. It had been a long and exhausting day. I should have known that I'd have a visit the minute I dropped off.

"Shelley."

I opened my eyes begrudgingly. "Oh, for goodness' sake. I need my sleep. I've got to have my wits about me tomorrow."

Shuffling up the bed to rest my head against my headboard, I saw my mum was sitting on a magic carpet that hovered mid-air. "But you believe it now? That I'm your mum?"

"Yes. Well done. You're no longer the strangest thing in my life." I might be facing the truth, but I was still bloody knackered and grumpy.

My mother smiled, ignoring my current mood. "I'm glad Frankie is teaching you how to use your magic. I can feel it in you now. It's getting stronger. You need to gain your strength so I can come back, and we can fight Lucy for your father."

I shot up, leaning forward. "YOU WANT ME TO FIGHT A DEVIL? ARE YOU OUT OF YOUR MIND?"

She raised a brow. "You need to harness that temper. Though it will come in handy when we face her."

Dropping back against the headboard, I groaned. "Can I go back to sleep now? This is not what I need to hear when I'm trying to relax and figure out my life."

"Sorry that I'd like to come back to earth and be in my body and reunite with your father. We'd quite like to be a family unit with our daughter, you know?"

Looked like my mum's mood was starting to become more like my own. I was too tired for this drama. Why couldn't she appear once I'd had some sleep?

"Hmmm, I wonder if my magic can push you out of my mind when I'm not in the mood? We'll speak soon, Mum, but I've had enough for one day."

"Shelley, that's so rude."

Psychic push

Hey it worked. Now I could go back to sleep.

~

It was only a ten-minute drive to Goodacre's Farm. As soon as I got in the car alongside Theo, I wished we weren't going anywhere except for my bedroom. I craved him like he must surely crave blood. I'd deliberately not done any magic so that I didn't smell, but as we started to approach the Withernsea countryside a strong smell of manure worked its way through the car vents.

"Jesus, I forgot how bad that smell can be." I pulled a face.

Theo looked at me, opened his mouth to say something, and then looked away.

"What?"

"Nothing."

"Out with it, vampire. What were you going to say?"

"Just that this is how you smell to me when you've done magic."

My jaw dropped. *I smelled like this manure farm smell?*

"Times about twenty."

I smelled even WORSE than this farm smell?

I took my mobile phone out of my bag and dialled Frankie.

"Dude. I smell like turnips to my boyfriend. Can I switch that off?"

The sound of laughter came down the phone. "It's fun watching those superior little noses turn up in disgust."

"Not when you're dating one."

He huffed. "Fine. It's easy to turn off. You just have to eat a slug every morning."

"Ewwww. I have to what? You've got to be kidding me. I retch every time I watch *I'm A Celebrity*."

Guffaws came down the line again. "God, you're easy to wind up. Just have a mouthful of rosehip tea every morning and you won't smell to the vampire. If he pisses you off, don't drink it and perform a series of spells. He might even be sick. That's such fun."

I heard a door creak and Kim's voice in the background.

"Who are you talking to, Frankie?"

"Gotta go," he said, and ended the call.

Theo sighed. "How well do you know this wizard?"

I brought him up to date with everything that had happened. "So you see, he knew my mum, and that makes me trust him. Well, as much as I trust anyone right now."

"Yes, about that. Do you still believe I bit your friend?"

I laid a hand across my breastbone. "No. I'm sorry, Theo. I panicked. You're my boyfriend, but she's been my assistant and best friend for a long time. I don't want anything to happen to her."

"That's understandable, but you have my solemn vow that the only person I intend to bite is you."

My betraying core went slick at his words. *For God's sake, have some control down there.*

As we approached the long winding driveway of the farm, Theo stopped the car. "Go on then, get this over with."

"Okay, you need to be completely quiet. I've only had the tiniest bit of practice."

He closed his eyes and sat preternaturally still. Show off undead bastard. I closed my eyes and concentrated on conducting a glamour to make him look different.

The trouble was that every time I closed my eyes, all I could think about was his cock. I opened one eye and sure enough his head was a giant penis.

Oh my fucking god. Please don't stay like that.

"I'm tingling, is this working now? Only I'm not sure I can cope with the smell much longer."

"No. Be quiet or it'll go wrong, and you'll look like a dick," I said. Not telling him how true my words were.

I needed to think of someone I didn't find attractive quickly, so I'd stop thinking of cock. I closed my eyes and imagined Simon Cowell. Good, now I'd calmed my libido down I could fashion a normal face for Theo. Except, I couldn't. Every time I opened my eyes, he was still Simon Cowell. Oh shit.

"Er, Theo," I told him. "There's a slight hiccough."

∽

When Jim Gilbert opened the door to his house viewers, his face paled, and he stood there in complete shock. "S-S-Simon?"

I stood forward and shook his hand. "Yes. I must ask you to not tell anyone about this visit to your property. It's highly confidential. Mr Cowell needs somewhere remote where he can escape his legion of fans and your farm looks ideal."

"Oh, of course. Of course. Please, come in," Jim said. "Can I get you a drink? I have tea, coffee, and I know it's early, but I have a really special whiskey I was bought for my 40th birthday that we could open." He looked at Theo, who said nothing. Of course, he couldn't because he didn't sound like Simon Cowell.

"Mr Cowell prefers not to speak and to let me handle everything for him," I said. "A drink will not be necessary but thank you for your kind offer. Could you show us around please?"

"Of course. I'll give you a brief tour and then I'll let you walk around by yourselves."

"That would be fantastic. If anyone asks you met with Shelley Linley and Bob Landry."

"Landry? God, don't mention that name to me," Jim said. "I know a freaking moron with that name."

I saw Theo's body stiffen.

"Well, we're short on time, so if we could move things along?" I asked.

"Sure."

Once Jim had shown us around, he left us to look around ourselves. Now I could see through glamour, I could switch my sight and see Theo, but poor Jim must have shit a brick when he'd opened his door.

"The farm has been modernised since I was here. There's barely a trace of my old home left."

"Does that mean you can leave it behind? Move on?"

"I don't know. It is rooted in my origins. I was born here, and I died here."

"But don't you have bad memories of your family dying here?"

"I have more good memories. It could be a happy place again. My childhood was extremely happy. We could raise our babies here?"

I looked at him. "Forgetting the fact that we've been dating a week; if we did have a baby, how does it age? Also, how can it have a brother or sister if you're only fertile every 101 years?"

He sighed. "Yes, it's likely we'd only have one. There's no knowing when a vampire will stop aging. It could be in childhood or adulthood. I was turned at 26 and aged a little more."

"And would you turn me?"

"If you asked me to."

"What if I carried on aging until my 60's or even older? I'd look like a cougar?"

"Then I'd see if Ebony had a makeup set that could make me look the same age."

"You were looking for a vampire wife when you applied to my agency. Wouldn't that be easier for you?"

"I was only looking for a vampire wife because I hadn't met you." He leaned over and kissed me. Unfortunately, in my surprise, I dropped my magic and so it was Simon Cowell who gave me a kiss. Jesus Christ.

Theo led me into an empty barn packed with fresh hay. "Ever made love outside?" he asked.

"No!" I answered. "And I'm not about to start right now. What if Jim comes in and sees Simon plugging his assistant? He could sell that story to a news channel."

"Dearest, Shelley." Theo stroked down my cheek. "There's a bolt on the barn door."

"What about security cameras?"

"I'm a technical genius, remember? Trust me. We're all alone."

"But I smell bad," I protested.

"I want you too much to care."

"Gee, thanks. I think."

The Vampire Wants a Wife

Then he leaned over and kissed my neck. My total weak spot. Goosebumps erupted across my skin. I closed my eyes, so the Mr Cowell lookalike remained at bay. Theo backed me onto some hay bales. Unlike in the movies, it was actually quite scratchy, but he really seemed to dig it here, so I didn't try to conjure up a bed or a blanket. Anyway, I'd probably make the hay bale into another giant penis with how my mind was focusing on Theo's right now. Theo unbuttoned his trousers, lowering those and his boxers and slipped my pants to my knees. Then he nudged into me, making me gasp.

But I couldn't help it. I started scratching my arse cheeks. The hay was unbearably itchy. As I began to writhe beneath him, Theo took it as my ecstasy and pounded into me, meaning that the hay scratched my butt even more.

"Gah. Stop. Stop right now," I shouted.

Theo opened his eyes. "Sorry. Is there a problem?"

"Yes. I just had anal with a few pieces of straw and my arse is being scratched to death. We need to stop. I'm sorry but this just isn't sexy."

Theo gathered me up and turned me over so that I was on my feet, resting my hands on the hay bale instead. He lowered himself down and licked all across my arse cheeks. I felt my skin tingle.

"All gone," he said. "Vampire venom at its finest."

I touched my butt cheeks. He was right. I couldn't feel a thing.

"Thank you," I said. "Sorry about us not, you know, doing it."

Theo's tongue began again, this time trailing from my butt cheek and down between my thighs.

"Who said we're not doing it?" he said before plunging his tongue inside me.

"Holy shit, Theo. Don't stop," I ordered him. He brought me to the brink before taking me from behind. Once again, he bit my neck as I came, making my knees give way as thunderous, multiple orgasms crashed through me. He pulled up my panties and gathered me into his arms.

"Please, Theo. Buy the farm. Pay the money. We can chase down your sire's sire later. You need to buy this place. I can see what it means to you," I told him.

"You just want to have outdoor sex again." Theo grinned.

"I can buy thick blankets. Think about how many places we've not done it yet."

Theo sighed. "If I transfer the money to you, will you purchase it? Then I've kept my solemn vow that I would not buy back my farm. It will be in your name instead."

"Theo..."

"Once I have the money back from my sire's sire, you can transfer the property to joint names, as married couples are advised these days."

"Theo, I am not your wife," I told him.

"But you will be. Why fight it, Shelley? You know you're never going to want another man's cock as long as you live. You're addicted to mine. My 110 years of experience is not going to be matched."

"Huh, conceited much? What gave you that impression?"

"The fact your hand is currently stroking the top of my trousers."

Oh shit. It really was. This was becoming quite a habit.

Chapter 14

Shelley

I seriously had no idea how to find Theo's sire's sire. It's not like there was a Vampires Reunited and he'd already tried Faceblood, putting out a random status about anyone who might have been in the area of Goodacre's Farm at that time. Theo didn't even know his sire's name. Anyway, I had lots of work to do today. Membership applications were coming in thick and fast. As I noted how many of them stated their supernatural status, I realised that my best friend was going to have to be brought into the fold.

I buzzed through to her office. "Kim, you got a sec?"

"Yeah," she said. She sounded like she had a cold. I wondered if I could do a spell for that.

Kim pushed open my door. Her eyes were puffy, and she'd obviously been crying.

"Shit, Kim. Is everything okay? I thought it was strange you'd not said hello this morning."

"Are you sleeping with Frankie?" she snapped.

I threw my head back. "What? Of course not. Whatever gave you that idea?"

"Well, I went into the bedroom yesterday morning and he was on the phone. I heard a woman's voice coming from the speaker. He rang off quickly and when I asked him who it was, he said it was no one important. When he went to the bathroom, I looked at his phone and the call was from you. He's saved you on his phone as Spelly Shelley. He's given you a pet name and everything. How could you?" She burst into noisy sobs again.

"Kim. I am not sleeping with Frankie. Ugh. I am however shagging Theo and enjoying it very much. Now, I'm getting the emergency wine out of my drawer because I need to bring you up to date with something, and when I do, you'll probably want to drink the entire bottle."

"Why? Is Frankie *dying?*" Kim wailed. "Did he confide in you? Does he need a kidney? I can give him a kidney."

For her own good I walked over and slapped her face. "Sorry about that, but you need to focus."

She rubbed her face. "*You hit me.* You cow! This had better be good or I'm going to bitch slap you right back."

I patted her arm. "There's no easy way to say this so I'm going to go for it like pulling a plaster off super-fast. I've discovered I'm half-witch, Theo is a vampire, and Frankie is a wizard."

"It's cool you telling me what you're dressing as for Halloween, but can you get to the fucking point?" Kim rolled her eyes.

"No, Kim. We *really* are those things."

"Fuck off. You're not funny."

I concentrated and put a glamour on the wine bottle, making it look like it was hanging in mid-air and pouring over the office floor. Kim quickly held her glass underneath it, her face contorting, trying to work out how it was in mid-air and how her glass wasn't filling with liquid. I took the glamour away.

"What the fuckety fuck?"

"I'm a half-witch. My mother was a witch. Half of Withernsea are supernatural beings. I don't know how many species but apparently werewolves are a real thing too."

Ebony bolted through the door just after Kim fell sideways off her chair. She grabbed Kim and the glass. "I saw this in a flash vision. Sorry I kind of broke your door. She gets it and it won't take her long, don't worry."

"She does? She'll be okay about it?"

"It's Kim. You'll wish you'd not told her. You need to phone Frankie, because in an hour she's going to call him and ask if he can magic an even bigger dick for her pleasure."

Sure enough, when Kim came to and had another ten minutes or so of asking me ridiculous questions like whether I could teleport Orlando Bloom into the office, (No. Though I may have tried. Don't judge me.), she's beyond excited that her 'Drab world has suddenly become technicolour'.

"Kim, there's a large reason why I wanted to share this information with you. Regardless of the fact you're my best friend, you're also my assistant and we are becoming overrun with new membership requests from our supe friends. So, I'm opening another wing of Withernsea Dating— The Supernatural Dating Agency. Totally off-grid, we interview our new members and place them under this agency. I've asked Theo, and he's going to alter our computer systems so if we're audited, only the humans appear. However, under the new agency, we can matchmake supes with other supes. I'm not sure how we'll progress if they want a human date, but let's take that as it comes."

"Maybe a legal disclaimer that they won't eat their date, or hex them if they don't like them?" Kim shrugged.

"Like I said, we have a lot to think about as we start our latest venture."

"I can't wait," said Kim, rubbing her hands together.

"Kim, you realise you're not a member, right?"

"Y-essss."

"You can't like ask them to strip or anything. Or send a nude photo with their application.

"God, you spoil all my fun."

"You were crying earlier because you thought I'd stolen your boyfriend."

"No, I wasn't."

"Erm, excuse me, you had snot running down your nose. It was gross."

"That was because I thought he'd ruined my friendship with you. Frankie is just a fuck buddy. He's not the love of my life. We know where we're at with things. Now, I have a whole new world to explore. He can give me the magic goods and I can still look around. What's happening with you and Theo, anyway? Is it going well?"

"He's giving me £430,000 to buy his old family farm until we can find his sire—long story—and then we'll own it together because it's going to be our marital home and we'll bring up our children there, apparently."

"Jesus, Shelley. That's a bit heavy. Shall we run off with the money and fly to Rodeo Drive?"

"The stupid thing is that I actually believe this is all going to happen." I sat back in my chair, only just realising this was how I was feeling. "It's like a gut instinct. Like everything is happening exactly how it should."

"I can't believe your mum comes to you in dreams and you can shut her out. Can you put my mum in one? She does my head in."

BOOOOOOOOOOOOMMMMMMMM. The noise was accompanied by an explosion of glass and the smell of smoke as my office curtains set on fire. I looked at Kim and realised we were within a protective shield that looked like a giant blown bubble. I pressed against it, and it felt spongy.

"Right, let me concentrate and get us out of here," I told Kim, whose eyes were wide. I slowly got us to the door and out into the hall. The bubble disintegrated and we ran like hell for the fire exit.

Everyone from the shops and offices was gathered outside. Jax ran over to us as we emerged. "Thank God. Are you alright? The fire brigade and the police are on their way."

"Yeah," I said, but I was everything but alright. Especially when I looked at the back of the crowd and saw the woman who was in Jax's coffee shop that time before our meeting. She looked directly at me, flicked her fingers and a little flame danced on the top of one of them. Was this Lucy? I tried to push my way through the crowd, Kim hot on my heels, but the woman was nowhere to be seen. It was like she'd just vanished into thin air, which I bet she had.

How was I meant to deal with Lucy if I couldn't get near enough to talk to her? Then the police and fire brigade arrived, and the afternoon was taken up with crime reports.

∽

My office just needed a little redecoration, and as Jax's older brother was a plasterer, painter, and decorator, he promised to fix things up the following week. For the time being I'd have to share Kim's office or take my laptop down to Jax's. I refused to be bullied out of my building.

We were sat in Kim's office shortly before five when a knock came at the outer door. I put the door on the latch and asked who was there.

"It's the police," the man said out loud, and then his voice dropped to a whisper, "The special division."

I let him in.

"Are you Shelley Linley?" he asked.

"I am. And you are?"

"Police Constable Darius Wild." He whispered again, "Werewolf."

"Oh," I said, not being able to help myself from giving him a once over. My subconscious no doubt looking for fur and claws. All I saw was a good-looking man with shaggy brown hair and a beard.

"Ebony's been keeping me in the loop and what happened today came up on our feed. Thought there might be something otherworldly to it. Best to check."

"Come through. We're working in my assistant's office at the moment." I walked in with him and heard Kim yell out, "Holy fuck."

She quickly covered her mouth. "Sorry," she said. "I have the hiccoughs."

But Darius didn't reply because he was frozen in place, staring at Kim, who was staring right back at him.

"Well, Darius, would you like to look at the crime scene?" I asked.

He shook himself, coming back to the land of the living. "Oh, yeah, sure." Then he followed me to my office with its scorch marks and soaked through interior.

"I've picked up all the details from the scene of crime officers, but sometimes we can pick up other things, extra clues, like signs of magic etc." He looked around and then walked over to one of the scorch marks. He muttered an incantation and it lit up with a dark red glow. "Yep, that's hellfire."

I sighed. "I've been told I've upset Lucy Fir."

"Oh dear," Darius said. "That's one woman you don't want to get on the bad side of."

"How am I supposed to reason with her if she's in Hell? I'm not going there." I described the woman I saw in the coffee shop before and in the crowd today.

"Yeah, that sounds like Lucy. She doesn't get to come away from her post very often, not unless Satan says so. You must have really upset them."

"Apparently my agency is making Withernsea too happy and loved up. Oh, and my parents have a longstanding feud with Lucy. She kidnapped my dad." I told him everything I knew.

"Ah."

"But how do I stop her?"

"And Satan. Chances are she's acting on his behalf. You have to offer them something they want in return for leaving you in peace. I'm afraid that's how it works. They're not going to bargain for the greater good, so you're going to have to think of something they want that's bad."

"Seriously?"

"I'm afraid so. Now, if we need to get a message down to Hell it's fine, because Rav is a demon, and he can visit there."

"Do you think we could bribe them with a good curry?" I suggested.

"I wish. Well, I'll leave you to have a think about it. I'll find out when you have the all clear to get this mess fixed up."

"Thank you, that would be appreciated."

"So, what has Theo said about what's happened?"

"You know Theo?"

"Yeah, he's one of my mates."

"Right, well, I kind of haven't told him yet."

Darius chuckled. "I'd love to be a fly on the wall when you do."

He followed me back into the office where another staring session followed between him and Kim. Jesus, was Derren Brown hiding in the cupboard? "Darius? Is that all?"

"It is. Oh, just to add that I sent in an application for the agency. I'm young, free, and single. Well, I'm not free on a full moon, but I'm available the rest of the time."

"Ah, yes. We're just updating the service, so it'll be even better, and we'll be in touch soon," I told him.

"Right, okay. I'll no doubt see you again soon."

Kim nodded her head, seemingly unable to speak.

I escorted him out of the office before they could start making goo-goo eyes at each other again.

When I got back Kim was tapping away on her keyboard.

"So, what was that all about? I felt like a third wheel."

"Sorry, I don't know what you're talking about. I'm dating Frankie, remember?" Kim said, going back to her screen.

"Okay then. Let's call it a night. I think we've had quite a day."

"Sure," Kim said. As I stood to get my coat, I saw her hastily click away from Darius' application form, recognisable from the photo on the screen. I decided it was better not to mention it.

"I will not allow you to reside by yourself any longer. I need to protect you through my waking hours, and if you will let me turn you, then you will be protected in my vault during the light of day."

"No. And you can stop with that manly protector shit. I can look after myself."

"But this is my role. To fight for your honour. I'm not sure how I could duel with a devil. I am entirely sure I would be dust in seconds, but at least I would have tried."

"Listen, I'd like my husband in my bed, rather than in a vase on the mantlepiece."

He grinned. A great beaming smile. "You said husband."

"What can I say? You're growing on me." I winked.

"I am growing right now, actually," he told me, and that was the end of the conversation.

Of course, the next morning when I woke, he was gone. It was going to take some getting used to, being the girlfriend and potential wife of a vampire. I wasn't sure whether I wanted to be made undead. What would happen to my witch powers? Then I remembered that I had a devil out to hurt me and the other things faded into insignificance.

∾

"You don't need to send Rav to Hell. Lucy comes to every Halloween celebration. She gets to be herself, but the people around her obviously don't know her horns are real," Frankie told me.

"So what does she get out of coming here?" I asked him. "Other than being able to walk around without a disguise?"

"That in itself is a major part of it, but also she has a quota for Halloween."

"A quota?"

"Midnight is the time when the veil drops, and she gets to choose one person. They have to have done something evil to be chosen. But she can go to their house and trick or treat them. Whatever they answer she can show them her true face. She touches them, and they burn from the inside out, then she escorts them to Hell."

"Please tell me being bad isn't running a red light or I've fucked it," I replied.

He chuckled. "No. Murder, child molestation. The kind of stuff that you think ah well, one less monster to worry about. It's sometimes a shock to see who goes. Last year it was my dog walker. Apparently, some of his charges never made it back to their owners."

"So in a way, she got to protect the animals. Aww bless," I said.

"Shelley—" Frankie yelled as a red-hot pointed arrow shot through the window and spiked through his wall. He froze it with water, and it fell to the floor with a crash.

"What the hell just happened?" I asked, shaking.

"Hell just happened." He raised his voice. "You just said 'Aww bless,' about a devil. Are you mad?"

"So, that's a no-no then, saying holy-type words?" I queried.

"If you want to live, I'd steer clear."

"Cool trick there with the ice. I can do that when I'm sent fire?"

"You can learn, but you can only control small amounts. No one has the capacity to stop hellfire but Satan, as far as I'm aware, not even the Lord himself. That's kind of the deal between good and evil. They have to keep a balance between the good stuff and the bad stuff. That's why sometimes shit happens, like earthquakes or tsunamis. Some people have to die so that others can live a good life."

"Shit, this stuff is deep. Anyway, so I can meet Lucy at the Halloween party down on the beach front?"

"If you can recognise her amongst the other devils, yes."

"Can I not do some kind of location spell?"

Frankie shook his head. "I'm afraid not. Only top-level witches can do location spells and you're only a half-witch. I would love to be able to do them. They could be so helpful."

"Damn. It would be a lot easier if I could just, for instance, wave at the wall and a map would appear and tell me where, like Theo is." I waved my hand, sighed, and rolled back against Frankie's sofa. "This whole thing sucks."

"Wha—" Frankie coughed.

"Have you got a crisp stuck in your throat again? How many times have I told you about eating too fast?" I sat up. Frankie was staring at the wall where above his television was a drawing of Theo's house and an X. "I thought you said I couldn't do it?"

"Y-y-you shouldn't be able to. This isn't right."

"Well, I can. Where is Kim?" I asked. A word came across the wall. U P S T A I R S. "My best friend is upstairs? Oh my god, have you got her waiting up there?" I pulled a face. "Am I after the event or before it?"

"Before. She's cool. She's watching *Emmerdale*."

I got up to leave. "You're weird. So very weird."

"Says the person who can make maps appear on my wall." His brow creased. "We need to test your magic again. Something's not adding up. Somehow, you've inherited more from your mother than your father, which is rare, though not impossible. Please be careful, it's very strong. Keep doing those protection spells and extend the wording to those innocents around you. You don't want them hurt by wild magic." He made some words appear across a piece of paper and handed it to me.

"Thank you," I told him. "Now roll on Halloween."

Chapter 15

Shelley

It was Halloween. We'd called a halt to supernatural matchmaking while we dealt with the issue of Lucy. In the meantime, Kim was adding applications to the new system and interviewing prospective clients—or should I say, she was adding the applications to the computer, interviewing the hot male applicants herself, and leaving the rest to me.

"Erm, not fair," I told her. "Leave some totty for me. I need eye candy too."

"You're getting married. I'm allowed to look at all the hot single guys."

"I am not getting married!"

"That's not what Ebony says, and she's a seer."

"I wish I'd never told you about the supe world." I sighed. "Has she said anything about you?"

"Just keeps going on about me dating a police officer."

"Oh yeah. I remember her saying that in Jax's. It's you and Darius. I bet you're going to date the werewolf."

"I don't think so."

"What have you got against Darius?"

"For a start I'm dating Frankie and for another thing, he has better hair than I do. I can't deal with that."

"I swear you were dropped on the head at birth."

"Not possible, my whole head and body are perfectly shaped."

"Come on," I told her. Looking at her attempt at a ghost outfit which was basically a powdered white face and a white bikini. She was going to freeze to death outside. "How are you a ghost?" I asked her.

"I died sunbathing," she said. "Overheated, had a heart attack."

"Every man out there will have a heart attack if they see you like that." I glamoured a white sheet over her body.

She looked down. "Take that off me right now." She tried to grab it but couldn't, seeing as it wasn't real. "This is an outrage. You're using your magic for bad things. Isn't this against some ethical code or something?"

"Let's go." I pulled her by the arm. "And remember, there will be children present in the café so no swearing at me."

"I'd better do it now then," she said, letting out a stream of expletives that showed me exactly what she thought of the outfit I'd fashioned for her.

∽

I'd thought Lucy might show up at the café open day, but she didn't, so it looked like I was going to have to look for her down at the beach. I agreed to meet Kim at The Marine bar at seven thirty.

"How will you find me in that crowd?" Kim asked. "You going to use a location spell?"

"No need. I'll look for the most naked person. The one surrounded by narrow-eyed women and men with their tongues hanging out. It shouldn't be difficult."

"So, you're going to take this monstrosity off me then?" she snarked.

"Yes, as soon as you get home, it'll disappear."

"Thank God for that."

"Look, you have to admit that when the local church's under-six choir walked in, you were pleased to be dressed."

"Yeah, whatever. Right, see you at The Marine. Are you staying dressed like that?" She pointed to my female vampire outfit which Theo had told me to save for later.

"Nope. I'm going as myself. Well, half of myself," I told her.

I figured if I was half-witch I needed to embrace it, so I'd bought a long dark wig and a pointy hat, plus a witch's costume. I looked pretty cute if I said so myself.

∽

Theo came to pick me up dressed as a werewolf, complete with Wolverine type fingers. We'd seen each other every night since we visited the farm, apart from Thursdays when he had a card night with his friends. I used that night to rest from all the sexual marathons we kept having.

"So, I guess I'll see Darius as a vampire?"

"You got it. We like to... what do you call it, 'take the piss' out of each other on Halloween."

We drove down to The Marine and met up with Kim who was standing next to Frankie. Kim was dressed as a corpse bride.

"Nice outfit," I said to her rather angry looking face.

"I *was* dressed in my ghost sunbather costume but another of the magical crew decided to dress me in another outfit." She gave Frankie a stink eye.

"Too many people were staring. I was at risk of turning them into snakes. It was easier to conjure you up a different outfit. In any case, you look even more sensational and will probably win outfit of the night."

"That's true. I do look amazing." She twirled. "Not like what *she* dressed me in earlier."

"Right, as fun as this is. I need to search for Lucy. Text me if you see her and remember our plan."

"You're not going alone," Theo said. "I'm coming with you."

"And me," said Kim.

"And me," added Frankie.

"Come on then," I said. "Let's get this over with."

"You don't smell of turnips this evening," Theo said to Frankie.

"Theo!"

"It's fine. I took something so you could avoid the odour. I'm nice like that. Whereas I'm failing to see any endearing qualities in your undead self." Frankie looked Theo up and down.

"I know, let's split up into two teams. I'm sure that would be more effective. Now, do you have your mobiles on in case we need to contact you?" I asked.

"We can communicate telepathically. Try it now. Just think of me and say 'Help'," said Frankie. I closed my eyes and imagined Lucy trying to set me on fire.

"What are you doing to him?" Kim screamed.

I opened my eyes. Kim told me Frankie had been buzzing.

"It's fine. I'll know to appear to wherever Shelley is," he said, then he and Kim went off in another direction.

Theo and I walked down the busy promenade and I stared at every devil. I didn't want to do a location spell if I could help it as it might give Lucy a signal that I was looking for her. I didn't know enough about how it worked. Music started up, and the crowds began to thicken. It became more difficult to stick together.

And then she was in front of me. Her eyes flashing red as she clutched my arm. She slashed open, what I knew from films to be a portal to her left, and dragged me through it.

I found myself sitting back in my own home.

"Well, well, well. If it isn't Shelley Linley. Or as you were born, Michelle Cast. I thought it was annoying enough that you were here in Withernsea upsetting Satan by creating love unions, but to find that you're the golden child... that was just the rain on my bonfire, and I don't like it damp."

"How did you find out it was me?"

"Because my boss hangs around Withernsea. He got all the gossip from dear Theo."

Theo. Satan knows Theo? What the actual fuck? "What do you want, Lucy?"

She looked at her blood-red pointed talons. "I ended up in Hell because of your parents, so I kinda think you can't offer me much in the way of a deal. Whereas I can play with you and make your life, well, Hell." She laughed and little flames sparked from her horns, two tiny protrusions atop her head.

I tilted my head as I met her gaze. "I get you were pissed that my dad went off with my mum. I would have been. To be honest, I'm on your side about the whole 'try to split them up thing' because to dump you before your wedding was pretty shit, but how is this my fault? I can't help that I was born."

She sat back on my sofa, which was annoying since she kept sparking and singeing the lovely leather.

"I knew Ebony's mother. She'd told me of her prophecy. That your father kept a secret, handed down through the generations. She saw a child, she said, who would be very powerful. She said that child's child would eventually rule all of Withernsea." She shot flames at my candles, lighting them all up. "I thought she meant me. My child. Our child. Mine and Dylan's."

"Oh."

"When your father met your mother, they humiliated me. Yolanda's predictions became clearer though. She said it was your mother that would have the baby."

"So you set the fire and killed Yolanda?"

"No." Lucy's eyes flashed with red, and my curtains set fire and dropped to the floor in ashes. "I stood near their flat, near the boutique, and wished revenge on them all for their betrayal. Your mother had just announced her pregnancy. A man approached me. He looked like a vampire. He said he could transport me and your father away to a different place if I would agree to work for him. He said he managed people, and it was somewhere hot and away from here. I loved your father, so I agreed. I guessed the stranger had a supernatural connection, most of Withernsea had. Apart from me. I was one of the ordinary people, yet not good enough for your father. I now know where the phrase *Hell hath no fury like a woman scorned* originates from."

She turned to me and reduced the cushions either side of me to ashes. I tried to raise a protective bubble around myself but that just made her laugh louder.

"I made a deal with the devil." Lucy smiled. "He looked so normal, but he was able to make a deal with me as I had evil intent in my mind. I'd been thinking about your parents, how they didn't deserve happiness, but ruin, and I had thoughts about killing them. Just anger, but that was enough for him to work with. He set fire to the flat, and it spread to the shop."

"The devil?"

"Satan himself. The minute I agreed to the deal, strands of red smoke wrapped around me. Your mother and father were caught up in the fire. The devil grabbed me and dragged me into the flames. They were trying to get out. I told your father that if he wanted to save you and your mother that he had to come with me. He could see I was corrupted by evil, but he agreed. Otherwise, all three of you would have perished in that fire. When the fire brigade arrived, I was placed on a stretcher. Your parents walked outside. I thought I'd hallucinated the whole thing. That somehow, I'd been in the fire and it had affected my mind, but then I found myself guarding Hell itself. Your father was bound to the same place, but he was there to suffer."

"But how could my father go to Hell if he hadn't made the deal himself?"

"Because when he saw me and realised I was going to split you all up, just for a moment he wished to kill me. His evil intent was enough. Of course, feeling even more bitter and twisted because I now lived in Hell, I told Satan about your mother's pregnancy. But it appears that the ones upstairs argued that Satan had upset the balance by taking your father, and so your mother was to be protected.

"So indirectly, Satan actually saved my life?"

"Yes, something he has never forgiven the gods for. Satan has ruled Withernsea for years now, walking around and living there as one of their own, while I tend the fires of Hell for him. While he was happy at the misery in Withernsea, I was left alone. You think I'm the enemy, but I'm just a puppet, *Michelle*. Now you're trying to make those he ruins happy, so you need to be taken care of."

"If it's Satan that wants to ruin me, why have you kidnapped me?"

"Because you're going to help me escape Hell. Now there's a deal you can offer me. Help me escape, and I'll free your father so he and your mother can get back together in Withernsea."

"But I thought you didn't want them together?"

She grimaced. "I've been stuck in one place with your father for 26 years with no escape. I'm sick of looking at his damn face, or should that be damned face? It's time for a change."

"It doesn't look like I have much of an option, does it?" I told her.

"Not really," she said. "Also, I get to take someone evil with me to Hell on Halloween and if you don't comply, I'll take Theo. He's a murderer after all."

I wanted to call her a bitch, but I knew from dealing with a premenstrual Kim when to keep my mouth shut and this was PMT x 1000 sitting on my sofa. "You said Satan has been walking around the streets amongst everyone for all this time?"

"Yes! He enjoyed taking a bite out of your friend. He wasn't impressed that you managed to heal the wounds. They were supposed to turn your friend evil. She would have begun to kill your other friends off one by one. You've pissed him off. He detects that the prophecy has started. That you have strong powers.

"Run this past me again. Satan's been walking around Withernsea as a vampire?"

"He has. He said tonight he's going to finish off the job he's started on your friend. He can't come after you directly, but he can kill some of your friends until you agree to make a deal with him." She looked at her red nails. "I'll bet he's there right now."

"Take me back," I demanded.

"Do we have a deal?" She smiled slowly.

"Yes. I will help you get out of Hell for the freedom of my parents."

"Excellent. As soon as I'm free, I will free your father."

"Now excuse me a minute while I do a location spell to find my friend," I told her. I stared at the wall and saw she was in a backstreet near the amusements.

"Can you take me there?" I asked Lucy.

"I suppose so," she said, then she grabbed me and back we went through a portal.

I appeared in the alleyway, Lucy standing behind me. Kim was lying on the floor.

Laying over her, his mouth on her neck, was Theo.

"Tell me this isn't true," I wailed. "Are you Satan?"

Chapter 16

Shelley

Theo stood up, Kim's blood dripping from his mouth. "Of course I'm not Satan. Have you been drinking? I got a call from Frankie saying they'd been in the bar and Kim didn't feel he was giving her enough attention, so she stomped out of the pub. He gave her a minute and then went after her, but she was nowhere to be seen.

"So how did you find her?"

"She's bleeding. It's like a homing beacon to me. I'm trying to close her wounds with my saliva, but it's not working."

"Because they're not vampire wounds. Here, let me." I moved towards Kim.

"Oh no, what's she doing here?" Theo asked, looking over my shoulder.

"Oh, yeah, Theo—Lucy. Lucy—Theo."

"Pleasure," said Lucy. "By the way, behave yourself or I'm taking you to Hell with me tonight."

I looked at Theo and shook my head. "Not the time to ask right now."

I put my fingers on the bite marks that once again marred Kim's neck and closed my eyes.

"Please show me with this spell. What ails my friend so I can make her well."

Opening my eyes, I saw a thick, red sticky liquid came out of Kim's mouth, heat making it sizzle.

"What has he done to her?" I closed my eyes again. "With my fingers on this wound, let it heal and make it good."

In my mind, I saw red-hot liquid in her system, so I imagined a cool, icy, nitrogen-style antidote, the white smoke chasing the hot liquid out of her body. Kim spluttered, and Theo held her while she vomited the red liquid again and again. Then she opened her eyes.

"What the fuck?"

I sent the psychic message to Frankie. He materialised in front of me and looked Kim over. "She's okay. She might feel off for a few days, but she'll survive." He looked at me. I nodded.

"But, Shelley, I don't know how you're doing this. I released the rest of your powers, but to be able to thwart Satan. This is beyond anything anyone in Withernsea has ever known."

"Really?" I turned around to Lucy. "I wonder if I can freeze you. Shall I give it a try?" I raised an eyebrow.

She looked back at me warily and took a step backwards. "Maybe you could. But you made a deal with me and that can't be broken now. Not even by a powerful witch."

"So how do I find Satan?"

"You don't. You wait for him."

I sighed. "Okay, while I wait, how do I get you free so that I can have my parents back?"

"You have to bargain with the devil himself," she said.

I placed a hand on my hip. "Excuse me? You said nothing about this before."

"I'm a devil. You have to anticipate I'll be devious. I'm a bad guy. You really need lessons in supes."

"So let me get this straight. I agreed to free you to get my parents back, not realising you meant I'd have to take on Satan?"

"That's right, babes."

"And I can't do a location spell?"

"Doubt it."

"You can do location spells?" Theo's face seemed to whirr with thoughts. "I know we're busy looking for the devil, but can you do one to find my sire's sire? I'll be able to get my money back if we survive hellfire."

"Sure." I flayed my hands in the air. "Not like I've anything better to do."

"Well, while you're pratting around with that, I'm going to get a gingerbread ghost," said Lucy, stomping off.

I conjured up a picture in the night sky that looked like I drew it with sparklers. "Where is Theo's sire's sire?" I asked.

"That's my house," said Theo.

"I'm going to try to find Satan," I said. "Just because other people can't do it, doesn't mean I can't." I looked in the air and pictured the stereotypical devil with horns. A red-hot light shone in the living room of the map of Theo's home. "That can't be right," I said.

Then the light opened into a flaming red portal and a voice shouted out. "Do come and join me. I've been waiting."

"Don't do it, Shelley. It's a trick," said Theo. "It's got to be."

"But if I don't go to see him, I don't get my parents back."

"What's going on?" said Lucy. "I felt myself being summoned."

"Bring them through, Lucy," the voice said again.

"Come on, it's fine," Lucy said.

"She could be lying to you." Theo pointed at Lucy. "She said herself that she lies."

I turned and looked at Lucy. "Not this time. She wants to be free. She knows this is the only way Withernsea is freed from his rule."

"But how has he been ruling? I've not seen any evidence of demonic power."

"He's not been walking around as Satan," Lucy said. "He's been living as a vampire, shagging around. Every one of his women has ended up in hospital with severe burns. I see it all where I am, but I'm powerless to stop him. Plus, one of them ransacked my flat when I disappeared and stole my Mac cosmetics—she had it coming."

"I'll drive us there," said Theo. "He'll just have to wait. It's only a couple of minutes' drive from here."

"Well, hurry," said the voice from the portal. "Or your friend Darius will be toast."

※

"I bet I could teleport with practice," I grumbled.

"I offered to take you; don't say I didn't," huffed Lucy.

"It's a couple of minutes up the street for Heaven's sake," said Theo, who had been struggling to get his car started.

A flame leapt out of Lucy's fingers and singed his back seat.

"We're in a petrol car, can you not blow us up?" I shouted.

"He's the one who caused that, saying words about the people upstairs." She folded her arms over herself and mumbled something about Hell being easier than real life.

We got out of the car and followed Theo into his house. As we entered the living room, we found two men playing cards.

"Darius? Reuben? I... I just spoke to, well, never mind. Er, did I invite you round for a game? I don't remember," Theo said, his face creased in concern.

"What's going on?" I asked.

"This is Darius, as you already know, and this is my best friend Reuben," Theo explained. "So... I'm a little confused."

"Really, you are so stupid," Lucy said. "I've already told you he's been living as a vampire."

"Say what?" I pointed to Reuben. "Is Reuben really Satan?"

"That's impossible," Theo exploded. "Reuben is my best friend. We play cards every Thursday night."

"Yeah, and Monday, Tuesday, Wednesday, Friday, Saturday, Sunday, he's either down in Hell or causing death and mayhem here," added Lucy.

"Lucy, my beautiful assistant. Are you enjoying Halloween? Have you decided who your new plaything will be?"

"Yes." She smiled sweetly. "I'm going to take Theo with me."

"What?" yelled Darius.

"Be quiet, wolf, or I'll be having a nice steak for dinner," snarled Satan.

Darius' face paled. "All those times we've played cards and had banter... you were the devil. I can't believe it."

"And you thought it was wereblood that made me volatile. You're so stupid."

"Is there someone else here?" I asked.

"No, why?"

"Because according to my spell, Theo's sire's sire is here as well."

Satan chuckled and raised a hand. "Oooh, that would be me, kind of. Basically, I watched Theo's ridiculously stupid sire get attacked, and then his sire, the original Reuben, came along, greedily wanting all the money from the sale of the farm, so I kind of tore out his evil undead soul and took over his body. I've had various assistants looking after Hell, and in the meantime, I've ruled Withernsea. It's been one of the worst places to live. Diabolical in fact. That is until you came along, Shelley. It was okay while you didn't have any powers and only wanted to match up the poor human saps who live here, but, *oh no*, Fate, the arse pain she is, decided to send Theo across your path, awakening your powers. I'm afraid that's not going to work for me. Take him to Hell, Lucy."

"I want to make a deal," I told him.

"Halt!" he shouted at Lucy. "It would appear a different option has been thrown my way." He stroked his chin. "I need a moment to ponder this. I don't want to waste the offer of a binding deal." His eyes flashed red. What was it with devils and vampires? Was there a shop somewhere with a deal on red contacts?

"Right. I want you to agree that you will not marry or give birth to this man's child," he said, pointing at Theo. "Also, that you will not arrange any more dates for supernaturals at your agency. I need my supes depressed. They create more death and destruction that way. Now, what do you want?"

"All I ask is that you let Lucy free of her duties and allow her to come back to earth. She was wronged. She didn't deserve to be placed in Hell. By doing so, she will free my father, and my mother will come out of exile."

"You're willing to give him up for this?"

"To save my family, yes. I want to know my father and mother." I looked at Theo, tears in my eyes. "I am so, so, sorry, but I have to do this."

Theo looked down at the floor. "I can't believe this. I've lost my best friend and my would-be wife in one night."

"Oh, and by the way, Shelley. How is your friend, Kim? She sure did taste nice when I bit her. Even better the second time around. It was easy to get Theo's tie from here. Stupid vampire never locks the door. I hope it didn't cause too much trouble between you and your boyfriend. Not that it matters now." Satan laughed, then stood up and shook my hand. "Deal," he said.

"Deal," I agreed. Red and white ribbons of smoke wrapped around our hands before dissipating.

I looked at Theo as the devil broke into laughter.

"Now," I said.

Chapter 17

Shelley

It all happened in seconds. The deal was binding and in front of me stood a red reptilian looking man. As he spoke, I noticed he did indeed have a forked tongue.

"That concludes our business," he said.

"I don't think so." A man walked through the door.

He had red hair the same as my own and I instinctively knew that this was my father, even before Lucy said, "Dylan."

He winked at me. "We kept one more secret from you, daughter." In front of our eyes, he transformed into a dragon-like creature. Standing on two legs, he had a dragon's head and wings on his back. His trunk and legs were reptilian, and he had a fishlike tail.

"This can't be true," said Lucy.

"What?" I asked.

"He's a wyvern," she said.

"Well, this has been fun, but I'm out of here," said Satan. "I need to tell Rav that he's back holding the fort."

"There's been a slight change in plan." A deep voice boomed from the dragon's mouth. "I think you'll find that Withernsea is mine."

I would have expected the devil to try to toast my father alive, but instead, he stood there with a bemused look on his face. "What are you talking about, lizard?"

"Did you not wonder how you were able to plunder this place unchallenged for the last 26 years?" said my father. "My family have held the secret of Withernsea for years. Its real name is

Wyvernsea, and it belongs to my family. With every child our line grows stronger as our children are born with even more power. I was born half-human and half-wyvern, but as you can see, the wyvern gene wins out, taking the best from the other half and adapting. I could pass for human when I was far from anything of the sort."

That's when the devil did as I'd expected. He shot fire at my father, who encased himself in an icy tomb and remained unaffected. "While ever I'm in Wyvernsea, I am stronger than you and the gods. It was only the fact you took me by surprise in human form, transporting me to Hell before I realised what was happening, that resulted in my imprisonment. Now, thanks to you, I'm back, my wife is coming back too, and we can be with our daughter."

"Yet, the prophecy isn't going to come true, boo-hoo," said Satan. "She made a deal not to marry the vampire."

"I didn't," I said.

He turned to me and his look chilled me to the bone. "You made a deal," he snarled.

"Yes, not to marry him," I said, pointing to Theo. "Or to have his babies."

"Is there something I'm not understanding?" spat Satan.

"Yes," I said, and the glamour fell away, revealing that Theo was in fact Frankie.

"Well, hello again," said Frankie. "Good job I knew all about Theo and you lot from our card games. The only thing I struggled with was his car. He really needs something more modern."

In a fury, Satan struck out and smote him. I watched as my friend and mentor fell to the floor, his body charred. Croaks of pain fell from his lips.

"Frankie, no!" I leapt to his side, placing my hands on his skin and began to say some words of a spell. But it didn't do anything."

"It's okay," he told me. "Ebony said this would happen. That I would sacrifice my life, but it would be for the greater good." He coughed. "Listen, tell Kim she was a great shag." He tried to laugh but coughed in earnest. "She wasn't meant for me," he said, and with one final scream of pain, his head fell to the side.

My own rage leapt to the surface. As I turned, my dad grasped hold of my hand. "Get ready, I'm passing on your legacy." An icy sensation surged through my body. My legs formed a lizard-like skin, and I grew wings.

"You have all the powers but because you're half-witch, your appearance should be kinder," my dad said, and he kissed my cheek.

Satan grabbed Lucy. "I agreed she could stay in Withernsea, but I don't remember stating she had to be alive, if we're being pernickety." He tilted his head. "Say bye, Lucy."

I shot out a sluice of icy water from my hand. It covered Satan and froze him in place. Lucy dropped to the floor, and I pulled her behind me. Heat burned through my ice until Satan stood there once more.

"Well," he snarled. "It would appear that for now I shall have to return home. But I'll be working on things while I'm down there. At least my supes will remain miserable now you can't arrange their dates."

"I can't," I told him. "But Kim can and seeing as I'll be getting married and having a wyvern/witch/vampire crossbreed baby, I think I'll probably be quite busy anyway. See yourself out."

Satan turned to Lucy. "I'm not removing your horns. Having spent so much time in Hell some of it will still be within you. See if you can find love with those on your head."

He vanished, leaving a trail of fire that didn't touch us but burned through Theo's apartment, reducing his belongings to ash while leaving the building intact.

I crouched down next to Frankie's body, and I cried and cried and cried.

∽

"How did you and Frankie do that? I didn't see you swap?" asked Lucy.

"We did it when you bought your gingerbread," I told her. "Frankie, Theo, Kim, and I had already worked it out as a potential back-up plan. It made more sense for me to attend with Frankie who could do magic, coax out my powers or tell me spells if needed, than with my boyfriend. I'm sorry we couldn't tell you, but you kind of can't be trusted."

"I understand. But I hope now I'm out of Hell and away from Satan's instructions we can try to be civil," Lucy said. "I'm going to go now. Your mother will no doubt appear at any moment and like I said, I'm sick of seeing your father's face." She sliced her arm through the air and then turned to me. "Forgot I can't do that anymore.

Looks like I'm walking. Time to find somewhere to stay." With that she walked out of the room.

Dad moved Frankie's body into the bedroom. Theo arrived with Kim shortly afterwards. He looked around his burned-out apartment. "Kim's been checked out at the hospital and she's fine," he said. "Looks like I need to find that sire of mine so I can move into the farm."

"I'm afraid Satan killed your sire years ago, so you're not going to get that debt settled," I told him. "And don't even think about looking for your sire's, sire's sire. The farm's bought now. End of."

"Ugh. Well at least technically you bought it." He harrumphed, then looked around. "Where's Frankie? I'd like to thank him for protecting my future wife," he said.

I began to sob again. "He died," I told him. "Saving my life."

"Died? How long since the time of death?"

"About thirty minutes," I said. "What does it matter? I've lost my friend and what am I going to tell Kim?" Kim was currently standing next to Darius. They were doing the weird staring at each other thing again. He was filling her in on things, and it was only a matter of time until he got to the part about Frankie.

"Where is he?" Theo asked.

"In the bedroom."

Theo leapt away from me and into the bedroom. I ran after him, once again shaken by seeing the body on the floor. He latched onto Frankie's neck and began to suck.

"You can't do that! That's disgusting. I know he's dead and can't feel it, but for fuck's sake, Theo, put him down, you sick bastard."

I dived into my handbag, pulled out a plastic Tupperware box and started throwing pieces of steak at him.

Kim burst through the door. "He's dead. Oh God, he's dead." She took one look at Frankie's charred body and ran back out heaving.

Theo glared at me. "Can you stop throwing food at me—again? And we'll be having a conversation about why you're walking around with steak in your bag when we get home. I'm not draining him. We have a one-hour window for me to bring him back. He'll be a vampire, and will have lost his magical powers on death, but he'll be able to guide you. He just won't be able to perform magic himself anymore. Do you think he'd want that? To be undead, rather than not be here at all?"

"Yes," said a female voice. My mother came through the doorway. "He's a very dear friend, and between us we'll show him there's a new path for him. Please, turn him."

Theo slit his wrist with a small knife he took from his pocket and let his blood fall into Frankie's mouth. After the first few drops, Frankie's body began to heal and his mouth fixed on Theo's wrist, where he sucked like his life depended on it, which it totally did. After a few minutes, Theo pushed him away and licked the puncture marks to close the wound.

"I'll take him," said my mother. "Dylan and I will take him to the caves until he has learned to master his new strength."

Theo nodded.

"We will speak soon, daughter," my mother said, giving me a kiss on the cheek. "But for now, rest up and take care of your friend. It's been quite an eventful evening."

I nodded, and she left.

Theo and I walked out of the room and back to Kim. Darius was with her in the bathroom. She crouched over the toilet, looking pale and wan.

"I can't believe he died."

"He didn't," I told her.

"You mean that overcooked chip is still alive?" she asked, her eyes wide. "That's even worse. No amount of *Extreme Makeover* can fix that."

"He's back to looking like himself, although much, much paler. Theo turned him and saved his life."

"He's not dead?" she asked.

"Err, yeah, he's pretty dead; well, pretty undead."

"Oh," she said. "But I don't think I can date him anymore because I'll keep seeing Chargrilled Charlie." She vomited again.

"I'll get you some water and then we need to all go to my house." I looked around the apartment. "I don't know what these devils have against soft furnishings."

Chapter 18

Shelley

It took a few days for us all to come to terms with the effects of Halloween. Kim was being monitored by a doctor at the local hospital who specialised in supernatural cases. I'd met him, and he was both human and fantastic looking, but Kim had no interest.

"I need time out from dating," she told me as we sat in Jax's waiting for the other businesswomen to join us. "In the last couple of weeks, I've learned Withernsea is full of supernaturals, had a near-death experience, and a boyfriend who went from wizard to fledgling vampire and is currently locked away for his own safekeeping."

"They have to do that when they're new or they do what Theo did."

She sighed. "I know. He's called me, you know? He says it's changed him, and although he remembers who he was, it's not who he is now. But we're going to try to be friends when he's eventually discharged."

"It's a shame. I can highly recommend having a vampire boyfriend."

"I've already told you that she's destined for the shifter." Ebony's voice came from behind us. "But not for a while." She stroked Kim's face. "You look pale. You must rest, and in the meantime, my cosmetics are fully stocked up so you can look less wan. I'll put a palette to one side for you."

"Seriously? I'll be okay?" Kim asked.

"Yes. Well, there might be a few little hiccoughs in your path, but it'll work out."

"What hiccoughs?" Kim panicked. "Like being half drained to death?"

"I'll just get my coffee ordered," Ebony said, walking towards Jax.

"I'm going off her," Kim said.

"I need to talk to you. You know my deal with Satan. I agreed to not run the Supernatural Dating Agency."

"You did what? Are you selling up? I'm no use at anything else. Do you think the new owners will keep me on?"

"You're such a dumb cow sometimes. I didn't say I was closing Withernsea Dating. I just can't run the supernatural side. *You're* going to run it—if you're willing of course. I'll do the humans and you do the supes. If there's any crossover, you'll have to manage it. I'm bound by my pact. I can't matchmake."

"Does that mean a pay rise?" she asked, smiling and winking.

"Yes, it does, and longer, less flexible hours."

"That's fine. I'm going to be a workaholic instead of a sexaholic."

I rolled my eyes.

Jax and Ebony joined the table, shortly followed by Samara from the groomers and finally Lucy.

"Everyone, this is Lucy," I introduced her.

"Hi again. Cute headband," said Jax.

"I said that too," said Samara.

"It's a great signature look," added Ebony. "They're from my boutique." She winked at Lucy whose floral headband was styled to cover up the two small protrusions that remained on her head.

"So, Lucy was just telling me she opened a steakhouse near the promenade," said Samara.

"Yes." Lucy nodded. "Barbecue is my speciality."

I went into my bag and brought out some cards. "You're all invited," I told them.

Kim shrieked. "You're getting married?! How did he propose? Tell us all."

I beamed and leaned closer. "Well," I said. "It was Thursday evening and Theo and I were in the bedroom. We'd decided that cuddling each other made us feel much better after recent events and then, erm, anyway..."

"Is there a point to this or are you showing off that you're having sex?" sniped Lucy.

"Anyway, afterwards we lay in each other's arms, and I realised that after everything that had happened, I didn't want to wait. Also,

I apologised for jumping to conclusions several times, and everything was just, at that moment, perfect." I sighed. "Then we both said it, at the same time, 'Will you marry me,' and then we both said, 'Yes,' at exactly the same time." I grinned stupidly again. So wide it was making my cheeks ache. "Then we totally had a ton of hot sex again, and yes I'm saying that to rub it in your face, biatch," I told Lucy.

"You realise you have to get me a date, don't you?" she said to Kim.

"That'll be a devil of a date," quipped Kim. "On your application we'll have to put something like raging PMT. No, PHT. Post-Hell tension."

Lucy sneered at her. "I throw out chips that resemble your last date," she bitched. "How is Frank-en-fried, anyway?"

"Still in training," I answered. "Anyway, back to me." I pointed to the invites. We're getting married at the farm... on Monday."

"Monday?" Kim said. "That's a bit soon."

"Maybe, but the guy agreed to move out super-fast," I said, failing to mention that it was because he thought Simon Cowell wanted to move in, and he got a photo and an autograph for his helpfulness. "Also, we already have the fireworks on Sunday in the park and I don't want to detract from that. So, Monday it is, for an extra firework party."

Then the *Female Entrepreneurs who do it with their Colleagues* talked about plans for the new year.

∽

"I can't wait to become Mrs Landry," I told Theo. "And I can't believe that I actually have a father to give me away." I'd met up with my parents a couple of times. Although we'd clicked, we were taking it slow. Plus, they'd not seen each other for 26 years, so I was keeping well away from their house. My mother had promised to keep teaching me magic and my father to tell me more about being a wyvern. He'd told me that I shared responsibility in keeping 'Wyvernsea' a thriving community.

"And after we have our baby and you're ready, I'll turn you into my vampire wife as well as my wedded wife," Theo said. I had to admit I was nervous about the whole 'undead, live for hundreds of years thing', but there was no immediate rush.

"The fireworks have arrived," Theo said. "So, all we need now is for the day to arrive."

"In the meantime, I do believe fireworks have started right here in my panties," I told my fiancé. "Fancy a bang?"

∽

Of course, our wedding took place on an evening. We stood in the grounds of our farmhouse, surrounded by family and friends. Even my adoptive parents had attended, along with Polly. Theo and I had decided we preferred to get married on our own land than in a church. I was kept warm by patio heaters and the bonfire. It was alright for my husband. Being undead, he didn't feel the cold.

My husband. Gosh it seemed strange to say those words.

But now the last of the guests were leaving, mainly because my best friend was telling everyone that they'd stayed long enough, and they needed to fuck off home. I didn't know who had the worst attitude: her or Lucy.

Speaking of Lucy, I stood in the doorway of my home unseen as she wandered down the driveway towards her taxi. I watched as she flicked her thumb and a flame shot out. She could still shoot fire...

But that was something to think about another day. Right now, it was time for my husband—there was that word again—to carry me over the threshold of our new home and take me to bed.

"Are you ready, Mrs Landry?" he asked me.

"Yes, Mr Landry. Very ready."

He picked me up, white gown and all, without effort and escorted me over the threshold, placing me down in the hallway. I'd been in close proximity to his body while he carried me, and I was ready to be a whole lot closer.

"Welcome home," a wavering voice came from our left.

I turned my head around and my jaw dropped. There in front of me was the hazy outline of a woman.

"Mum?" said Theo. "Is that you?"

THE END

A Devil Of A Date

SUPERNATURAL DATING AGENCY
– BOOK TWO

Chapter 1

Lucy

Leaving Hell, was, well, hell on earth.

Oh, don't get me wrong, I was glad to be free of the furnace and back to Withernsea. It's just that—everything had changed.

I'd watched an episode of *Eastenders*. Phil Mitchell was now old.

Nerds had become cool with *The Big Bang Theory* and the *IT Crowd*.

Stars in Their Eyes wasn't on anymore.

I was going to need counselling.

I'd kept up with certain things in Hell. We had computers though the internet was limited to what Satan felt we needed to know, and that wasn't the latest on Kylie and Jason (who'd just released *Especially for You* when I was kidnapped). Fashion was easy to keep up with as the new residents came fully dressed and I gained an envied designer wardrobe from the many rich wives who'd killed their cheating husbands. That's how my love of Louboutins had started.

But television. This was all new to me.

When I'd left earth, Grant and Phil Mitchell had just joined Eastenders, my favourite soap opera. I needed to watch twenty-seven years of episodes to get caught up. Seeing as that was impossible, instead I was trying to read episode guides on the fan wikis I'd discovered on the net, but that was taking a long time.

I'd spent the best part of two months when I wasn't working, sat in front of the television while my roommate was at work or sleeping, trying to work out why the latest craze was to watch people living their romantic lives on the television.

When I'd left, *Doctor Who* had just been pulled off the television due to poor ratings. Now it had been back on for years and I'd missed this Tennant bloke. The sexiest doctor ever. I'd lost a week out of my new life catching up on him alone.

The Fresh Prince of Bel Air didn't appear to have aged as much as Phil Mitchell. I wondered if Will Smith was an undercover supe.

Then there was food. I'd not needed to eat while in Hell. We filled up on the souls of the evil. Now I needed to eat. I was plowing through the latest pizzas while trying to keep healthy via drinking these probiotic things that apparently helped my bowels.

Everything was taking so much getting used to. It was like entering a disco: the bass thumping, the lights flashing—but sped up. At times I'd been glad to get to bed, to sleep and block it all out, and wow these Memory Foam mattresses were the bomb. I'd forgotten how much I'd enjoyed sleeping so I made the most of it while my roommate was downstairs.

I heard footsteps thumping down the stairs.

Shit. Shit. Shit.

I desperately tried to turn *The Only Way is Essex* off, but Gemma was so loud and she yelled "Arg," at the top of her voice.

I tried to rip a portal in the air, then remembered I couldn't do that anymore.

The door banged open, and my housemate stood there in his boxer briefs. His hairy, portly belly spilled over, and I glanced up at his middle-aged, balding head. Funny I'd been thinking about Phil Mitchell, I seemed to be sharing an apartment with someone who could be his brother.

"Who the fuck are you?" The guy scratched his bald pate though I noted his nostrils flared. He seemed stuck between thoughts he might be sleepwalking and ones of bashing his glamorous intruder's head in. A smell emanated from him. Great, I'd made him nervous and now I had to suffer. What the hell had he eaten?

I wished I could focus on just his head and didn't have to see his gut. "Do you have a t-shirt by any chance?" I asked him. "I'm finding it hard to talk to you when you're half naked."

"Are you kidding me? You break into my home and you're asking me to get dressed?"

"I didn't break in. This is my home."

He edged towards me slowly, raising his hand up. He was acting like I was a cornered frightened dog like the ones on *Dog Rescuers*, which I'd got a little hooked on. If he came at me with a net, I'd bite his nose off.

"Okay, now take it easy, love. You're just a little confused. Maybe you live down the street and you've had a bit too much to drink and I've somehow left the door unlocked. It's an easy fix. You just have to tell me your address."

I huffed. "I live here. Fact is, I moved in around April 1991. Then I had an extended holiday somewhere hot and now I'm back."

"The previous tenant's lease was given up by her parents because she went missing." He looked at me and his brows creased. "Which isn't you as you're too young. Anyway, she ran off cos her fiancé got his leg over with another woman. She must have been a moose whereas you're fit as fuck even if you're crazy."

I zoned out as he carried on with lewd suggestions on how we could flat share. He was yapping through TOWIE which was unacceptable.

"Oh! Now I see why my electric bill has gone up. I complained to them that it was too high. It's been you. How long have you been here, sneaking around?"

Another stench wafted over. I scrunched up my nose and tried not to breathe.

"Do you know? I thought fuck I have a crazy woman in my house, but now, seeing you lying on my sofa, looking all sexy in that tight red chemise, I'm thinking either I'm hallucinating or you're a gift from God."

As his curtains set on fire and his eyes went wide, I guessed he was quickly changing his mind.

Chapter 2

Kim

Zoella coffee mug—check.
    Zoella desk tidy—check.
Zoella natty pencils—check.
The most awesome job in the world? Check. Check. Check.
I ran the Supernatural division of Withernsea Dating Agency. My promotion had taken place two months ago, and I was finally finding my feet and settling into the post after a handing over period from my best friend and owner of the agency, Shelley. Or should that be two months of lectures of what I could and couldn't do.
Well, today she wasn't here.
Oh no.
Because today was her husband's 127th birthday. Yes, you heard me right. He was 127 and his fertile window had opened today. As it only lasted for a week, and then would be a further one-hundred-and-one years before it reappeared, Shelley was having a week's holiday to concentrate on the making of a little supernatural baby. Her husband was a total stud muffin: all dark and delicious, even if he was one of the undead, and I wouldn't have been human if I wasn't envious that Shelley was having a whole week of down and dirty shenanigans. And I was human, though my bestie had discovered she was a witch/wyvern cross. Yes, she'd had quite the adventure the last few months. We all had.
But I wasn't jealous she was making a baby. Nah, she could keep that. The only thing I wanted drooling near me was a hot man, or even a cute puppy. But babies? No way. Far too much fun to be had

when you were single. Though I was swearing off any repeat performances with any man for now, human or otherwise, with where my last relationship had got me.

Anyway, today it was time to make a few adjustments to the dating contract. I rubbed a little *Soap and Glory* hand food into my palms as I cast my eyes over the current agreement on my laptop. The smell of it was divine—the hand cream, not the computer. I made a mental note to stop by *Boots* on the way home for another tube and then remembered that a quick trip to the shops wasn't so easy anymore. Shaking my head, I looked at my screen once again.

Terms of agreement

I (insert name here), of (insert address here), hereby declare that my membership of Withernsea Dating Agency shall be kept secret from all of human origin unless prior checks have been made.

Checking was Theo doing his vampire mind mojo, asking humans on the books if seeing a supernatural being would freak them out, then making them forget he'd asked the question. Shelley ran the human side of the operation and with Theo's vampire speed it was easy for her husband to just 'pop by the office', when required.

By signing this document, I agree to cause no intentional harm to another human or supernatural being.

I agree that the facts here are true and that I give permission for this document to be passed through a truth serum. Any lies will result in instant cancellation of membership.

We'd had to add this because some supes such as demons never stopped bloody lying.

Now it was time to add in my extra bit.

I agree that should the agency deem it advisable, I will go on a 'dummy date' with a member of the team in order to practice dating.

There, done. Now I could pick out all the good-looking supes and date them under the pretence of it being to help them. Keeping things nice and casual, just as I needed it right now. As if on cue, the pain in my ass spoke up.

"That's deplorable. If I still had my magic, I'd make that disappear. You're taking liberties."

I flicked my gaze towards the vampire hanging upside down in the corner of my office.

"Yeah, well you don't. And I'm sick of telling you that we aren't together anymore. I'm free to date whoever I choose."

And here was my current problem and the reason I did not want a regular date. My ex-boyfriend, Frankie–well, ex-fuck buddy to be entirely honest—had been killed on Halloween by the devil, then turned by Theo into a vampire. He'd lost all his previous magical powers, but something had gone awry. Whereas all other vampire's body clocks called for slumber between dawn and midday, Frankie didn't sleep at all. Not one wink. He could however hang upside down for hours in a kind of 'rest-mode'. The minute I moved, walked, talked, he was all ears, and they were super-charged hearing ears now. As a new vampire, Frankie should have been desperate for blood, but instead he'd developed a neediness for me. As in, he was scared to be away from me. I'd been the last constant in his life and once his initial blood thirst had dissipated, he'd start craving Kim. Now, I had to say I couldn't really blame him. I was an amazing shag, but having a vampire in the corner of my office or bedroom for the past two months had been draining, even if my blood had stayed in my body.

It had proved impossible to keep him in the 'caves', the place where fledgling vampires were taught about their new bodies and where some vampires went to die. Shelley had told me that the caves were a place of rebirth and death. If a vampire had tired of the endless night, they could attend for counselling, say an incantation, and turn to dust. They also cared for vampires whose turnings had not gone to plan, like Frankie's. Shelley's mother and father volunteered there to give back to the supernatural community of Withernsea.

Frankie had been so tormented to be without me that Margret, Shelley's mum, had asked if I could visit there, to see if it would calm him down. I'd ended up bringing him home as he wouldn't detach himself from my leg until I promised he could stay with me a while.

Bearing in mind that Shelley had mad witch skills, she'd done her best to turn his obsession off, but it showed no signs of abating. While I had my house guest, I figured I may as well do a little harmless flirting with the supes of Withernsea and yes it had crossed my mind that while I was at it, I could quiz them to see if they had the power to sever a dependent vamp from my life.

I wouldn't have minded so much maybe, if Frankie could have still been my fuck buddy, but currently his extra intake of blood wasn't circulating ALL the way around his body, if you got my drift.

I stared at my Zoella Hb, my eyebrows squishing together. "Oh, there's no lead in this pencil."

"You're making it worse, you know, drawing attention to it all the time. I'm getting a complex." Frankie's gaze was cast towards his loins, and he wrapped his arms over his front.

"I'm on about one of my new set of pencils, not your dick." I sighed. "Please. Can you go somewhere else today? Either that or cheer up."

He swooped to the floor and sat in a chair opposite me. "I think I'm depressed, Kim. It's like I've had an extreme makeover and basically no one knows who I am anymore because the outside of me has changed, and it's changing the inside of me too."

"You look exactly the same on the outside, Frankie."

"No, I don't. I'm a little paler and I was always congratulated on my natural glow."

I started to open my mouth.

"No, I don't want to buy one of Ebony's cosmetic palettes. My skin is extra sensitive since my change."

Well, he had been burnt to a crisp by Satan before his regeneration so that wasn't entirely surprising.

"Look, Frankie." I sighed. "We're going to have to come to some kind of an agreement about you giving me some personal space. It's been a month now since you left the caves. I want to date. I want to work in peace. Heck, I want to have time with my battery-operated boyfriend or even take a dump without you being pressed against the outside of the bathroom door."

"I can't help it. I can't be without you. When I left your side, the devil killed me."

"But you're not dead, you're undead, and you can have an amazing life. Hey, I can even get you a date." I pointed at my computer screen.

"No! I'm not ready for the world of dating and I can't be away from you. I get all worked up if I can't see you."

"I'm taking you to see a doctor. There's the one at the hospital that specialises in supes who looked me over when Satan bit me."

"I am a doctor."

"You *were* a doctor. Now you aren't. Anyway, thinking about it, it's probably a psychiatrist we need to visit, not a physician. This situation cannot go on. I need sex."

"Hit a guy when he's down, why don't you? It's not my fault I can no longer perform." Frankie bit on his lip forgetting he had fangs and a drop of blood slipped off his bottom lip. "Oh crap, this is really annoying. You need a bloody license to own these things. They're always sticking out when unwanted."

"Frankie." I scratched my chin. "Do you think you're kind of having boner problems but with your fangs?"

Frankie covered his ears, his mouth gaping open. "I beg your pardon. Could you insult me anymore?" He kicked the bottom of the chair, so the casters moved it slightly to the right, so he was looking away from me. "Carry on, I've not topped myself yet. Oh, hang on, I'm already dead."

I rolled my eyes. "You are being beyond dramatic today. I'm being serious. You haven't got control of your fangs and if you think about it, it's similar to getting an unwanted hard on. I'm not a dude obviously but maybe there's some similar chemistry there with how to gain control of them."

"You can't control getting a hard on. Even thinking of your dead grandma with her rotting teeth doesn't work 100%."

I made a retching sound.

"Hey, you were more than willing to pretend to be a corpse when we were role-playing."

"Only because you had a decent sized dick and knew how to use it. I just overlooked your weird kink."

"I want to bring something to your attention. Just because we are no longer having sex doesn't mean we can't snuggle. Hanging from the ceiling can get monotonous and lonely you know. I might like to slip between the sheets every now and again and get some comfort from my new terrible life."

Sighing again, I leaned forward on the desk, resting my elbow, and placing my head in my hand. I'd done more sighing the last month than I had coffee drinking—and that was saying something.

"Look, tonight—just for one night—you can have a cuddle. For five minutes. That's all. Then you'll have to go back on the ceiling until we can get you that appointment."

"Five minutes? Is that all I get?"

"Frankie, you don't sleep and you're a vampire. I have to put my wards around me at night, so you don't have a midnight feast on my neck."

"I wouldn't drink from your neck." He winked.

When he did that, I saw a faint glimmer of the old Frankie. In truth, I wasn't surprised at his level of distress, after being incinerated by the Boss of Hell. It was going to take time for him to come to terms with his new personality and new non-magical body. We needed outside help though. I was a human and couldn't give him the support he needed. Plus, if this carried on, I was going to get deep frown lines and I'd never forgive him for that, especially when he might not age any further himself.

"Look, do you think you could manage to go to the coffee shop and get me a latte?" The coffee shop was only a small walk down the back stairs and then round to the front of the block of shops the business was part of.

Frankie shook his head. "I can't leave you."

"What if I FaceTimed you all the way there and all the way back?"

Frankie looked upwards. "That could work."

"Excellent. You see, this is progress." I gave him some money for a coffee and a chocolate doughnut from Jax's.

"I miss doughnut's," he said. "They should do doughnut flavoured blood. Then I might like it more." At the moment, Frankie was surviving on donated blood, but he hated the taste. However human food didn't taste the same either, so he really was struggling.

He left the office, and I propped my phone up on my desk so he could still see my face while he went downstairs and next door to the coffee shop.

Finally, I might get a minute's peace to get some work done. I turned back to the agreement on my screen.

Bang. Bang. Bang. Bang. Bang. I jumped a foot as the door almost fell off its hinges.

"Oh, I fucking give up," I muttered to myself as Ebony came barging into the office.

"Take that paragraph out right this very minute," she said in her cut-glass accent as she pointed at the screen.

"God, you fricking seers are so annoying with your know-it-all-ness."

"I will keep repeating to you that I don't know everything. I'm not a mind-reader, I'm a seer. The reason I know my Christmas present is not 'out of stock' as you keep stating and is actually down to the fact you haven't bothered to go to the shops yet, is because I'm still waiting for the gift from last year also. You should just say you're not buying it if you're too lazy to do your bit. It's much easier."

"I've been rather busy if you haven't noticed, what with my new career and my new permanent accessory. Hey, I could give you a poorly turned-out vampire for Christmas?"

"I'll pass, but if I don't get my real present by the month end, I'm buying myself some Pandora and coming to collect." Ebony swept her manicured nails towards the computer.

"If you're not a mind-reader, how come you know about my extra paragraph?" I complained.

"I've had a vision. You were on a date with a shapeshifter who wasn't your one."

I sat with my head in my hands taking deep breaths. "How many more times? I'm not looking for my one. I'm looking for two, three, maybe even four. Reverse harems are the in thing right now, you know?"

"You will end up with the wolf. Delay all you want. But if you go on dates with others you will end up in incredible danger."

A girl could really start to get annoyed with seers. They came out with all these dramatic words like incredible danger, but could never tell you exactly what it was, so you know, you could just avoid that one thing. Like for instance if she said don't date the hunky faerie fireman, then you could just cancel that date and carry on with your life, but no, she had to do the bursting into the room drama, the dramatic statement, and then, like now, she just flounced back out to go raid the stash of vodka she kept behind the boutique counter that 'helped' with the visions.

I saw just a glimpse of the door moving and then I was up against the wall held in a tight embrace. "Frankie. For the love of God, you're taking years off my life."

"I missed youuuuuuu," he wailed. "I couldn't smell you. The phone is no use; your attention was on Ebony, not me."

I attempted to extract myself. "Fuck, you're freezing. There's no way I'm snuggling you tonight. Not a chance in Hell." I pushed him off me. Thank God he didn't have full vamp strength yet. He'd probably have crushed every bone in my body. "Where's my coffee, Frankie? And my doughnut."

"They're here." I turned to see Lucy, the demon ex-manager of Hell walking in. She carried my coffee cup in her hand—her glowing amber hand. "Kept it super-hot for you," she said. "Couldn't do the same with him unfortunately." She pointed a red talon at Frankie. "He's still pathetic, I see."

"I'm going to take him to see someone. Hopefully they can help with separating him from me."

She flicked a flame from her thumb. "Vamps and fire don't mix. Just say the word."

Frankie whizzed up to a far corner of the ceiling where he folded into himself and shut down. It was like having a vampire edition Alexa.

"Lucy. For God's sake you've frightened him even more."

She set fire to my new Zoella notebook. I threw my coffee over it distraught. "God, what did you do that for?"

My pencils turned to ash next.

"Stop saying those words. I can't help my response," she shrieked.

I thought back to what I'd said. Oh yeah, the 'G' word had come out. Shit.

"Now I have no coffee and no nice notebook and pencils," I told her. "There'd better be a good reason you came in here."

"There's an excellent reason." She smiled wide and adjusted the headband that covered her horns. "It's been way too long since I had any romance in my life. I need you to find me a date."

Unfortunately, that proved the end for my new desk tidy. I really would have to work on my blasphemy.

Chapter 3

Kim

"Hold up there, hot stuff." I needed a second to process this. I turned back in my chair and put my hand over my mouth. The worst tempered woman in the world wanted a date. Deep breaths Kim.

I swung back around on my chair to face her. "So let me get this straight. You want a date and romance? You're not just using Withernsea Dating as an escort agency in a bid to get laid?"

"Well, obviously I'd like to 'get laid' as you term it, but no. I've been without a romantic partner for almost twenty-seven years and it's time I got back on the horse so to speak. I guess they call it a ride for a reason. Plus, you never know, if I fall in love maybe my horns will fall off."

I felt sorry that Satan had left her with her horns intact as revenge for escaping Hell. She'd had no choice but to adopt a boho look so she could wear a lot of floral headbands.

I picked up a notepad and pencil from my drawer, unfortunately not able to use my brand new Zoella ones as they were now ash or dripping in coffee. "Okay, Lucy, take a seat and let me go through the initial set of questions."

Lucy tapped a Louboutin clad foot. "Is this going to take long? Can't I just look at the photos and pick one?"

I folded my arms across my chest. "No. If you want the help of Withernsea's most fabulous dating agency, we're doing this properly."

She harrumphed and sat down. "Very well, and we have to do this with Frankly Batshit stuck above our heads?"

"Unfortunately, right now, where I go, he goes. So until I figure something out, he'll be here."

"Well, if he repeats anything he heard here today, I'll incinerate him."

Frankie's arms folded in even closer around himself.

"Leave him alone and let's get started on my questions. Okay, your name," I asked her.

"You know my name. I do hope we're not going to spend thirty valuable minutes with you asking me things you already know."

I typed in Lucy Fir.

"No middle name then?"

"Not one I'm admitting to," she said under her breath.

"Aww, come on, Luce. To get the best from the machine I need full and frank answers."

After a series of disgruntled facial expressions followed by flared nostrils, she spat out, "Connie."

I snorted. "Pardon?"

"Okay, okay. My middle name is Connie, after my mother's mum—my granny."

"Lucy Connie Fir." I wrote down trying to keep a straight face. It was no good. "Connie-fir. Pahahahahaha."

I smelled the definite odour of burned hair and sniffed around me.

"You might need a trim," she said, pointing at a singed piece of my hair.

"Oh my fucking—"

"STOP," Lucy yelled. "Or you'll end up bald."

She sat back. "Look, Kim. You can't blaspheme near me or really take the piss because Satan has left me with residual powers, and I don't know when they will fade. Quite frankly, I'm still a little evil. So please can we go forward without any more drama, or I'll be getting a jail sentence instead of a date. Only, I've spent quite enough time trapped in a dark place over the last few years."

"Fine. I'll go carefully," I said. She had no worries; she'd nearly burned my fucking hair off. Shelley would have to work out additional protection spells for us all while Lucy was still volatile.

"What's your date of birth?"

"The second of March 1965."

"You'd think Hell would have given you wrinkles, with all that suffering."

Lucy looked me directly in the eye. "I didn't suffer though, or age. While you're there you turn evil like your surroundings. I had a jolly old time watching people being tortured, especially if I needed to whip them."

I made a side note to ask her later if she might still like the whipping.

"Okay. Hair colour is ginger, skin colour: pale. Height: I'm guessing around 5 foot 8 inches; you seem a couple of inches taller than me."

"I'm five foot nine."

I asked for her weight. No way was I guessing that wrong and being flambeed.

"Any distinguishing features?"

"Other than two red protrusions on the top of my head? Nope."

"Your place of birth was here in Withernsea." I wrote that down. "Okay, current address."

"Hmmmmm. I have a little problem there." She chewed the side of her mouth for a moment before her green eyes brightened. "Oh actually, I just thought of a solution. My current address is 73 Holly Avenue, Withernsea." She broke out into a wide smile displaying those perfect white teeth.

Have you ever seen a vampire fall off a ceiling?

I did. Right then.

"That's my address," Frankie shouted from the floor.

"Yes, but you're not living there are you? You're staying with her." She pointed to me. "So really I'd be doing you a favour by staying at your place. It'll keep intruders away. Where are your keys?"

"Hang on," I interrupted. "I thought you went back to your old home?"

Lucy crossed one leg over the other and sighed. "I did, and I've lived there ever since I returned, but you see, my family had presumed I was dead and had given up my let and so I've been having to share with this middle-aged dude who farts all the time. And well, he realised this morning that I was resident in the loft and he had a little panic attack. When he'd calmed down, he told me I could remain sharing and even get a bed to sleep in. It just had to be his and I could share as my part of the rent."

"And?"

"And so I've burned my bridges there, so to speak."

"You set the place on fire?"

"It might need a little redecorating. But it was his fault, methane and fire. BOOM." She smacked her palms together and then pulled them apart.

I could feel panic settling in. Who the hell was I going to set her up with? I could put them in grave danger. The only person I could think of was Satan himself and he wasn't dating, he was in Hell, raging at no longer having Withernsea as his playground.

"I'll get you Frankie's keys, as long as you sign a legal document stating that you're responsible for any repairs resulting from your special powers. Also, you need to pay him rent. You can stay there until Frankie is a) ready to move back into his own home or b) he moves elsewhere and needs to sell up."

Lucy smiled again. "Oh yay! My own home! No one but little old me. It's been so long since I've had any me-time, as you call it these days."

It was strange seeing her genuinely happy—quite unnerving in fact. "About that. You won't be completely on your own. Frankie has a cat that the neighbours have been feeding. Maisie's now temporarily yours."

Frankie made a strange noise like a laugh but from under a bitten fist.

"Anyway, moving on. Any family history of note?"

"No. I have a normal family. They've moved to Bridlington apparently."

She looked at my expression and answered my question without my having to ask.

"I'm not sure about getting in touch or going to visit them. It's hard to explain to mortal parents why you haven't aged and where you've been for twenty-six years. I need to think things over, and I know for a fact that you only want to know this because you're a gossip queen and it has sod all to do with my application."

I stuck out my tongue, ever the professional.

"What's your favourite food?"

"Anything but barbecue. I smell that at my current place of employment and did at my previous." Lucy now owned a steakhouse near the promenade. Where the money had come from to buy it had not been shared, but I knew Shelley's father had a lot of money and a guilt complex for leaving her all those years ago.

A Devil Of A Date

"Almost there now. What is your ideal date?"

"Most definitely NOT a restaurant, or a bonfire, or a sauna, or a beach holiday. Nowhere hot. Maybe building snowmen, skiing, walking around the chiller cabinets in the Asda."

"I'll write down a winter's stroll. Okay, finally your reason for application to the agency. Here I'll give you a piece of paper and a pen and you can write that bit out yourself as it needs to come from the heart." *If you have one,* I thought.

Lucy sighed but took the pen, paper and a magazine I'd given her to rest on. At one point steam actually came out of her horns but I thought it best not to comment.

"There." She handed me the paper back.

"Okay, just give me a few minutes and I'll type this into the computer."

I hit the keys, copying over her reason for application.

Twenty-six years ago, my boyfriend left me for another woman. I later found out that the important future child of Withernsea who I presumed I would carry, would be carried by this other woman. I therefore made plans with Satan and split them up. Since then, I have had a lot of time to reflect on my actions and realised from keeping Dylan in Hell that he wasn't the one for me anyway. We didn't really have a spark and when I recently found out he was in fact a Wyvern and from the sea, maybe that's why. Fire and water don't mix.

Since I've returned, I've had to put up with seeing Dylan and his wife Margret newly reunited and with their daughter, Shelley—the picture of a perfect happy family and it makes me want to ~~burn the fucking lot of them to a crisp~~ *look for my own new love so I can put the past behind me and move on with my life now I am back resident in Withernsea.*

"So no water sprites then, or mermen?"

"Most definitely not."

"Okay, leave this with me, Lucy. I might need to do a follow up interview before I see what the computer algorithm brings up for you. I'll be in touch."

I crouched over Frankie and got his house keys out of his pocket. At one time that would have led to an immediate hard on and sex, but this time he just whimpered.

I threw them at Lucy, and she caught them on first try. Quick reflexes. I'd add that to my list of features.

"If you plan a housewarming, please don't take it in the literal sense."

"Ha ha," she replied sarcastically and with that she sashayed out of the room.

I stood there looking at the quivering wreck that used to be my boyfriend.

What was I going to do with him?

Chapter 4

Lucy

I didn't know why Kim, Shelley, etc had to give me such a hard time about my fiery accidents. I had just escaped Hell. Did they expect I'd be down here repenting, granting wishes, and doing charity work? I had twenty-six years to catch up on. The first thing I intended to do was to have as much fun as I possibly could. My real age on my birth certificate might be fifty-three, but my body was twenty-seven and me and my perfect hourglass figure were going to paint the town red. Oh, come on, what other colour was an ex-devil going to paint it?

I got a taxi to my new home and was pleasantly surprised as it pulled up outside a detached bungalow. As I let myself in and walked through the hallway, I noted all the boring masculine tones of blacks and greys. Looked like I might have to grab a few accessories for the place. Pushing open the living room door, I anticipated looking around the space, but instead my vision went black and severe pain struck my face.

"Hisssssss."

"What the fuck?"

I finally managed to extricate myself from the cat's claws and threw it onto the couch. I felt at my face and then glanced at my fingertips that were coated in red blood—my blood.

Hissing myself, a flicker of flame licked at my fingertip. "I suggest you don't do that again, Maisie, because your owner doesn't seem to like hot pussy anymore, so you'd better not attack your new handler."

The black cat trembled and then in front of my eyes, limbs elongated and there in front of me, a woman with green eyes, cocoa coloured skin, and long, jet black hair appeared.

"So you know who I am? Who the fuck are you?"

"Interesting," I said glancing over her. "Kim didn't tell me you were a shifter. She thought you were most definitely a pet."

Maisie folded her arms across her waist. She was wearing a shimmery black dress, and I thanked God that when she'd shifted she hadn't appeared in her birthday suit. The only pussy I wanted to see was when she was in feline form.

"Well?" I probed further.

She shrugged. "They don't know. Frankie doesn't know. He stitched me up one day at the hospital and I thought he was caring and would look after me. So I shifted, and he adopted me after I'd hung around here a little."

"And he has absolutely no idea?"

Maisie moved and laid down on the sofa, tucking her legs up under herself and yawning. "See, I'm always tired. I like being a cat. I get fed, petted, and get to sleep all day. Frankie watched TV a lot so that was good. I've been happy being a couch potato. But then he didn't come home. The neighbours have popped in and they keep saying things like 'Poor Frankie,' but obviously as a cat I can't ask where he is."

"Your neighbours believe Frankie is in a psychiatric establishment."

"And where is he really?"

"He got burned to death by Satan, brought back as a vampire, lost all his magical powers, became some weird vamp reject that never wants to sleep, developed an attachment disorder to his lover and is currently hanging around upside down wherever she is."

Maisie sat up, her mouth hung open. "You're playing with me, right?"

"Do I look like I have a little ball with a bell in it? He's lost it. Kim's taking him to the doctors, but for now he's staying with her. Whether she likes it or not. Seeing as I was of no fixed abode, I asked if I could stay here until he feels better."

"And you are?"

"I'm Lucy. Lucy Fir. Ex-watcher of Hell."

She hissed again, her green eyes going wide. "Sorry, that was rude."

A Devil Of A Date

I shrugged my shoulders. "Don't sweat it. It's not every day you meet an ex-demon."

"Ex? So you don't have evil powers? How did you do that flame trick then?"

"Satan wasn't happy about my freedom, so I've been left with some residual powers, hence the fiery fingers. He also refused to remove these." I pulled my headband off which was giving me a headache anyway and moved my hair to give Maisie the full effect of my horns.

"Whoa." Maisie got up and brushed past me, then stared at my horns and batted them.

I startled. "What are you doing?"

"I'm part cat, duh. Just like you can't stop your little flame, I get attracted to tiny objects and want to play."

"Must be difficult if you date a man with a small penis."

She stood and stretched. "I don't date. I was happy here with Frankie. If you're staying, will you feed me?"

"I have no problems opening a tin of cat food."

"Would you pet me, stroke me?" She pouted, brushing past me again.

"Hell, no. I don't bat for that side. Go visit the neighbours for that."

"Well, I sleep on Frankie's bed, so you'll need to take the spare room."

"Yeah, planned to anyway, and I'll buy fresh bedding."

Maisie tilted her head to one side. "Please don't tell anyone that you met the real me. If Frankie comes back, I will probably remain his pet as long as his ability to care for me is intact."

"You have my word. So when was the last time you went out? Properly out? As in for a drink or something and I don't mean a saucer of milk from next door."

"Erm, two years ago maybe?"

"Excellent. Tomorrow night you and me are going out on the town. I need to see what the Withernsea night life looks like and check out the human men until the dating agency match me up with my new love."

Maisie's brows drew together. "What would you need from a dating agency? You are beautiful, with your pale skin and glorious ginger hair. Men should fall over themselves to date you, especially my fellow cat shifters. Female gingers are rare in our world and revered."

"Yes, well, I'm out of practice and things have changed a lot since I last dated. I mean what's that app thing? You didn't swipe people away like a piece of toilet roll across your shitty arse back in my day. I have applied to the dating agency, but that costs money so in the meantime we shall see what is available for free."

"I suppose I could go out. As long as we don't stay out too late." She yawned again.

"Right, well are you going to give me a tour of the house because I'm due at work for the evening shift later."

"You have a job? Where?"

"I own Red's Steakhouse near the Promenade."

Maisie's eyes lit up. They looked like they were almost twinkling. "Oooh, I quite often hang around the backyard when I'm out on the prowl. The smells from that place are divine."

I shook my head. "Most definitely not divine. Tantalising, tempting, but not anything from up there." I pointed heavenward. "You mustn't mention those above in name to me. I have a strange reaction. Like I'm allergic to goodness."

"Interesting. Well, I'll attempt to not say anything about up there if you can bring me home a portion of your special grilled and smoked salmon home from the restaurant."

"Deal." I held out my hand but instead of shaking it she knelt down and pushed her head into it. I could see we would need to teach her some skills on how to behave back in the human world. Between us we were a right pair.

∽

After unpacking the few items I had collected, namely a couple of changes of outfits, underwear, and some toiletries, I headed over to the restaurant. Red's had become my safe place. Amongst the smell of chargrill, I felt at home, comforted. I know I'd told Kim I didn't like the smell or heat, but as much as Hell had been hard work, (torturing could be tough on the arms from all that whipping), it had been my home for the last two-and-a-half decades and I couldn't leave it behind as much as I'd have liked to. Somehow, here where the barbecuing smells led to nice meals for the residents of Withernsea, rather than a punishment for someone who'd been too naughty for upstairs, I could stop worrying about my future for a couple of hours.

Although I could cook, I wasn't restaurant standard, so I had my Head chef, a guy called Grant, and a team of other personnel. My job was to ensure that all the ordering was done, financial accounts kept in order, and rotas organised. I'd been an office secretary and bookkeeper before Hell. Only a few of my staff—the supernatural ones—were aware of who I really was. One day, I hoped we supes could stand tall amongst the human population and live as one.

I shook myself. Where had that statement come from? All live as one? Panic gripped my chest. An unfamiliar and unwelcome feeling. I didn't have thoughts like that. The people upstairs had thoughts like that. I needed to get a grip.

You used to be like that once upon a time.
You used to be young and in love and... human.
Now you're human again.

Okay, I'd had enough of the crap spilling out in my inner thoughts. It was time to go out onto the restaurant floor, as this alone time wasn't doing me any good.

Henry, one of the wait staff, came walking over to me as I made my way to the front of the restaurant. "I think we've got one about to try to escape, table six."

"What's he been doing?" I nonchalantly looked around the restaurant, sweeping my eyes over the suspect runner.

"He's had a full three courses with three beers. Now he's sweating and looking around the exits. He visited the bathroom a few minutes ago. I followed him in, and he was opening the window, saying he 'needed air'."

"Leave him to me. Go back to what you were doing."

"Okay, Lucy."

Henry walked away, and I slipped out of the back exit and waited around the corner for the familiar sound of my restaurant door jangling.

A couple of minutes later the noise came. He was so busy looking behind him to make sure he wasn't being followed that he failed to see me.

Anger fuelled me and I caught his arm and dragged him back to behind the restaurant. It would appear I really wasn't fully human just yet, my demon strength giving me an advantage over a man who was half a foot taller than me and about five stones heavier. He was an obvious gym bunny, and I wondered why he'd tried to steal from me.

"You didn't pay for your food," I reminded him. "Would you like to explain why?"

He sneered at me. "They sent a woman after me? Have the men in there got no balls?"

I clicked my fingers until a flame appeared. "They have, but I'm a demon and so my balls are bigger. Let me demonstrate." I watched as the flame hovered and grew in mid-air until a massive ball of flame hung there. "Now, how was it you liked your dinner? Well done, I think you said."

I made out like I would throw it.

"Nooooooo. Oh fuck, here, here. I'll pay, I'll pay." The man went into his pockets and threw his wallet onto the floor. I picked it up, the ball of fire still hovering in front of his face, and I withdrew the exact amount he owed, then an extra twenty. "That's the tip for your wait staff tonight. Very generous of you," I told him.

"So, you'll let me go right? I paid. I'm free to go, yeah?" The man trembled in front of me, his frightened eyes reflected my flames.

"Well, you've paid but you haven't been punished," I said. "So let me see. What would affect a man like you the most?"

I looked at his suit, at his appearance. Was that fake tan? I guessed his appearance was important to him.

I dropped the ball of fire and singed off his eyebrows. The smell of burning lingered in the air and he felt at his face while he sniffed.

"What did you do? My eyebrows, where are they? Crap, my eyebrows. I've a date tomorrow night. What am I going to do? That's why I didn't pay tonight. I wanted to try the place out, but I can't afford to eat out tonight and tomorrow."

"Have you heard of internet reviews?" I snarled. "They'd show you that my restaurant is the best in Withernsea without you stealing from me. Do not enter my establishment again or next time I will burn your bollocks off. Are we clear?" I said, my voice deepening.

"Your eyes, your eyes," he said, and the smell of urine pervaded the air.

I let a flame lick out from my fingertips again.

"Do you want me to dry your trousers?" I asked and laughed.

With that he took off and as he ran away, I laughed again. I felt so much better now. Much more myself.

I heard a slow clap from behind me.

"Well done, Lucy. I thought I'd lost you, but it appears you still have potential."

I pivoted. A tall pale man with dark hair stood there. He told people his name was Reuben and he was a vampire, but I knew him as Satan. I had seen his true self, and it was so frightening he wouldn't be able to stand here in Withernsea in that form.

"I thought you weren't allowed here?"

"Shelley may be more powerful than me, but it doesn't mean I can't sneak down here now and again when she's busy shagging the vampire. I must keep an eye on things for when I work out how to get the place back. It will be mine again, Lucy."

I started to walk away.

"The fight is within you, Lucy. Whether to let your human side through and become just yet another boring inhabitant of Withernsea, or whether to enjoy that evil inside yourself and let it go free. I know what it looked like just now. You enjoyed tormenting that man, admit it."

"I was just fed up that he tried to rob me, that's all." I pretended to check out my nails.

He smiled, his mouth curving up at one side.

"You keep telling yourself that. I'll be nearby though, just in case I get the chance to take you home."

"Hell is not my home," I shouted, my voice clipped in anger.

"If you say so," Satan said. Then he ripped a tear in the air and disappeared through it.

I sat down on the steps at the back of the restaurant shaking.

I couldn't go back there. Ever. I would have to work hard on restraining my temper and on becoming, I gulped, good. I knew I needed to fall in love, fast. Love might be the only thing that could redeem me.

Chapter 5

Kim

"Hello?"

"Shelley? I'm sorry to phone and interrupt your marathon baby-making session, but I need help with Frankie. He's got worse and I know I bought a gym membership in January, but I've only been once because it was a free workout with a trainer and he was well fit. Anyway, basically he's too heavy to drag around and I need some assistance."

"It's fine. Why would you need to drag him around though?"

"Because he won't move. He's sitting on the floor trembling. It's only when I threaten to leave him by himself that he gets up. He's in a bad way, Shell, and I don't know what to do anymore. I know you only have one week to make a baby before you have to wait another hundred years, but I seriously can't carry on. I need advice. Can Theo help?"

"Hold on, let me just have a word."

She put me on hold.

"You're talking about me like you want to be rid of me," wailed Frankie.

"I do want to be rid of you. You're my ex. You're totally cramping my style," I yelled, exasperated.

He curled back up in a ball, so feeling like shit for shouting, I stroked his back soothingly while I waited.

Shelley's voice came back down the line. "Theo says to bring him over. We need to get a look at him. It might be you need to stay here for a night or two, so bring a change of clothes for you both."

"But Shelley, it's your—"

She interrupted me and whispered down the phone. "I can barely walk; he won't leave me alone. I need a fucking break, like literally, a break from fucking. It's alright for him with his stupid vamp strength. Get yourself down here, even if Frankie makes a miraculous recovery, you hear me?"

"Okay then. See you in about an hour," I told her.

I carried on stroking Frankie as it seemed to be relaxing him a little. "Hey, we're going to Theo and Shelley's farm. They've loads of space for us there. Theo's going to assess you to see if he can help."

"What's the point? Why don't you just stake me? You don't care." He rolled away from me.

"Hey, fuckface." I flicked his ear hard using my thumb and middle finger, back to my usual take-no-shit self. "I do care because I've been with you all the time, ever since you changed and went all pathetic. However, I'd like my friend back. I don't want to be lovers anymore because I'm focusing on my career, but I got your back, Frankie, and people will want to be around you more if you're not lying around like some poor pathetic slug when you're supposed to be a cool-ass vamp."

"Focusing on your career? By picking out the hot men and taking them on test dates?"

"Hey, them's the perks. You, my man, need to realise how hot some women will think you are. You have watched Batman right? I mean blow me, Christian Bale in that bat suit. You could give him a run for his money you know, and the best thing is, you're not fiction, you're the real deal."

"I'm defective."

"That's why we're going to take you to Theo's. If anyone knows how to help, it's another vamp. So come on, let's get you up off the floor and into my car. We need to call home for some clothes and then it's operation 'Get Frankie His Freak On'."

∽

We pulled up at the farmhouse. It had belonged to Theo's family back in the day, and he and Shelley had recently bought it back. It was a decently sized place and to me seemed too big for a small family, but Shelley said Theo had plans for the place. Those plans would need to work around the fact that Theo's mother's ghost frequented the farm.

I turned to Frankie who'd stared out of the window in silence the whole way here. "Okay, we're here. Remember, this is all to help you. Yes, I want you to be able to spend time on your own eventually, but I know that might not happen overnight. I'm your friend, okay?"

He carried on staring out of the window.

"Frankie. I *am* your friend. I'm not doing this to abandon you. I'm doing it because we need you back. Where's Frankie, my red-hot lover gone? Yes, you are now a vampire and no longer a wizard, but you still have a dick if you look down your trousers."

"It doesn't work. Like my vampire genes." He still wasn't looking at me, but at least he was now talking.

"And that's probably all related to how you feel. However, I'm not a trained counsellor, and I know barely anything about being turned into a vampire, so let's go see the people who do, okay? Let's treat it like we're having a little holiday."

He finally turned to me. "What if it does nothing?"

"Then we try something else, buddy." I rested a hand on his arm. "I won't give up, even if you do."

Frankie surprised me by giving me a tiny hint of a smile and I was amazed at how much that warmed my heart. He even opened his car door and got out by himself.

"You're a great friend, Kim," he said. "I'm sorry for all the trouble I'm causing."

"You just died, Frankie, and got brought back from the dead. I'd rather have you here causing me grief than be mourning the loss of a good friend. Now that said, if you tell Shelley about the change I made to the contract, I'll stake you before you get the sentence out."

Shelley appeared in the doorway. "Come through and I'll make you both a hot drink. It's cold out there today."

We followed her through to a large country kitchen complete with an aga. It was lovely and warm and we both took a seat around the large oval oak dining table towards the rear of the room. "Okay, so I know what you'll want, Kim. What about you, Frankie? Tea or O-neg?"

"Tea please."

She looked at him strangely and then met my gaze. I shrugged my shoulders.

Footsteps were audible, and I turned around to look for Theo, but there was no one there. I thought I'd imagined it until Shelley put my coffee on the table and I watched as a coaster sailed through the air, my mug lifting up and the coaster sliding underneath. Then a thin apparition of a woman who looked to be in her mid-thirties appeared.

"That table has been in my family for years. Would you mind not marking it with cup rings?"

"Sorry about that, Mary. I forgot."

It was the first time I'd actually met the ghost of Theo's mother, as I'd only ever been to the outside of the farmhouse before when I'd dropped Shelley off after a night out. She had long dark brown hair, tied up in a bun and wore a plain white cotton dress that went past her knees.

"Mary. This is my friend and business partner, Kim; and this is Frankie, who—"

"Oh I know all about him. I eavesdrop on most of your conversations, honey, and while we're on the subject, I think you overuse the blasphemy a little in the bedroom. Maybe try not to take the Lord's name in vain quite so much."

I giggle-snorted as I witnessed Shelley's jaw drop.

"What have I told you about the bedroom being off limits? I'll fix wards if you don't behave."

"I haven't set foot in your room. You're just so loud. That's my son in there, how do you think it makes me feel? Although I'm very excited about the prospects of a future grandchild."

"I swear I heard clapping outside our bedroom door yesterday," Shelley said to me.

I needed to change the subject—fast. "It's lovely to meet you, Mary. You know then that Frankie here is having a few problems so we've come to stay for a day or two?"

She hovered next to him. "I understand, son," she said, which was weird cos they looked more or less the same age. "My transition to a ghost was a shock. One minute my son was helping me milk the cows and the next he was draining me of all my blood. All I can say is time is a healer and you'll adjust. At first, I thought it was the Devil's work, but now I see it was in God's plan. Instead of us only having a limited time together in the mortal realm, I can now spend eternity with my son. There's no greater gift than that, even if he did have to murder me painfully for us to get there."

Hmmm, it seemed like she still harboured a little grudge.

Theo walked in. "I've apologised profusely for that, mother, and I will continue to do so until the day I'm staked or visit the caves to be put to sleep."

"Hush your mouth talking about places like that. You can't leave your mother behind."

"I think you'll find that there's a little thing called The Light, that you can follow anytime you want out of here."

"It's more difficult for those of us who encountered traumatic deaths. I'm tethered to the farm."

"Yes, and we love having you here, as long as you give us a little space. Right now I need to focus on Frankie if that's okay?"

"Huh, I know when I'm not wanted," she said disappearing.

From the "Ow," that came from Theo's mouth and the clutching of the right side of his head it would appear she'd given him a thick ear on departure.

"Are you sure we're okay staying here?" I asked. "You already seem to have a lot on your plate."

"You're fine." Shelley waved a hand in front of her. "We're used to her now. It was a shock when we first moved in, having expected to have our marital home to ourselves as newlyweds, but she's lovely, and very helpful around the place. She loves to clean. Says it's a woman's work. She's not impressed that I have a job. Thinks us modern women are strange. She thinks I'm stopping work when I have the baby."

"You'll need to," said Theo. "Childbirth is not easy."

"Oh my god, next you'll be telling me that the baby could hurt me and bring me almost to the point of death like on Twilight. I know now that it's all stereotypical nonsense."

"Actually, that can happen, but not frequently."

"Whaaat?" Shelley screamed, a hand flying to her chest. "My bones could break? The baby could drain me?" She slapped his arm. "What have you done to me, you stupid shit?"

"Joking," Theo said, before grinning.

Shelley gave him his second thick ear in as many minutes. Then she pulled out a chair and sat down.

"That was so not funny, Theo. I thought I might die for a moment then."

"You are going to die. You're going to be turned eventually, and if anything started to go wrong, I would turn you, just like in the film. But stop believing everything you see on the television." He turned to me. "She shouts at the soap operas like they are real people. I've told her as an ex-actor, it can lead to strange stalking behaviour. I had several people believing I was my characters and following me around calling me by my character's names. It's very disconcerting."

Shelley looked across at Frankie. "Anyway, mate. How are you holding up?"

Frankie had helped Shelley understand her witch powers and had known Shelley's mum. It was plain to see from her expression that she was very fond of him, though her own powers had grown to far encompass those Frankie had had in the past.

"I'm not so good, Shelley, to be honest. I'm a little lost given I'm no longer a wizard and yet I'm not a vampire either. I don't know who I am."

Theo took a bottle of blood out of the freezer, popped the cap and sat down so that now all four of us were seated around the table.

"We shall get to the bottom of what is happening, Frankie. I am sorry that my saving you has led to these difficulties. However, it's not all bad. You no longer stink like rotten vegetables."

Shelley gave her husband the stink eye. "So, tell us what's happening, Frankie." She patted his arm softly. "I know it's hard but tell us how you feel. Can you go back to the beginning and explain what's happened since you were turned?"

He took a deep breath. "I can't stop thinking about how it all happened. One minute I was standing there with you at Theo's feeling exultant, and the next I was in some kind of waiting room. I kept looking around as I wasn't sure how I'd gotten there and I kept trying to use my magic to get back to you but it wouldn't work. The room was plain, just magnolia walls and a wooden floor. With a loss of anything else to do, I sat on a wooden chair and waited. The door opened, and an angel stood there. I just knew she was about to call my name. She was so beautiful—her wings like snowflakes spun with silk thread and the glisten of teardrops. I stood and took a step towards her and then there was this horrendous pain. I fell to my knees, and I remember her expression was one of fear, and then I wasn't there anymore. I found myself back present in my body in an amount of pain I can't put into words."

Frankie visibly shook at this point, and we were all looking at him with concerned expressions. He looked about to go into shock. "Then there was nothing. Like I passed out but I was aware of it.

A Devil Of A Date

Just a kind of suspension. This went on for what seemed like forever. The next thing I knew I was awake, and back in my body, but I was sucking blood out of Theo's wrist. It seemed like the most natural thing in the world, but at the same time as I was enjoying the drink and gaining comfort from it, I was also horrified, as if watching myself from a distance, not understanding what was happening."

"I understand that. It happened to me too," said Theo. "Those thoughts do fade in time, but of course I can't speak about the smiting by Satan part as that hasn't happened to anyone I know."

"Do you feel okay to carry on?" Shelley asked him and he nodded.

"Of course then your mother and father took me to the caves. I had the blood thirst as normal, but it wore off and I found I didn't need much. Instead, I still wanted to eat human food, but that also tasted strange. Things I loved before tasted strange. The others all slept the sleep of the dead from nightfall to dawn and I didn't sleep at all. At one point I decided that Theo bringing me back was a mistake, and I opened the door and went outside. I'd thought going out in daylight would kill me."

"You tried to kill yourself?" I gasped.

"Huh. I couldn't even do that. It turned out that vampires can walk around in daylight. It just goes against their body clocks to do so and can make them very ill. I confided in your mother, and she told me I must be some kind of special vampire hybrid. A kind way of saying that my turning hadn't worked. Your mother was so very patient, Shelley, and spent lots of time with me, but as the weeks passed, I realized I didn't fit in at the caves. Margret offered for me to stay with her and Dylan, but I knew they'd only just reunited. I couldn't do that to them. Then I started to crave the company of Kim. I hungered for her the way I felt I should be hungering for blood. You know the rest. I've been by her side ever since. I can't leave."

"Whoa," said Shelley. "Any ideas, husband?"

"Well, from my short stint as a physician..."

Shelley's eyes bugged out, and she mumbled, "Just when I feel I'm getting to know him."

"...I'd say that you are suffering from a kind of post-traumatic stress disorder and have transference issues with your cravings. You know it should be blood, but your psyche is denying it and keeping you from fully transforming. That would be my differential diagnosis. I also think you are severely depressed. You've admitted you tried to end your life."

I put my hand across Frankie's and he put his other one over mine.

"I'm sorry," he said.

"Don't you dare apologise. We're the ones who should be sorry. You fought with Shelley and Theo against Satan. Satan! The Boss of Hell. I'm not surprised you are having PTSD."

"And attachment issues," Theo added. "You were the last safe thing he knew. That's why he feels he can't leave you."

Theo got up from his seat. "You are safe here, my friend, and we will work closely, you and I, over the next few days, and see if I can help you. However, today is the final day I can make babies with my dear wife, and so if you'll excuse me, we need to leave. Right now," he said locking eyes with Shelley and cocking his head in the direction of the door.

I watched as Shelley got up slowly. "Okay, well, if you need me tomorrow, I'll be sleeping for most of the day, in fact make that about a week; yes, a week's recovery sounds about right. Help yourself to any food or drink and Mary will be back shortly to show you to your room. I didn't know your current sleeping arrangements so there's a king size bed and a chaise longue." Then Shelley disappeared as her husband used his vamp speed to whizz her out of the room.

"Well, I feel like there's hope, don't you?" I said, squeezing Frankie's hand.

"Maybe," he replied, and I looked at my friend and hoped to God he could be saved.

Chapter 6

Kim

As Shelley said, Mary came back and showed us up to our room. "I've put you in this one, as far away from those two as possible. There's a TV and a radio in there. I suggest you have them on loud."

"Oh dear, is it really that bad?" I said, biting my lip.

"Well, I thought he couldn't shock me any more than the day he brutally murdered me, but it seems he's doing his dang best to try. No one wants to hear their child shouting about how much they love pussy unless there's a family pet."

As she pushed open the door, I was pleasantly surprised. I'd expected a country look like downstairs but it was actually sleek and hotel like. We even had our own tea and coffee making facilities.

"This is gorgeous," I exclaimed.

"Theo's considering opening the farmhouse as a bed-and-breakfast."

My eyes opened wide. "Really?"

Mary placed a finger across her lips. "But you haven't heard it from me, because, well, he didn't actually tell me this information to my face. He's done this one room up so far, so I guess you're kind of test subjects."

"Oh, I don't mind that at all," I said resting against the mattress. "This bed is so comfy. I'm going to have a nap."

"Well, if I were you I'd order a takeaway, because you might be waiting a long time for Theo or Shelley to make you anything to eat and I can't manage that, it expends too much energy."

"Thank you for everything, Mary. It's much appreciated, and we'll send for a pizza or something later. We'll get settled in now."

Mary left us behind, and I looked at Frankie.

"Look, this bed is huge. Why don't you try to sleep in it tonight? If you want to get out later and rest on the ceiling, do that, but for now get in. In fact, I'll tell you what, I'll fill up the kettle and make my hot water bottle. Then dressed in my fluffiest, warmest pyjamas, I'll give you a cuddle for as long as I can stand the cold."

"That would be lovely. Thank you again, Kim, for everything."

Fully clothed, he got under the covers and once I had made my faithful hot water bottle that I had to confess I sometimes used even in summer because I got dreadful cold feet, I also got under and got on his back for a bit. It was nice and something we never did as fuck buddies. He was cool, but not as cold as I imagined he'd be and I fell asleep.

When I awoke, I turned to find Frankie out of bed and reading.

"What's that that's holding your interest?" I asked him as I stretched.

"It's a book about supernaturals. All the different kinds and all their characteristics and idiosyncrasies. It does point out that it's only a generalisation as there are exceptions to every species. It's made me feel a little better. That there isn't one way of being a vampire, like I thought. There can be variations."

"Well that makes perfect sense because humans have many, many variations. None of us are the same. Even identical twins have different characteristics," I replied. "So you see, we just need to work out who Frankie is now. Not the vampire. Not the wizard. But Frankie. I mean, look at me. There's only one of me."

"Thank fuck," he said. "One's enough."

I almost fell out of bed.

Then he laughed, and I saw a glimmer of the man I once knew again.

∾

After spending the day at the agency, we returned to the farmhouse after six pm. Theo insisted on Frankie following him into his home study, and with a look of panic in my direction, he eventually went, leaving me alone with Shelley in the living room.

"You look as tired as I am," Shelley said, yawning. "I've told Theo he's having no sex for at least a week. I'm exhausted."

"Huh, at least you're exhausted because you're enjoying yourself. I'm just finding it really difficult not having a second to myself."

"Well, Theo is not letting Frankie leave his office for the next hour. It's part of his therapy. He's making him go cold turkey with you. So go run a bath and enjoy yourself before your shadow re-appears."

"Really?" My face lit up. "You don't mind? You won't think me rude?"

"Nope. I will just curl up on this sofa and go to sleep. Grab us that slanket on your way out, would you?"

Well, she didn't need to look quite so happy I was leaving her alone. Rude! Then I thought of the peace and quiet and all that lovely hot water and I bolted up the stairs as fast as my legs would carry me to my en-suite.

It was perfect. There were Molton Brown toiletries and the most luxurious Egyptian cotton towels. Theo really had done his research. Sinking into the warmth, I felt the tension melt away from my bones. I had to believe the present situation would eventually resolve, but I knew no matter how much I moaned and whined at him, Frankie had helped my best friend when she first came into her powers and had put his life on the line for her to get her parents back, and for that I would do whatever I could to help him while he needed me.

I realised I was spending my time without Frankie thinking about Frankie, and so I changed my thoughts to a naked Chris Hemsworth and enjoyed the rest of my free time 'playing' in the bath.

Ahhh, total bliss.

Chapter 7

Lucy

"Please, Maisie." I moved closer towards her. "You said you'd come out with me tonight. I want to check out the dating scene."

Maisie stretched out in front of the fire. "But I'm so warm. Do I have to?"

"I'll buy you a milkshake? And fish on the way home?"

"Okay," she said swivelling around and sitting up. "Bribery is everything." She held up a hand. "But here are the rules. One: I won't cop off with just anyone. I have standards, I'm snobby like that. So if you meet someone you like, don't expect me to fawn all over his ugly friend. Two: if you pull, then you can bring them back here. Just let me know and I'll meow at next door's window and stay there."

"You do that and they let you in?"

She stretched out her arms and fingers. "Yes, and Mr Smith, who looks like Jason Momoa, picks me up and puts me on his knee." She smirked. "Then I curl up in his lap. I mean who else but Mrs Smith could do that? Sometimes I'll even tread him, my little paws massaging that sausage packed in his Y-fronts."

"Ewww, Maisie. That's disgusting." I pulled a face.

"He just thinks I'm an innocent cat. It's not like he gets hard or anything." She huffed.

"I didn't mean that. I meant the fact he wore Y-fronts. Who does that these days?"

"Oh yeah. I know. His sense of style is lacking, but he makes up for it with what he's packing."

"I need to see this neighbour if he looks like Jason Momoa. Do we need any sugar? Anyway, I digress. Any more rules?"

"If we see Frankie—and I know that's doubtful given he's gone a little insane—you do not reveal who I am."

"Well, while I don't understand it myself, that's fine with me. I don't care if you don't want to tell him you're a shifter. You do realise don't you that you're just as insane, right? Pretending to be a house cat almost all day every day."

"Do you want to go out or what?" Maisie hissed.

I really had no idea what to expect in the way of nightlife, and I wondered if Hell had opened a new portal when Maisie took me to Brandy's, a new-ish Prosecco bar in the centre of Withernsea. The owners had done their best to style it with sleek and modern furniture, but the hard fact remained that next door at one side was the busiest fish and chip shop in the town, and at the other was a Pound shop.

I cast my eyes around the place. The music system pumped out Taylor Swift's *Look What You Made Me Do,* which to be honest could have been my signature song as a newly departed-from-Hell demon. The bar was two deep and Maisie made her way to the front, smiling at all the men who moved to let her through. More than one cupped her ass as she passed them, but she didn't try to bite any of them like I thought she might. She was like a cross between Meghan Markle and the woman who played Maze in Lucifer, which of course I had binge-watched as soon as I got back to earth. Some parts of it were quite accurate except Satan looked nothing like Tom Ellis. Anyway, I wasn't surprised she got all their attention. Then there was me, tall with bobbed ginger hair. It had to be said that we were two hot chicks, hot as hell in my case.

It was no surprise that two minutes after we sat at a booth, two guys came to join us. We were in luck. Both were dark haired, dark-eyed, and hot as sin.

"Mind if we sit here?" one said. His brown eyes gleamed under the light. I heard Maisie purr and shot her a look.

"Not at all. Please." I gestured to them to take a seat.

"We've not seen you here before?" The man—who introduced himself as Martin—said as he slid into his seat, alongside the other guy, Stan.

"No, this is our first time," I replied. "I'm Lucy and this is Maisie."

"And how long have you been together?" he asked.

I stared at him. "We're not together. What gave you that idea?"

He stared back. "You know this is a gay bar, right? Though I know you don't *have* to be gay to drink here."

"Her face is telling me she didn't know that." Stan smirked at Martin.

"Oh, you didn't think...?" Martin said, and then he started laughing. "Oh, Stan, she thought we were hitting on them. Oh my. Sorry, darling, you look like a nice girl, but if I had to see you naked, God, I'd barf."

Whoosh.

Oops.

"Aaaaahhhhhhh, Stan. Help me, Stan. My beard is on fire. Help me, help me."

I reached over and pulled his face towards his pint pot and immersed his charring beard in there. The beer sizzled in the glass.

Stan sat there stunned. "How did that—"

"The bloke behind you dropped a lit match. Disgusting really seeing as it's no smoking in here. His foolhardiness almost cost your partner his life," I said. Stan stood up leaving poor shellshocked Martin with his hand on his beer-soaked singed beard.

I watched as Stan started threatening all the men behind him asking which of them had a match. Of course, none were forthcoming, but one seriously objected to being accused of being an arsonist and threw a punch in Stan's face, splitting the corner of his lip.

"Jesus fucking Christ, what have you done?" Maisie said, her fingers touching parted lips as her blasphemy brought on another round of fireworks. The flames on every single candle in the building shot up a foot high scaring the clientele of the bar half to death. I was a fire hazard.

"I objected to them drinking beer in a Prosecco bar. I mean how gauche," I joked.

"Let's get home before you actually kill someone, Lucy," Maisie scolded.

She grabbed hold of my arm tightly, which of course would have looked perfectly natural to others in the bar and like I had a possessive girlfriend. However, they were all too busy screaming or running around hysterically trying to work the fire extinguishers. I was halfway across the room, attempting to reach the exit when I saw him at the back of the bar—Satan. He saluted me and laughed. I narrowed my eyes at him, before pushing people out of my way so I could get out. My horns—the ones that had been entirely dead—were tingling. I needed to do something fast as otherwise I feared I was headed back to Hell.

"Why on earth did you bring me to a gay bar when you knew I wanted to find a date?" I yelled at Maisie, just outside the bar.

She shrugged. "Can't blame a girl for trying, but I accept now that you're totally straight."

"I thought you liked Jason Momoa next door?"

She nodded. "I do and I like Mrs Momoa too. You must have heard the expression 'not enough room to swing a cat?' Well, baby, I swing all ways." She winked at me.

"Well, I don't, so can we concentrate on finding me a man?"

She sighed. "Fine."

I looked in the queue for the chippy. It was mainly families waiting, apart from one very small man at the end of the queue. I extricated myself from Maisie's arm and walked over to him.

"Are you single?" I asked. He wasn't bad looking, with wavy, light-brown hair, and he revealed a cheeky grin with good teeth. The smile made around his eyes crinkle and I noticed they were a lovely shade of green, almost like the palm plant I used to have on my windowsill years ago.

"I am if you two are offering."

"It's just me. Now are you really single? I'm in enough hot water with a man already. I can't be doing anything else bad tonight." Then I leaned over to him. "Apart from in bed that is."

"Do you know, I think I could forgo chips if you're inviting me for coffee," he said.

"Can I just have a quick word with my friend?" Maisie yelled loudly, and she yanked me back.

"What are you doing? You need to get back to the house, calm down, and we need to talk about how we're going to get you to stop setting everything on fire."

I shook her off me and whisper-shouted. "Once I find love it will stop. So I need to look. This man could be the man of my dreams."

"A four-foot-tall pixie?"

"Don't be so mean. How come I'm the ex-demon when you say such nasty things?"

"No, he is. He's a four-foot-tall pixie."

I blew out a loud breath. "I don't care what he is. I'm taking him home, so get ready to molest Mr Smith's penis tonight."

Maisie sighed. "Do you have your key?"

"I do."

"Fine. I'll be back in the morning, and I expect that fish you promised me." She stalked off.

I fixed the pixie with my best smile. "Shall we get that coffee then?"

∽

I can't say I'd really thought things through. Walking through the street back to the house holding his hand—something which he'd insisted on—looked like I was bringing my eight-year-old son home to anyone walking behind us. When we got through the door, he had to climb on the top of the shoe cupboard before he was tall enough to lean over and kiss me. Oh well, as my dear mother used to say, we were all the same size lying down. I just hoped he hadn't really wanted a coffee first.

"Shall we?" I indicated down the hallway to my bedroom.

"Yes, we shall," he said, his voice husky.

Opening the door, I was grateful I had my own bathroom. "I'll just go freshen up," I told him as I headed into my en-suite. "Make yourself comfortable."

"You got it, baby."

As I checked out my reflection in the bathroom mirror, I had it all worked out. We would fall madly in love and he would wear platform shoes with lifts in order to make him a little taller. Anyway, what would his height matter when we fell in love? I would love him for his beautiful personality, and I'd be able to be a perfect wife, living a normal life in Withernsea at long last.

I walked out of the bathroom with a dreamy look on my face and then stopped at the foot of the bed, my jaw dropping open.

Tristan—as I'd discovered he was called—was lying back on my bed naked, his legs splayed open. I couldn't see his penis for the mass of pubic hair between his legs. A giant bush, it looked like tumbleweed had blown in and landed atop his cock. Maybe that's why I was so fucking quiet right now.

Where was it?
Where was his cock?

He patted the bed next to him and so I crawled alongside him wearing just my black lacy undies, worn in the hope of getting some action.

I gingerly lowered my hand into his thatch and I shivered.

Sometimes to grab a tricky soul to take to Hell I'd been sent down direct to Withernsea's graveyard where I had to shove my hand down through the earth until I could burn through the coffin. Then placing my hand on the body's chest, I'd release the resistant evil soul. Now and again all you got for your troubles was a handful of grass and a worm, and that's what I'd got right now. I fastened my hand around him and pumped, hoping he'd engorge, but he remained a worm, and this bird no longer wanted to eat it.

"Your cock..." I started to note my disappointment but was interrupted.

"Yes." Tristan smiled. "We pixies are known for our splendid members. It is good, yes?"

I reassessed the worm. I guessed that in relation to his height the dimensions were quite good, but not in relation to my vagina. I let go and laid on my back pulling the duvet up around us so that I could pretend he was really six feet tall and that his feet didn't finish near my knees. He moved astride me and shortly after started making groaning noises.

"How is it for you, baby?"

Whaaaattt? Was he actually inside me?

I couldn't tell. I actually could not tell and all I could think of was what if he impregnated me and I had a houseful of tiny creatures to look after, like my own living Trolls? I pushed him off me, but hadn't realised how hard until he landed on the floor at the side of the bed with a thud that released a dust cloud.

"What the fuck, you lunatic?" He clutched at his back. "You nearly broke my spine, what's wrong with you?"

"I'm sorry, this isn't going to work for me."

His face turned puce. "You do realise you were the one who invited me here? I could have been eating a fish and chip supper by now."

"I'm sorry... they still might be open?"

"For God's sake, there's no wonder you're single," he spat out as he stood up.

Blasphemy and insults combined in a volatile con-cock-tion as his pubic hair mountain burned off in front of my eyes.

"Oh there it is," I exclaimed in wonder, now able to see the little bird now its nest was gone.

But it was only a fleeting glance as with a curdling scream, Tristan had picked up his clothes and dashed for the door.

As it banged shut, I sat back, resting against my headboard.

I needed Kim to find me a date fast, because from now on I was only dating those the computer algorithm suggested, and I was definitely researching supernatural men's physical characteristics before I took any more to bed. I wondered if Kim could add a section about attitudes to manscaping to the application process?

CHAPTER 8

KIM

"Anything else I need to know on my return from annual leave?" asked Shelley as she sat back at her desk.

"No, I told you everything at your house. Anyway, your people, the humans, are all behaving."

"Huh, I'm sure they won't be. They like to complain when their first date doesn't yield them wedded bliss. I get sick of reminding people we're a dating agency, not magicians."

"Except you do have magical capabilities," I mused. "I wonder if you could make people fall in love with each other?"

"Nope. I'm a witch/wyvern cross not a fairy godmother. Now be a love and fetch me a coffee, would you?"

God, back one day and she was already bossing me about.

"I have my own division to run, you know? Those supernaturals can't find their own dates. They need me."

"Do you want me to stay in this mood all day?" She quirked an eyebrow.

"Do you want a chocolate doughnut with it?" I said, and I backed quickly out of the door.

~

I walked into Jax's cafe. There was a queue of three people in front of me, so while I waited I looked around to see if there were any familiar faces seated within the vintage inspired landscape of Jax's. My eyes landed on *his*, and as if he could feel my gaze upon his face,

Darius Wild, policeman and werewolf, stared right back from where he was sitting with a fellow officer.

"It's terrible form to stare at another man in the company of your ex," moaned Frankie.

"I'm not staring at him," I snapped. "And hopefully you won't be chained to my side much longer, even though I love you dearly *as a friend*."

"If you aren't staring, then why haven't you noticed that not only did you reach the front of the queue, but people have rolled their eyes at you and walked past you to get served?"

"What? How long have I been here?" I gasped.

"Ten minutes you've been staring at the animal," Frankie said with derision.

I walked up to the front of the queue and ordered coffees for us all and a chocolate doughnut each.

I was staring at the other baked delights on display when I caught sight of a reflection behind me in the queue. Fuck, *he* was up close and personal.

"Is that everything, Kim, honey?" asked Jax.

"Yes, babes," I replied, about to hand over a tenner.

"I'll get those, Jax, and another two teas please," a husky voice barked out.

"That really won't be necessary," I said, and despite my desire to ignore him, instead, I turned to face him.

"Well, I insist," Darius said. "How are you, Kim? Have you found me a date yet?"

I sighed and was about to offer up my usual excuse of there being a computer problem still when my Siamese twin piped up.

"Yes, the computers are all working now, and we have your first date all ready for you. We'll email you the details over later and you can finally start looking for your ideal woman," Frankie announced.

"Really? Wow. At last," Darius replied, a smile coming over his lips that I noticed did not meet his eyes. "I'll look forward to it. I was wondering how you were managing to stay financially afloat with all the gremlins affecting your computers."

"Yes, all fixed now. Hopefully, you'll be all settled with a lovely were in no time," added Frankie.

"Well, she doesn't strictly have to be a were. A human woman would also be acceptable if she was willing to date me."

I couldn't meet Darius' gaze, so I made a point of picking up my coffee and doughnut. "Can you grab the others?" I asked Frankie.

"Sure. Be seeing you around, Darius. Thanks for the coffees," Frankie added, helping me out in that all I had to do was nod my head in Darius' direction and get out of there.

We strolled back toward the office. "I don't know why that man cannot get the message that you aren't interested." Frankie held the bottom of the stair's door open for me.

"Maybe, because I don't have time to tell him before my vampire friend interferes? Just a thought."

"I realise I'm being entirely selfish, but I can't see any man wanting to go on a date with me as a third wheel so that about kills your love life for now."

"Yes, thanks for reminding me. Anyway, I don't want to date right now."

I climbed the stairs, thankful that Frankie was behind me and couldn't see the truth in my face.

As much as I wanted to deny my feelings for Darius, the moisture pooling between my thighs said different things to my mouth. But my dating a supernatural had brought me nothing but grief and when I was finally rid of Frankie as my ever-present companion, I was in no rush to have another supe around constantly. No matter how attractive I found Mr Wild and no matter how many minutes-come-hours I lost staring at him—and I'd yet to discover why I went into a trance-like state around him and him with me—it just wasn't happening. Mainly because I got the feeling he didn't want just a date with me—he wanted more. So, as much as it pained me, I really was going to have to run his details through the machine and get him a date. But just until I got used to the idea there was no harm in changing a few of his details was there?

"It's so good to be back at work. Playing Cupid, being a Boss Babe and then going home to my man." Shelley looked so happy it was actually nauseating, or was that down to the fact I was eating my third doughnut?

"And your best friend, a vampire accident, and your mum ghost-in-law. Yeah, amazing," I replied sarcastically.

"You're full of the joys today, aren't you? Stick your doughnut in your gob so it makes your voice stop."

"You do realise that the minute you're up the duff, your lovely husband will want you to stay at home, don't you? You know, your 127 years of age, old-fashioned vampire husband."

She shrugged her shoulders. "Well, he married a modern-day girl, and just like his computer skills, his woman handling ones must be updated. He works from home, so actually there's no reason why he can't bring up the baby."

"The fact he killed his own family doesn't worry you?" I asked honestly.

She sighed. "No, because that was all to do with him being turned."

"Ah, so actually, it's you who will need to avoid your child once you're turned then?"

Shelley went pale. "Oh my fucking god. I never thought of that. Kim, what if I don't know what I'm doing and I drain my own baby, or toddler, or well, you get the picture… whatever its age is when I'm turned? I'd never forgive myself. What am I going to do?" she screamed.

"Sometimes it's like there's nothing between your temples at all," Frankie's voice was full of scorn. "Expectant parents have enough worries about things they don't know, without you adding to the list. Of course, she'll not drain her own baby. Even in the changeover, you'd be fiercely protective of them, Shelley."

"Really? I won't try to eat it?"

"No. Now please, haven't you been around this one long enough to know to ignore half the crap that comes out of her mouth? Hell, why do you think I was only a fuck buddy? I didn't want to actually have to converse with her."

"For someone who can't leave my side, you're being awfully impolite there, buddy."

Frankie looked glum. "Hopefully, Theo will manage to treat me and then you can be free to make doe eyes with the wolf all day."

"Oh no. Not again," said Shelley. "Why don't you just bump uglies with him once and for all?"

I sighed loudly. This was getting boring. "Because a) I'm not into having a voyeur, and b) I'm not dating, I'm just concentrating on my career, and c) all of you shut the fuck up about the wolf.

"Do you know wolves can smell a female's arousal? Makes sense really, doesn't it?" Frankie fixed me with his gaze. My eyes went wide. Please God, no. Did that mean Darius knew I had damp panties in the cafe? Although for all he knew they could have been damp for Frankie. They had been frequently before he'd turned into a vamp wimp.

"Well, Darius has a date with a fairy called Glenda on Friday, so that will take his mind off me," I said.

"You finally algorithmed him?" Frankie's jaw dropped.

Shelley scratched the side of her temple. "Why has it taken so long to get Darius a date? He's been on our books for months."

"Yes, but according to Kim, she's kept having 'computer glitches' when she tries to put his details in. He's had to have two months membership refunded so far."

Shelley's eyes narrowed at me. Great, he'd dropped me in the shit. "Might I remind you that those memberships pay our salaries and without the agency members we wouldn't have employment? Is there anyone else you've been unable to process?"

"No." I looked at the floor.

"So, you are completely uninterested in Mr Wild, yet somehow he's the only dating club member to encounter 'glitches' in his application. Hmmm."

The phone thankfully interrupted the conversation at that point, and I got ready to make my escape back to my own office.

"Yes. What? Seriously? You sure about this? Hmmm, okay, I'll pass the message on." Shelley ended the call and looked at me.

"That was Ebony. She said—and these are her words not mine, so don't shoot the messenger—that 'Your actions will put you in great danger, but this is the only way you will accept your destiny'."

"Did she sound like she'd been on the vodka again?"

"Look, Kim," Shelley said, and she'd gone into mother-mode, so I had to pretend to listen. "If Ebony has 'seen' something in your future, some danger, you must be very careful."

"It's a good job I'm around to protect you," said Frankie, then he saw our faces and scowled. "Hey, there's no need for the look either of you gave me then. I'll gain my vamp skills. It's just taking me a while longer. I'm a slow developer."

"The only thing I'm in danger of is going insane around the lot of you," I said in a huff, going out and slamming the door behind me. Of course, it didn't actually slam because my permanent shadow was behind me and it smacked him in the face instead, making me feel bad.

God, I couldn't even have a tantrum in peace now.

I stormed into my own office to find Lucy sat waiting in front of my desk.

"What do you want now? I'm having a hell of a day already."

She raised an eyebrow. "Like you have any real idea of what one of those is like."

I huffed. "Sorry, Lucy." I pointed to Frankie who had sat in a chair in the corner. "This is all getting to me now."

Frankie glared at me. "I'm having treatment. It's not like I want to sit with you all day, every day."

"Hmmm." Lucy crossed one leg over the other, revealing a shapely thigh through the split in the side of her black wrap dress and the red flash of her Louboutin sole. "He's not as clingy. What treatment are you having, Frankie? I think it's doing something."

"I'm having talking therapy with Theo."

Lucy scoffed. "No, there's something else going on. Some trickery. I can feel it. It makes my horns tingle and they're tingling right now." She got up and walked over to Frankie. "Hmmm, I don't know exactly what Theo's doing, but there's something you're unaware of. Theo is being a naughty vampire." She clapped her hands. "Ooh, goody, he's been so boring since he slayed his own kin."

"I can assure you that the only thing we've been doing is talking while enjoying a really fine vintage of a sherry-casked scotch."

At this point Lucy roared with laughter.

"Sherry-casked? Has your scotch got a little of a red tinge to it, Frankie?"

Frankie's nostrils flared. "What are you saying?"

Lucy stroked Frankie's cheek. "Oh, baby, I think you're being weaned."

He glared at me. "Did you know about this, Kimberly?"

Whoa, full name alert.

"Don't be ridiculous. Look at my face. I'm as shocked as you are. It makes sense though as to why you've been a bit more jovial and insulting towards me."

He folded his arms across his chest. "Well, I am not impressed at being tricked."

"But Frankie, it's working, whatever it is. For all we know it might really have been sherry-casked scotch. You can't believe the she-devil. She's not exactly a trustworthy specimen, is she?"

Frankie exhaled loudly.

"Can you sit back in your seat?" he asked Lucy. "You're freaking me out."

She smirked at him but did as he asked.

I clasped my hands together. "So, what can I do for you today, Lucy?"

"I need you to expedite my first date. It is most prudent that I find love immediately, as I fear I shall slip back into my old ways otherwise."

"What do you mean?"

"I'm feeling, well, evil. More evil than usual since I've been back on earth. I don't like it. I can't go back there. Therefore, I need you to find me love, pronto."

She placed a hand down the top of her dress and adjusted her breasts. "What is going on with these things? They're straining my brassiere at the leash."

"Erm, Lucy. Do you also want to eat sweet stuff, and maybe have a few pimples?"

"Yes. This turning human thing is no joke. I also weigh a few pounds more."

"Have you had a period since you came back down to earth?"

Lucy tilted her head and looked up to the right. "No. Oh fuck, that's what this is? I'm not going back evil? I have pre-menstrual tension?"

"It certainly sounds that way."

Lucy smiled. "That is so very wonderful. I can embrace my current evil then because it will wear off in a few days." She looked over at Frankie calculatingly.

"Try anything with me and I'll pray to you know who to stick you in the menopause. I hope my house is still in one piece too."

"Yes, I'm making myself quite at home there. However, if you're improving, I'd better find love quickly, so I have somewhere to go on your return."

"He-who-can't-be-named help them," Frankie retorted, earning a red-eyed flash in return.

Chapter 9

Lucy

It made the most perfect sense now. I wasn't becoming evil again after all. I was getting my cycle back! No one would ordinarily be ecstatic that their period was coming, but on this occasion, I was going to be an exception to the rule. For a start, I had permission to be bad-tempered. Also, I could eat chocolate without guilt and curl up at home with a hot water bottle as I kept getting chilly up here in Withernsea, despite saying I didn't want to be around any heat.

"Could you please run my details through your system and get me my first date? Please?" I begged, which pained me. But I knew the way around someone like Kim was to suck up and tell her how brilliant she was. "Come on. I know you'll find me someone. I bet since you took over, Shelley's so jealous of how fabulous you are with the supernaturals. Do you know, I bet she's feeling a tad redundant," I stirred, warming up to my PMT.

"Actually, Kim's hardly set anyone up yet. She's been 'learning the ropes'," Frankie responded using air quotes.

Kim sat back straight in her chair. "That was true, but now I'm about to prove myself as queen of supernatural dating and you, dear Lucy, can indeed have a date. Give me a moment to load up your profile."

I waited as she keyed some information into her computer.

"Ah, here we are. Your first pairing is with Jared. Jared is an Eagle shifter."

"Is he flame retardant? Do you ask that question by any chance?"

I tried to say the question as an aside, but Kim just leaned forward over her desk.

"Is. He. Flame. Retardant?" She slapped herself in the forehead.

"It's really hard not to blaspheme here," she raised her voice, looking at Frankie. "Fuckety-fuck, she's going to flambé all my clients. They don't make a Scotchguard for supernaturals you know?"

She swung her chair to the left as she made a large huffing sound, and she banged some more keys.

"Right. Your first date is now with Todd. Todd is a ghost."

"A ghost? You want me to date a ghost? Where's the future with someone wispy? Can he turn stiff? Actually, forget that question," I said noting her reaction.

"He'll be a good practice date. Todd is an ex-swimwear model who drowned a few years ago on a shoot."

"He drowned modelling swimwear? How ironic."

"Yes, he couldn't swim, which didn't matter as it wasn't required on a shoot. However, he'd been two-timing his co-models and one of them slipped him a sedative before knocking him over the side of the boat. She subsequently killed herself rather than face jail."

"Christy?" I queried, recalling the large-breasted blonde. "I liked her. Ohhhh, this is that *Todd*. Apparently hung like a horse. It was a shame having to torture her as I always had sympathy with people who were two-timed."

"I should have known she'd go to Hell. You met her? Well, Todd learned his lesson. Now, although he's a ghost, in answer to your question, he is able to become solid."

"Whey-hey," I said rubbing my hands together.

"That is not what I meant. I meant he can come out on a proper date. Now the downsides of dating a ghost. Should he come to terms with his traumatic death, he may see a light, travel towards it and that's him done. Off to the place that shall not be mentioned, *or*, your old place of work, depending on how his life on earth balances out. Also, he can only solidify for two hours at a time, then he has to kind of charge himself back up for ten hours, so you have to work around that with any dates. The big advantage however, is you can't set him on fire. He's totally untouchable by earth, air, fire, or water. Hence, he'll make a fantastic first date."

"Okay, and when is Todd available?" I asked, taking out my iPhone and opening my calendar.

"How's Friday?"

"Friday night would be very acceptable. Where shall I meet him?"

"What about *Jetty's Ice Cream Parlour*? The temperature of the place is warm, but of course the ice cream is cool, meaning you can choose what temperature you need to be. As a ghost, Todd doesn't feel the temperature, so it won't bother him." She scratched her chin. "Now, what I can do if you like... and I wouldn't ordinarily offer this to a client..."

"Yes?" I wished she'd get to the point.

"Seeing as it's your first date and you are, at your own admission, very out of practice, what would you think of having a double date? With me and one other?"

"I wonder if I will be able to taste the ice cream?" said Frankie, and I saw Kim's face dull.

"Oh no, I forgot about you."

"Gee thanks. And don't think I don't know what's going on here. Wolfman has his date Friday night too. I wonder where you suggested he take her."

"Shut your pie-hole before I stake you," Kim snapped.

Ooh, this was getting interesting. So Kim liked a wolf? If my date got boring, I could play with all the other human and supernaturals.

"A double date sounds just the thing," I said. "Now what are you planning on wearing?"

∼

I returned home feeling very pleased with myself. I had a date for Friday night! With a swimwear model no less. He was sure to be dead fit. I chortled at my inner joke.

I wondered if Maisie would have returned yet from her overnight next door. I pushed open the front door and hanging up my bag and coat in the hallway, I ran towards the living room after hearing the most horrendous hissing sound.

Halting at the doorway in shock, I witnessed Maisie in female form surrounded by about fifteen male pixies. They were throwing stones at her, their faces alight with mischief.

"What's going on?" I demanded.

"It would appear they're upset that I've offended their leader. Except I wasn't the one who took him home was I? If you could just explain that to them, then maybe, 'Ow, stop that', they'll let me go."

"But then they'll start on me." I drew my brows together in thought. "Just a minute." I took out my phone and punched in a number.

"Kim. How do you deal with pixies? As in get rid of them?"

I waited.

"What do you mean you're not an encyclopaedia of the supernatural? You run a dating agency for them. I'd suggest you learn so you can match-make better, you sarcastic bitch. Thanks a lot. I have a pixie situation at home. Yes, in Frankie's house. Oh, he'll talk to me. Good that someone cares."

I waited again.

"Frankie? Can you help me? I have a house full of evil pixies."

"They'd better not be destroying my home."

"They're not, but they're picking on Maisie. However, I didn't think the RSPCA would believe me that I had pixies being cruel to the animal."

He sighed. "I brought a book back from Theo's to read while Kim's working. It's all about supernaturals. Pixies you say? Poor Maisie. She's not hurt, is she?"

"No, she's fine."

"What are they doing in my house, anyway?"

"Look, tell me how to get rid of them and then I'll tell you how they got here. They're throwing stones right now and your mirror is getting chipped."

"That's an antique," he screamed down the phone.

"So, get looking them up."

I heard pages being flipped. "Iron."

"Typical, I'm always being punished for not doing housework. Where do you keep it?" I sighed.

"Keep what?"

"Your iron."

"Not an iron! Iron the element. I have an iron knife hung in the kitchen among my other kitchen tools. Just wave it about at them though. Don't kill them."

I took the phone through to the kitchen with me. He had so many cooking implements you'd have thought he was Gordon Ramsay. "Got it. Thanks." I hung up and walked back in the room.

"Back off." I waved the knife around and they screamed with

fright and raced to the back of the room, fighting to put others in front of themselves. The noise was like nothing you had ever heard. Like multiple people screaming after inhaling that gas from balloons.

"Silence," I roared, flames flickering at the ends of my fingertips.

"P-P-permission to speak?" asked a pixie at the front.

"Permission granted."

"We came at the command of our leader, Tristan, who suffered a large embarrassment here. You see, as our leader, Tristan is held in esteem as being a very skilled and practised lover, and you have sullied his reputation by the loss of his, erm, hair. In our realm, the, er, hairier the better and so by divesting him of this, he is now considered weaker. Should rumour go around our court he could be challenged as pixie leader."

"What does that have to do with you throwing stones at Maisie?"

"We thought she was you and Tristan had sent us here to get you to apologise and to somehow find a way to mend his reputation. You caused the incident and so in pixie law you must solve it. Otherwise, you will have pixies visit you until you make amends, and believe me, that is not fun."

I drew in a breath. "Let me think on this a while. What do pixies like to eat and drink while I consider things?"

"We would love a drink of milk." The pixie stepped forward. "I am Lornan."

I shook his small hand in mine. I must have been rat-arsed last night to take a pixie home. What had I been thinking?

"They can't have my milk." Maisie's eyes narrowed into slits.

"You have special cat milk; they can drink my semi-skimmed," I reassured her. "Now, while I get your drinks, I need you to tidy all these stones up if you don't mind, Lornan. Only this isn't my house."

"Oh we like to tidy up," Lornan said. "We'll repair any damage too."

They set off to work while I returned to the kitchen. I phoned and asked for Frankie again who told me to pour it into bowls for them to share. Who'd have thought the vamp reject would have a use?

While the pixies enjoyed their milk, I walked back into the living room to see how Maisie was doing.

"Had they been any smaller I'd have changed to my feline self and chased the bastards," she said.

"Yes, well talking about your kitty side, I have an idea to get me out of this scrape I've got myself into and all I can say is you'll benefit, so turn and lie down please."

"Oooooh," said Maisie. "You've decided to give me a try?"

"Nope. Now turn into a cat, like pronto." I held out a cat brush. "I'll tickle your chin with it if you're good."

It was hard to reconcile a black cat with my new friend. She sat on the carpet at the side of me while I gave her a good brush. Very pleasingly, lots of fur came off into the brush and while her fur gleamed silkily, I kept cleaning the brush out with my fingers and piling it up. I brushed around her chin and she head-rubbed back, clearly enjoying her little cat self. She was purring away, and I tickled the top of her head.

By the time the pixies made their way back into the living room the job was done. "Maisie, time for you to go out now," I said and with a prance she was out of the room and I heard the cat flap smack shut behind her.

I held up the pile of fur. "Will you be able to make a merkin out of this for Tristan?" I asked Lornan. "And please offer my sincere apologies. I would offer them in person, but unfortunately, my powers are a little awry and I would hate to accidentally set anything else on fire."

Lornan looked at the fur. "This will be gratefully accepted. How black and shiny it is. I think he may even dye his hair to match. Thank you, lady."

He bowed. "You have made reparation and we shall now be on our way."

And with that the group of pixies filed out of the house. God knows what the neighbours thought. That I was organising my own panto no doubt or had a Tyrion Lannister fetish.

I decided that between now and my date on Friday I would concentrate only on the restaurant and on keeping control of my powers at this time of the month. I headed to the kitchen in search of a bottle of coke and some jelly babies, then realised I couldn't face eating little bodies after spending time with the pixies. Instead, I opened a chocolate cake. Stuff it, I thought, and that's exactly what I did to my mouth.

Chapter 10

Kim

"They are being very kind in trying to help you and having us live with them temporarily, so you mustn't be rude when we walk in there," I reminded Frankie, who had spent the rest of the afternoon chuntering about trust issues.

"I will be very tactful in my approach."

"Good." I rang the doorbell, and the door appeared to open on its own. When I scrunched my eyes, I could just about make out Mary's outline.

"Mary, are you alright? You look very washed out." I stepped through, concerned about her translucence. She opened her mouth, but then she was gone.

I stepped into the kitchen where Theo was sat at the table nursing a cup of tea.

"I just saw your mum. Well kind of saw her, then she disappeared. Is she alright?"

"She's worn herself out with busy bodying. I had Margret and Dylan around earlier to discuss the next stages for Frankie's treatment and what with that and riffling through your things while you were out, she's expended too much energy."

I saw Theo's hair move slightly as if it had met a small breeze.

"Can't clip me around the ear right now, can you, mother? Go and lie down for pity's sake, woman."

Frankie pulled out a chair facing Theo and sat down. "Have you been feeding me blood?"

Theo sighed. "Let me get you a drink of tea, Frankie, and I'll explain everything. Coffee, Kim?"

"Please."

Drinks in front of us, Theo sucked on his top lip for a moment and sighed.

"I was at a loss as to how to help you, Frankie, so I experimented. I knew that our talking could help in you coming to terms with your new existence, but every time I offered you a bottle of blood to drink you gagged, which is most unusual. So, I talked to Dominica, one of the elders from the caves, and she said she'd come across a case like yours only once before and they'd decided to give small donations of the founding vampire's blood to them in order to see if they could spark the usual change."

"You admit to giving me blood?"

"Yes, minute amounts, so my apologies about the sherry-cask. It was indeed what I said, but I also put in a few drops of this very powerful blood. Have you felt any different?"

"He's not been quite as clingy," I declared. "He stayed on a chair reading a book today. I managed to get quite a lot of work done. Also, at times he was quite surly towards me. It's all very encouraging."

"Charming. Most women covet attention, but you want me to be distant and insulting. No wonder you're single," Frankie huffed.

"See? He's more like his old self."

"That's good news. What we'll do is keep on with the talking therapy and also a daily ration of the original source."

"Why do I need shower gel?"

"Not that Original Source. Blood, you dummy." I rolled my eyes.

"I don't want the blood. So forget offering me any more sherry-cask whiskey. I just can't face it. I'm so not a vampire. Now can I have more of this Rosehip tea because it's delightful. I've missed it since I no longer need it as a magician to turn off my 'turnip smell' as you so-call it."

"You like that?" Theo poured Frankie another mugful.

"It's delicious. I love herbal teas. They're far superior to English Breakfast or Earl Grey." He drank his second cup down. "I can't believe we've found something I like the taste of. Gosh, I'm really thirsty today. Did I read so much I forgot to drink?"

Theo filled him up a third time, and I tried so hard not to let a smirk reach my mouth, but come on, it was impossible.

"What? What's with your face?" Frankie gave me a surly look and turned to Theo. "Could you tell me the name of this particular brand? I want some for the office."

"It's English Breakfast mixed with, erm, original source," said Theo. "Mainly you're drinking blood, Frankie. Now we need to go through to my office so we can work on you accepting that fact."

"I'm—I'm—" Frankie looked down at his mug.

"You're a vampire, dude." I lifted my own coffee mug and chinked it against his glass.

〜

Frankie was subdued when he returned with Theo to the living room later.

When Shelley opened a large packet of cheese and onion kettle chips and placed them in a bowl in the middle of the table, he didn't try to eat any. I wish I could say the same myself, but they are so more-ish and I must have eaten over half the packet easily, dipping my hand in for great handfuls until Shelley slapped my fingers away.

"When might you know if you're pregnant?" I asked her, getting brave after drinking two glasses of wine.

"It can be anything from one week to five weeks apparently."

"And how long are vampires pregnant for?"

"Around six months," Theo said. "Obviously with our little mixed breed baby, we're not altogether sure what's going to happen. No one mixed a vampire with a half witch/half wyvern before to my knowledge."

"It's certainly not in the encyclopaedia," Frankie added.

"Are you nervous?" I asked Shelley.

"Nah. I can't think why anyone would be nervous about having a baby come out of their hoo haa. Especially when you're a witch/wyvern cross, only learned that a few months ago and do not understand how that will impact on giving birth to a vampire's baby. Not shitting myself AT ALL."

"Well, there's no need to be sarcastic. I was only showing interest." I rolled my eyes at Theo.

"Could you possibly not say that you're shitting yourself, darling? Apprehensive is such a better word."

"Do you want me to insert a melon somewhere so you can practice what I have ahead of me?" She glared at her husband. "Oh it has gone very quiet in here now, hasn't it?"

"I will care for you no matter how difficult it gets or how uncouth your mouth, my darling wife, of that you have my word."

Frankie stretched out against the back of the sofa. "I'm thirsty. Do you have any more tea?"

∼

The strangest thing happened the next day. As the sun rose, I heard a groan. Startled, I turned to see Frankie dive under the duvet. "I'm knackered," he said, and then, he fell asleep.

I was so shocked that I couldn't get back to sleep myself. I sat up against the headboard, a bit uncomfortable that there was a vampire under the bedcovers.

"Oh, love, I'm sorry to disturb you. I didn't think you were dating anymore," came a whisper to my right.

I jumped, seeing Mary's form.

"What are you talking about?"

"We didn't do things like that in my day. It was very just do the deed and clothes back on, but I should think if the fella is busy down there under the sheets, the least you could do is act like you're enjoying it."

"Oh my god, Mary, he's not doing that! His vampire gene is kicking in a bit. He saw a little of the dawn and dived underneath. I should be so bloody lucky at getting any other action."

"Oh, well, that's alright then, I'm not disturbing anything after all."

"Except for floating around my bedroom in the very early hours of the morning."

"I like to check on everyone, make sure you're all okay."

I sat up and swung my legs out of bed. "Well, I might as well get up now. It's not that long before my alarm's due to go off, anyway."

"I'll make you a drink, shall I? Then I'll come keep an eye on Frankie here."

"Coffee would be lovely, and would you?" I said, looking at the lump under the duvet, genuinely grateful that she'd look out for him.

"Of course. It's what I would have done with Theo had he been around." She screwed her face up. "No actually, I'd have tried to stake the little shit. It's a good job I've had time to forgive him for the thirst that was beyond his control."

I bit my lower lip. "I worry about Frankie. I know he's not mine to worry about, but I've kind of been his guardian of late."

"Well, I would guess by the fact he's sleeping that he's evolving now into a full vampire? I should imagine you'll find it strange him not being by your side all the time."

"Well, it's early days so we'll see how it goes."

I wasn't sure how I'd feel about it. Probably a short sadness followed by a loud cheer and a party.

Downstairs, I had several cups of coffee and fixed myself a bacon butty while I waited for Shelley to wake up.

She wandered into the room bleary-eyed at seven forty-five. Now I'd always been lairy with the time, but Shelley was always an early riser. Things had changed since she'd married a vampire.

Mary placed a coffee in her hand and Shelley slumped in a chair at the kitchen table. "I think I'm going to need to be turned soon." She leaned over towards me and whispered. "It's a bit much when your husband is at his brightest in the middle of the night and keeps you awake. No matter how nice it is, I still need some sleep. I can't keep staying up until the early hours."

"It must be difficult having a different sleep schedule?"

"Well, I guess it's not any different from someone whose partner works night shifts, but just sometimes it would be nice to spend the whole day together.

"That's ironic. We're trying to get Frankie to become nocturnal when you'd like Theo to be able to come out in the day."

We both looked at each other.

"Do you think there's something in Frankie's body that might be found, some DNA or something, that could be looked at by scientists to see if a vaccine could be made? Maybe vampires could start being around in the daytime?" Shelley said, looking quite excited.

"That's what Theo said happened to the last vampire like Frankie," Mary said, refilling our cups. "They dismembered and tortured them trying to find a cure for daytime slumber."

We looked at her in shock.

"I may have overheard that when he was talking to your parents about Frankie," she said.

"I never thought of that. It would put him in extreme danger if people found out. It's better that he carries on being given blood and we try to turn him fully," Shelley said.

"Right, have a good day ladies. I'm off to keep an eye on Frankie. I'll hit the burglar alarm if there's a problem. That will ring your phone won't it, lovey?" she asked Shelley, who nodded.

"What will you do about the agency when you're turned? You'll not be able to work during the day." I asked her.

"Oh, we'll cross that bridge when we come to it. I've enough to think about now with the prospect of potentially being pregnant. It's a shame though about the fact Frankie could be put in danger because of his current ability. Life would be a lot easier if vampires could keep the same hours as humans."

A crash came from near the kitchen window, and we rushed over to see what it was. "Umm, there's nothing there," I said.

Shelley went out of the front door and looked around, then an angry expression crossed her face and she stormed back in.

"For a winter's day it was awfully warm out there under the window."

"Meaning what?"

"Meaning that whatever was there either carried their own radiator or came from a very hot place."

"Lucy?" I queried. "What would she be doing here?"

"Not Lucy." Shelley replied. "Satan. I've had my suspicions that he keeps hanging around. It would appear he can't accept that he needs to stay downstairs."

"She means Hell, not the basement." said Mary, reappearing.

"Hmm, I wonder what he's up to?" I mused.

"Down to, more like," corrected Mary.

∽

It was so peculiar not having company at work. I kept speaking to the corner of the office and then realising that Frankie wasn't there. I did however get lots of work done and answered an email that congratulated the agency on its ability to bring love to the supernaturals of Withernsea. Hopefully it wouldn't be long before I got my first wedding invitation as a thanks for my matchmaking abilities.

It was around three fifty pm when I heard a loud bang at the back door, an ear-splitting screech, and I only had time to realise the door had flown open when I found myself pinned against the wall, vampire fangs descended and touching my neck.

My body froze in shock. The last time I'd been bitten was by the devil disguised as a vampire and he'd almost killed me.

"Frankie. Frankie, don't do it. Please, just take a step back. You don't want to feed on someone without their permission, right?"

He licked up the outside of my neck. "But your blood is singing to me, Kim. Maybe just a little taste?"

His teeth punctured the skin, eliciting a sharp scratch like that from a needle, but then adrenaline flooded my veins and as I heard him suck, my legs turned to jelly, and my body craved his touch. I wanted him to feed from me, to keep feeling the euphoria racing through my body.

Then Frankie wasn't there anymore, and I hit the ground hard, landing on my bony ass.

"Ow," I said rubbing my neck.

Although I found it difficult with the buzz in my system that was spacing me out, I saw that Shelley was now in the room. Her eyes shone silver blue and all I could think was 'whoa'. Whatever drug I'd had was really fucking trippy. Frankie was pinned against the wall wrapped in silver-blue webs as Shelley's raised hands were held open in front of him.

"Are you okay, Kim?" she asked me.

"Yeah, why, what happened?"

"Frankie escaped the house and decided you were dinner. I knew something was amiss as the house alarm went off and rang my phone."

"God, I was only having a sip. I was in control," he said.

"Did Kim give you permission to drink?" She turned to me. "Shit, was I disturbing something?"

"No." I said as the shock hit, and I realised what had just happened. "Fuck, he bit me. Shelley, he bit me. What if he'd have killed me?"

She looked at her watch. "I'll ring Theo. He should be up now. We need him here fast."

Chapter 11

Kim

"We should have seen this coming," Theo said, pacing the room. "I fed him the strongest blood in our history. That of the Founder. How could I fail to realise that he would crave more? He was continuously thirsty last night. I obviously gave him far too much."

"Theo, you were doing what you thought was right. You can't blame yourself," I said as Shelley tended to my neck, doing her healing mojo.

"Well, if you can stay a couple more days, I will restrict the amount of blood I give him. In the meantime, I need to confer with those at the caves more. He may have to go there again."

"But what if they decide they want to experiment on him?" Shelley said. "Let's just keep this to ourselves for now. We'll work something out. It's early days yet."

"Can you stop discussing me as if I'm not in the room? I'm not having any more of that blood. I could have killed my friend," Frankie said. He turned in my direction. "Do you still have those handcuffs we used to use?"

"Now is not the time to proposition me again, Frankie. We are very much over," I huffed.

"Not for that. Look, I want you to cuff me so that I can't try anything. I need to go cold turkey. I'd rather be a pathetic half-vamp than accidentally drain you."

Theo sighed. "I can't help but blame myself. After my own turning, I should have known you'd thirst for more. It's basically like you're being turned again."

"Well, I don't want it. So leave me alone and let me go back to how I was."

Theo sighed, but it didn't look like we currently had any choice.

∾

By Friday, when date night rolled around, Frankie was back to his clingy self. Now not only was he in my space all the time but added to that was a thick layer of guilt because of him feeding off me.

"I'm paying for our dinner tonight," he told me.

"We're going for ice cream." I rolled my eyes.

"Well, if you want a waffle as well, it's on me," he said.

I really was getting to the end of my rope now. I had Frankie hanging around and tonight I'd got to witness Darius on his first date with our agency. I'd deliberately chosen a fairy as they were known as being skittish and unable to settle, so I thought she might get on his nerves. She would certainly be no use as a wolf's mate. Fairies were light on their feet and slight, and wolf shifters seemed to prefer a woman with a bit of meat on their bones. This was in no way connected to the fact I'd stopped doing Slimming World, was eating extra chocolate doughnuts and had put on half a stone in the last three weeks. No, that was just me allowing my winter body to develop. We all needed extra fat stores in winter you know, it was how animals survived.

"Frankie, can I just have a minute on my own to get dressed?"

"Sure." He turned around.

I sighed heavily. This was going to be a long night.

∾

I'd decided not to do much with myself. I didn't want to attract attention to me. Rather, I wanted to assist Lucy on her date, survive yet another few hours with Frankie, and spy on Darius and the fairy. Therefore, I'd come out dressed in a black hoodie, a pair of jeans, and I had my dark hair tied in a ponytail, with my fringe combed over to the side. I coated my head in hairspray and added a little perfume to my pulse points.

As we stepped inside *Jetty's*, a waitress came over to show us to our table. Lucy had already arrived. She was sitting there, dressed to impress in a curve revealing bodycon dress in black lace, her Louboutins still on her feet. From behind the waitress, Todd appeared. He just appeared right behind her. Poof, there he was. She jumped as she turned around, for Todd was standing there in nothing but his swim shorts, muscles flexing everywhere.

"Oh my," I said.

"Erm, sir, we do actually have a dress code," the waitress said.

I stepped over. "Oh, Todd. I'm so sorry." I laughed. "Go along with this," I whispered in his ear. "We forgot to tell you we weren't doing fancy dress anymore."

Todd turned to me. "I'm sorry. I only have the clothes I died in. I never thought."

"Here, would you like to borrow my jacket?" Goose bumps trailed up the back of my neck at Darius' voice. As we turned towards him, he handed over a full-length, fake fur jacket. "This should keep you warm."

I looked at his date. Her photo had shown a dark-blonde haired plain Jane. It appeared Morgan had had a makeover. She was a wisp of a thing, with long blonde curled hair, the most bewitching green eyes, and she seemed to be dressed in a slip—a red, very thin slip.

"I think perhaps your lady friend might need the coat more?" I suggested.

"Oh no," she said, shaking her hair. "I'm hot."

She was as well, the bitch.

"So, what's happening here then?" Darius asked, with a quirk of his eyebrow. "A little double date?"

Todd put the coat on and thanked Darius. "Yes, kind-of. I'm here to meet Lucy, and Kim and Frankie agreed to join us as we're both new to the dating scene and a little nervous. Why don't you both join us?"

"No, it's only a table for four," I protested.

"Oh that's okay." said our waitress. "It's no trouble to move another little table across and two chairs."

If looks could kill, that lady would have been an ideal date for Todd right now.

"In that case we'd love to join you," Darius said, and I didn't need to know he was staring right at me as he said it. I could feel his stare burning through me.

"When you've finished playing musical chairs, I'd like to be introduced to my date." It was time for Lucy to make herself known, and as she stood up, her breasts heaving to stay enclosed inside the tight embrace of the fabric of her dress, three sets of male eyes moved as if hypnotised to her rack.

Great.

So that's how we ended up out on a triple date. Lucy was in the farthest seat, and so I steered Todd opposite her, then I sat next to Todd. Frankie sat opposite me, and Darius sat next to him, leaving Morgan, the fairy, to take the seat at my other side. Super. I was twice her size. I couldn't even complain because I was the one who'd set her bloody date up.

"Sorry again about my outfit and thanks for the coat," Todd shouted across the table at Darius.

"No worries."

"Actually, I should have worn my Halloween outfit then we'd have matched," I informed Todd. "It was a white bikini because I was being a ghost who died sunbathing. Quite the coincidence, yeah?"

"Really? Wow, yeah, that's totally so coincidental. And my shorts are white too, so we would have been like a total twinning couple if I'd known you then. You're single right? I don't see a ring."

"Actually we were dating at the time. I was concerned she'd catch her death, it being winter, so I magicked her some clothes," Frankie added. "You did look lovely as the Corpse Bride."

"You do magic? Whoa, man. Can you make me disappear?"

"I wish," shouted Lucy.

Oh dear. This date wasn't going well.

"No. I'm a—"

I could see Frankie didn't want to explain what he was to Todd, so I tried to divert his attention.

"So, Todd. Do you like steak? Lucy owns *Red's Steakhouse*?"

"Uhm, I'm a vegetarian," he replied.

"Oh, I don't remember seeing that on your application?"

"Nah, I thought it might cut down my chances to date a hot chick."

"Oh Frankie, please talk to me. My date is a dullard," I heard Lucy say.

"I wanted to talk to you anyway. You never explained how my house ended up full of pixies."

Pixies? I couldn't have heard that right.

"Hey, Todd. If you don't mind me asking, how did you die?" Darius asked.

"Oh yes, tell us all the juicy details. I never met a ghost before," added Morgan.

"Well," Todd sat back letting his coat part slightly which caused his pecs to appear. They rippled as he moved. "Basically, I was on this shoot in Greece, and—"

"Are you ready to order?" asked the waitress.

That interruption over and ice creams and refreshments on the way, Todd carried on.

"So you see, I'd been two-timing them, and well, Christy decided to kill me and knock me overboard."

"Or maybe she'd just had to listen to you drone on for thirty minutes like I have," Lucy muttered under her breath.

As the time ticked on and our drinks and various ice cream concoctions arrived, it was like spinning plates trying to keep up with conversations. Todd never stopped talking about himself and I tried to be polite listening; Frankie was telling Lucy about what had been happening to him the last few days; Lucy was talking about Frankie's house. Then I'd been trying to keep an ear out on what was happening to my left with the progressing fairy/were date.

"Darius, did you really just pick up your bowl and slurp the remains or am I imagining things?" Morgan queried.

"Oh, as a wolf, that's what we do. Sorry if it looked a little slovenly."

"It's not that. But you need to leave a little in your bowl for the fairies to have tonight."

"As soon as that woman takes our dishes they'll be going straight into the dishwasher," Darius answered.

"How do you know that? They may leave them out for my brothers and sisters."

"No, I know the staff here and they kind of don't want the food standards agency on their backs, so they clean up."

Morgan gasped. "Then I cannot remain here. They do not support my kind."

She stood up.

"I apologise everyone and especially to you, Kim. Thank you for setting me up with Darius. He is a very good-looking man. But I can't stay in this restaurant as it's not fairy-friendly and I regret there is no spark between Darius and myself. If you could pick me another date for next week, I would be delighted, but I shall choose the location if that's okay."

"Of course. I'll be in touch."

With that, Morgan bid farewell and walked out of the parlour.

"Ouch, that was a little abrupt. You alright?" Frankie said turning to Darius.

"Don't feel you have to stay if you're upset. It's fine if you want to go home," I told him.

His eyes narrowed, and I was sure a little flash of yellow hit them although it could have been a reflection from the parlour's lighting. "No, I'm perfectly fine where I am, thank you. I'm thinking I might have a hot drink now to warm me up."

I turned back to Todd so as not to show Darius how much he was getting to me.

Todd was stirring his ice cream into a gloopy mess.

"What are you doing?" I asked.

"I love making it all one colour and if you stir it really well it goes like a drink, a bit like a—"

"—milkshake. Of which there's a selection on the menu," Lucy interrupted.

"Really? Oh wow. I like doing this though. It's so fun and tasty."

"Todd, do you hold a grudge against the woman who killed you?" Darius asked.

He stopped stirring. "Well, of course. She murdered me and yet she is free to do as she pleases."

"Are you talking about Christy?" Lucy interrupted. "She's not free, honey. She's in Hell. Babes, all I had to do was take away her fake tan and implants and she screamed for hours."

He stared at Lucy, finally giving his actual date some attention. Unfortunately, only in order to discuss his ex-girlfriend. "Christy is in Hell? Really?"

"Yeah, she begged me for forgiveness, to be allowed to go to heaven, blah blah blah. They all do, it's sooo pathetic. Why not be evil and own it, right? Anyway, she was saying how sorry she was for murdering you, but that she'd loved you so much and wanted to marry you, but you cheated on her with, let me see if I can remember. Hmmm, Susan, and Katie, and Yasmin and Katya, yeah? Anyhow you get the point I'm trying to make, right?"

"D'ya hear that, Todd?" Darius leaned over the table, capturing Todd's rapt attention. "Christy loved you. She only murdered you because you cheated on her. She wanted you so much she couldn't bear to share you."

Todd's eyes began to water. "You think so?"

"I know so," Darius said. "Do you think you'd forgive her if you had a chance to spend all of eternity with her?"

For fuck's sake. He was upsetting my, err, *Lucy's* date.

Todd placed a hand over his heart. "I did think I loved her. It was just, there was so much other pussy around, you know?"

"I know, friend. But you can understand why she got so jealous, can't you? She just wanted you for herself and now she's stuck in Hell... all because she loved you."

Was Darius trying to audition for an agony aunt stint on *This Morning* or something?

"Maybe you could find it within yourself to forgive her?"

I watched as Todd's body wobbled. He went translucent for a minute before solidifying again. *What the fuck?*

Then I got it. Oh my god, was Darius trying to get rid of my, erm, LUCY's date. *I really needed to stop forgetting that I came with Frankie.*

"I can see a golden light," Todd said.

"Don't walk towards it," I yelled.

"Walk? It's coming out of her fingers." Todd pointed at Lucy.

"My date is as boring as fuck. If he doesn't move on, I'm going to test out the elements theory," Lucy said, watching the flame climb higher on her fingers.

The waitress popped over. "Erm, sorry, but this is a no smoking establishment."

"Could I have another sundae please?" Todd requested.

I'd hoped it was almost time to go home, but now we'd need to sit here in purgatory awhile longer so Todd could finish his next ice cream.

As it got delivered, Todd picked up his giant spoon and began to stir it again.

"Fuck that," Lucy said, and reaching out she grabbed the glass. I saw her hand take on its amber glow and she passed back a glass full of steaming liquid.

"So, about that forgiveness?" Darius reminded him.

"Oh yeah? Well, thinking about it, if she's been punished and everything then that's alright, isn't it? I wasn't innocent myself. So like I totally forgive her and hopefully we'll meet again." He cocked his head to his right sharply. "I could swear I just heard her. Wow, what a coincidence, she's over there," he said pointing towards the wall. Before I could warn him, he'd gone, out of his seat and then just completely vanished.

"What have you done?" I yelled at Darius.

"I've assisted a restless spirit in moving on. It's my good deed of the day. Or good dead of the day," Darius quipped.

"That was Lucy's date." I gave him the stink eye.

"Was it really, because from where I was looking it was more like you were on a date with him?" Lucy snarled. "Not that I protested too much because it was obvious he was brain dead before his body joined in the party. Even his looks couldn't make up for the fact that the lights were on but no was even in the area, never mind home."

"I was just trying to keep him in conversation because you spent all night talking to Frankie."

"You think she'd be pleased. She's always moaning that she doesn't get a break from me and that we're over, and then I talk to someone else, and she complains." Frankie turned to Darius. "You never know where you are with women, do you?"

There was clicking in front of my face, and I came to.

"For fuck's sake, you're staring at each other again. What is it with that shit?" Frankie whined.

"I bet it's in your encyclopaedia thingy. Look it up when you get home. Well, to her home." Lucy pointed a shiny red talon in my direction.

The waitress wandered over. "Would you like the bi—"

"YES," four people shouted in unison.

A deathly silence came over the table. The trouble was I didn't like silences. I always felt I had to chatter to fill them.

"You owe me for Todd's membership fees," I almost growled at Darius. "Because you cost me his custom."

"Well, if you ever prove that having a membership with your agency is worth it, I'll gladly hand the extra money over, but so far I've had one date with a fairy."

"I gave you a refund of your other fees."

"I want dates, not a refund."

"Fine. I'll set you up with someone every single day this next week."

"Fine."

Silence descended again until Frankie spoke up. "Kim, I need the toilet."

I puffed out my lips on a sigh. "Come on then. You'll have to FaceTime though. They aren't going to let me come in with you."

"I need to go; I'll go in with him."

"Thank you, Mr Wild, but he'll still need to FaceTime. He can't be without me."

"You have my sympathies."

"Thanks, it's very restrictive." I said, surprised he said something so supportive.

"I was talking to Frankie."

"Bastard."

"Pardon? What did you call me?"

"Can we save the pissing contest for the bathroom, please," Lucy said. "I think I actually had a better time with the pixie."

I tilted my head looking at her. "What's all this about a pixie?"

"Never mind. Come on, Frankie. You can do this. You managed without Kim for hours earlier. This is a few minutes to take a leak, so don't make her FaceTime. It's not very gentlemanly."

Frankie looked unsure.

"Darius is coming in with you. You'll be fine."

"You'll be right outside?" he queried, checking with me.

"Yes, of course I will."

Frankie went into the bathroom with Darius.

"I'm sorry, Lucy. This evening was dreadful. I'll get you a much better date next time."

"Thank you. I'll be happy to come to the next date on my own though. I think it'll be better that way, without you and the wolf trying to make each other jealous."

"That is not what—"

"Don't actually give a shit, Kim. I just want to find the love of my life so I can be settled and no longer evil, so get me more dates. I want one every night next week like Darius."

"You want Darius?"

"No, I want a date every night like you've said you're doing for him. Waste of bloody time setting me up with him when you're destined to be together. Ebony told me all about it over coffee," she said to my shocked face.

"Not a chance. I'm not into the whole man bun thing."

"God, you are so shallow sometimes, and if I can see that, you should worry. I know you're capable of more with how you are with Shelley and with Frankie. Why not try a relationship for once instead of a fuck buddy?"

"I have my reasons and you don't need to know them. Let me concentrate on getting you a date."

"I tell you what, if you find me love, you have to go out with Darius on one date. *If*," she emphasised the word, "he's not already settled with someone else that you've matched him up with—which he won't be, because he's your *des-tin-y*."

"Fine." I shook her hand and wisps of red and white smoke?—that's what it looked like—wrapped around our hands.

"Ooh, it would appear that I am definitely still a little demonic, and you know what that means, don't you?"

"What?" I said flailing my hand in the air as it was having a hot flush.

"You made a deal with a devil. It's binding."

"Gaaahhhh." I stomped my foot. "I forgot about that."

It was then Darius came bursting out of the door.

"Is there a fire?" I quipped.

"You could say that," he gasped. "We were in the bathroom and then he came out of nowhere. Just tore a hole in the air. It was so hot, flames licked around it, and then he pulled Frankie through it, and it closed up."

I looked back at Lucy.

"Satan's got him." She confirmed my dreaded thought.

CHAPTER 12

LUCY

Kim clutched at my arm, squeezing her eyes closed. "Fuck. He's dead. Let's face it, If Satan hasn't killed him, the shock will. What's he got against Frankie? Well, other than being tricked back to Hell. This is not good, not good at all." The pitch of her voice got higher with every new sentence, and she grasped at her throat. I could hear her getting breathless as her panic increased, so I slapped her. Truth be told I'd wanted to do that earlier anyway for her monopolizing my date, but at least right now I could get away with it as being a necessity.

"Calm down. Being hysterical will not help him."

Kim clutched the left side of her face. "Right. Yes, yes, you're right, I need to focus. We need Shelley. She's the only one with the power to get him back."

She pulled out her phone, and I noticed how her hand shook as she pressed the contacts button.

"Shelley, we're at *Jetty's* and Satan took Frankie." The words flew out of her mouth so fast it was like they were all one.

After waiting valuable minutes while Kim explained the situation, I noticed that Darius was pacing around like a, well, wolf waiting to pounce.

"Is there anything me and my pack can do?" he asked as she pressed end call.

All the tension between them became forgotten as they focused on the matter at hand. "I don't know. It's all down to Shelley really.

They're going to meet us in front of the amusement arcade. Let's go."

We walked down the street and watched as Shelley appeared from around the corner, no doubt having travelled by portal, and then a freak breeze whipped her hair before her husband appeared at the side of her, having travelled using his vampire speed. I missed being able to appear via a portal. Now I had to catch the bus everywhere which was a complete arse pain.

I took in how Theo was with his wife. He touched her shoulder lightly and fastened his gaze on hers, checking in with her that she was okay. I didn't need to hear his words though, his non-verbal cues saying everything before his mouth opened. I turned my gaze to Kim. Worry etched her features, and the wolf, Darius, hovered just behind her. Although she was oblivious, being preoccupied with concern, I saw Darius rubbing at his eyebrow, his other fist clenched at his side where his knuckles were white.

I'd spent a lot of time in Hell, and many hours watching people. Seeing their faces when they first entered and realised where they were. I knew that so many people didn't believe there was anything after death and I understood. We were brought up with lies about Santa and the tooth fairy, and so why would anyone believe there were really angels and demons? They'd enter Hell and I'd watch as their mouths slackened, and their eyes widened. Then they'd look around at their new environment with a confused gaze upon their face. Their eyes would blink rapidly as if by doing so their fiery hot surroundings would disappear, and then as they accepted this was not a dream after all, not a nightmare, their arms would fold over their stomachs, their cries of 'No' lost in a sea of screaming.

"Lucy. LUCY." I looked up quickly in the direction of the sound and saw Shelley frowning at me. "Is he able to take him to Hell? I don't think he can, can he?"

"No. He has to be here somewhere, so you need to do a location spell. You know, your Spot-a-Satan map."

Alongside the flashing lights coming out of the amusement arcade, no one noticed as Shelley focused on the wall at the side of the building and a location map appeared with its shining red dot.

She turned in my direction. "According to this, he's at your restaurant."

And so he was. Sitting there at a table in the window as bold as brass. Frankie was sitting opposite him shaking and looking for all the world like some kind of druggie sat with his dealer.

Henry finished taking payment from a table and then walked towards me. "Thank goodness you're here. I've asked but they won't leave." His lips pinched together, his jaw taut. "It's putting people off coming in."

I sighed. "It's fine. I know them. Leave it with me. We're going to move to a larger table. Take a drinks order so it doesn't look too suspicious."

"Okay, boss. But if you need me for anything, just give me a signal, like tug on the bottom of your ear, okay? I'll keep watching." He bowed his head and walked away. I was lucky to have such good staff. I'd inherited them along with the restaurant, the previous owner having moved away to be nearer to family as he'd reached retirement age. I made a note to get to know them all a little better, to be a better employer than I had been.

Moved to the larger family celebration table at the rear of the restaurant, we were less conspicuous. Shelley sat right next to a grinning Satan and spat out angrily. "What are you playing at?"

Satan sat back, smiling, in his charming vampire guise—a devil of a disguise. "I was just chatting to Frankie here about a business proposition. I could make him a very rich man if he'd let me bottle that non-sleeping vampire juju he has going on. Trouble is, he's not been very talkative. Just keeps sitting there shaking and stuttering. Have to say I'm getting a little impatient."

"The last time you met, you killed him," Shelley pointed out, completely unnecessarily if you asked me. Indeed, Satan just glowed. Yep, he really did get a bit of a redness about him as he laughed. "So, shall I use some of my own juju to get you out of here and back down under?" she threatened, and she didn't mean Australia.

"Now, now. That's not very civilised behaviour, is it?"

"And kidnapping our friend is?" I queried.

Satan tilted his head toward me. "Awww, the lovely Lucy. I wondered when you'd join in and dazzle us all with your opinion." He pouted out his bottom lip. "I have to say I'm a little disappointed that you've sided with the defunct vampire though. Don't you fancy teaming up with me again? We could have fun working out how to get the DNA out of him." He winked.

"Sorry but hanging with you has gotten kind of old," I told him. "Now I'm looking for new experiences."

"Yeah, she's going to find a new man to hang with. She's going to fall in love," Kim blurted out.

Satan looked bemused before pointing at me. "Her? Fall in love?" Then he burst out into raucous laughter. "If she starts dating, I'd test the meat in the kitchen to make sure she's not gone all Hannibal Lecter. Only a vast amount of char-grilled bodies would be obvious, but missing people and a reduced meat budget? Win, win."

"We can't allow you to take Frankie anywhere," Theo interrupted, sitting forward in his seat.

Satan clasped his hand to his chest. "Oh, my best friend, Theo. How I've missed you, dude. Every Thursday night I feel at a loss." He turned to Darius. "Don't miss you at all," he said in the most insulting tone he could afford.

"Likewise, Satan," Darius replied. "It's a lot cooler without you."

"Nice one," Satan said, holding out a bro fist which Darius bumped.

"When you've finished with the reunion, we need to talk," Shelley interrupted. "You can't just keep coming back here when you damn well feel like it."

"I can though," Satan replied. "I went over the finer details of our agreement and all we agreed was I would release Lucy. Nothing said I couldn't take her back with me again. Also, although you're unfortunately stronger than me, I never agreed that I would stay away from Withernsea. It's just a little more boring now you can rein me in."

"So you decided to kidnap Frankie, knowing full well that I would come after you?"

"Of course."

"You know you can't have Frankie, so why did you really kidnap him? It's not to experiment on him. You know I wouldn't let you."

"True. However, you can't stop me spreading his secret around Faceblood can you?"

He held up a hand to Theo. "I'm not on there as Satan or Reuben, so there's no point trying to block me if that was your idea. I can make no end of fake aliases. So for me to not do that, well, we perhaps need to come to some new kind of arrangement..."

"What do you want?" Shelley asked. "And having Lucy back is not on the table."

A Devil Of A Date

"Oh, my little Lucy will come back all on her own, I'm sure." Satan grinned. "No, I want to be able to come back down here and recruit. All the potential evil people are walking around unguarded. You're putting Withernsea in danger."

"I can't allow you to come down and kill people, even if they are evil. You know, he-who-shall-not-be-named and yourself have to keep the balance and Fate decides who dies when."

Satan actually sulked. "Fate's such a lucky bitch. Why didn't I get her job?"

"So, I'm sorry, but on this occasion the answer is no," Shelly said. "Now, however, I do agree that you can come down here if you wish to visit from your workplace. I understand it might take some time to adjust that you no longer rule things down here. I sure as shit haven't got my head around everything I need to do here yet, but no smiting, you hear me? Or I'll find out how to banish you from Withernsea forever. Why don't you go somewhere else, anyway? Why here?"

"So many questions, but you see, Shelley, answers have power and so I don't think I shall avail you of them. I'm sure we'll be chatting again soon. Anyway, what about if I just torture anyone evil here, rather than actually kill them? If you let me do that, I'll keep quiet about Frankie here's talents."

"Oh, Satan," sighed Shelley. "The problem with your selfishness and your vanity is that while I've kept you enrapt in conversation about yourself, Theo whizzed home and back. I don't think you have anything to bargain with now."

I turned around to see Frankie drinking what looked like a pint pot full of red wine, but I knew it was nothing of the sort. A tear ran from Kim's eye as she stroked his back.

"I don't know what will happen to me now, but I couldn't let you do this," Frankie said to Satan. "So because of you, I'm probably dying again."

Then he fell to the floor, his body shaking as seizures overtook him.

"Damn you," Satan spat, banging on the table with such force that the crockery shot everywhere, and the table splintered down the middle. Then he and Shelley were gone.

Theo looked around in panic. "Where's my wife?"

There was a clattering of dustbins. "They could be out the

back," I said. "Kim, Darius, go with Theo. I'll get Frankie and take him to my house, *his* house."

Kim hovered, undecided. "Go. I'm a demon, I got this. Your best friend needs you."

She leaned over Frankie, kissed his forehead, and then ran outside.

I stared at the convulsing vampire. Henry came running over. "I told the patrons there had been a family argument that had resulted in an epileptic fit through shock."

"Well, that's exactly what it was," I said to my human waiter.

"Lucy. I'm not stupid. I may be human, but my best friend's a pixie."

Dread ran through me. It couldn't be, could it?

"Wh-what's his name?"

"Cornelius. He lives in Montreal now though. Haven't seen him for a couple of years."

I exhaled. "That's brilliant."

He looked at me strangely. "Your friend seems to be sleeping now, but what's happening?"

"I honestly don't know, but what I do know is he's probably not safe to be around humans. I need Allan to drive me to my house. Can you go ask him for me?" Allan was a cook and a bear shifter.

Then Frankie went into another seizure which looked even more painful than the last.

"Hold on, my friend," I whispered to him and then I looked at him in shock thinking of my words.

He really had become a genuine friend.

"You're not allowed to die, you cretin, you hear me?" I whisper-shouted. "I'm taking you home."

Chapter 13

Kim

That minute spent dashing out of the restaurant seemed to last a lifetime. Seriously, time seemed to stand still, and we moved in what appeared to be slow motion, Matrix style. Theo's expression was haunted, before he disappeared leaving me with Darius. I turned to the man whose company I'd been doing my best to avoid and watched as he reached out and grabbed my hand. The most powerful electric type force buzzed down my skin, but I had no time to think about why. All I knew was it energised me as I stepped outside, ready to fight to the death if I needed to in order to save my best friend's life.

But as I rounded the corner and dashed out of the back exit of the restaurant, I saw I was of no use.

For Satan was hanging in mid-air, looking like he was choking, in a stranglehold of the same blue web type material she'd fixed Frankie with. My bestie was stood there complete with her reptilian legs, and greenish-blue wings standing proud of her back. She'd harnessed her inner wyvern.

She turned to us, keeping one arm up in place, and that on its own held Satan in position. My God, she was strong! I needed to remember not to protest the next time she asked me to get her a coffee and a doughnut.

"Sorry I worried you, but I needed to take this outside, away from the human eyes. Only this guy was getting very annoying."

Only the strongest person in Withernsea could call Satan annoying.

She dropped him down to the floor where he clutched at his neck and spluttered before dropping his vampire glamour and standing there in his burning red skin. His too was reptilian looking. He spoke, giving us a glimpse of his forked tongue. This was the evil that had fed from me at Halloween, poured sizzling venom into my body. My heart thumped in my chest, so hard I thought it would kill me where I stood.

"If you ever step out of line and do something evil, I shall come for you," hissed Satan. "You may be more powerful than me in Withernsea, but in my domain, I rule, and I will take great personal delight in torturing every single atom of your body."

Then he ripped a hole in the air and went through it.

"My darling, are you okay?" Theo ran to his wife and threw his arms around her.

I realised I was still holding Darius' hand. Had been the whole way through. I dropped it and ran up to Theo and Shelley, throwing my arms around the both of them. "You utter shit. You gave us such a fright," I told her.

When I turned back to say thank you to Darius, he had gone.

~

Back in the restaurant, Henry told us that Lucy and Frankie had been taken to Frankie's house.

Theo spoke. "I'll go back home and get some further supplies of blood and a few other things. Shelley, I need you there in case you have to secure him. I don't know what's going to happen. No one has ever had such a large dose of the founder's blood before."

An attractive woman with long, black hair let us into Frankie's home. She threw her arms around me and nuzzled my neck, before running towards the furthest bedroom, my ex-lover's bedroom. I wondered how she knew which it was. As Frankie had been by my side since this whole thing happened, I could only suppose she was a friend of Lucy's, but her familiarity with the home made me wonder if she'd been staying here too, in which case Lucy was seriously taking the piss.

"He's in there. He just keeps having seizures." The woman, bless her, looked really worried about him, pacing around the door.

"And you are?" I queried.

She smacked herself in the forehead. "Oh, of course. Silly me. I didn't intend to ever reveal myself, but seeing as my Master might not survive, I thought it best to be here, like this."

Master? Was Frankie a Dom? Had he had a sub all this time?

"So, I'm Maisie. Or as you know me best, Frankie's pet cat."

My hands and legs felt jerky, my muscles tightened, and I leapt back drawing my arms across myself.

"Come again? You're Frankie's cat? Maisie the cat?"

"Yeah." She smiled, rubbing her body alongside mine. "Good to meet you in my other form. I'm a cat shifter. Anyway, I don't have time to explain further because of course we need to see what's happening with Frankie."

"God, yes. Sorry, you threw me with the whole looking like Miss World thing."

"Oh thank you very much," she said, grasping my arm. "I won Miss Werecat in 2015 actually. Beat a shit ton of tigers which didn't go down well. Anyway, of course, being unconscious, Frankie doesn't know I'm his cat. He doesn't even know I'm here, so if he comes round if you can let me tell him? That cool with you?"

"Err, yeah, sure," I replied, still a little overawed by the woman and the current situation.

"By the way, you have some am-az-ing moves in the bedroom, lady."

It was then I realised that all the times we'd turned around to find we were being stared at by a cat, it wasn't accidental.

I was about to shout, 'Oh my god', when I realised I was in hearing distance now of Lucy, so I reined it in.

I pushed open the door to see Frankie once again laid still. "What's happening?"

Theo turned to me. "So far he's having convulsions and then resting. This is quite normal for a vampire turning, so at this stage all we can do is wait and see what happens."

"What did the people at the caves say?"

"That his case was unprecedented. No one has been given such a massive transfusion. There was only that one other vampire before who didn't sleep and as I said he didn't survive the experiments. They've sent over a little more Founder's blood but now I've to dilute it with regular O-neg as he can't become dependent on the stronger blood."

"What if he's the same? I don't think he's strong enough to survive that."

Shelley came over and touched my arm. "We'll support him in whatever way we can," she said and the look on her face told me that if at the end of all this there was nothing left but a trip to the caves to say the incantation, then she would take him there herself.

I made a silent prayer, given present company, that it didn't lead to that.

∽

"Thank you so much, Lucy, for bringing him here," I told her.

"It's his house after all, and, well, I realised he's my friend," she told me, looking sheepish, a look I'd never expected to see on Lucy, and to be honest one that made her look a little, well, human. Which was unnerving at the same time as I processed that twenty-six years ago that's exactly what she had been. A human woman, in love with a man, thinking she was about to get her happy ever after and marry the man she loved. It was the first time I'd ever considered that the demon in front of me had been wronged herself. Shelley's father had hurt her so bad she'd lost her human self completely.

"You're my friend too," I told her, and she looked at me in shock.

"And mine," Shelley said, before nudging her husband.

"And erm, mine, but it's a distant friendship, we don't hang-out or anything," Theo said awkwardly.

Lucy smiled. "Thank you." Then she scratched at the left-hand side of the top of her head as if she had a violent itch. When she brought her hand away, she held a red horn between her fingers.

"One of my horns came off," she said in astonishment.

We all stood around her slack jawed.

"You've just become a little more human, Lucy," I told her. "Congratulations."

∽

The following day, after a night where everyone had had next to no sleep, Theo sent us all to stay at the farmhouse. With a couple of other vampires from the caves helping him, he banned everyone from the house, while Frankie's thirst began in earnest. Maisie went to stay next door once more, but Lucy came to the farmhouse with us. Mary made up a bed for her in one of the un-modernised rooms. Lucy said she didn't care what the room looked like, she was just glad of some peace and quiet. I didn't think the shock of losing one of her horns had quite sunk in yet.

As a human, I was strictly forbidden from being anywhere near Frankie, given his previous attachment to me. I decided to throw myself into work, given that it was so strange him not being around.

But by day three I'd got used to my own company again and wanted to go home.

"You can't," Shelley told me, stroking my forearm. "I completely understand that you want to enjoy your own space again, but if Frankie escaped, it would place your life in danger. So, I'm sorry but you're staying here."

I protested, but she pulled me into a hug and whispered in my ear. "We can do this the hard way if you like and I'll bind you in webs, or you can shut up."

I sighed, but hugged her back. "Thanks, bestie. You must be missing Theo like crazy."

She shrugged. "I am missing him, but it's nice spending time with you girls. I know we're concerned about Frankie, but I think we should take our minds off things tonight by having a girly night. What do you say, Luce? Movie, snacks, and paint our nails?"

"Sounds good to me because it's my last free night this week. My date nights start tomorrow. Five evenings, five dates. I have to anticipate Frankie wanting his house back and so I need to find love and new accommodation."

"You can stay here if you need to. We've loads of spare rooms."

Lucy placed a hand on her chest. "Thank you for the offer. That is so nice of you given that you're still basically honeymooners."

"Honeymooners living with the mother-in-law," Shelley interrupted.

"Well, I am really hoping to find my own love to snuggle with, and if not, then I need to get my own place. Learn to stand on my own two well-heeled feet."

Part way through girly night the phone rang. Shelley picked it up. "It's Theo," she said before pressing the answer button.

Shelley did a lot of saying 'yes' and 'okay' before ending the call.

She smiled before speaking. "Frankie is through the worst. He's settled and is now accepting normal O-neg. It looks like the Founder's blood has worked and he's completed the change. But he's asking to see—"

I interrupted. "Oh God, so it's not completely worked." I stood up, grabbing my bag. "This is my life now. Frankie's companion. Destined to never be left alone to find my own love."

"—Lucy," Shelley finished.

My jaw widened, and I slumped back down on the sofa. "Say what? Not me? He wants to see Lucy?"

"Yep. Looks like you're free again, Kim. Theo says you can return home now if you like. That the threat to your safety has passed." She turned to Lucy. "Don't worry, he's not transferred his attention to you. He wants to talk to you that's all, about your accommodation."

"Looks like I'm being evicted already," Lucy said.

"You can come back here afterwards if needed. I promise it's no trouble if you want to stay a few days."

"Thank you. Well, I guess I'd better get my coat on and phone a taxi."

She left the room, and I looked at my best friend.

"It's really over? I no longer have a permanent vampire shadow?"

"That's right. You're a free agent now, Kim. So the question is, are you still committed to your career, or are you back on the market?"

I thought about my added 'dummy date' bit to the contract. I could go on tons of dates now and have some one-night stands. Then I thought about how lovely it would be to be completely on my own for a bit. I decided I was re-amending the contract and taking that section back out.

"Career only for now. Plus, nice quiet evenings in. I just need to swing by the supermarket for a packet of batteries for my B.O.B."

Shelley laughed. "You'll be buzzing in every sense of the word."

Chapter 14

Lucy

As the taxi drove me to Frankie's house, my body became consumed with feelings I hadn't experienced in years. I felt dizzy, my stomach churned, and my heart suffered palpitations. After the first minute of believing that with the loss of my horn I was becoming ill, I realised that I was experiencing feelings of apprehension. My humanity was most definitely returning. I didn't know what I would face at Frankie's. I would be one of the first people to see his new form. Would he be the same, or was this Frankie version three? Not a wizard, not a half vamp; maybe none of Frankie would be left at all and instead I'd find a cold, calculating vampire.

As the taxi pulled up outside the house, it looked like I was going to be getting my answers soon.

Theo greeted me at the door. I looked behind him, noting the seemingly quiet house.

"Where are the vampires from the caves?"

"They've returned home. Frankie doesn't need them anymore. He'd already had all his vamp training even though he'd not turned properly, and so with his refrigerator stocked with O-neg, he's been discharged from their care. He's passed all his tests and is now a fully-fledged vampire."

Theo had thrust his chest out such was his pride. I guessed he was now a 'proud dad', having sired Frankie. A strange warmth radiated through my body. Whoa, was this... joy? I was happy for Frankie and Theo. All these new sensations would take some getting used to though.

"Is it safe for me to enter his room?"

"Oh, he's not in his room. He's sitting on the sofa with Maisie." He beckoned me inside.

Theo explained he was staying over one final night as he accompanied me to the door of the living room where I knocked and waited. It was very strange having lived here for a short while to now be feeling so uncomfortable at being here.

"Come in," Frankie's voice could be heard like a mumble through the wood of the door.

I opened the door and there he was. Sitting on the sofa, looking exactly the same as ever in appearance. The difference was all in his posture. No longer was he folded into himself, or trembling, or looking anxious. Now he was sat back on the sofa relaxed, with a laptop on a tray on his knee, and Maisie curled up at the side of him in her feline form.

"Lucy," he said jovially. "Come sit, we have much to discuss. By the way, congratulations on the losing of a horn. Is there a horn fairy who takes them away and puts money under your pillow? Oo-er, horn fairy. Sounds like a job I'd enjoy."

Hesitant, I walked over to the armchair and sat down in it while Theo took a seat at the other side of Maisie. I watched as Maisie stood up and stretched out her legs, her back arching, before her head looked around as she decided how and where she was going to sit back down.

"I'd stay away from Theo's lap unless you want trouble from Shelley, and bear in mind she won against Satan," I said.

Maisie fell back down against Frankie's side.

"How are you getting on with the fact that Maisie is a werecat?" I asked him.

He shrugged half-heartedly. "Makes no difference to me. I'm a vampire now and there's a longstanding truce between vamps and weres in Withernsea, so she has a home here as long as she wants. That's one of the reasons I've asked you over."

I slumped a little in my seat. "Oh, of course. Maisie will need her own room now. That's fine. I can stay at the farmhouse a few more days while I look for new accommodation. It's been kind of you to let me stay."

"It's weird you turning a bit nice. Good weird though."

I picked imaginary fluff from my sweater. "It's taking a little getting used to. I'm having feelings I've not experienced in years."

He raised an eyebrow. "Tell me more."

I rolled my eyes.

"Anyway, in terms of letting you stay, well, I think you kind of moved yourself in, but no that's not what I want to say. After a chat, Maisie said she'd prefer to stay as a family pet and curl up on the end of my bed still. So, what I want to ask you is would you like to keep renting the room? I'm going to be asleep through the main daylight hours and you can make sure Maisie gets fed etc. I'll be around in the evenings, but I guess most of the time you'll be at work at the restaurant. We shouldn't get under each other's feet too much, but it would be nice to have company."

I smiled. "I'd love that, Frankie, because I class you as a friend. I can't tell you how pleased I am to see you in such good shape."

He looked himself over. "I really am, aren't I? Good to see a change of species hasn't ruined my physique or exceptional good looks."

I started laughing. "This new you will take a little adjusting to."

"Yeah, me too. Daily O-neg." He shook his head. "It's all very new and strange. However, I found a new interest." He nodded towards his laptop.

"Oh yeah, Pornhub?" I quipped.

He winked. "Not while Theo's here, but I might check that out later, now the equipment should be working again. No, Theo here is an absolute legend at investigations. Do you know he tracks vamps' mortal enemies as his career?"

I looked over at Theo, my lips parting. "Really? Wow."

"Yes." Theo straightened up. "It's quietened off of late as people are getting better at doing their own internet searches and apps are being developed all the time. I'm probably going to wind the business up soon to be honest as I'm considering running the farmhouse as a bed-and-breakfast."

"I think that's an amazing idea, Theo, and I don't know if you've realised but you kind of already are. You've had Kim, Frankie, and me all staying there. It makes sense to open and start charging."

"That's very true, Lucy. I think when I return to my home, I will begin to draw up some business plans."

"Anyway, back to me," said Frankie. "Theo saw how I was with the supe book and my interest in learning about all species. Now you know there's the prophecy about Theo and Shelley's child and how it will be the complete ruler of Withernsea? Well, I've started researching that. Theo had done a little research on it, and I've taken it over. I'm going to write my own book. All about the different supernaturals in Withernsea—an updated version—and try to find out what the correct details of the prophecy are."

"That sounds fantastic," I said genuinely pleased for him.

"Well, a doctor's shift patterns don't align with vampire hours, so I'm going to ring my managers tomorrow, end my period of sickness, and hand my notice in. I have plenty of savings to tide me over, but Theo is going to help me develop a paid app where each species can log on to find out all about their ancestry and develop their own family trees using all the research I'll have gathered. It's a lot of work but I'm looking forward to it."

"In the past, I worked in admin and was a bookkeeper, so if there are any small tasks I can do to help, I will. Obviously, I have my own job, but it would be interesting to learn about my place of birth."

"Thank you. I may just take you up on that. Anyway, the room is there if you still want it. Most of your belongings are still in it I presume?"

"Yeah, I just took a few bits to Shelley's while you were busy completing the turning. Other than packing those things up, I'm ready to move back, so maybe tomorrow?"

"That's fine, and by the way, no need to be quiet when you come in. Theo assures me we aren't light sleepers. We do sleep like the dead. You can put music on, etc. Just act like I'm not there."

"Okay. I'll go back to Shelley's shall I, and get my things for tomorrow?"

"No need," said Theo. "I'll pop back now and get Shelley to collect your belongings if you like, seeing as it doesn't cost me cab fare. You begin to make yourself at home and many congratulations on your new official place of residence."

After I agreed he went whizzing off.

"He's had a few nights without his wife and wants to bone her in an empty house, doesn't he?" I said to Frankie.

"His balls will be bursting." Frankie guffawed.

"Poor Mary," I said. "They will really have to find a way where his mother can have some peace."

"Hey, you never know, I might turn something up with all my research."

"I might be able to help you with some of that." I grinned with mischief.

A Devil Of A Date

"Oh yeah?"

"Yeah, Kim's set me up with five dates in a row after the disaster which was Todd. I have a different species each night. I'll ask them questions for you, if you like? It'll give me something to do on the date if they're boring as all hell."

Frankie nodded, his face turning more serious and losing some of his humour. "Sure, if you don't mind. I don't want it interfering with your love life though."

"It won't. It will give me a chance to get to know them better, and then each night I can come and report back. Unless things go brilliantly, and then you'll have to wait for my report until I get home." I winked.

"As long as the report stays PG."

He looked like he was going to say something else, but then Theo whooshed back with my travel case. "Here you go. Shelley says you'll both have to come over for a meal one night soon. You'll find you get used to eating human food again, Frankie. It usually does taste as it used to, but you will gain no nutrients from it, so no more worrying about getting your five-a-day. That's all in your bottles now. I think he'll be okay now you're staying, so I'm going to go home. Can you make sure he has his drink regularly, Lucy?"

"I will do," I agreed.

"Okay, well, I'm off back to the missus," said Theo. "We're at the end of the phone if needed, but if you could try not to call tonight, I'll love you forever."

And with that Theo left once more.

"I suppose you'll want to go get settled in your room now?" Frankie said, and I felt a little dismissed before I realised this was his first night alone in months and one of his first nights as a proper, fully-fledged vampire.

"Yeah, I'll leave you to it. Night, Maisie," I said, tickling under her chin and getting a purr for my troubles.

I hesitated in the doorway and turned back around to him, "I'm glad you survived, Frankie. Withernsea is a better place with you in it."

Then I went to my room.

CHAPTER 15

KIM

There I was, batteries changed over in my battery-operated-boyfriend. My electric blanket had warmed up my bed and I had an erotic novel and my Captain America collage on the top of my duvet. I was just about to climb into my bed when the phone rang. I picked it up and the caller's name was displayed across the screen.

FRANKIE.

Oh, for pity's sake. He was cured and he was still bugging me!

"Hello?"

"Hello to you, my ex-lover. I'm ringing with my most heartfelt apologies of my behaviour of the last few weeks. You'll be pleased to know I'm entirely cured and now don't want to be in your company again in the slightest."

"Hurrah!"

"We still good though? Friends, right?"

"Yes, absolutely. Friends who barely see each other except for in passing or when in group activities."

"Oo-er, tell me more about these group activities."

He certainly was back.

"I meant like if there was, God forbid, another triple date, or a get-together or anything like that."

"Oh, I knew what you meant, but I couldn't help myself."

"You really are you!"

"I am, Kim. Albeit a supercharged vampire Frankie."

I climbed under my duvet and sat with my back against the headboard. The warmth from the blanket sank into my bones. It was heavenly.

"So it all absolutely went okay? You are like Theo now?"

"Yes. Everything that went wrong has been overwritten. I'm on normal blood and I'm developing a new app with Theo's help and so not going back to the hospital as a doctor."

I'm really pleased for you, Frankie."

"Thanks. Well, I'll let you go, it's getting late. I just wanted to apologise, but also to say thank you. For all that I drove you mad, you looked after me. You were a fantastic friend, Kim, and if anything similar happens with you when you're turned into a were, you know where I am."

I spluttered. "W-what do you mean turned into a were? There will be no such thing happening to me."

He chuckled down the line and then hung up.

Twat.

I looked at my Captain America collage and my B.O.B. and knocked them onto the floor. Frankie mentioning weres had killed my libido. That man was a B.O.B. blocker.

∽

Shelley was late in to work, and when she eventually dragged her sorry looking arse through the door at ten thirty, she popped her head around my door sheepishly, clutching two coffees.

"Come in, slacker."

She flopped into the chair opposite my desk. "Theo returned home. Mary made herself scarce."

"Lucy?"

"Returned to Frankie's. He offered her a regular room rental."

"Ah, so then the traveller returned to his own bed, board, and lodgings, and wished to lodge in your bed and board you, right?"

"That would be correct, and so once he had finally gone to sleep, I snuck into one of the guest rooms and had another couple of hours sleep. I apologise, but I think I'm the undead one in our house today."

"Hey, you're the boss. I was never exactly on time when I was playing hide the sausage with Frankfurter. So you do what you need to do and I'll cover while I'm being a career woman. Because..." I drum-rolled my desk. "Ladies and gentlemen, Frankie has now left the building."

Shelley giggled.

"Are you going to pass me my coffee then?" I asked her.

Her mouth cocked to the side.

"You have not...? There isn't one for me is there? You've bought two for yourself."

"I'm very, very tired," pouted Shelley.

"Unbelievable." I turned my attention back to my laptop.

"So, Lucy was saying tonight is the first of five dates you've set up for her?"

"Yeah, that's right. Because of the double/triple date fiasco."

"And is it the start of Darius' five dates too?"

Shelley had the audacity to wink at me. I completely ignored it; a fact for which I felt I should be rewarded. Later, I would buy myself a coffee and two doughnuts seeing as my boss wasn't on the case.

"It is, and I feel I've chosen him five fabulous matches and shouldn't be at all surprised if he isn't completely besotted with one of them by the end of the week." I span around in my chair.

"So you inputted all of his details correctly and put him through the algo totally on point?" Shelley said sarcastically.

"Yes, I did."

"Hmmmm."

"I really did!"

"Who has he got tonight then?"

I let my eyes adjust from my going dizzy from all my enthusiastic chair spins. "Well, perfectly, two days ago we had an applicant from a female were. She's the correct age bracket. She's from his pack but located within a small offshoot of the main pack, in Hornsea. If Darius quoted from last year's Love Island, he would say she was '100% his type on paper'. I've outdone myself."

"Ohhkay then. I have to presume you know what you're doing, and in terms of finances it would certainly be good to actually get Darius' membership fee this month. What about Lucy? Who have you set her up with?"

"Her application is a little more difficult because she's changing all the time. Have you noticed?"

"Have I? Not half! She's not set anyone on fire this week at all to my knowledge. Not one single person."

"It also means that her original application form data is off and so I've tried to adjust it as to her current self, but really, she's half-human now. I was thinking, maybe you might look for a human date ready for her final date on Sunday? Kind of a wildcard? It would need to be someone who you felt wouldn't freak out if she revealed a horn. What do you think?"

"I think that's a great idea. Could be a film, *Four Supernaturals and a Human*."

I laughed. "When you've drunk all your own coffee, could you log into her application and see who you have who could potentially be a suitable match? But for her date number one, I've gone in the opposite direction. You know how on those house programmes they nearly always show you what you don't want first?"

"Yeah?"

"That's why her first date is with Rav from Hanif's."

"A demon?"

"Yep, thought we'd see if it truly is better the devil you know, or whether she is heading towards complete humanity."

"Where are they meeting?"

"At *Beached*, the seafood restaurant in town. Why?"

"So I can know where to avoid this evening as me and Theo are going out too."

"Date night? Oh, have a fantastic time."

"To be honest, I'm just hoping we make it. That he'll leave me alone long enough so I can eat. I need to keep my strength up. How about you? What are you doing this evening?"

"Catching up on Hollyoaks and getting smashed on vodka. I can't wait."

"This Frankie thing really has cramped your style, hasn't it? Right, I suppose I'd better let you get on and fire up my own laptop. If you want to fetch coffees in about another hour, I'll love you forever."

"And a doughnut?"

"Do you know what? I don't feel in the mood for one today. Just coffee please. I'm too tired to eat."

She left, and I sat back at my computer. I typed in Sierra Forrester and stared at the woman on the screen. She had reddish-brown, long, curly hair; plump cheeks and lips; and freckles crossed the cheeks and nose of her golden-toned skin. She was beautiful, and according to her application, ready to find a mate for life.

I switched over to Darius' application and there he was. With his long shaggy brown hair and beard. He was stunningly handsome. I could admit that to myself. They would have beautiful little werebabies if it worked out for them.

I sat back in my seat and closed my eyes.

'You're a waste of space, Kimberly Fletcher'. I could hear my father's voice like he was in the room with me now. *'A good-for-nothing tramp. You've made a laughingstock of me and your mother. How does it look when the vicar's daughter is caught having sex in the graveyard? Well? No one will ever want you as a wife, you're tainted. Just a hussy'.*

'I don't want to be a wife, ever!' I remembered screaming back. *'Look at my mum. Who'd want to be like her? Having to be at your beck and call all day long with no life for herself? She's like a walking dead person'.*

'How dare you speak to me like that? Get out'.

'No, Kenneth, no'. My mother had tried to touch his arm, but he'd just shrugged her off.

'Let the tart go. If she wants to live an amoral life, she can. But not here. Get out of my house'.

I came around from the memory. He'd never forgiven me, nor me him, and he'd passed away five years later after suffering a stroke. I saw my mother infrequently with the odd phone call in between. Things remained strained between us, and I knew she felt I'd contributed towards that stroke because she was aware I'd carried on with my 'wanton' behaviour. In fact, if anything, I did it more. Partly because I enjoyed sex and partly in spite. I'd enjoyed a healthy sex life and I had no doubt the rumour mill back home had been strong. I could imagine it now.

Poor Father Fletcher. That tramp daughter of his is back to her old tricks. Such a shame, she seemed such a nice girl growing up.

It was the main reason I resisted anything that could lead to a serious relationship. Because if I did, what if my father was proved right? What if I was tainted in some way and never destined for a happy ever after? I knew what Ebony kept saying, but half the time she was pissed on vodka. It was better I kept things simple.

Just casual dates and no big romances.

I clicked out of Sierra's application first and then with one last glance, Darius'.

Have a nice date.

Chapter 16

Lucy

Wednesday

I met Rav, my first date of the week, outside Beached.

I appraised him. He had lovely dark skin and chocolate brown eyes and his hair gleamed. He wasn't tall for a man, about an inch taller than me, maybe, but at least he wasn't a four-foot pixie, so I called this a triumph.

"I've never eaten here. I'm looking forward to it," I said after shaking his hand.

"Yes, well, erm, I looked at their prices and I, erm, changed our reservation. I hope that's okay?"

"Oh. So where are we eating now?"

"Hanif's."

He took me to the Indian restaurant where he worked, and more to the point, when we got there and they told him they were short staffed, he sat me at a table near the kitchens and grabbed an apron, serving customers and sitting and talking to me in between service.

Did he once ask me about myself in terms of hobbies and interests?

Oh no. All Rav wanted to know was how to source a 'Get out of Hell Free' card.

"Please tell me how you managed to get away?"

"It wouldn't make any difference to you, Rav. Because all demons aren't created equal, and you were born to a demon parent. It's in your blood, whereas I was tricked."

He sighed before the words, "Service," had him getting back up from his seat again.

After forty or so minutes of this, I beckoned over a different member of staff and ordered a takeaway. Then once it was at my table, I paid and left, leaving Rav to his work. He could go to Hell as far as I was concerned.

I walked back into the house to find Frankie in the kitchen finishing up a bottle of O-neg.

"Oh dear, back so soon and... is that a takeaway? I thought you were going out for a meal?"

I sighed, grabbing a plate from the kitchen cupboard and warming it using my inbuilt heat mojo before dispensing my chicken vindaloo across it.

Frankie sat down at the kitchen table, and I pulled up a chair in front of him. "Seriously, no word of a lie, he changed the venue and took me to where he works and then..." I paused for effect, "...he started working."

"Oh, so that was the end of the date then? Did you rearrange?"

"Oh no." I felt my fingers clench around my cutlery. "He sat me near the kitchen and kept sitting back down opposite me in between serving."

Frankie snorted.

"And the best thing? He never even took my own order."

That was it. Frankie clutched his stomach as mirth hit him. It was a good job he no longer needed to breathe as he'd have struggled with how hard he was laughing. I couldn't help but join in.

"Hence my takeaway. Also, he just wanted to use me anyway."

Frankie's face turned serious. "Oh yeah, just wanted a shag, did he?"

"No. He wanted to know how to escape Satan."

"Oh. Well having met the guy, I guess I could understand that."

"Me too, but he's a born demon. There's no way out of that for him, and it was all he talked about on the few occasions he sat down. I'm so glad to be home." I looked around. "Where's Maisie?"

Frankie sighed. "She's spending more and more time next door. I don't think she's comfortable now I know she's a were. It's not the same, because if I'm busy with the computer and she wants milk, I tell her to get off her lazy arse and get it."

"I guess there are a lot of different things for us all to adjust to. You're a vampire, Maisie's come out of the catflap, I've lost a horn.

Anyway." I raised a vegetable samosa towards Frankie's now empty bottle. "Here's to the new us and let's hope for less drama and a better date for me tomorrow."

∽

Thursday

"Yes, fricking brilliant idea." I slammed the door as I came home. "Theo needs to look at that algorithm because opposites attract does not work when a devil meets an angel."

Frankie peered around the edge of the doorway. "You're home even earlier than last night." He held onto the doorframe for support as he once again dissolved into laughter.

"You're not funny," I said as my one remaining horn emitted sparks of flames. "It brought my demon side out more. It's been tingling all night."

"Sorry," he said but the way his lips trembled showed me that he wasn't the slightest bit sorry and was trying his best to contain further eruptions of laughter.

"Look, come through to the living room, calm down and tell me all about it," he said. "And please don't set fire to me, cos I'm rather flammable these days."

I threw myself into the chair, a pinched expression on my face as I tried to calm my temper. I felt like I wanted to start an inferno.

"What on earth was Kim thinking?" I complained, my jaw tensing. "I'm going to visit that dating agency tomorrow and give her a piece of my mind."

Then I fixed a death glare on Frankie. "You need to stop laughing, seriously." I felt at my head. "What if this causes my other horn to grow back?"

I let out a scream, feeling like I was gasping for air. The next minute I felt my hand being enclosed with a cool one and my brow being soothed by cool fingers.

"Lucy. Lucy. Calm down. It hasn't grown back, and if it does, we'll deal with it. Hiccups can be overcome, as my own turning demonstrates. Now, look at me and try to breathe properly."

I opened my eyes and stared into Frankie's.

"Ar-are my eyes red, Frankie?"

"No. They are your normal human colour."

"Would you tell me if they were red?" I frowned.

"Not on your life, but..." He dragged me unceremoniously to standing. "Look in the mirror. Not red."

I let out a large exhale.

I turned back to him. "Sorry for my outburst."

"Getting used to them to be honest."

"Oh, piss off."

"See what I mean? Now sit back down. I'll go get you a cuppa. Then when you're calmer, you can tell me about this date."

I glared at him.

"Purely for the purposes of updating my species manual."

I sniffed the air. "Strong odour around here, like, erm, bullshit."

He chuckled and left the room.

~

"So, I finally think I'm going to get my seafood meal and then he can't get in the door because his wings are too wide and he's new and can't get them to fold away. Of course, the humans can't see them and so the staff are wondering why he's hovering around the doorway. I had to tell them he had social anxiety. This he met with scorn because it was a lie and of course angels don't like lies. So that was strike one for the demon. Anyhow, I figured we'd just settle for fish and chips and a walk up the seafront because I needed to eat—by now I was starving—but I knew already this date was going nowhere. Well, sods law, someone had to be standing next to the seafront in all this bad weather. Idiot drunkards."

Frankie continued to nod in all the right places.

"The next moment, one of the idiots decides to stand on the railings, and that's it, over he goes. And he's drowning, so Andrew, that was his name by the way, tells me he doesn't know whether he's supposed to save him or escort him to heaven. He's just standing there like a great celestial idiot.

"In the meantime, the coastguards have been alerted, but before they can get there, Andrew decides to jump in and save him. He then flew up in the air in front of all the onlookers, clutching the drunk in his hands. The minute he put him on the pavement, I quickly phoned Theo and he whooshed in and mojo'd everyone around so that they didn't go into Supe-shock or start snapping pictures on their phones.

"At that point another angel appeared and took my date away, which was good because I was now sharing my date with the coastguards, Withernsea, humans, and Theo. Then I discovered with all the drama *my fish and chips had gone cold*," I spat out.

Frankie leaned over to his side table and took out a selection of takeaway flyers. "Come on, what do you want to eat? My treat for you having such a bad date."

"Pizza. The cheesiest, greasiest pizza money can buy," I replied, finally letting the angst leave my body. "Frankie, I'm not sure I can do a third date."

"So don't." He shrugged his shoulders. "I'm not exactly forcing you out of here, am I? You have a room here for as long as you need it."

"Thanks," I said. "I'll have a word with Kim tomorrow."

∽

Friday

"No way," Kim shouted at me. She actually yelled. "I've set up those dates and you cannot let those people down now. You're to go on every one of them. You hear me?"

I didn't think I'd ever seen Kim in such a mood. She even scared me, and I was still part demon.

"Whatever is the matter?" I took the seat opposite her desk as I watched her pace around the office.

"Nothing."

"Doesn't look like nothing from here. Does someone need to be flambeed? You could ask Rav. I'm kinda trying not to do that while I attempt to lose my other horn."

Kim threw herself onto her chair dramatically. "I've had four disgruntled customers, because Darius, apparently, is so enamoured with his first match, that he cancelled his other dates. Instead, he's seeing Sierra every night this week. My customers are extremely pissed off that they no longer have a date with a good-looking werewolf." She narrowed her eyes. "Their words, not mine."

"Your *customers*, right?" I said, getting up and backing out of the doorway.

She sighed. "Look, I can cancel them if you want. It's not your fault, I'm vexed. It's Darius', trying to ruin my business."

I shouted around the door, almost clear of the office now. "No, it's fine. I can still go on mine."

∼

Friday evening's date was with an incubus. Luckily, as a fellow demon, I wasn't vulnerable to his womanizing charms. I had to admit he was fit as fuck and if I wanted a lay, not to find the love of my life, he'd have been perfect. He definitely matched up to everything I'd asked for physically and with his interests. However, to me he just came across as a sleazeball rather than a seducer.

"Just to double check, you don't want me to visit your dreams tonight then?"

"Not a chance."

He swung a finger across his neck. "Do you mind if we cut this date short and I go find someone else? Only I have a weekly quota, and last night I had a rest night. I was literally fucking knackered," he said.

"Not at all," I said honestly.

He beckoned the waitress. "Can you cancel her order? She's not staying now."

My mouth dropped open. I'd gotten as far as a seat at Beached this time and even placed an order, but actually managing to eat here was becoming a distant dream.

Putting on my coat and grabbing my Chanel handbag, I headed for the door. By the time I swung my body around to take one last look through the doorway, Ian the Incubus had three other women in his booth.

As usual, Frankie's head appeared around the doorway when I returned home, his eyebrow raised. "Don't ask," I told him. "Just get a movie out—the more murder in it the better—while I fix myself a sandwich, and then I'm drinking this baby." I held up the bottle of Fireball I'd bought from the offy on the way home.

"On it," he said. As I made my sandwich, I realised how grateful I was that Frankie was around this week. Soon he'd be confident enough to go out at night, so it was fortuitous that right now when I most needed it, he was able to give me support through these nightmare dates. I just hoped things couldn't get any worse.

∼

A Devil Of A Date

Saturday

"Why did I have hope? That's a 'them upstairs' kind of feeling."

I smelled burning. Oops. "Sorry, Frankie. I owe you a new coat. I hope that one didn't have any sentimental value."

"Kitchen," he shouted from the living room.

Wandering through to the kitchen I saw a buffet laid out: little sandwiches, crisps, sausage rolls, etc, and a choice of wine, lemonade, or vodka.

I heard footsteps and turned as Frankie hovered in the doorway behind me. "I took a wild guess at the outcome." He shrugged his shoulders. "So grab a plate, load up, and come and tell me all about it. Again."

I piled my plate high. Stress eating, that was what my life had come to.

Walking back into the living room, I sighed. "One more date to go. It's a wildcard apparently. I have to humour Kim. It can't be any worse than tonight's."

Frankie got comfortable on the sofa like my stories were from CBBC bedtime. Glad someone could find them entertaining.

"Tonight's date was a Brownie."

"As in a Girl Guide? What sick shit is Kim dealing in now?" Frankie laughed and winked. "Just joking with you. So. A Brownie. As in a male fairy?"

"Yes. He came for our date, and I hadn't even attempted to book Beached with my latest adventures there, so I thought oh I'll go back to Jetty's and take him there. Anyway, he was fantastic, Frankie. On the small side but really attentive. He kept stroking my hair, tucking it behind my ears; he pulled out my chair for me. He even cleaned around my plate when I spilled ice cream. That's how attentive he was."

"Oh dear," Frankie exclaimed, and I guessed he knew what was coming.

"I thought, it's happening. I found someone. Kim's finally worked her mojo. He was handsome, just, kind of perfect."

"So you didn't understand what a Brownie was?"

"No. He just said he was a male fairy, so I thought he must fly around the bottom of people's gardens at night."

"But Brownies are house fairies..."

"I know that now, knobhead."

That earned me a raised eyebrow.

"Sorry. I'm just rather frustrated," I huffed. "So, we're approaching getting the bill when he jumps up and starts tidying all the tables. All of them. Well people looked at him very strangely and then at me. The next thing, anyone who had ice cream or cream left in their bowl—he drank it down. Right in front of them! The staff there became agitated, and so I went over to him to ask what he was doing and that's when he explained, that he cleans up in restaurants and in reward he's given cream. Except, Jetty's hadn't asked for his help. He'd just taken it upon himself to tidy up. Then," I said the word again with emphasis, "then, I realised he hadn't been *attentive* to me. He'd been tidying me up. Placing my hair behind my ear and smoothing it: tidying my appearance. Holding out and then tucking my chair in: making sure the chair was away tidily. Cleaning up my spills: well, you get the picture. I never want another ice cream as long as I live. I looked at my plate. "I'm going to stuff my face with this feast and then I'm hitting the vodka."

"I'm about to watch the latest episode of *The Big Bang Theory* if you're interested?"

"Yeah, stick it on," I said. "A date with the television is what I need right now."

Chapter 17

Kim

I'd not had time to brood about Darius today. Other than Lucy's failed dating attempts, the rest of Supe Dating was going amazing, and I'd been rushed off my feet. However, we were receiving a special guest at three pm and so all dressed up with my best business suit on, I sat with Shelley and Theo in her office.

And such as it was that just as the sky was darkening on this winter afternoon, the office shone bright as Angel Sophia, the Archangel of Love, appeared in the office with Andrew at her side.

"Thank you for seeing us," she said. "Please take a seat, Andrew."

Sophia looked directly at Theo. "My many thanks for your quick actions last night in ensuring that Andrew's identity as an earth angel remained a secret."

"You are very welcome," Theo replied.

"I wanted to give my thanks in person and Andrew would like to add something."

Andrew coughed. "Yes, I would also like to give my thanks to you, Theo. Also, erm, Kim, if I could be removed from the dating agency site?"

"Oh, yes, sure," I said. "Any reason why?"

Sophia smiled. "Angels mainly belong with other angels, unless I decide there's a specific reason for a different union, and our love is entirely different in that Andrew will find his companion in time naturally. He's had a few forks in the road, so to speak, and last night's dalliance with a part-demon... well, it's not gone down too well in the higher echelons. So, I'm taking him under my wing, and I shall guide him on his future journey. We've decided that the life of an earth angel is not suited to Andrew and so he's moving on up, shall we say?"

Her smile almost knocked you sideways in its beauty and power.

Sophia produced a silver envelope seemingly from nowhere and handed it to Theo.

"Shortly, you will need this. It's an angel calling card. I met with our oracle to discuss how I could repay you and this is what she advised. There is no point in you opening it as the words will only appear on the card inside at the correct point in time. I would suggest you give the card to your wife. As she is currently the most powerful of those in Withernsea, it will fare her well."

She tapped Andrew on the shoulder. "It is time for us to leave."

"Thank you for this," Shelley said bowing her head. "We are most honoured to have met you."

"And I you," Sophia replied and then with a blast of bright light her and Andrew were gone.

"Did that really happen?" I asked Shelley and Theo, just as a large, white feather drifted down and landed at my feet.

"I guess it did," I said.

∼

Just before closing a knock came at my office door. "Come in."

I blinked rapidly when I was faced with the sight of Frankie in front of me.

"Frankie! You left your house."

"I did." He smiled.

"Oh, you look amazing," I said, vaguely recollecting the times I'd been up close and personal with him. "Do you know, I've actually missed you a little."

"And me you, just the tiniest bit you understand, not in that whole attachment disorder way."

"What brings you to the agency if it's not little old me?"

"It's about Lucy and her disastrous dates. I wondered if you'd help me with a little plan for in case her final date tonight goes awry?"

"Take a seat and let me know what I can do," I instructed him.

When he left, his talking about the fish restaurant had made me hungry. That and talk of dates had brought Darius back to my mind. I needed to get myself back out there. I fired up the computer and looked at all the attractive males who had recently signed the contract while it included the 'dummy date' clause.

Satisfied that I'd pulled up a hunky male who I'd have some fun with, I called to see if he was free.

A husky voice answered the phone.

"Hello."

"Jett?"

"Yes?"

"It's Kim from Withernsea Supernaturals."

"Oh. Hi there. Everything okay?"

"Yes. I just wanted to inform you that you've been randomly selected by the computer to attend a 'dummy date'. Are you free his evening to meet with me at the seafood restaurant, Beached?"

"Err, I'm not entirely sure I can come into Withernsea. Could you possibly come out to Hogsthorpe?"

I looked closer at his application and sure enough he was not a Withernsea resident. Trust me to choose someone not from here. I didn't feel like travelling though.

"Not on this occasion. Don't forget it's not a date, it's more of a training exercise."

"Okay. I'll chance it. It's just I'm not very welcome there with a few folks from a time I've visited before."

"Just wear a hat and glasses," I said, by this point willing to beg to get the man here. I needed a date, and he looked like he'd take my mind off current circumstances.

A throaty chuckle came down the line. "Okay, I like dress up. Let's do role play for our dummy date. I'm coming as Beast, so are you gonna be my beauty?"

"We'll see what miracles my make-up can perform."

We arranged to meet at nine pm and I ended the call.

Fuck you, Darius Wild. Well, no, not *fuck* you. *Oh for goodness' sake body, stop with the damp pants and the tightening nipples just because I said Darius and fuck in the same sentence.*

I closed down the screen where the photo of Jett Conall, wolf, had been opened. What was that phrase again, 'the best way to get over one is to get under another?'

Either that or I was barking mad.

Fifteen minutes later I was panicking, wondering if this was such a good idea. What was that about him not being welcome? What if he was a big, bad wolf? I didn't own a red coat, but I was now feeling very apprehensive.

I tapped my finger on my desk. What should I do? Should I cancel the date?

But that wouldn't look good on the agency, and he's probably set off by now anyway.

Congrats, Kim, on another spectacular fuck-up.

My phone rang, and I hoped it was Jett cancelling.

"What have you done?" Ebony's voice screeched into my ear.

"Is it my date? I knew it was a mistake. You warned me and I didn't listen. I'm sorry, Ebony. I'll cancel," my words rushed out.

"It's too late. Whatever you've started cannot now be halted. The chain of events has linked together and will have to see itself through to its conclusion."

"What do you mean? What do you see? Ebony, tell me what I have to do?"

"I don't have that information. I already told you to be with the wolf and you discarded my advice like a knock-off Kylie Jenner lipgloss. Now you will have to find your own path. Good luck, child."

And with that she hung up. *Child?* I was two years older than her. She didn't half go weird when she was seeing things. Plus, yet again with the random stuff. She couldn't tell me anything for certain. She was like a bloody weather forecaster. They told you what to watch out for, but you had to actually step outside to see what it was really like.

I ran through to my colleague's office.

"Shelley," I yelled.

She startled at her computer. "Whatever is up? Has someone died?"

"Only my brain cells. Please would you and Theo join me on a double date tonight?" I begged.

If I'd started the Apocalypse, I needed the most powerful person in Withernsea with me.

Chapter 18

Lucy

Frankie had gone out. He'd actually left the house. I should have celebrated with him, but I wasn't sure I liked it. He'd been in every night these last few days when I'd got back from my crap dates, and kept me company. Now, as I started to get ready, he wasn't here. And he'd been dressed up.

I sighed. He was completely comfortable in his new vamp skin now. Next, he'd be dating and shacked up with some cute little female vampire and I'd be looking for a new place to live again. I noticed I was banging cupboard doors around. Keep calm, Lucy.

I actually crossed my fingers about my date tonight. We were meeting at Beached where I hoped I was *finally* getting to eat from that seafood menu.

Ready, I made my way there.

Tonight, I'd dressed simply in a pair of black leggings, a black-and-white striped tunic top and a black leather jacket. Louboutin heeled black boots were tonight's shoe of choice.

After waiting about ten minutes at the entrance of the restaurant, I saw Henry from Red's approach. It must be his night off.

"Hey, Henry!" I shouted out. "Fancy seeing you here. Are you on a date too?"

Then the penny dropped. My date was called Henry. My employee *was* my date. He was also human.

Our faces both fell at the same time.

"I can't do this, Henry. You work for me."

"Yeah, I feel exactly the same. Do you still want to get a drink though?"

Rubbing at my forehead, I sighed. "Truthfully? No. To be honest I've had a belly-full of dating this week. I just want to go home, grab a snack pack of Maltesers and watch Game of Thrones."

"I'm gonna give my mates a ring then. Look, please come and have one drink with me at the bar in Beached. I'll look a right saddo standing there on my own."

I sighed. "Okay then. Only one though."

Walking inside, I was surprised to see Kim sitting at a booth with Shelley, Theo, and a guy who I could only make out had jet-black, shoulder-length hair. Huh, so she managed to get herself a date. "Can you just excuse me a second?" I asked Henry as he waited to be served at the bar.

I wandered over to my friends.

"Well, at least you've managed to eat here. I'm keeping it on my bucket list, though I'm sure I'll have kicked it before I ever end up seated here with an actual meal in front of me."

Kim's brows creased. "Are you here on your own?"

"No. Henry's at the bar. We're just having a quick drink. Only as one of my employees we don't want to date. He's waiting for his friends to arrive. I was just about to ring you to say another one hadn't worked out."

Kim smiled, which wasn't the expression I was expecting to be honest when I was telling her that her dating business had failed me.

"I was about to ring you in the next thirty minutes funnily enough to see how it was going. You see, since you applied at the agency, you've completely changed. You're no longer the angry she-devil you were. Earlier today we had an extra client drop by and ask to be added to our database. I checked to see if he was a match for the new you, and well, who'd have believed it, but it brought you up as 96% compatible. So, you have another date should you wish to eat here tonight, Lucy. Your date is waiting at the back table, just over there."

I followed her finger to where a blonde-haired man sat looking more like his old worrying self than the confident man of the last few days.

"Frankie?" I queried. "Frankie's my match?"

"Absolutely."

"But he's not interested in me. Going on a date with him would be weird."

"Lucy." Kim raised an eyebrow. "What do you think you've been doing for the last few days?"

And then it struck me. Every single date that had gone wrong, I'd gone home to Frankie. We'd watched movies, had takeaways. Basically, we'd had in-house date nights.

And I'd loved every single one. The truth was that as soon as the dates had gone spectacularly wrong, my first thoughts had been to go back to Frankie's, knowing he'd be there to comfort and spoil me.

I stared over at him and as if detecting my gaze, he looked straight at me. I could see the apprehension in his eyes, but really there was no need. Completely forgetting I'd been talking to Kim at all I almost ran to the back table.

I held out my hand. "Hello, you must be Frankie. I'm your date for the night, Lucy."

He clasped his hand in mine and it just felt right. His cold touch suited my extra devilish warmth.

"May I say how beautiful you look this evening. Would you like to dine with me? I hear the food in this restaurant is remarkable."

"I really would," I told him and sat down.

And as I eventually got to sample the wonderful food of the restaurant, I realised that the right man for me had been under my nose from the very beginning.

CHAPTER 19

"It looks like everything is going very well over there and you've brought another successful result to Withernsea dating." Shelley clinked glasses with me.

We'd had a very enjoyable evening. Jett was great company and extremely hot to look at. Hopefully, I'd see if that hotness extended to the boudoir later.

"I hope so. I have to say they look good together," I replied peering over my shoulder. "They can't take their eyes off each other, can they?"

"I know how they feel," Jett said, as his hazel gaze swept over me.

I smiled, trying my best to look coy.

Then the door to the restaurant crashed open and Darius strode down the aisle towards us, Sierra in tow.

"I knew I could smell filth. What are you doing on my turf, mongrel?"

Jett slowly wiped his mouth with a napkin.

"Sorry, Kim. I told you I kind of wasn't welcome around here."

"Damn straight. Get the fuck out of here before I rip you apart," Darius growled, his eyes alighting on mine.

Jett looked from Darius to me. "Oh. I see what's going on here. Do you have designs on this human, pretty boy? And what does your date think about that? Let's ask her, shall we?" He looked behind Darius.

Jett's eyes rolled. "Oh, it's just the loyal best friend. How boring. I thought there could be some girl-on-girl action."

He stood up and threw five, ten-pound notes on the table. "Thanks for a lovely evening, Kim, but I have to return to my own territory. Pack rules. However, I want to see you again, so I do believe, Mr Wild, that you and I will be having words at a later date, about my visiting privileges." With that he strode out of the restaurant.

Best friend? Sierra was his best friend? But they were dating. I didn't understand.

Darius sneered at me. "Cavorting with the enemy pack? You went too far this time, Kim. You've made your point that you're not interested. I get it. We're done. You can take my name off your books. I can find my own dates. Come on, Sierra, let's go home."

This was all happening so fast. I didn't know what to do. One minute I'd been enjoying a date with Jett, the next I was involved in some kind of spat between the packs, and now Darius was done with me? What did I do?

As Darius also turned and walked out of the restaurant, I felt my legs moving. I needed to go after him. But as I stood, I heard a blood-curdling scream from the back of the restaurant.

Chapter 20

Kim

Shelley, Theo, and I raced to the rear of the restaurant where Satan had Frankie held by his shirt collar, a red sizzling knife at his throat.

"Please?" Lucy was almost falling to her knees, her eyes feverish and her plea coming out in a shaking voice.

"Oh, Lucy, my darling. Don't worry. You see, you can save your loved one. All you have to do is agree to come back to Hell with me. Simples."

"I warned you." Shelley glared at him.

"Oh yes, you did, but other than that bit of blue web type stuff, you can't actually do a great deal against me, can you? Like you said, you have power over me in Withernsea, but in Hell, not a jot, and that's where I'm taking Lucy. So why don't you mind your own business, bitch?"

Theo launched toward Satan but as his knife sparked and sizzled further, he found himself pulled back by his wife by blue threads.

"P-please. Let him go. Haven't you done enough against Frankie?" Lucy begged again.

"It's okay. There's no way you are going back to Hell. He can do what he wants to me. Can I just say how much I prayed that your dates would all go wrong? You see, I love you, Lucy. I'm prepared to die for you."

Lucy's eyes appeared wet. "You do? Oh my god, Frankie. I love you too."

I watched as Lucy felt at her scalp and the other horn came away in her hand. "It's gone. I'm *human* again," she exclaimed.

"Nooooooooooo." Satan turned into his original form, his forked tongue striking out towards Lucy.

It was then I realised something. Something incredible. "She said God. Lucy said God," I yelled, "and none of us set on fire or anything. I bet that's why Satan has turned into his original form."

"The card!" Shelley's eyes widened, and she felt in her pocket. "Theo! I need that card."

Through trembling fingers, she pulled out the envelope and extracted the card. I watched as a large white feather appeared and fluttered across it, words appearing.

"It's an incantation of some kind, but we need some ingredients. A glass of water, a wedding ring, and some cat fur."

"There's water on their table." I pointed at it.

"I'll put my wedding ring in," said Theo, throwing it in the jar of water with expert accuracy.

Satan roared with laughter. "Yes, you get a lot of cats in restaurants. I'm just going to watch your pathetic attempts for one more minute, and then Lucy, I shall be giving you your ultimatum once and for all. It's either your horns back or you lose the man you love. Your choice, hun. Sorry to spoil your fun and all but I really can't be doing with all this love and happiness crap that's going on." He shuffled around. "It gives me the heebie-jeebies."

Shelley's shoulders slumped. "I could hold him in my thread, but any sudden movement and Frankie's dead."

"Lucy!" A man walked up to the table with a group of small men behind him. Pixies. "Is everything okay?"

"Henry. Will you look after Red's for me? Make sure the staff are okay? It looks like I've got to leave Withernsea." Her chin trembled, and she wiped under her nose with a napkin.

Then her gaze centred on one of the pixies and she launched out of her position like a lovesick crazed stalker of Harry Styles, front row at a One Direction concert.

"Oh no. Not her, help me. *Help me!*" yelled a pixie with dark-blonde hair. He looked petrified bless him.

"Drop your trousers, right now," she screeched.

Everyone in the restaurant stilled and turned towards the screaming banshee who had wrestled a pixie to the ground and who currently had her hands in his pubic region.

Even Satan looked dumbfounded, and Frankie's face was one of unease crossed with devastation.

Then there was a ripping sound, followed by a sharp scream of pain from the pixie. Lucy held a wad of dark hair aloft before running to the water jug.

"I don't have time to explain, say the sodding rhyme," she yelled.

Shelley shook herself and read.

> *"With the purity of water,*
> *the fur of one so smart,*
> *May love bind you together,*
> *And you never be far apart."*

A glowing tendril of white smoke rose from the bowl wrapping itself around Frankie, another around Lucy, and then the tendrils entwined together into a heart shape before disappearing.

"I'm going to hurl," said Satan, and with that he slit the knife straight across Frankie's throat.

But it did nothing. As it pressed against his flesh the fiery blade fizzled out.

Then Sophia appeared.

Satan rolled his eyes.

"Great. What are you doing here? Always the party pooper with all your lovey dovey stuff. I mean, a heart at the end. Talk about overkill."

His eyes fixed on the box in her hand and his own widened. "What's that?" He looked to escape, renting a rip in the air, his escape portal, but Sophia put a hand up and froze it. Shelley added her blue strands which knitted it back together.

"We've been having meetings. Urgent meetings. You see, you've not been keeping to our agreement about the balance between good and evil. For that, you have outgrown your position. It's time for your renewal."

"You can't do this," Satan yelled.

"It is not our doing. If you have kept to the agreement of balance, nothing shall happen when I open this box. In the end we are all accountable for our decisions, even you."

She opened the box and a small white arrow floated out. As it approached Satan it turned black as night before it punctured his neck.

"Aarrrrrgh."

In front of us Satan crumpled to the floor, flames enveloping him in a way that surely he couldn't survive.

But of course this was Satan, so we waited with baited breath.

The flames died away and the man who remained was someone entirely different.

"Fuck me. Has he regenerated like Doctor Who?" I shouted before I realised I'd just cussed in an angel's presence.

"Angel Sophia. My apologies for my language." I bowed.

She smiled and her face glowed brighter. "No apologies necessary, my child. It is just a human thing. It's when your words cause harm, I take offence."

Satan sat up and rubbed his head. Then he looked at Sophia.

"Where am I? Why am I on earth?"

Sophia walked closer to the table and whispered something in Lucy's ear before walking over to Satan. "Come, there have been changes. We need to go to the Angel realm and discuss." With a blinding light they were gone.

Theo looked around, and we finally took notice of the mass hysteria overtaking the restaurant. "Group hypno session coming up. I'm going to be one tired vampire tonight."

Was it me or did his wife actually look pleased about that fact as she magicked his wedding ring out of the bowl and back onto his finger?

∽

Once the restaurant patrons had been dealt with, we took a seat back down at the table to enjoy a well-earned drink. I ordered a red wine; Shelley, a coke because she was erring on the side of caution; and Theo ordered a red wine himself which he tipped into my glass as soon as I'd downed my first, before extracting a small bottle of blood from his pocket and pouring it into his glass.

"What a night," Shelley said for about the thirtieth time before picking up her glass and taking a swig. She licked her lips. "I was ready for a drink."

"Err, Shelley," I said, pointing to her.

"What? Oh there's not another drama is there? I need a rest. I'm feeling wiped."

"You just drank my O-neg, darling. I think the tiredness might be that you're having my baby," Theo said, looking into her eyes with such tender love.

Shelley's phone rang and as I saw the ID, I picked it up first.

"Yeah, yeah, Ebony. We know already."

"The baby will bring great joy to Withernsea. If only the same could be said for you."

I hung up. This night was now for celebrating, not for worrying about werewolves.

Lucy and Frankie approached our table hand-in-hand.

"We're leaving now," she said, her eyes glittering. The pair of them were bouncing on their toes such was their haste to get home. She turned to Shelley. "We just wanted to say thank you for everything, especially for smoothing things over with Tristan. You declaring him the hero of the hour meant that he wasn't deposed of his pixie position and I won't now have to make reparation again, although I have promised to comb Maisie for him the next time I see her."

Shelley smiled. "It was a little fur-raising, but it all worked out in the end."

"Yeah, and now you can go be all loved-up," I said. "Congratulations you two."

"About that. Our agreement means you now have to date Darius." Lucy smiled.

I shot back in my seat. "I don't think so."

Then I yelped as a strange heat radiated up my arm.

"It was binding. You have no choice. Sorry." Lucy exchanged a knowing look with Shelley. Then she and Frankie left.

"Can I have the bill please?" I asked our waitress. I wanted my bed, and probably to thump my pillow a few times.

Chapter 21

Lucy

Having a vampire boyfriend was so cool. No longer did I need to catch buses. He just whooshed me back to his, well, *our*, house.

"Which room?" he said throatily in my ear.

"Mine," I whispered.

With my door kicked off its hinges, and an "Oops, oh fuck it," from Frankie, he deposited me on the top of my duvet and I thanked God, yes, this was my thing now, that I'd kept my room tidy.

Frankie nuzzled my neck. "You smell divine."

I sure did.

I kicked off my Louboutins with a whispered apology to them for my lack of attention, and then the rest of our clothes followed as we got ourselves naked. Skin to skin we lay together now under the duvet.

"Who'd have thought this was going to happen?" Frankie said.

"Mmmmmm." I snuggled closer. "Not me but thinking back it makes perfect sense. We were two people searching to find our new selves and not only did we do that, but we found each other too."

"Thank goodness you got that cat hair. I can't believe that was the real story of why there were pixies in my house."

"There's more to our story though, Frankie."

He propped his chin up on the pillow at the side of me and gave me his full attention.

"When Satan smote you. I was responsible. I'd brought Shelley to that house, had tricked her. She'd not realised that to release me and therefore her parents, she had to make a deal with the devil. I brought her to Satan's attention and that led to your death. That was me. Tonight, I saved you from him. It came full circle and now it's over, we're free."

"I love you, Lucy Fir, and sometime in the future, when we've dated a while, I think we need to change that name of yours. I think Lucy Love sounds much more suited to the new you."

"Lucy Love," I sighed. "Infinitely better."

Frankie laid me back on the bed and trailed kisses over every inch of my body. I felt his erect cock next to my thigh and shivered in anticipation of what was to come.

When he eventually entered me, it felt like everything and more. I rocked against him until explosions overcame me like a tsunami wave.

Frankie moved to my side, and I laid back, enjoying the aftershocks of this amazing moment.

"Lucy? Are you supposed to be floating?"

I opened my eyes and found myself around five inches off the bed, the duvet having been thrown back during the throes of passion.

"Oops," I said coming back down.

"Are you glowing a little or is it my eyes?"

I patted his arm. "When Sophia came over to me, she whispered that the balance had to be restored. I've spent years being evil and creating harm. With Andrew of no use as an earth angel, she made me one."

Frankie gasped. "What does that mean for us?"

"It means that like my vampire boyfriend, I will no longer age," I told him. "Angels aren't supposed to be with vampires. For us, she made an exception. When she bound us together, it was for eternity. I hope you're ready for that." I bit my lip. "I'm not sure what it means in terms of children though. Can you cross an angel with a vampire?"

"Ah, we have over a hundred years to think about and research that one," he told me, then he leaned over and nibbled at my neck causing another flush of desire to run through my body.

"And that research is continuing right now," he said.

THE END

Hate, Date, Or Mate?

SUPERNATURAL DATING AGENCY
– BOOK THREE

Chapter 1

Kim

What was the wolf equivalent of the doghouse? Because I was in it.

My misdemeanours? Well, let's see...

Dating a wolf from an enemy pack - check.

Losing five werewolf shifter clients in one evening - check.

Pissing off your newly pregnant, mega hormonal boss - check, check, check.

I was sitting in Shelley's office right now while she glared at me. It was most off-putting. I couldn't even bribe her with a coffee and a chocolate doughnut because she'd started drinking blood, which she was decanting into a tomato juice bottle to fool other clients.

Shelley's arms were folded across her chest. "You have until the end of the week to get me five new clients."

I sighed.

"You lost us Darius, Sierra, and Jett. Plus, two more of Darius' pack quit."

I pouted. "Sierra doesn't count. Darius only got her to join to make me jealous."

"She was still paying her fees."

I held a hand to my breastbone. "Can you stop thinking about your business for a moment? I'm in deep shit, Shel. Ebony says I'm going to cause a pack war. A. Pack. War. Also, I have to date Darius because of my binding deal with Lucy. How do I do that when he won't speak to me? Huh?" I shook out my right arm. "This stupid appendage keeps feeling like it's having its own menopause and Lucy says it will continue to feel occasionally like it's burning until he goes out with me. Jett won't answer my calls either. I need understanding, not more pressure. I don't deal with stress well."

Shelley snorted. She actually snorted at me. "If you don't have clients, you don't have a job, do you? Now that's stress."

"It's not faaaiiirr," I whined.

"Oh, for goodness' sake. You have five minutes to moan on, during which time I'll be your best friend. Then I'm back to being a boss and you have to bring in five more clients to replace the income you've lost."

"Supernatural ones?"

"Ideally, but I'll accept any at this time."

"Okay." I lowered my chin to my chest. *God, I have a great rack.*

Shelley looked at her clock. "Five minutes starting from now."

Fuck, I'd better get it all out quickly, like when you're trying to name everything you remembered on The Generation Game. "It's not fair, Shelley. I found the sexiest red chemise with a hooded robe. I was gonna go all Red Riding Hood on his arse."

"Whose? Jett's?"

"No! Are you even listening? I dated Jett to make Darius jealous."

"Um, you've been telling us all you didn't want to date Darius."

I slapped myself in the forehead. "I lied, okay? I've been having a crisis. I don't do relationships, and Ebony said I was destined for him. That's a relationship, right? Like a bloody long one. So I panicked. How come if a normal person panics, they just might need to buy a bunch of flowers and say sorry, but I start a pack war? A Pack. War."

"What exactly is a pack war? It doesn't sound good in any case. Anything with the word war in it is a little worrying."

"You think? I don't know but I've started one. What if they all die? What if Darius now dies? Or Jett?" My traitorous mind imagined Sierra Forrester lying bloodied on the ground. *That's just bitchy, Kim, and an evil thought too far. Why am I smiling? Stop it.*

"What's the plan then? Just sit back and see what happens? I'm sure if there was any immediate danger to Withernsea I'd have been alerted."

A sip of my coffee was required. God, that was lush. "I've asked Frankie if he can send me a history of the shifters. Of both the packs, both here and at Hogsthorpe, and a potted history of shifters in general. The more information I have at my fingertips, the more I'll know what to do next."

"Well, I don't see that there is anything else you can do right now. Just keep trying to phone Darius to apologise, and wait until your reading material comes through. And in the meantime, stay out of trouble and get me those clients."

I blew a huge breath out making a puh noise and then sat up straighter and crossed my legs. "How are you anyway? Are you adjusting to life as an expectant mama?"

Shelley nodded. "To be honest, I wouldn't know I was pregnant if it wasn't for the O-neg I've started drinking. I have five months to go with having a vampire baby, maybe even eight if it ends up being like a regular human/wyvern/witch baby. I'm quite chill about it all."

"Like a regular human/wyvern/witch? Have you heard yourself? Will it come out with fangs? Scales? A broomstick? What about red eyes? Are you having a home birth because how do you explain its potential peculiarities in the labour ward?"

A serious amount of eye rolling occurred. "It will come out like a regular baby: without teeth and with blue eyes. And there's Dr Fielding at the hospital, along with a whole host of other medical staff who know full well that Withernsea is full of supernaturals. Mine isn't the first supe baby to be born here."

"I still can't get over that. Even though we run a dating agency for them, so many people here are like the undead, or have real life talons. Must be a twat having a manicure if you're a bird shifter."

Shelley ran her hands through her hair. "Can you go to your office now? Time's up and you're wearing me out."

"Thanks a bunch."

As I stood up to leave, the door banged open, and Lucy walked in clutching two coffees. She passed one to me, sat opposite Shelley, and put the other one in front of her on Shelley's desk.

"What's happening, dudes?"

"We are not dudes," I protested. "I hate people use that word for everyone. Makes me think I've grown a penis, and I didn't realise."

Lucy tilted her head towards me, then looked back at Shelley. "What's got into her today, or rather not got?" She cackled.

"Oh just because you're loved up." I did a mock vomiting impression. "Anyway, how come you're up at this time? Shouldn't you still be at it with lover-boy?" Lucy was dating my ex, Frankie.

"He's sleeping. Vampire, remember?" She rolled her eyes. *Why was everyone rolling their eyes at me today?* "But for your information, I'm up keeping an eye on a client. The quicker I get my earth angel duties done, the quicker I can become an angelic housewife and just stay at home serving my man."

We both gawped at her.

"Oh my god, you didn't seriously believe that bollocks, did you?" She guffawed.

"Are you supposed to blaspheme and swear when you're a helper of the angelic realm?" I creased my brows at her.

She wafted her hands as if wafting my words away. "I can't help blaspheming. After not being able to hear those words for twenty-odd years, I can't stop saying them all. Holy moly, oh my god, oh my fucking god, Christ almighty. It's so refreshing. Anyway, Angel Sophia told me that as long as I wasn't actually harming anyone, I was fine."

"I'm not sure that's what she meant, Luce. I think she was referring to that one specific occurrence of a rude word you did right in front of her."

"Po-tay-to, po-tar-to."

I stared at her, my hands on my hips. "Why was I expecting you to be all lovely now you are no longer a demon?"

"I'm a beginner earth angel. I don't think we're quite ready to move to the miracles stage yet."

"Who's this client then?"

She smiled brightly and rose an inch up off the floor, just hovered there and didn't even notice. "He's called Seth, and he's a new assistant in Jax's coffee shop, so I shall bring you regular coffees while I do my job."

"And what do you have to save him from?"

Lucy pulled a dramatic face. "Oh, I'm not allowed to tell you that. It's a celestial secret. I can tell you one thing though. That man is hot. H.O.T. hot."

"How else would you spell it?"

"Kim! Your grumpiness and rudeness are out of order today. Go to your office, right now." Shelley glared at me again and pointed at the door.

"Huh." I stomped out, taking my coffee with me.

It was seriously like I'd been sent to the naughty corner. I powered up my laptop. No new clients had applied. FFS. If we'd had five—or even better, more than five—new applications for membership, I could have got away with having to find any. I moved onto my own emails. I'd start work in half an hour when my coffees had had a chance to kick in.

There was an email from Frankie.

From: Frankielove@yahoo.com
To: Kim@withernseadating.com
Date: Wed 25 Jan 2018 Time: 10:02 am
Subject: General shifter information

Hey Kim.
While I dig a little deeper into the specifics, here are some factoids about the shifters in general. Document attached.
From your mate (get it? Lol)
Frankie

I clicked on the attachment and opened the document, saving it to a brand-new folder I named 'get self out of the shit'. Then I sat back and read it.

GENERAL WOLF SHIFTER INFORMATION
(Not to be reproduced. Copyright F. Love, 2018)

Werewolf (werwulf, man-wolf, lycanthrope)

The ability to shift into a wolf from human form.

The rumour that you can become a werewolf from a scratch is untrue folklore. In reality, you have to either be born a were, or in the instance of a mate, bitten during the mating ritual under a full moon.
Weres are vulnerable to silver and can be killed by being shot by a silver bullet to the heart.
Weres can shift at any night through choice, but on the night of a full moon will always change. This is when mating rituals occur. It is not true that wolves rampage at this time with a lack of control over their animal selves.

Mates primarily come through the pack. However, due to a lack of female offspring (8 out of 10 were births result in male children), mates are often selected from out of the pack. Weres mate for life. A male werewolf is expected to take a mate no later than at the age of thirty years and can be ostracised from the pack if still single by then.

I clicked into Darius' profile. He'd recently had his 29th birthday. That was a plus for me. I could just wait it out until he got desperate. Although what if he was already desperate and mated with Sierra? Yes, they were friends, but we all knew it was nigh on impossible for males and females to really be friends. Did that mean he might have shagged her before?

He will have slept with people, Kim. You're no saint yourself, remember?

I rang his mobile phone. Once again it went to his answering service.

"I'm not able to take your call right now, and if you are Kim, quit ringing. I told you we're done."

Rude.

We're done. Were done. Hahahahaha. He'd said a joke without realising.

Not to be thwarted from my current mission, I sent a text.

Kim: I really am very, very, sorry. BTW your voicemail is rude and unnecessary.

My phone soon beeped with an incoming message alert.

Darius: Stop texting.

Kim: I will if you'll meet me to talk.

Darius: I have nothing further to say to you. You brought shame on me.

Kim: Give me a chance to make amends, pleeeaaassseee. Pretty please with cherries on top?

This message failed to send <<communication error>>

Had he blocked me?

My bloody arm set off with another hot flush. "Ah, Hell, it's not my fault he won't date me," I yelled in the direction of the floor. Then I realised it was my fault, so I sat and sulked for a minute.

Then I tried to ring Jett.

"I'm not able to take your call right..."

"For crying out LOUD." I ended the call and threw my phone on the desk in temper. Thank God, it had a protective case. Well, there was nothing else to do. I should just get on with my work, which included finding five new customers. I stood up, grabbing my jacket and handbag. I'd go to Jax's coffee shop. Not only could I look for potential new clients and get some lovely coffee, but I could have a nosy at this sex god, Seth. It would take my mind off other things.

∽

Whoa!

The queue to the front of the coffee shop counter extended out of the main door. No way was I waiting in that. Jax was my friend. I passed a load of women in the queue and then as I got halfway, I stopped—stunned.

In front of me was a blonde-haired guy in jeans and a white t-shirt wearing a barista apron that said 'Jax's' on it. What played in my head was a fantasy movie-reel of him in a shower, the spray bouncing off a hard, ripped man chest, while he bit his lip and looked at me with a lusty wink.

"Kim!" Jax shouted. "Come meet the new guy, Seth. He's proving a hit. We've never been as busy."

Much to the consternation of the rest of the queue, I stalked right to the front making sure my skinny-jeaned ass sashayed as I did so. I held out a hand. "Hey, Seth. I'm Kim. I work at Withernsea Dating just upstairs and along."

He gripped my hand. Hmmm, firm handshake, smooth warm skin. Clean fingernails. All good signs.

"What can I get you? I guess as a regular I'd better make sure to remember your order."

A bed and your cock please.

"A latte and a chocolate doughnut please."

Down, girl.

"Coming right up." He beamed a huge smile at me. Oh God, he had cheek dimples. I was going to be a puddle on the floor in a minute.

When he served me my coffee, I leaned in closer. "Erm, Seth. Sorry to be so direct with this, but I'm looking at this queue. Do you have a girlfriend?"

"No. I got divorced recently. My ex cheated on me." He shrugged.

"Do you fancy joining the books?" I asked him. "Say, one month's free trial?"

"Sure, why not? Drop me a form in."

I went into my purse where I always carried a few copies. "Can you get it back to me by five?"

"Okay." He served me my order and a side of another beaming smile.

As I walked back up the queue, I stopped to talk to the other women waiting. "Hey, I'm Kim from Withernsea dating. We just signed Seth onto our books, and we have several other men just like him if any of you are interested in signing up."

I walked out with twelve new applications. I'd eaten my doughnut and drunk my coffee while women filled out the application, so I walked back to the office and knocked on Shelley's door.

"Come in."

Her face flashed with annoyance as I walked towards her.

"Where have you been? You'd think given our conversation this morning that you might have actually stayed at your desk and worked."

I placed the application forms on the table. "Twelve new customers, and a 'lucky' thirteenth shall be here and on your desk by five-thirty." I high fived myself. "You were saying?"

Shelley grinned. "I was saying what an asset to my company you are, Kim. Thank you. Enjoy the rest of your day."

I felt good, so I sashayed out of Shelley's office too.

Now there was just those pesky wolves to deal with.

Chapter 2

Darius

"How long are you going to be wearing that face?" My younger sister Alyssa asked.

"I'm not wearing a 'face'," I protested.

She tilted her head to one side. "You look like someone tea-bagged you with a sweaty bollock."

"*Alyssa Dakota Phelan*, you'll have your mouth washed out with soap if I hear you say that again."

"Sorry, Mum," she said, while simultaneously rolling her eyes at me.

Fifteen-year-old sisters were a challenge. I couldn't imagine trying to parent her.

"Look at him though, Mum. He's been like it for days now."

My mum came over and sat beside me on the sofa.

"It's true you're not yourself, Son. I know you were disappointed about the woman, but she still might be the one. We have to wait now."

"I really liked her, Mum. But what she did, dating Jett. I'm not sure I can forgive that. I don't understand why she'd date him and not me."

"She's asked to meet you. Why don't you go and see if she can explain? It's better than sitting looking constipated," Alyssa sniped.

"How do you know she's asked to meet me? Have you read my messages again?"

"Well, you do leave your phone hanging around."

I stood up and got right in Alyssa's face. I saw the yellow flash of my wolf eyes reflected in the shades she was now wearing. She thought they looked cool. It wasn't even sunny, and we were indoors.

"Keep out of my stuff and my business, or I'll borrow your DKNY sunglasses and accidentally sit on them."

"Darius, sit back down. It's not your sister's fault things have been a little rough for you lately."

Alyssa moved her glasses up to the top of her head so I could take in her smug smile.

"Alyssa, the dishes need taking out of the dishwasher. Go make yourself useful."

She huffed and left the room.

My mum stared at me a moment and then began speaking. "I went to see Ebony today."

I scrubbed a hand through my hair. "Mum, why did you do that?"

"Honestly? Your dad had pissed me off, and I decided to go have a good spend, and her boutique is the best in Withernsea. But as soon as I got in there she started with the visions. I actually felt sorry for her. They give her terrible migraines."

"She got the vodka out then?"

"Yes, and I had one, so she didn't look odd. Poor woman, it's the only thing that helps her."

I clasped my hands tightly, my knuckles whitening. "Go on then. You know you're dying to tell me what she said."

"Darius, I'm not dying to tell you. You're my oldest son and I'm looking out for you, that's all."

I sighed. I really was a grumpy bastard of late. "Sorry, I know. I'm just frustrated with all this mating stuff."

Now I was in my thirtieth year the pressure had ramped up. I'd wasted months trying to pursue Kim Fletcher, the super-hot woman at the dating agency who handled the organisation of dates for our kind. My mind floated back to when I'd first properly met her...

I'd seen her before, around Withernsea. Her long dark hair framing a heart-shaped face. But it was her smell that appealed the most. She smelled to me like the finest scotch mixed with sex. She smelled like she was mine. I'd been called to the agency after there'd been a fire bomb aimed at Shelley's office. I'd made sure my police uniform was on point, my police shirt tight against my pecs and my trousers hugging my arse. One thing all the running around in the woods did was give you a great arse and thighs. I knew I looked like a walking Magic Mike stripper.

As soon as I'd walked past her, she'd yelled "Holy fuck," before covering her mouth and pretending to have the hiccoughs. I'd tried not to smile at her reaction, which wasn't all that difficult because when I met her gaze something strange happened. It was like we were locked in a staring competition. I couldn't take my eyes off her.

It took Shelley to remind me I'd come to view a crime scene before I'd been able to break away.

When I'd returned to Kim's office, I'd started staring at her again. There was something in me, like an invisible thread that was dragging me to her, and that smell... I just wanted to leap over the desk and bury my nose in her neck and nuzzle her.

I'd needed to leave but didn't want to. What could I say to get her attention? I decided to remind Shelley about my application, hoping Kim would take the hint and date me herself.

"Just to say that I sent in an application for the agency. I'm young, free and single. Well, I'm not free on a full moon, but the rest of the time."

But Kim only nodded her head before her gaze had returned to her computer screen.

She'd been in a casual relationship with a magician called Frankie before Satan had smote him and he'd ended up turned into a vampire. Since then, I wasn't aware that she'd dated anybody. I'd thought I was in with a chance, but then she'd arranged dates for me with other women, and she herself flirted with other men.

When I'd seen her in a restaurant with Jett Conall—one of our enemy pack—a few days ago, it had been the last straw. If she knew what she had started I'd never be able to forgive her, and that's why I'd been putting off seeing her.

"Earth calling, Darius." My mum nudged my shoulder.

I turned to her. "I'm listening."

"Ebony says Kim's actions will set in train a challenge between you and Jett for Kim's heart, but there is also a shadow hanging around, a third suitor. She foresees not only a challenge for Kim, but also one to our pack as the wolves of Hogsthorpe will be able to challenge Withernsea for power if Jett mates with a Withernsea resident."

"How come they haven't already made such a challenge? There are plenty of single women in Withernsea."

"The rules are that they can't seek a date, but in this case, Kim asked him. She looked him up on the computer. They were finding a loophole anyway. Applying to the agency was a way of meeting a woman. If he'd gone out on an arranged meet and convinced his date to ask for a second date that would have done it. It was only a matter of time. The wolves are bored in Hogsthorpe—restless. Ebony says she can hear their inner wolves howling with confliction."

"So Kim did this, but the chances were it would have happened anyway?"

"Yes, Son."

"And not only is Jett my enemy, but there could be another man?"

Surely it couldn't be Frankie? He was loved up with Lucy now.

"That's what she said. Now you need to have a really clear think on whether or not you're going to pursue Kim. If she is the one for you, I will help you all the way, Darius. But it will not be easy. We must speak to Alpha Edon and listen very carefully for his directions. This is very much pack business, Darius, even though it's your mating and your heart."

I sighed. "I know. Why does it have to be this complicated though?"

My mum stroked my hair. "Because it's love, Son, and love is complicated, but worth its challenges."

She left me, going to the kitchen. We lived in a large wooden cabin built in the woods at the edge of Withernsea. No residents here knew it existed as we'd surrounded the land in front of the woods with a caravan park and had got a wizard to erect a glamour which meant that anyone staying in the park only saw farmers' fields when they looked out of their window. A perimeter fence with security warnings stopped anyone venturing any further than the caravan park boundary. Some of the pack had chosen to live in the caravans, preferring that to a wooden structure. I would have the choice once mated to build a home in the woods or accept a brand-new caravan or lodge. I would let my mate choose our home. All I would be interested in was making sure she was happy and satisfied.

I decided I would speak to Alpha Edon before I made any

further decisions about Kim as my possible future mate. I'd need to be sure to accept my responsibilities as a member of the pack and put that before love. The safety of my pack was paramount.

"Have your balls dropped yet? Are you going to get your woman? Or do you want to borrow a tampon?"

Alyssa was back.

Yes, safety was paramount, even that of annoying little sisters.

Chapter 3

Kim

"You do know I had your boyfriend resident in my office for months, don't you? I just got rid of him and now you're hanging around. What gives?"

Lucy looked up from her eReader. "I'd gotten to a really interesting bit then. Can't you just get on with your work? Seriously, you spend a lot of time distracted from your duties, you really do. I mean twenty-three-and-a-half minutes looking between Darius, Jett, and Seth's profiles. I suppose that's due to your selfless dedication to find them dates, even though two of them aren't even on your books anymore, and you used the other for recruiting purposes."

I narrowed my eyes at her.

She placed the eReader on her lap. "It's a good job Satan regenerated because the old one would have really seen your potential." She flicked back her fringe. "Anyway, in answer to your question, I need to be around here for my whole earth angel post. I have to keep an eye on Seth, and also an eye on Shelley to make sure that her baby is safe, but don't you be telling her I'm doing that."

I dropped my pen in shock. "Is her baby in danger?"

"Not at the moment as news hasn't got out yet. She's yet to announce it beyond close family, right? But her and Theo, and her parents, are very aware that this child is prophesied as the ultimate leader of Withernsea. The most powerful supernatural ever. There are going to be a few folks not so happy with that idea."

"I never thought. Poor Shelley. It's bad enough dealing with morning sickness when you're drinking blood—seriously, it's like the exorcist or something—but to have people want to harm you and your baby? That just doesn't bear thinking about."

"Which is why she has an earth angel hanging around. If it's okay, I need to stay around here a while. Well, between here and the coffee shop. If there was a spare unit, I'd look at renting a space because I'm putting together Frankie's encyclopaedia of all the supernatural species while I'm between angel duties. I'm just reading through the first chapter now." She picked up the eReader and shook it at me. "He's in his element putting this together and learning about all the different kinds of supernatural beings."

"Just stay there a moment. I need to have a word with Shelley about something. I'll be right back."

"I've no intention of going anywhere, but it's kind of you to make the gesture." Lucy picked the eReader back up. "I'll be leaving at four pm when Frankie is due up though, because he's due *up* if you catch my drift and I'm going to oblige him."

I shuddered at the thought. Lunch could wait. It was even worse given that he was my ex because my mental image of him with Lucy was a little too vivid given our past. I knew she was guaranteed a good time and didn't blame the woman for going home promptly. But still, I didn't need to know he was an alarm cock so to speak.

I wandered through to Shelley's office. "Hey, you got a minute?"

"Ooh sounds serious. Sure, sit down."

"Lucy's here again. She has earth angel shit to do and needs to be around. Do you think if I got the staff room emptied of the junk in it, she could go in there? We don't use it and she has the money to pay a monthly rental. Also, she has spare time when she's not earth angeling. She's got managers in at Red's now because she wants to spend her evenings concentrating on Frankie's meat and two veg instead of any at the steakhouse. I was thinking she could learn the ropes and cover your maternity leave?"

Shelley raised her eyebrows and shot me a questioning gaze. "Do you think she'd be up for that?"

"I don't know. I thought I'd sound you out first, but she's typing up Frankie's manuscript which means she's learning all about supernaturals. God, what if she ends up better at my job than I am? Please don't sack me when she's awesome!"

"She might end up awesome at knowing things, but as an employee I think she'd be even harder to control than you are. Can you see me setting her regular hours? She got damn selfish spending all those years in Hell. She's getting better now she's with Frankie and has lost the demon horns, but she's a way to go with developing her good side. I mean she set my office on fire last year."

"Yeah, but that's when she was evil, and she can't flick fire out of her fingers anymore."

"Oh yeah? Have you checked her handbag? She's started carrying lighters... and she doesn't smoke."

"Do you think Angel Sophia was having a mental breakdown when she gave Lucy this job?" I asked.

"I trust our celestial beings know what they are doing. I have enough to think about down here, never mind up there."

"Of course. How's your training going?"

"My father feels we need to meet more regularly now with the baby coming. Now Satan has been replaced by a new version it means that other supernaturals are likely to descend on Withernsea, not believing I am a worthy opponent while pregnant. They'll try to use my pregnancy to their advantage in gaining control. It might be worth keeping an eye out for any strange applications to the dating agency, as gaining an interview here would give them direct access to me."

"That's true. Listen, if Lucy comes on board, we will vet all the new applications and do all the interviews. You can focus on the rest of the work."

"Appreciated. Being pregnant with a vampire's baby is hard enough without all the stress of the ruler of Withernsea crap."

"And how is the Daddy-to-be?"

"Smothering. Thank goodness he has to sleep during the day and also that he doesn't need to breathe, or I might be smothering him too—with a pillow."

I laughed. "Right, I'm going to go back and see if Withernsea Dating is recruiting a new employee. Can we afford it?"

"Sure, I have a rich vampire husband anyway to fall back on if things get tight while I have the baby."

"I think things are likely to get loose," I quipped.

"Yeah, well, I'll be doing Kegels daily, don't you worry about that. I've got to keep my vampire lover happy for many, many years. Hey, actually that's another point in the favour of being turned before the birth. I'd keep my pussy tight."

"I thought you weren't interested in being turned? That you

wanted to wait until after the birth?"

Shelley fiddled with a paperclip on her desk. "I've been speaking to the medics at the Caves and there's no risk to the baby. In fact, I'd probably be a healthier mum if I was turned. It's just the whole feeling like I have the flu, dying, agonising thirst thing that's putting me off."

"I don't know why. That was your every Friday and Saturday night pre-Theo."

"Ha-ha."

I left Shelley's office and returned to my own.

∽

"Lucy? I have a proposition for you."

The eReader went onto her lap again and she sighed. "I knew this would happen. That you wouldn't be able to accept me and Frankie together. I'm sorry but I don't swing that way. I already told Maisie this. So, no. No threesomes."

"Eww." I actually did gag. "That's not it."

"God, you are dramatic. If I did swing that way you'd be thoroughly satisfied and begging for more, so drop the norovirus look."

I shook my head as if I could dislodge her thoughts from my mind. "I'm starting to regret my looking out for you now," I told her. "Now get up and come follow me."

She sighed but stood and followed me out of the room and across the small landing. I pushed open the door to our staff room. It was a small room with a table and four chairs, sink, kettle, cupboards, and boxes full of crap that needed sorting out—mostly electronic equipment that had broken and it had been easier to just dump it. We'd not used the staff room as we had Jax's below. Jax's coffee and doughnuts were legendary.

"What is it you're showing me? The world record for dust bunnies? There's a whole fucking warren in here. You need pest control." She sneezed.

"This potentially is your new office. We could work through the boxes together. I'm sure between you and Shelley you could come up with a redecorating budget. Jax's brother would do a good deal on it. It would give you an office of your own, and also, if you want it, there's a job to go with it."

"I'm not going to be your cleaner. Just because you're a filthy whore."

"I'm sure your ex could vouch for that fact, but no that's not it, you ungrateful cow. Now shut it and listen up before I change my mind and just lock you in here."

"Fine."

"You're here all day, and your earth angel duties are intermittent, right?"

"Correct."

"You're helping Frankie put his guide together..."

"Also correct."

"Shelley needs someone to cover her maternity leave. Our proposition is why don't you work for us freelance? You can use the office and juggle Frankie's guide, earth angel duties, and working for the agency. You'd be helping me interview potential new clients. Plus, with you working on the guide, it would be fantastic to have your expertise on all the supes. You're bound to learn all about them as you put the guide together."

"I would have to ask Frankie if I could share his work with you, given that he is going to make a living from this masterpiece."

"How much will his guide be?"

"Four dollars ninety-nine a month to access his database. A complete bargain."

"Then sign me up as an early-adopter."

She squealed and clapped. It was scarier than anything she'd ever shown me as a demon. "His first client. He'll be ecstatic."

"So, what do you think? Do you want to rent this room and work for the agency?"

"Yes. That would be fantastic. Would you be okay if I set up CCTV in here? I want to be able to keep an eye on Shelley and on the coffee shop."

"Is this legal?"

"Not in the slightest."

"I never heard you ask. Keep it in a lockable cupboard and if you ever grass on me, I will paint your office red, turn the heat up full blast and be such a damn cow to you, you'd think you were back in Hell."

"You are very mean to me sometimes. I heartily accept all proposals. I shall go and get us coffees to celebrate and thus do a little earth angeling at the same time while I check what Seth is doing."

As she walked past me, she knocked a cobweb off my skirt. "I hope that's from the room and not your vagina."

The door swung shut behind her and closed before my mouth did.

Chapter 4

Darius

I headed to an area at the edge of the woods where the community hall stood. This was where we held our pack meetings and ceremonies. We weren't a huge pack, with around thirty adult males, twenty-five adult females and then the kids. Altogether our group totalled around seventy. We had different duties around the park. I did some security detail alongside my job as a Police Officer.

Our Alpha, Edon, was around sixty years old and had been the alpha male for the last twenty-nine years. Alpha's were elected by the rest of the adults in the pack. Edon was a charismatic leader with a huge presence. With short salt and pepper hair and a long grey beard, he stood for no nonsense. He was like an uncle to me. The whole pack were family to each other whether through blood or circumstance.

Any adults could attend the pack meetings, but it was mainly the adult males who attended, following meetings with a game of pool, and a beer or scotch.

I walked into the meeting room looking at who was here already. There was Edon; his sons, Reid and Sonny; my stepfather, Billy; my younger brother, Rhett, who was twenty; and about another eight of the pack males. Alyssa had assured me that she would kick sexist butt when she was eighteen and could attend the meetings. I gave her two meetings maximum before she was bored out of her brain and back to taking selfies on Instagram. No one willingly wanted to attend, it's just how it was. Back in the old days, tradition deemed it the man's role, and because it was boring, the women still let us get on with it.

Some things were worth fighting about in equality, pack meetings weren't one of them. Everyone got a say in pack business anyway. My stepdad always warned me that when women put their mind to something not even being a scary arse wolf would stop them. "Your mum goes feral without changing if I'm not careful."

I took a seat around the large meeting table and poured myself a scotch.

Edon cleared his throat. "Okay, all, if you're ready. I'd like to get down to business."

We nodded and murmured our agreement.

"Right, the first thing on the agenda is I would like to announce the engagement of my eldest son, Reid, to Sierra. Their mating ceremony will take place in three full moon's time with their civil ceremony here in the hall. Invitations to come.

We all clapped and patted Reid on the back. He and Sierra had been together a long time. He was a good friend and Sierra had been my best friend for years. She was a year younger than me, so three years older than her fiancé. The pack had always thought Sierra and I would get together but we'd never felt that way about each other. As soon as Reid hit twenty-five the mating call had passed between them. I was pleased for them both.

However, at the same time I felt a pang that Reid at twenty-five would be mated before me. It might have been my imagination, but I was sure I'd felt some of the others looking at me when Edon made the announcement. In one year's time I'd be an embarrassment to the pack if I remained single.

Edon went through some other more mundane business before tapping his papers on the desk and then placing them down.

"Okay, the final discussion of the evening relates to the future of the Withernsea pack. Now I know there have been rumours going around. That ends right now. I'm going to tell you the truth and you make sure this gets back to those who need to know."

There were murmurs of agreement in the room.

"Darius was fated to mate to a human female, by the name of Kimberly Fletcher. However, things have gone awry and Kim ended up contacting Jett Conall and asking him on a date."

More murmurs along with surprised gasps circulated.

"That means at some point soon she will be forced to choose between them."

"Shame it's not the olden days when you'd just go in and bloody carry her out. Tell her to be quiet, she was yours and that's that." Said Bryan, our oldest member, at eighty-six.

"Yes, well times have moved on and you'd be arrested if you did that now."

"Can't arrest himself, can he? Can't he have a word with the bosses? Just go into that agency and get her, lad. Tell her who's boss."

"If I may carry on..." Edon gave Bryan a cool-eyed gaze and Bryan sat back suitably chastised. "The woman will have to choose and being a modern-day woman could accept neither of the wolves and someone else entirely, a possibility given she has an entire database of available males at her disposal."

"Does Darius have to court her?"

"No. The Seer says that the woman has to do her own choosing. If she requests his company, Darius can attend but he can't tell her that the pack are under threat should she choose Jett."

"And if she doesn't want either me or Jett?" I asked.

"Then they can't come back to Withernsea. Unless they find another female. The other option is we take them on in a pack challenge and run them out of the area altogether but that would be a last resort."

"What's the plan of action?" I asked.

"If she asks to see you, you go. If she wants to speak to you, you speak. If she wants you in her bed you make sure you fuck her until she wants to scream no one's name but your own."

I guessed I needed to unblock her telephone number then.

"And what if she dates the other wolf as well?" I needed to clarify the arrangements.

"You can't interfere. Not until one of you mates with her. Once she agrees to be your mate, she is in effect engaged to you and will have to make a date for the mating and civil ceremony. We wish you luck, son." Edon said.

Everyone raised their glass. I drank several. The challenge was on and I knew that if I didn't win, I might be out of the pack soon and more catastrophically we were all potentially out of Withernsea.

Back in my room, I unblocked Kim's number and waited. There was nothing. It looked like I'd succeeded in driving her away. I called Sierra.

"Congrats, lady. I'd better be going to be the best man."

"Of course you are, silly. Thank you. Now how are you doing? Reid's just filling me in."

I'd bet he was. Newly engaged males were randy as all hell.

"I need a favour. Could I buy you a coffee tomorrow and one of the nicest doughnuts around?"

"Oooh Jax's?"

"Yeah."

"Okay. What time do you want to meet?"

"Well, that's the thing. I want you to go without me."

"Huh?"

"Let me explain."

The following morning just after 10am my mobile phone pinged.

Kim: I demand you meet with me, so I can explain everything. Stop being an arse Darius Wild.

I sat back and laughed, waited five minutes and then sent a reply.

Darius: Fine. Where then? This better be good. I don't like my time being wasted.

In seconds I had a reply.

Kim: Eight pm. Hanif's. I'll pay.

Fuck. It went against every bone in my body to let a woman pay for dinner. I thought about my sister's face if I said this, growled, and typed my response.

Darius: See you then.

I opened up a new message to Sierra.

Darius: Thank you so much. You're a star!

Sierra: My pleasure. Her face was a picture. She deffo likes you, so something else must be holding her back. Anyway, good luck, bestie.

Hmm, could that be true? Was there something stopping Kim from being mine? I guess I needed to find out.

Chapter 5

Kim

I'd spent the night catching up on *Stranger Things* on the television. I'd had a good night's sleep. Life was good.

Today me and Lucy were going to get the staff room cleaned up. Therefore I'd tied my hair up in a ponytail and put on my painting clothes. No point in getting dressed up if we were going to be knee deep in dirt. Shelley would man the phones and keep an eye on the emails. All I needed to do was go get a coffee and doughnut from Seth to get a head start on the day. The eye candy wouldn't go amiss before all I could see was dust.

Once again, the coffee shop was bustling. Jax spotted me and motioned for me to take a seat. Even better. Table service. She wandered over.

"The usual, babes?"

"Yes, please. Wow, it's not letting up in here, is it? Are you this busy all the time?"

"This is slow. I don't know what Seth has, but I need to bottle it if he leaves."

I laughed. "If only you knew before that the way to a successful coffee shop was a hot barista. Now the other women, and some men, of Withernsea will be getting hooked on your superior brand of coffee. They are so lucky."

"They are. I'll be back in a moment with your order. Are you staying in, or taking it back to the office?"

"Staying thanks. I don't start for another twenty minutes today."

"Do you know, I'm going to come join you. I could use a rest. It's been relentless."

I was pleased for Jax. She'd been running the coffee shop for three years now and it really was an amazing venue. Choose what had brought in the extra custom—her products reputation or the hot new assistant—she deserved every success. I looked around the space. The atmosphere was amazing with everyone laughing and chatting.

Then I saw *her*.

Seated at a table near the counter.

I'd been so distracted ogling Seth, I'd failed to see the other person under my nose.

Sierra Forrester.

There she sat with a friend. The large beaming smile on her face revealed her white movie star style teeth. Her chestnut curls bounced as her head went back with laughter. Even her freckles seemed to dance across her nose and cheeks.

Bitch.

Then her friend grabbed Sierra's hand. Her left hand. They both stared and admired a ring on her finger. My eyes zeroed in on it. At a large oval diamond. I checked out which finger it was on and felt my heart plummet. No. He wouldn't do that. Would he? Had Darius proposed to Sierra? *What had I done?*

I only realised I was staring rather rudely when Sierra's gaze caught my own.

Fuck, she was coming over! I froze.

"Hey there. Kim, isn't it?"

"Yes, that's right." *Look at her. Smile. Come on body, do something!*

"The coffee here is fabulous. I shall have to come here more often, although I'm not sure my fiancé will approve of me hanging here with that hottie behind the counter. Am I right?"

"The coffee really is lovely here," I forced out, refusing to acknowledge her use of the word fiancé lest I leapt up and pulled a few of her curls out.

She swept a few said curls out of her face, using the aforementioned hand. The dazzle almost blinded me as the sun hit the diamond.

Just then, Jax arrived with my order and a drink of her own. She sat down. "Am I missing anything then?" she asked me. "Any gossip. News? I get so bored sometimes stuck behind that counter all day. We've not had a girls' night out for ages. We must have one soon."

"No, nothing of any excitement to report," I said.

"I got engaged!" Sierra squealed. "Sorry. I know Kim. My name's Sierra." She held out her hand for Jax to shake. "Your coffee is delightful by the way. I shall tell all of my friends and the pack. I know Darius comes here a lot already. Now I know why he was always hanging around. I couldn't understand why he was always here before. Now I know. It's the coffee and doughnuts."

And me you cow. Before you stole him.

"Is that who you're engaged to? Darius Wild?" Jax looked shocked as well she might.

Sierra giggled for longer than she needed to. *Yeah rub it in, cow. You won. I was an idiot.*

"Oh God, no. Ewww. Darius is my best friend. He's like a brother to me. No, I'm engaged to Reid Woodland."

"I don't think I know him. You'll have to bring him in and have a coffee and bun on the house from me in celebration," Jax said. "Won't she, Kim?"

I was still trying to find my voice. She wasn't engaged to Darius. SHE WASN'T ENGAGED TO DARIUS.

A massive smile lit across my face, and I grabbed her hand. "Where are my manners? Let me look. Oh my, that ring is amazing. You'll have to be careful you don't start a fire with that baby. Why wait for Reid? Why don't we celebrate now? Let me buy you and your friend a drink and bun, whatever you like." I was rambling, but my mouth wouldn't stop.

"Have you seen Darius lately?" I asked her. "Only I've tried to call him, but there was a fault with his phone."

"Yeah, he said there had been, but it's fixed now. You should ring him," she replied.

Jax got up to get the drinks and buns leaving us alone.

"I don't know what was going on that night at Beached when you ate with Jett, but it has caused problems for the pack."

"I didn't realise. I'm sorry."

"Why did you date Jett anyway? Are you serious about him?" Sierra's voice had softened.

I shook my head. "No."

"Look, it's none of my business but you need to be honest with

Darius. He's my best friend. If you don't want anything to do with him in a romantic way, that's fine. Just let him down gently, okay?"

"I'm going to ask him to meet me, so I can explain."

"Great." She smiled at me. Fuck, I was beginning to like the bitch now. "Well, thank you for the coffee and cake. I'd better go back to my friend now."

I took out my phone and scrolled through to Darius' number and typed him a message.

Kim: I demand you meet with me so I can explain everything. Stop being an arse, Darius Wild.

Now I just had to wait.

Chapter 6

Shelley

I was in my office—alone.

Thank fucking God.

The last four months had been a crazy whirlwind. I decided to write bullet points on the notepad on my desk, to try to get my head around everything.

- Discover supernaturals exist.
- Meet and fall in love with a 126-year-old vampire.
- Discover your mother is a witch.
- Find out you have witch powers.
- Discover father is a wyvern.
- Inherit wyvern powers.
- Be informed that your future child shall be the most powerful ruler of Withernsea which started out as a place called Wyvernsea.
- Marry the vampire.
- Discover the ghost of your vampire husband's mother lives in your new home.
- Have to defeat Satan.
- Find out you're pregnant.
- Vampire husband decides this is a good time to redecorate and turn the farm into a Bed and Breakfast.

I think that was all. I stared at the list. There was no wonder I was having a little meltdown moment right now. On top of this, the dating agency business needed attention, and I was worried about my best friend. I knew Kim's past, knew about her awful father and why she was hesitant to commit herself to a relationship. Headstrong, stubborn, and impulsive, my bestie had made some rash choices of late and was now living with the consequences.

But picking dates off her work computer as she had with Jett had been a step too far.

One minute she did something crazy like this, the next she rocked up with big ideas for the place like the awesome plan to bring Lucy in. I really did believe that Kim needed a steady influence in her life. She didn't have parents or siblings around, and despite my best intentions, with work and my personal life getting ever busier, I wasn't able to be there for her all the time like I could when I was single. The time when I didn't have to look out for Withernsea, when I was just a normal resident and could have a piss in peace without a ghost floating in to tell me some gossip she'd heard, or a husband coming to make sure I was okay.

Thank fuck he slept all day, so I was able to spend the majority of my work hours in peace. Well, as peaceful as it got around here, bearing in mind we'd had Frankie hanging around for months and now we had Lucy. I didn't know what her earth angel duties were about—she couldn't say—but I hoped they didn't have repercussions on my decision to let her have an office here.

The reason I had peace and quiet today was that Lucy and Kim were sorting through all the crap in the old staff room. I'd said I didn't know if dust could affect vampire babies and so they'd agreed to keep me well out of it.

The only thing I was allergic to right now was drama.

I sat back in my chair and closed my eyes.

Peace and quiet at long last.

I woke with a stiff neck from being laid back on the office chair. For a few seconds as I came around, I stared at the clock at the bottom of my computer. I'd been out of it for fifty minutes. Swiping my bag off the floor, I took out a bottle of O-neg and downed the contents, giving a satisfied belch at the end. What was happening to me and my life? I had to consider being turned into a vampire along with everything else. I think I was about to have a panic attack.

Instead, I had a small heart attack when a middle-aged woman with long dark hair with a white stripe zapped into the room.

"Jesus Christ, Mother. You can't do that. You're going to spook the baby out of me."

"I detected anxiety in my firstborn. I had to come. What's the matter, sweetheart? Can I help?"

"Yes, you can start by not doing that again, so I manage to stay alive a few years longer."

My mum sat down opposite me. "What's going on, Shelley?"

"I'm stressed. Overloaded. This time last year, the most I had to think about was if I had any clean knickers. Now I'm worrying about being turned into a vampire, birthing a healthy child, keeping everyone in Withernsea alive, and my HUSBAND," I began shouting, "starts decorating the house. Like there isn't enough happening! Now there's dust and mess everywhere and I'm not at the nesting stage, mother, NOT EVEN CLOSE."

"Oh dear. I think your pregnancy hormones have kicked in a little, darling."

"You think?" I spat out as I looked around at the papers that had shot off my desk and were falling all around the room. I'd never had a good handle on my powers mixed with my temper.

"As was," I shouted, and they started to lift up and gather back into piles before they floated back down onto my desk. At least I knew how to rectify my disasters now.

"Is there anything I can do to help?"

I sighed. "Seriously, I doubt it. I'm just fed up is all. My life isn't my own anymore. Bloody Withernsea. I'm just glad the new Satan's on vacation so there might be a little peace around the town."

"No mother's life is their own anyway. Comes with the commitment. Even though I had to give you up for adoption, I never stopped searching for you or trying to put things in place for when I could come back home."

"What if I'm a useless mother? I mean if there's a supernatural crisis in Withernsea I'll have to deal with it won't I? What if my baby hates me?" I started crying.

My mum rummaged in her bag and passed me a tissue. "Try not to cry, honey, because the blood stains."

"What?" I wiped my eyes. Sure enough, my hands were stained in red.

"Jesus, I can't even cry properly now," I wailed, and the papers went flying around the office again.

"As is!" I yelled.

My mum stood up. "Come on, let's go to Jax's."

"But I've gone off coffee. I mean that really is the devil's work, it's got to be. Making me go off coffee and doughnuts is the worst evil I've ever encountered."

"Well, I sure need one. Let's go before I suffer death by a thousand paper cuts. Now come here and let me wipe your eyes because you look like one of those statues that weeps blood. We don't want people stood staring at you praying for miracles."

"I don't mind if they pray for me to be able to drink coffee again," I grumbled, but I let her dab at my face, and then I stood up grabbing my bag and chucking my notepad and pen in it.

Jax's had people queuing out of the door and was packed inside. Kim had mentioned it, but I'd thought she was over-exaggerating again. I looked at the front of the queue at the new barista. He was sexy, but this was a little bit overkill. Surely the women of Withernsea had seen a sexy man before? I certainly had. Theo was gorgeous. Darius was a hunk. Here at Jax's they were acting like sex-starved women at a male strip club.

I mumbled some words so that to me and my mother everyone else was muted and then I magicked another table leaving all the room with the suggestion that it had been there all along.

"You aren't supposed to use your magic for personal gain," Mum said.

"It's for the safety of these people here, or I might kill them all," I snipped.

Mum tilted her head at me. "Pregnancy hormones really are the pits. Right, stay there while I go queue for my drink." She held up a hand. "No more magic, Shelley."

I had to sit there for twenty minutes while she queued, but rather than find it a hassle, it was bliss. With everyone muted, I could watch all their interactions but not get a headache from the noise. I started to realise how much people gave away with their body posture and mannerisms. There were so many hair flicks and smiles in the new barista's direction. I focused in on him. The way the women were in here, I would have thought he was an incubus, but he gave off no supernatural vibe whatsoever. He'd sent in an application form for the agency, and I was in the process of inputting his application. Maybe he really was hotter than the coffee, and my recent marriage had dulled my attraction switch. That and my current condition.

My mum returned and sat in front of me with a coffee and a chocolate doughnut. I had all on not to leap across the table and pull her hair out.

"Pass me your bag," she said.

"What?"

"Stop questioning me and just do it."

She brought out of my bag a flask and a doughnut.

"What on earth?"

"It's a full glamour, you idiot. I'm surprised you didn't think of it before. The flask that to you will taste of Jax's coffee, is in fact your bottle of O-neg and your portion of liver will now taste and look like a doughnut."

Why hadn't I thought of that?

Because I'd been too busy drowning in self-pity, that's why.

"Mum, you're a genius!" I told her as I bit into my doughnut, the chocolate oozing out of the middle. For the first time in days a beaming smile broke across my face.

My mum took a drink of her own coffee and smiled. "Mmmm, I swear this gets better."

"Thanks, Mum. I needed this."

"I know, honey, you basically sent out a mental SOS."

"Did that happen when you were on the astral plane?"

She shook her head. "No. Until you came into your powers, I couldn't locate you at all. They were the worst years of my life and I thank the powers that be every day now that I was returned to your life."

It was hard to believe that my separation from my parents was due to the fact that my dad had left Lucy for Mum, resulting in years in Hell for my father, trapped by Lucy when she was a demon, and my mum stuck on the astral plane. I couldn't equate that Lucy to the one I knew now, and that was probably a good thing. There'd been fault on all sides anyway, and it had cost each of them dearly.

"How is Dad?"

"He's fine, lovely. He's spending a lot of time swimming out at the Caves. Oh, that reminds me, he says everything in the sea is calm, so you don't need to worry about that anyway. Your father's happy to keep an eye on the water."

"You mean to tell me I have the whole sea to govern as well?"

"Well, of course. You're taking over the rule from your father. At some point we'll need to have a coronation and that will be one ceremony on land and another under the water so you can meet your subjects. You'll be their queen."

I necked the coffee. Okay maybe it wasn't able to give me the same effect with it being a glamour, but the blood gave me a buzz and it stopped me from screaming out loud while my mouth was full of liquid.

I picked up my bag and rummaged inside until I found my pen. I placed that and my notebook on the table and added to my list.

Rule the seas of Withernsea and meet supernatural water creatures.
Then for dramatic effect I added in capital letters.
HAVE A NERVOUS BREAKDOWN.

My mother grabbed the notepad and looked down the list. "Oh, honey. Why haven't you told me about all this? I could have helped you. A problem shared is a problem halved after all."

"Not unless you're taking on half my to-do list," I grumbled.

"Let's have a look and see if there's anything I can do," she said, completely ignoring me. I vowed to always listen to my child and attend to their every whim right there and then.

"This isn't a to-do list. It's just a list. We can scratch out half the things on it," she said, picking up my pen.

"Right, 'discover supernaturals exist'. Yes, you discovered it and what? How is that a problem? It's helped you double your business, hasn't it?"

"Well, yes."

"Right, I'm crossing that off. 'Meet and fall in love with a 126-year-old vampire.' Oh you're madly in love, oh how life sucks. Well, your husband does, at your neck. I'm crossing that off." She struck through my writing. "'Discover your mother is a witch. Find out you have witch powers. Discover father is a wyvern'. Yes, undoubtedly this will take some getting used to, along with the next one about your powers and being the current ruler of Withernsea. But we are here to help you now. Before you didn't have your parents around you, so think of it as a good thing that you're reunited with your mother and father."

She took a sip of coffee. "'Be informed your future child shall be the most powerful ruler of Withernsea which started out as a place called Wyvernsea'. You have the advantage of knowing your baby's future. What about mums who don't know their future treasured offspring will grow up to be a serial killer, or a thief? Yours will be powerful and held in high esteem by the community. Boo hoo."

My mother had a point. I was being a mardy arse, wasn't I? I took the pen off her and scratched a couple of things off the list.

~~Marry the vampire.~~
Discover the ghost of your vampire husband's mother lives in your new home.
~~Have to defeat Satan.~~
~~Find out you're pregnant.~~
Vampire husband decides this is a good time to redecorate and turn the farm into a Bed and Breakfast.

"'Discover the ghost of your vampire husband's mother lives in your new home'. Well, a lot of women have the mother-in-law from hell, yours is just floating around earth, be thankful. You've a permanent babysitter on hand, and she can help with the bed and breakfast."

"I don't think seeing a ghost is going to help business much."

"Shelley, make it supernaturals only. It won't hurt to suggest to human enquirers that you're full. I know Theo's excited about his new business venture, and it must be difficult for him to get his teeth into something that excites him after 127 years on earth. Gosh, that came out wrong, didn't it?" she said as we both burst into guffaws of laughter.

"Aw thanks, Mum. I've been ruminating about things that are in the past and things in the future that are beyond my control. Not only have you helped me with that, but you even sorted my coffee and doughnut problem. I love you, Mum. You're amazing." It was the first time I'd said the words to her since I'd found out who she was and had started the process of getting to know her.

I watched as my mum's face crumpled and she began to sob.

"I'm sorry I had to leave you, Shelley. It was the biggest mistake of my life and I suffered every day."

"It's in the past, Mum. Let's just enjoy the here and now, shall we? That's what I'm going to do from now on," I said, and then we heard the coffee shop door burst open and a voice screamed, "We're all doomed."

Chapter 7

Shelley

My jaw dropped open as Ebony almost fell through the doorway before she practically bounced off the nearest table. My mum and I ran towards her holding a side of her each, and steered her to our table where I made another chair subtly appear and plopped her onto it. This chair had arms so she couldn't fall off, given that she was rip-roaringly drunk.

"Ebony, how much vodka have you had?" I whisper-hissed.

"I don't remember. I don't remember anything." Her eyes went wide. "I got to the boutique this morning for eight, and then it's all blank, and my visions have stopped."

"Well, duh, isn't that why you have all the vodka?"

Her hands flailed around her face. "I drink to lessen them, but they've gone. My mama always said if they went then that meant major evil was around. I can't protect people right now with no visions. What if you all die?"

Ebony then headbutted the table as she passed clean out.

Jax came running over. My mute spell had dropped the minute I'd started talking to Ebony, and I was more than aware of the gossip and stares happening around us. I picked up my mobile phone.

"Kim? Stop tidying, we have an emergency at Jax's. No, the coffee hasn't run out. It's Ebony, there's something wrong with her. Can you or Lucy mind her boutique? Lock the office up and get down here will you, quick as you can?"

I carefully lifted my friend's head up to make sure she was just passed out and hadn't broken her nose or anything on her face's date with the tabletop.

"Can you get some really strong coffee for her, Jax?"

"Sure, coming right up." Jax went over to some customers seated on a sofa. After she'd talked to them, they got up and came over to us, a look of concern on their faces.

"We're gonna help you move your friend over to the sofa, then she can lie down with her feet up," one of them said. "We can move to your table."

"Thanks so much," I said, and I went to help move Ebony.

"Hold it right there! You shouldn't lift anything in your condition," yelled my gobshite best friend from the doorway. She then realised she'd announced my unannounced pregnancy to half the female population of Withernsea. "With your bad back," she shouted louder. "The doctor said you weren't to move anything with your BAD BACK."

"If only I had Ebony's foresight, I could mute your damn mouth," I said to Kim as she came over. At least she went to the gym and was good at helping move the dead weight of our friend.

Finally, after some huffing and puffing, Ebony was laid on the sofa with her feet elevated above her head. She was starting to come around and started groaning. On my mother's advice, we murmured a spell suggesting that the other customers in the cafe had had enough coffee and cake and they gathered their coats and left.

"Oh dear, Ebony's drama has scared off my customers. I hope they come back," Jax said, unaware that anyone in Withernsea had supernatural powers.

"I'm sure they'll be back soon. At least it gives you a chance to get cleared up and have a breather."

"Why am I thinking about my customers? It's Ebony I should be worried about." She shouted over to Seth. "While it's quiet, why don't you take a break, Seth?"

He removed his apron and came around from the back of the counter. "Is there anything I can do? I'm sorry I couldn't help move her, but I was stuck behind the counter serving." He looked around. "It's strange how everyone left like that. Can I help at all?"

"We're okay here, Seth. Thank you. Either get your break or if you could help by tidying up…" Jax said.

"I'll clear up."

"I'll help you," my mum told him.

"Thanks, Margret," Jax said. "Help yourself to anything from behind the counter."

"Is Seth included?" Kim smirked.

"If you fancy a sandwich or a bun or anything," Jax added.

I took a baby wipe out of my bag and started wiping Ebony's brow with it.

"Aww, look at you, you're already being all…"

I glared at Kim.

"Efficient." She exhaled. "You are so, so, efficient."

Ebony continued to come around, and we gave her some sips of water and then strong coffee. I decided she wasn't in a fit state to stay by herself back home. "Listen, we're going to stay here for a while. Just here on the sofa and then when it gets to four o'clock, I will call Theo and ask him to take us to mine."

Ebony started to protest.

"No. You're coming to our house and that's that, until we work out you're okay. We've loads of room. I'm not leaving you on your own until your visions are back. You can't carry on like this anyway," I said looking at her. "I'm going to ring the *doctor*." I emphasised the word doctor so that Ebony knew I meant the one who helped supes.

"Frankie," Ebony said. "Frankie might be able to help me."

"Okay, we'll call Frankie. Again, we'll have to wait until later." Frankie used to be a physician at the local hospital before he became a vampire, so as long as we waited until he was awake, he could well be able to help Ebony.

I looked at my friend. To say she was dark skinned she looked pale. I was so used to her dramatic behaviour I'd never really stopped to think about what it was doing to her mental and physical health. There must be something I could do to help her live with her visions because from what I'd seen today, if not, they were going to slowly kill her.

Theo had to use his car rather than whizz here by vampire super speed. Luckily, we didn't live too far away. Ebony had spent most of the afternoon sleeping. Theo walked in and picked her up like she weighed the same as a Barbie doll. "Subtle, husband, subtle," I whispered, knowing his vampire hearing would pick it up. He started to act like he was struggling with her weight.

"Let's get you to the car," he said. Then he stood stock still and stared at Seth. "I don't believe we've met," he said, and no word of a lie, while he was holding my friend, he let one hand go and held his other out to Seth. God help me.

"Seth Whittaker," Seth said, shaking his hand. "I'm the new barista."

"Oh, my wife didn't mention there was a new barista. Good to meet you," Theo said, and then he stared into Seth's eyes. "You will never find my wife attractive. When you see her, you will think of your grandmother naked."

"Theo!" I yelled.

Seth was staring into space as the compelling took place. I knew as soon as it had worked because he glanced over to us and then heaved. Bloody insecure vampire husbands.

"Let's get out of here before someone gets hurt, and I mean you," I yelled at Theo. He put his hand back on Ebony and pretended to struggle again.

"Take that image out of Seth's mind." I mimed to my mum, who nodded. Otherwise, poor Seth was going to be a basketcase.

˜

When we got back to the farm, Mary, Theo's mother, greeted us. Mary was a ghost but could solidify while ever she could summon the energy. "Who have we here?" she asked. "And I don't think drugging people is the way to get boarders."

"It's my friend Ebony. She's not feeling well, so I've brought her here in order that we can take care of her."

"Oh, the poor love. I'll try to put the kettle on." Mary bustled off.

"Come on, Ebony, let's get you settled on the sofa." Theo helped me get her there and then I sent him to the kitchen to help his mum to make a lot of black coffee.

Ebony looked up at me from the sofa. "I'm sorry, Shelley, for causing all this trouble. I panicked when my visions went."

"It's probably that you're exhausted, Ebs. I really do think we need to find a way other than vodka for you to deal. Now just lay back for a moment while I phone Frankie, okay?"

She nodded. I settled a couple of cushions underneath her head and neck, and then she closed her eyes again. I took the opportunity to call for extra assistance.

"Frankie, I need your help."

"Anytime, lovely. What can I do for you?"

"Can you come over to the farm? Ebony is having a lot of trouble handling her visions and now she says they've disappeared. She turned up to Jax's so drunk she was knocking furniture over."

"Oh shit. And you say the visions have left her?"

"Yeah."

"Okay, babes. Give me some time to look into that and then I'll come over. It could be late."

"That doesn't matter." Since I'd been drinking blood, I'd found my body clock was changing, and I was going to bed and getting up later. It was giving me a taste of what would probably happen when I was turned.

I ended the call and sighed. I hoped we could help her.

"Wife. You need to rest now for an hour. It's been a stressful afternoon for you. Ebony is asleep and mum is looking after her." Theo grabbed my hand and pulled me in the direction of the stairs.

"I'm wide awake, Theo. I don't need a rest," I complained.

"Even better," Theo said, continuing to pull on my hand.

"I need to look after my friend."

Mary floated out into the hallway. "Love, go upstairs, because you know what men are like when they've got the horn on; can't leave us alone until they're spent. I'm okay here. Listen, I'll make a ghostly wail outside your room if you're needed. I need to practice it as when the Bed and Breakfast is open, I'm going to start haunting the customers. Ghost sightings can bring in good trade."

I placed a hand on my temple. She was going to haunt the customers? It was definitely a good idea to stick with boarding supernaturals only, or the incidences of death by heart attack at our establishment could be significantly higher than average amongst other B&Bs in the area.

She floated back off, and I looked at my husband. "You have the horn, huh?"

"I fear if I wasn't already dead the need would kill me. It's like my groin is trying to burst out like the creatures in that film *Alien*."

"Well, I guess you'd better take me upstairs then."

. . .

Theo wasn't joking. He quickly stripped off his trousers and his cock sprung out like a jack in a box. After shedding the rest of his clothes at vamp speed he helped me out of the rest of mine.

"I cannot wait to be sunk inside your depths," he announced, making the corner of my mouth turn up in amusement. Sometimes it took some getting used to that my husband was 127.

He walked over to our chest of drawers and opening the top one pulled out a pair of handcuffs.

"Theo! What are you up to, you filthy boy?"

"I have been acquainting myself with that series all you women like, so lie on the bed. Now. Do as you're told."

Hmmm, not quite sure 'do as you're told' was the usual Dom command, but my pussy went slick anyway at the thought of a little playtime, so I climbed onto the bed.

Theo climbed alongside me and leaning over, he grabbed my wrist and clicked a cuff around it, fastening the other to a bedpost at the top of the bed.

"I could only get one pair and I need to secure your other wrist. Ah, my tie," he said, climbing off the bed and going through his discarded clothes. He restrained my other wrist and then sat at my feet.

"Oh, lovely wife. What shall I do to you now?" He winked.

He licked, nibbled, and kissed from my feet all the way up to near my core. His cool touch set my body to goose bump and by the time his cool tongue met my clit I was in a frenzy of need. "Oh my god, yes."

My back arched, and the chain rattled on one wrist while the tie tightened on the other.

Theo continued to lick me and suck on me while his right hand travelled upwards to tease my nipples, which pebbled under his touch.

"Please, Theo. I need you." I was desperate to have him inside me.

"If it wasn't for our guest, I would keep you in here all evening. Alas, I suppose I should move things along." He sighed, climbing up my body and rubbing along my slit with the tip of his hard dick. I spread my legs wider, and he pushed inside.

"Ooohhh, yes, yes."

Theo pushed deeper, and I raised my hips matching him thrust for thrust. Being pregnant was making me even more horny than I usually was for my sexy husband. I hoped he was going to bite my neck because that made me come so hard I'd see stars. He nuzzled my neck, and I nuzzled him back.

And as we came together, the bite was amazing. My pussy climaxed so hard around Theo's cock I was surprised it didn't cut off his circulation.

Then Theo pushed me back away from him and withdrew, feeling at his neck, a look of horror on his face.

He pulled his hand away, and I saw blood on his fingertips. My vision travelled to his neck where I saw puncture wounds. My mouth felt funny and as I ran my tongue around it, I felt the two protrusions.

I had fangs?

I. HAD. FANGS.

I tried to feel my teeth with my hands but of course my arms were restrained.

"Whath the fuck isth happening, Theo? Why do I haveth fangs?"

"You bit me. You bit me!" Theo said. "How can you have fangs?"

"Justh geth me outh these cuffths." I was beginning to panic now.

Theo undid the tie and then looked at the handcuffs and froze.

"Whath?" I glared at him. "Whath up? Leth me go."

"Erm, when I borrowed the handcuffs, I forgot to get the keys." Theo looked at the floor while biting on his lip. Then feeling blood running down his neck, he licked his finger and ran it over the puncture wounds sealing them.

"Then cuth them off or go backth to the shop."

"I didn't get them from a shop. I kind of knew Darius wasn't working and so I just 'popped' there for a second to borrow them."

"They're Dariusth?"

Theo looked sheepish.

"Didth he know you borroweth them?"

"I was going to take them straight back."

I tried to demonstrate my frustration by letting my head flop back against the pillows. Here I was, handcuffed to the bed by a were shifter policeman's handcuffs while I seemed to have grown fangs, and in the meantime, there was a guest downstairs who needed my help.

"Go geth them," I screamed.

Chapter 8

Kim

Lucy was running Ebony's shop until closing which left me, Seth, and Margret helping Jax to cope with the swarm of people who descended once Shelley and Theo had taken Ebony home. At closing time, we were happy to swing the open/closed sign around and lock the door.

"Jax, you'll need some more staff at this rate."

"I know." She stretched out her body and rolled her neck. "It's killing me. I just don't know what's caused it."

"There's probably been a mention in a magazine or on Twitter or something," Seth suggested. "These things happen and go viral. It'll settle down in a day or two, I'm sure."

"I wish I knew the future." Jax sucked on her top lip. "If I knew it was going to stay busy, I'd hire, but I don't want to do that if it might stop. Trust Ebony's visions to stop now. I could have asked her to read my palm."

"Well, I'm not going anywhere," Seth said.

"You've been amazing, but now go home." She pushed him towards the door, or rather she tried to, but her five-foot waif-like frame versus his six-foot muscular one meant he didn't move. In fact, if he hadn't been looking, he probably would have thought a fly had landed on him.

"I'd better get back. Dylan will be wondering where I am." Margret bid us goodbye and left.

"I'm just going to ring and see how Ebony's doing," I told the other two.

It rang a few times and then a faint voice came onto the line. "Helllooooo."

"Mary? It's Kim. Is Shelley or Theo there?"

"No, lovey, they're in bed. Can I help you at all? You'll have to be quick though, I keep fading in and out."

I shook my head then realised she couldn't see me.

"In bed? What about Ebony?"

"She's fast asleep on the sofa and I'm keeping an eye on her. My son came home acting very possessive and whisked Shelley upstairs. I don't know what happened while they were out, but I'm surprised he wasn't beating his chest or dragging her around by her hair. He'd gone all caveman."

I laughed knowing he'd met Seth.

"Okay, as long as everything seems settled. I'm making my way home now as I need to get ready to go out later. Tell Shelley to call my mobile if she needs me."

"Will do."

"Oh." Seth had puckered up his delectable lips and scrunched up his nose. "I was going to see if you wanted to come for a quick drink? Only I'm knackered and could sink a pint. I didn't fancy being there on my own."

I had to admit that with the nerves hitting my body about my upcoming date with Darius, a drink was exactly what I needed. One couldn't hurt, could it?

"Sounds good to me. Let's go. I'll take you to The Marine. Have you been there yet?"

"No."

We nodded at Jax. "Do you fancy a drink, Jax?" I asked her.

"Nah, I'm buggered. I want my sofa. Enjoy yourselves you two. Have a drink for me."

~

It was a ten-minute walk to the pub which gave me a chance to try to get to know Seth better. I told myself it would help me find him a date, but really, I was just a nosy bitch.

"Are you from Withernsea? I don't recall seeing you around here?" *And I would have because you're one hot fucker.*

"No, I was born in Hull. I just decided a couple of weeks ago that I was fed up and fancied a change. I was sick of going to

Cleethorpes, so I looked what other beaches were close and chose this one. Thought I'd do a few months casual work and then go back to Hull and my mundane life."

"I bet your life isn't really mundane."

"I'm an assistant manager at a supermarket. Or rather I was before I handed in my notice and came here. They've promised me a job on return but said it will be most likely back on the shop floor. I can't seem to care." He looked down at me. "How about you?"

"Lived here all my life. Met Shelley when we went speed dating. We were supposed to find dates, but I found a best friend instead. Been working at the dating agency now for almost a year and a half. Got a promotion to run..." I was about to say the supernatural side. Shit, my mouth had been trying to get me in trouble all day. "To help run the agency with Shelley, now she's all married. Plus, the agency has got a lot busier of late. So that's it. I live in a house on my own and at the moment I'm happy that way. You said you were divorced?"

"Yes. I'm renting a flat above a chippy right now. I'm going to get fat with a chippy below me, and a job at a coffee shop with the best buns I've ever tasted."

I looked over his buff body and the thought of tasting his buns crossed my mind. The firm ones packed inside the arse of his jeans. I really needed to calm my libido. Jeez, I'd bet I was ovulating. I was like a bitch on heat when I was halfway through my cycle. I'd need to be careful not to try to mount Darius when I saw him.

"Yes, I agree. Jax has the best buns and the best coffee. If she ever tries to shut up shop, you'll find me on the nearest bridge."

We reached the pub and went inside. Luckily there were a few spare tables. Seth chose one near a window and we sat down. "What would you like to drink?"

"Erm, half a beer please. You choose which one, they have a lot of guest beers on here."

He nodded and went to the bar.

Returning with my half pint and a pint for himself, he sat down opposite me. He picked up his glass and chinked it against mine. "Cheers," he said.

"Cheers," I replied.

He picked up a food menu. "If you want to eat here, it's my treat. I've nothing to rush home for."

"Actually, I'm going out," I told him.

"Oh," he said, placing his menu down on the table. "Anywhere nice?"

I was about to tell him about my dinner date when my phone buzzed with a text notification. Opening my bag, I rooted around, upending tissues, pens, my purse, a small hand gel, and some painkillers. I needed one of those handbag compartment things to help organise me, I thought, and then realised that there was one right at the very bottom of the bag, and I'd just been throwing things on top of it. Eventually, I located my mobile phone underneath it and lifted it out.

Darius: *An emergency has come up, so I can't make it. I'll be in touch.*

I sighed. Huh, I'd bet there was no such emergency, and he was just putting me off. When would I get it into my thick head that he wasn't interested anymore? What I needed was a nice human male to date, and oh look, here was one right in front of me.

"My plans are cancelled, so if the offer of dinner is still on, then yes, I'd love to stay and eat."

"Great." Seth put his hand on top of mine. "Not that your plans have fallen through, but that you can stay for dinner." He passed me a copy of the menu. "My treat."

"No, I'll pay my own way," I told him.

"Not a chance. Look you get them next time."

Next time?

I sat back, placing my mobile phone back in my bag, and picked up my drink. "I think I'll have a burger and fries. You'd better get a salad though, fat boy."

He tilted his head, raised an eyebrow and then slowly lifted his t-shirt showing me a six pack, then he rippled his abdomen.

I needed to pour my drink over my head to cool me down.

"Think I'm okay a bit yet," he said, winking, then he went to the bar.

I watched his buns move.

Fuck Darius. I was moving on.

The evening was fun, and we caught a taxi home, calling at my house first.

"Just a moment," Seth said to the taxi driver, and he ran around my side and opened the door for me.

"How very gentlemanly of you," I said.

"I do my best," he replied. "On a first date anyway. Can't promise to be so gentlemanly on a second."

I looked up at him. "Is that what this was? A date?"

"We spent time together and shared food." Seth shrugged as he followed me up the path to my door.

"I do that with my friends. I'm not dating them."

Then I wasn't speaking anymore because my lips were otherwise engaged. Seth's warm mouth met my own in a sweet, chaste kiss.

"Thank you for a lovely evening," he said, walking backwards down the path. "And we kissed, so I think that most definitely makes it a date."

I watched as he climbed back inside the taxi, and it drove away. I wasn't sure what I felt about the evening. Mainly as I was supposed to be out with Darius, not Seth, and I'd thought we were just grabbing a bite to eat as mates. Now I seemed to have a new boyfriend. Shelley was going to murder me for dating another guy off our own books. But was I actually dating him? I needed some time to think about everything. My mind was confused.

And then I saw him, standing across the street.

Darius.

He shook his head at me. He must have seen everything.

"Darius, wait!" I yelled, running down the path.

But he was a were, and even without shifting, he could still outrun me by a mile. He was gone before I'd reached the edge of the path, leaving me with nothing but the fading roar of a motorbike engine.

There was no wonder Ebony was losing her mind with my antics. I was driving myself crazy.

Chapter 9

Darius

A few hours earlier...

Alyssa kept smiling at me from her position on the sofa as I paced around the floor.

"What time are you meeting her?"

"Who?"

"Your date?"

"Who says I have a date?" I shrugged my shoulders.

"You've shaved, smell to high heaven of Lynx, you're in your favourite jeans, and you can't stand still."

She tilted her head at me. "Your date. It's with Kim, isn't it? That's why you're in such a state."

"I am not in a state," I growled.

"What time are you meeting her?" she asked again.

"Eight at Hanifs."

"Yeah, boy." She stood up and raised her hand for a high five. Teenagers were so frikking weird.

"Why are you so interested in my love life?"

"Cos when it comes to you getting a mate it means Mum stops looking at what I'm doing."

I narrowed my eyes. "And what are you doing?"

She gave a big fake smile. "Nothing at all, big brother. I'm being my angelic self and behaving perfectly."

I placed my palm to my face and rubbed at my eyes. "I can't think about what you're up to right now."

"Exactly." She mimed a mike drop and said the word, "Boom."

I started pacing again, then found her in front of me staring at me again.

"What *now*, Alyssa?"

"Undo your top button. You look too formal on top. Now roll up your sleeves." She stood back appraising me. "That's better. Now take your hair out of that man bun. That's so last year. In fact, we have two hours before your date and time to fix it. Let's see if Zara is free to cut it."

"I'm ready. The man bun lives another day. Now sod off and leave me alone."

Alyssa rolled her eyes. "If you've been dreaming about her undoing your hair and running her hands through it, I'm gonna barf."

"Out."

"It's my living room as well as yours, dufus."

My phone ringing stopped further arguments. Theo's name flashed up on the screen.

"Hey, pal. How's it going?"

"I've got an emergency. I need your help."

My posture stiffened. "Police help, or friend help?"

"Erm…"

"Theo, tell me. I can't help unless I know."

There was a pause. "Alas, I feel this may affect our future friendship, and your trust in me."

"You've killed someone, haven't you?"

"No."

"There's been a murder? Can I come, can I come? Is there lots of blood? I watch *Game of Thrones*. I promise I'll be quiet."

"Just a minute," I said down the phone, then I turned to my sister. "There hasn't been a murder. Now go and have underage sex or drink too much and just get from under my feet."

"Okay, bro. Very open-minded of you. I'll be sure to tell Ma I had your permission when I'm a barefoot, preggo lush."

My mind was going to explode soon between delinquent sisters, panicked friends, and my upcoming date. I decided to leave my sister in the living room and head up to my own room.

"Right, Theo. I'm back. You need to tell me what's going on."

"Verily, I may have happened upon your handcuffs, looked after them for a time and forgotten the key."

All of a sudden it became crystal clear.

"You rogue. Well I never, Theo Landry. We'll talk about the fact you went through my belongings without asking later. Right now, on a scale of one to ten, how mad is Shelley?"

"Three thousand and twenty-six, as a rough estimate."

"I'm on my way."

⁓

When I arrived at the farm, Theo greeted me at the door looking even paler than his usual vampire self if that were at all possible.

He clasped his hands in front of him. "Before you enter, you need to be apprised of the full situation."

"Okay..."

"There is a seer on the sofa. She's hungover because she has lost her visions."

"Right."

"My mum is looking after her. Now you haven't met my mother yet, but I think she will be making herself known soon enough. She's currently watching over Ebony."

"Okay."

"Frankie and Margret are both on their way over to help with another delicate matter. I would be grateful for your opinion on whether I free my beloved wife now or later."

"Why would you not free her now?"

"Please follow me upstairs," he said and began to walk up the first step.

"Erm, not sure about coming into your chamber, Theo. Isn't your missus kinda tied up?"

"I have put a robe around her. Only her wrists and ankles are on show, and... well, her mouth."

"Come on then." I checked my watch. I was due to meet Kim in an hour, so the sooner I was out of here the better.

When I walked into their room, it was like a scene from a horror movie. Shelley was pulling at her handcuffed wrist, her mouth covered in red blood, and fuck, were they fangs? She actually hissed as Theo walked in the room.

"Get me out of these handcuffs now, you bastard. Oh my god, you brought Darius? How am I supposed to show my face in front of him again, you utter twat?"

"Wife, you aren't lisping anymore. Are you getting used to your teeth?"

"Bite me, you motherfucker."

The image of a woman floated into the room before solidifying in front of me. I blinked twice, and when I opened my eyes, there was a woman dressed in a long white gown, with dark hair in a bun standing in front of me.

"I assure you there was none of that going on between me and my son, young lady." She stopped in front of me and froze in place, her mouth open. Her image trembled and then she moved and dropped to a curtsy in front of me. Looking up from under her lashes she spoke. "I don't believe we have met. I'm Mary. Could I be of assistance to you at all? A drink perhaps, or I could launder your clothes?"

"My clothes are clean."

"We could dirty them?" She giggled.

"Mother, behave yourself," Theo shouted.

Mother!

"I do apologise. She's been dead a long time and so hasn't seen many men in quite some years."

"Or had sex," Mary added.

Theo held his forehead. "On the rare occasion I bring a male to the house, she gets a little... excitable."

Mary winked at me and did a 'call me' mime.

"Mother, we already have been blacklisted from Domino's Pizza delivery and they'll no longer deliver newspapers to the house. Could you please gather yourself?"

Mary huffed. "I'll go back to Ebony."

"Are you all quite finished?" spat Shelley, a few drops of blood splattering from her mouth. "Only I could use some help over here."

"Do you see my predicament now?" Theo asked. "Do I keep her restrained until her mother arrives? She's very volatile and unpredictable."

"Unfasten me, you wanker, or I'll cut off your balls when I eventually get free."

I stepped forward. "Shelley. Shelley, are you in there?"

She gave me the side-eye. "Where else would I be, Darius?"

"Oh," I said, surprised. "I thought you were, well, possessed."

Theo sighed. "No, this is just my wife in a bad mood."

"Shelley, I will undo the cuffs, but only if you promise that no violence will occur. Your wrists will be numb anyway. While I do that, Theo, get some warm water and a flannel so Shelley can clean her mouth."

Theo nodded rather enthusiastically at being able to leave the room.

I walked to the right-hand side of the bed and undid the cuff from her wrist. She pulled her arm towards her and rubbed it frantically.

"My husband is an idiot."

"He is, a total idiot, but it's because he's blinded with love for you. The dingbat nicked my handcuffs to please you. Now I'm gonna be having words about his invasion of my space, but I know he would never have done anything like that a year ago. He's just trying to please you."

Shelley folded her arms over herself and exhaled.

"I suppose."

"Look, when I eventually find my mate, I will make acts toward her that are out of nature. I will cook for her when I have hardly ever been in a kitchen in my life because to feed our mate is something we are duty bound to do. Once she is my mate, I will learn to cook then I can cherish her when she's with cub."

Shelley fastened her gaze on mine. She was calming down, but her body posture was still taut. I was used to dealing with unpredictable behaviour in my line of work. If she launched, she'd be cuffed again, and it wouldn't be for sexy times. "Aren't you meeting my friend tonight?"

I looked at my watch. "Shit. Shit. I need to get out of here."

Shelley put a hand on her stomach. "Oh God, I don't feel good."

I rushed to her side. "Is it the baby?"

And then she puked. Red spray all across my shirt and jeans.

At that moment, Theo walked in with a flannel and a small bowl of water. Shelley was looking mortified, and I was trying not to be sick myself.

"Oh, I'll be back again in a moment... with a bucket." Theo announced, leaving the room once more.

And that's how I found myself sat with a towel wrapped around me in a guest room, while Theo laundered my clothes as nothing of his would fit my wide frame. I texted Kim to cancel, knowing there was no way my clothes would be ready on time. It would just have to be rescheduled; it couldn't be helped. I put that it was an emergency, so she'd know I wasn't messing her around. She knew I worked in law enforcement. She'd think it was that. I was bitterly disappointed. I'd wanted to clear the air and take her on a date, see if she really was the woman I'd like to eventually make my mate.

In the meantime, I kept having Mary pop in to 'See if I was alright'. Trouble was she never looked at my face when she said it. She might only look in her thirties, but she was still my friend's mother, ghost or not. It was weird. I think Shelley or Kim needed to find a date for her. There must be other unsettled ghosts around the place.

While I waited for my clothes, I heard voices from downstairs and presumed Frankie or Margret had arrived to see what to do about Shelley and the appearance of fangs. I was in no rush to go say hi. The further away I was from Shelley's pregnant 'Mouth Vesuvius', the better. I'd just stay in this guest room and lament my lost date.

Part of me wondered if it was a sign. Before Ebony's predictions, I'd thought the idea of fate was a bag of shit, but when Ebony started telling me Kim was my destiny, I'd wanted to believe it. I'd been hooked on the woman since I first set eyes on her, despite the fact she was cocky as fuck. You see, I felt it was surface bravado and that underneath there were layers to get through to find the real Kim. I wanted to peel back those layers and peel off her clothes.

"Ooops." Mary giggled, and I realised my thoughts had produced a hard-on which was tenting the towel.

Fuck my life.

⁓

When my clothes had finally been returned, and I'd dressed again, I headed down to the living room. It was a benefit that the room was large because Shelley, Theo, Margret, Ebony, and Frankie were sat in there, and now there was me and Mary to add to the party.

"Mother. You're fading. Go rest," Theo ordered.

"Yes, love. I was just about to say goodnight. It's been a busy day. Goodnight all."

"Thank you for caring for me when I was indisposed," Ebony said in her cut-glass accent.

"Not a problem at all, lovey. I hope they get you all sorted. Okay people, I'm out of here. I look forward to seeing you all again under better circumstances. You too, big boy."

I felt my face burn.

"Darius is fated to end up with Kim. It's been seen in Ebony's visions. Sorry, Mary," Shelley told her while wearing a sympathetic look. It appeared her fangs had gone.

"Oh. What a shame. I'll just have to order some more takeaways and see who turns up," she said and then she disappeared.

"She burned herself out," Shelley said in explanation. "She'll be back in a few hours."

"I must apologise for my mother's behaviour. It is most unusual. She was never like this in life."

"Yeah, her death gave her a new lease of life. Weird or what?" Shelley said to him.

"Alas, no one should have to witness their mother trying to flirt with their friends."

"Have we found anything out about your fangs, or why Ebony's visions have stopped?"

Frankie stood up from the sofa and began pacing. "Shelley's fangs are easily explained. It's an anomaly. She's not turning into a vampire. It's the fact she's carrying a part-vampire child. The child is thirsty for blood and so it has caused a temporary genetic change that means Shelley can grow fangs in order to procure the blood. Obviously, she needs to be careful that pregnancy cravings don't cause her to drain anyone. If she increases her intake, the cravings will be kept at bay, and everything should be fine. Once the baby is born, Shelley will no longer grow fangs. Of course, she's considering been turned soon anyway, but we'll cross that bridge when we come to it. For now, mother and baby are doing well."

"And Ebony?"

"No one knows." Ebony looked up at me. "I shouldn't have lost them. I thought it meant I might die, but Frankie says that's a myth, that seers don't lose their visions, unless someone is doing this deliberately to me."

"So someone could be trying to block them?"

"Yes. But I don't know who or why. Unless something happens to reveal if that's the case, there's nothing I can do. In the meantime, I shall take a recuperative break. It will be nice to be sober for a time. I'm having a visions and vodka detox."

"Frankie and I are going to research if there's some kind of spell or potion we can make so that Ebony no longer has to reach for the vodka. It's not healthy and they're preventing Ebony from having a life of her own." Shelley reached across to Ebony and placed a hand on her arm. "I've been a crap friend. I'd not thought about the fact that you'd not been able to rest and had been relying more and more on alcohol."

"Oh, darling. It's not your fault. That's the life of a seer. It's a fact that many do not live until old age. Suicide rates are high in my kind."

"That's not happening to you, Ebs. No way."

"Right, so we think there could be someone in Withernsea tampering with your visions? Putting up a block?"

"It's a possibility." Frankie nodded.

"I'll do some investigating. See if there's anyone new to the area who's been in close proximity to Ebony. I'll open a 'black file' police report."

Frankie gasped. "What has her ethnicity to do with this? I did not have you for a racist, Darius Wild."

Ebony burst out laughing. "It's what the supernatural cases are called, Frankie. Darius has to be careful being around human colleagues."

"Oh." Frankie looked sheepish.

Ebony stood and hugged him. "Thank you for looking out for me. It's much appreciated."

White feathers rained down over them both and the next minute Lucy appeared in the room. "Hey all. I've been sent here, so you must be talking about something connected with my earth angel job. Care to enlighten me?"

"Long story short. I grew fangs, but it's because of the baby. Ebony's visions are blocked and that could be because someone is interfering with them."

"Oh they are," Lucy said, perching on a sofa arm.

"Pardon?" we all said at once.

"It would be helpful if you could explain what's going on?" I told her.

She shrugged her shoulders. "Sorry, no can do. Angel vows. I'm on it though, you'll just all have to trust me."

Trust the recent manager of Hell?

That was a new one.

Hate, Date, Or Mate?

This lot had exhausted me and the fact my date with Kim had been postponed itched at my skin. I looked at my watch. It was half past ten. I decided to call around to see her. Just to explain I'd been with her friends and that I wasn't playing games. Enough of that had gone on between us. It was time for honesty. I said goodbye to everyone, got on my motorcycle, and drove down to her house. My bike was powerful and made a lot of noise, so being considerate, I parked it at the end of the estate and walked down. There was a taxi outside the front of her house with its engine running and as I walked closer, I saw that Kim was standing outside her house—with another man. On closer inspection, I saw it was the new guy from the coffee shop. Huh, she didn't waste any time. And then he kissed her. No more than a quick brush against her lips, but he kissed my mate. I felt my wolf churn inside me and had to resist the change as my body trembled with the urge to shift. He got in the taxi, and it passed me as I stood on the pavement. As her eyes watched the taxi move away, I noted the moment she saw me standing there. She froze.

"Darius," she shouted.

I couldn't fight my change any longer. My wolf thrashed and twisted inside me to get free. Instead, I ran, jumped on my bike and sped away for the woods. I needed to let loose with my animal. There was no way I wanted my human thoughts right now. I wanted to tear the ground up beneath my feet, and howl until every bit of the frustration had left me.

Chapter 10

Kim

I'd not slept well. My mind churning with thoughts of yesterday. I'd decided against texting Darius or trying to call him. There was only seeing him face-to-face now that could sort out this mess. Even worse, despite my tiredness, my day would be free of Jax's coffee, because there was no way I was stepping foot in there. The last person I wanted to see was Seth. Not today.

Seth was lovely, but he was a potential friend. His kiss had produced nothing more than a warm sensation against my lips; it certainly hadn't spread that warmth down to my core. Whereas seeing Darius had made my heart almost thud through my chest. I sat for a moment with my head in my hands. Then I pulled myself together, made a flask of instant coffee, pulling a face throughout, and then I grabbed my handbag and set off to work.

Giggles came out of Lucy's office and I could hear Frankie mumbling. What was he doing out in the daytime? It went against his body clock which could make vampires feel really ill. Squeals erupted. Oh for God's sake, what were her and Frankie doing in there? Okay, it was nothing I'd not done with him myself in my own office in the past, but come on. Have some respect for the ex. We'd only been fuck buddies, so how did I term myself. Did ex work if you'd not been a girlfriend? Maybe now I was a no-fucks-buddy? I wish I gave no fucks certainly, about anything right now. Whatever was affecting Ebony's mind, I could do with a dose of it.

I wandered through to Shelley's office where I saw her drinking a large coffee with a flushed face.

"Hey, you look better. And you're back on the dark stuff."

She shook her head. "No, it's a glamour." She shook it off to show me a glass of O-neg, then placed it back on. "It was my mum's idea. Don't know how I'd not thought of it. I'm drinking blood but I have it looking and tasting like coffee."

"Now I know why your cheeks are pink. I thought it might have all been down to your randy husband." Shelley's brow creased. "I called you yesterday, but Mary said he'd taken you to bed. Had got all caveman about Seth."

"Yes, well, the less we talk about last night the better. It was quite eventful."

"Oh? I thought Ebony had come around."

"She did. But then we had to get other people to come around. My mum, Frankie, and Darius."

"What?" I pulled up a chair in front of her desk and sat down leaning closer.

"First, in the throes of passion, I grew fangs and bit my husband."

My jaw dropped.

"Did I hear you right? Did you just say you grew fangs?"

"Yep, fangs. Frankie looked it up, and it's all the baby. But I have to drink loads of blood so that I don't try to take a bite out of anyone else."

I pulled the lapels of my jacket up around my neck. I'd already suffered random bites in the past, I didn't need my best friend munching on me.

"And then most embarrassing of all..." Her face went red and this time it wasn't to do with her blood intake. "Theo had handcuffed me to the bed."

"Get Theo, going all Christian Grey."

"Yeah, but Theo being Theo, had forgotten the keys to undo them."

"I'm not following. He left them at the shop?"

"Oh no. My loving husband had left them at his best friend's house. He'd borrowed Darius' cuffs... without asking."

My mouth dropped open again.

"Darius had to come free me and do you know how I repaid him? Well, you must because he ended up cancelling your date because of it."

I sighed. "No. No I don't."

"Oh. I threw up down him. All over his shirt and his jeans. Blood everywhere. We had to launder them while he waited. I'm sorry we messed up you two finally getting together to talk."

"Oh, that's okay," I said, although it couldn't have been further from okay. I stood up and started backing away towards the door. "It does sound like you had quite the adventure. I'd better get on now. I have a lot to do today."

"Okay, bestie. See you later. Sorry once again for messing up your evening."

I nodded and left.

Back in my own office I almost threw myself down in my seat. Fuck. He'd ended up involved in Theo's mess and then Shelley's vomit. He couldn't make the date because he was stuck at the farm, and what had I done? Had tea with Seth and then let him kiss me. I was a mess. I was the trollop and whore my father had always said I was. A waste of a person. I'd be better off staying on my own than trying to find a partner.

I'd brave it to the coffee shop just before closing and let Seth know nothing was going to happen between us. At least that was one mess I could get myself out of.

There was a knock and Frankie and Lucy burst into my office.

"Kim, we're engaged!" Lucy yelled excitedly. "I've no ring yet, but I'm going to be Lucy Love. Oh my god, I'm excited. I must tell Shelley." She ran from the office down the corridor to Shelley's.

"Wow. Congratulations," I told Frankie, who looked more shocked than happy.

"Kim. My actual words to her were supposed to be, 'Babe, can I finger your ring?'. But I messed them up and said, 'Can I ring your finger?'"

I burst into noisy guffaws. "Oh thank you for making me smile. Oh Lord, hahahahahahha." I creased over.

"Kim, you have to help me."

I tried to catch my breath. "I'm not h-helping you get out of an accidental proposal."

"No." He shook his head vehemently. "I do want to marry her, even though we've only been dating for nine days. I can live with having proposed. She's my one. But I need to do a new one. That can't be it. That's no story to tell our future children."

He took a lingering look at my face. "I can see you're going to be no help whatsoever today. I'm glad my life is so amusing." He went into his jacket pocket and extracted an A4 manilla envelope. "We'll see if your face is still as creased with laughter when you've read this lot. The history of the Withernsea and Hogsthope packs. And thank you, Frankie, for staying up all night. Oh, that's okay, Kim. You're welcome."

My face froze.

"Yep, thought as much."

"I'm sorry, Frankie. But I'm having a shit time and that did make me chuckle. I will help you plan an amazing proposal, okay? And thanks for this information."

His face relaxed. "Okay, I'd better get to bed because I'm starting to feel a bit queasy." He raised a warning finger at me. "Don't you dare say a word about what I just told you."

"I won't. I promise. No woman needs to know her proposal was accidental and if you were going to propose anyway, what's the problem?" Then I launched into Beyoncé's 'Single Ladies' and sang about putting a ring on it. Frankie huffed and zapped away.

～

I sat at my desk, poured myself a cup of instant, and began reading. I took a swig of my drink and winced. It wasn't what I was used to. *This is why you don't shit where you eat, Kim. Leave all the dating agency customers well alone.*

I opened the envelope and began reading.

WITHERNSEA AND HOGSTHORPE PACKS - A POTTED HISTORY

(Not to be reproduced. Copyright F. Love, 2018)

Until 1989 the pack was united as one - Withernsea. One member of the pack at that time was Arlo Wild. Arlo was mated with Freya Wild and she was carrying his cub. Arlo had been almost thirty years old when he had mated with Freya.

Arlo became the alpha of the tribe following the death of his predecessor in battle. Two months before the birth of their son, Darius, Arlo met another wolf shifter from the Hull pack, Renee Thorn. His mating instinct kicked in and he was forced to confess to the pack that he had faked his 'calling' to Freya due to his age and worry about being cast from the pack.

He was thrown out of the pack in disgrace, leaving Freya to care for their newborn son alone. He started the Hogsthorpe pack and declared himself alpha. Those that sided with him joined him, along with other rogue weres from other packs. The result was that Hogsthorpe has always been a volatile pack, and Arlo ended up ousted as leader and killed in 1992.

Freya Wild had been swept along with the romance and only realised Arlo had not been her true mate when William 'Billy' Phelan joined the pack, having moved from Derbyshire. They mated and married and had a further son, Rhett; and daughter, Alyssa. Darius remains a Wild although his mother, stepfather and siblings have the surname of Phelan.

After finding out the above, I sought an audience with Jett Conall, from the Hogsthorpe pack. There he confirmed my suspicions. What follows is for your information only and will not appear in my records.

Jett Conall is ALSO the son of Arlo Wild. His surname was changed in 1992 when his mother remarried.
Jett is Darius' half-brother.

This is the reason the two factions remain separate. Darius and Jett refuse to acknowledge each other as siblings and their mothers remain bitter enemies. Jett is alpha of the Hogsthorpe pack, whereas Darius refuses to accept his place as alpha, instead deferring to Edon Woodland.

Although no clear statement has ever been made, the rumour is that Jett intends to do a hostile takeover of the Withernsea pack and take what he feels is his rightful place as alpha of the united pack, to honour his father.

There were other words in the text. Stuff about the set-up of both packs and the members but I scanned it, my eyes reading the above words repeatedly.

Oh Christ. And I'd managed to select Jett from the agency's database and call him for a date.

There was no wonder Darius had acted like he had.

I put the document on the table and picked up the envelope to put in the recycling, but noticed another page still inside.

THE MATING OF WERE SHIFTERS - FACTS AND RULES
(Not to be reproduced. Copyright F. Love, 2018)

To ask a wolf on a date is stating your interest in becoming their mate.

To attend the date and eat with a wolf is part one of courtship. Part two is to find out if you are physically compatible through the act of sexual intercourse. Part three is to complete the mating process under the full moon and be bitten by the wolf at which time non-pack members become both wolf (if not already) and pack.

Most wolves determine their mate by a scent. This scent is so intoxicating it can lead to periods of overwhelm until mates become accustomed to it.

Should a female show interest in more than one wolf then they must let the female decide. Alternatively, they can take out the other wolf.

To cook for a potential mate is a demonstration of the fact you will care for that woman and her future cubs.

When I'd read that, I was ready to throw myself out of the window. I had serious reparation to do. Ebony was right. I really had started a pack war. What if Darius and Jett tried to kill each other now? I needed to do my damnedest to end it. It was just that to do so I would have to confront every demon I had inside me. But I'd do it, for Darius' safety.

My door burst back open and the beaming smile of Lucy greeted me. It was still unnerving seeing an ex-demon happy.

"Many congratulations again, Lucy."

"Oh thank you. But that's not why I'm here."

"Oh?"

"You're one of the reasons I've been hanging around here too. I just had to wait for you to realise that you needed to work on your own demons and then BOOM, here I could be, to let you know I was here to help you."

"You're here to help me?"

"Yes. To avoid a pack war and get your man. Are you ready, Kim? I might be an angel now, but it's going to be one hell of a time."

Chapter 11

Lucy

I left the office in high spirits. Life was good. I was engaged. I had a fantastic job. Finally, something was going my way.

I heard coins tinkling behind me and pivoted to find Andrew, my predecessor, a few feet behind me. He was supposed to be in Heaven, having been transferred after almost exposing angels to humanity (not in that way, get your head out of the gutter).

"Andrew? What are you doing here?"

He picked up the coins, putting them back in his pocket and scratched around his neckline. "Oh, I'm back down here, second chances and all that."

"Oh, and have you got a project?"

His face flushed. "Yes, yes, I have, and I need to make sure that this time nothing goes wrong."

I smiled at him. He stepped back a little which I thought was mean. Was my being happy THAT much of a shock to people?

"Well, anything I can do to help, just ask."

"Thanks, Lucy. Well, see you around." He turned and started walking in the other direction. Hmmm, he'd been coming this way before, now he was walking away from me?

Having been one of the devil's top employees, I had a large bullshit-ometer, so I carried on walking for a few minutes, and then I turned quickly, fast enough to just see the edge of Andrew's leather jacket disappearing into a shop doorway. I stalked over to where he was pretending to look in the shop window. Unfortunately for him it was a sex shop, and he was currently looking at very large butt plugs.

"The way I look at it, either way right now you're screwed, Andrew. What's it to be, fess up, or shall I go purchase the extra-large?"

Andrew sighed deeply. "I'm so going to get fired again. I wasn't supposed to be seen on this job."

My mouth dropped open. "Andrew." I tilted my head at him. "Am I your project?"

"Well, erm, yeah." Another deep sigh escaped him. "Now I suppose you're going to report me?"

"Hell, no." My eyes widened. "If you have an earth angel job to do on me, then get on with it, right now. Save my life or whatever it is you're supposed to be doing."

"I can't tell you what it is, but it's not saving your life. All I can say is that a test is coming."

"Right, I need you to be with me at all times then to get this done. The sooner you're finished, the sooner you can pass your earth angel exam and the sooner I can get back to my life, because..." I beamed again. "I am about to get married."

"Cool," Andrew said, but his face didn't look happy, which made the hairs on my neck stand up.

"Come on, let's go to mine," I told him. "We have a spare room."

Frankie got up a little later than usual due to his having been up in the daytime. He wandered into the living room and saw me sitting beside another man and his eyes flashed red.

"What's going on?"

"Frankie, darling. Andrew is coming to live with us for a while."

"He's what?" The next moment Andrew was pinned to the wall while a vampire with exposed fangs got up in his business. My fiancé turned to me. "I'm not into sharing."

"Put him down, Frankie. It's not like that. He's an earth angel like me, and apparently, he's doing me."

Frankie hissed. "Doing you?"

"As in I'm his project. He's saving me in some way. We're not romantically involved for God's sake. Put the poor man down before he urinates down his own legs."

Frankie dropped him and returned to his usual look and held out a hand to Andrew. "Nice to meet you, pal. Thought about getting a Chinese for tea. You fancy it?"

Andrew went and sat in the furthest corner of the sofa. I heard a clatter at the back door and then a black cat sauntered into the room, walking over to Andrew and jumping up on his knee where she curled up on his lap and started treading his groin area. His surprise at that coupled with an almighty sneeze meant that Maisie was thrown a foot away onto the floor. She landed on her paws, upper back arched, turned around and hissed at him.

I walked over to her with a pet friendly wipe. She hated water but could tolerate a wipe. Then she shifted into her beautiful brunette self.

Andrew's eyes went wide. "You're the cat?"

"I am," she said. "And now I'm wondering how I'm going to inflict punishment on you for throwing me on the floor and coating me in your nose juice. Do you like to be whipped?" she asked him.

"Andrew is an earth angel, Maisie. There'll be no whipping or punishments with him."

She sat at the side of him, far too close, invading his personal space. "Do you earth angels have to be all celibate?"

He swallowed hard. "Well, no, but it's frowned upon if it would distract me from my job and this is my last chance, so all my attention needs to be on Lucy."

Maisie rolled her eyes. "Huh. It's always all about Lucy. Everyone loves Lucy. They even made a stupid TV show about her."

"*I love Lucy* is not about me," I told her.

"She has red hair. You should totally sue the company, they obviously copied you."

"That programme came out in 1951."

"Is it you that's completely unoriginal then? Hah."

Andrew's nose started twitching again.

"I think Andrew here is allergic to cats," I told her, just as she dived across the room, landing on my lap, before another huge sneeze rocked him.

"Ugh. Get off me." I pushed her up.

"Oh well, never mind. I'm in a ménage with the couple next door anyway." Maisie smoothed down her hair.

"Being their pet cat is not classed as being part of a ménage."

"For an angel you are always so goddamn mean. Cut me some

slack here. My love life is seriously lacking, and you bring a hottie here, and he's allergic to me. All-er-gic. And my paws tell me he's packing so I'm really depressed right now." She pouted. "Have you got some of that nice salmon?"

"Oh for heaven's sake. Let me get you some dinner. I'll be back in a moment, gentlemen, please try to not kill each other while I'm gone. I'll fetch you an antihistamine, Andrew, to stop the irritation, although she's following me, so it should go off."

Maisie followed me out into the kitchen where I took out some fresh salmon. I put the kettle on ready to poach it, just as she liked it.

"He's hot. It's not fair."

"Can you behave? He's staying here for a while. Hopefully, not too long though. Apparently, he has an earth angel job to do for me."

"For you? Is shit about to go down in your life?"

"There's no need to look happy about that potential fact."

She leaned against the side. "I'm sorry. You know how it is. When your life is crappy, it hurts even more when you see people getting along with theirs."

I patted her arm, and she started purring and pushing into my hand. It was really off-putting when she did that in human form.

I took my hand away and she eye-rolled. "You're so uptight and missing out. You've seen my tongue, right?" She licked my hand.

"Ewwww."

"Feel how raspy that is? Imagine it there." She nodded at my crotch.

"Maisie. For the umpteenth time, I do not fancy women. I am very happily engaged to a MAN."

Her eyes narrowed, and she hissed. "What's that? I'm sure you just said engaged." She grabbed my recently licked hand. "No ring. Explain yourself."

I put the salmon in a pan of boiling water which distracted her for a few seconds.

"Frankie proposed this morning, in my office. It wasn't the most romantic of proposals, but he did it all the same. We've not had chance to talk about details or a ring or anything yet, because of Andrew." I nodded in the direction of the living room. "I don't know anything else other than I said yes."

"Can I be a bridesmaid?"

"If you promise to stay in human form. Only I don't fancy untangling cat claws from my wedding dress."

"Lace feels so good in my paws." Maisie went into a daydream. "I used to be able to swing off people's net curtains when they were in fashion. Now everyone's windows are bare. Bare is in fashion: windows and pussies. It's about time net curtains and rugs were all the rage again."

I was beginning to feel the onset of a tension headache and rubbed at my right temple.

"A few minutes and then your salmon will be ready. So, are you happy next door?"

Maisie had popped around there a lot while living with Frankie and they'd taken her in when Frankie was ill (in reality he'd been changing into a vampire). They'd asked if they could keep her as they'd got used to her, and Frankie had said yes. But they were human and had no idea that they'd actually moved a third person into their home. Maisie was under strict instructions not to reveal herself, especially when the husband next door looked like Jason Momoa.

I went into the cupboard and got a couple of antihistamines out and filled a glass with water. "Just wait a second while I take these through," I told her. "Make sure the pan doesn't overboil."

Voices quietened as I got near the room, and as I entered, I had that feeling that they'd been talking about me. I guessed Andrew might have been instructing my fiancé on something earth angel related. I passed Andrew the antihistamines and water.

"Thank you."

"I'll be back in a moment. I'm just feeding Maisie. Would you like a hot drink, Andrew?"

"I'm okay with this water, thanks."

I returned to the kitchen to find an empty pan and an empty room. "That bloody cat." I should have known better to leave a cat unattended in a kitchen with fish. She must have eaten it half-raw.

I threw the pan in the sink and began tiptoeing back towards the living room. Now I know they said eavesdroppers never heard anything good about themselves but well, I did use to be evil, and I wanted to get a heads-up about why Andrew was here. I would have to be beyond stealthy as my hubby had vampire super-hearing. I went back and put the radio on in the kitchen. That would interfere with his hearing and put him off long enough for me to get to the room door.

"What was I saying? That bloody radio. Oh yeah, basically I've told Kim, that she's to keep it secret because if Lucy finds out, I'm a dead man."

"I'm sure she'd forgive you."

"Forgive me? Are you joking? Can't you tell me what to do to make things right?"

"I can't. I'm here for Lucy, but it sounds like talking it over with Kim was a good idea. You're sure she won't say anything?"

"Lucy would kill her too. It's not cool to deceive a friend like that is it?"

"And Kim's your ex, so that wouldn't go down well either, you two being together like that."

"Exactly. I don't know what to do right now. I need time to think. To hatch a plan."

I stood in the doorway feeling like I'd been hit by a thunderbolt. What was he saying? Had he cheated on me, with Kim? Is that why the proposal had appeared to come out of nowhere?

I went into the room, both men looking startled. "I'm not feeling good. I'm going to go up to bed, okay?"

"Alright, darling. You need anything, just shout down. I'll hear you."

I nodded and went up the stairs to my room. Then I laid on my bed and burst into tears. History was repeating itself. I was losing my man to another woman.

I didn't think I could go through it all again. Look at what had happened last time. Sheer Hell.

Chapter 12

Darius

"Bro, can you stop thumping around the place? Some of us are studying you know?"

My sister sat at the dining room table, her schoolbooks in front of her. I kicked a chair away and sat down on it. "You're a female. Explain something to me."

Alyssa sighed and sat back. "It must be bad if you're actually going to listen to anything I have to say."

I pulled out my tongue. If there was such a thing as a mature male, I certainly wasn't feeling it today.

"The date went well then?"

"There wasn't a date."

"She cancelled?"

"No." I sighed. "I did."

"*Are you out of your freaking mind?*" Alyssa's voice could have been heard in Australia. "Is this something to do with the emergency you rushed out on?"

"Yes, it meant I had to cancel."

"Oh well, that couldn't be helped, just rearrange."

"I went to see her at her house—after I'd dealt with the emergency—and well..."

"Spit it out, brother."

"I saw her with another man. They kissed."

She was out of her seat. "The bitch. I will go kick her arse."

"Alyssa, sit down."

"Do you want me to drag her here by the hair? I can do that you know. They've accidentally left that paragraph in the Shifter Handbook."

I rubbed a hand over my brow. "No, Alyssa. I want you to sit down and shut up for a moment so I can TALK. TO. YOU."

"Spoilsport." She flopped back down into her chair. "Okay, I'm listening."

"This was a different male. Not the shifter scum, but a human who works at the coffee shop. I don't know why she's doing this. Our connection. It was strong. She's my mate, I know it."

"Have you heard anything from the mutt?"

"No. If he sets foot near here, or near her, I will tear him limb from limb."

Alyssa sighed. "Look, Darius. Have you tried talking to her? She's a human. She probably doesn't understand any of this."

"I want to talk to her, but I need her to ask me out again. Those are the rules. She has to do the instigating. I can't see it happening. Especially if she's started dating one of her own kind."

"Look, Darius. Do you want her, or are you prepared to let one of the other two have her? The way I see it, it's like she's playing a real-life version of that Marry, Date, or Dump, and right now you are definitely the dump, a turd. It's time for action, man."

I ran a hand through my hair. It cascaded down around me.

"Come on." Alyssa got up.

"Where are we going?"

"For a haircut. Time to ditch the stereotypical werewolf look. I don't think she wants to date Fabio."

∞

"Oh no! You look like Liam Hemsworth. Now I can never watch *The Hunger Games* for sexual stimulation again. You spoiled Liam for me for life." Alyssa mock-shuddered. "But in terms of a lady-boner, Kim's will be raging when she sees you."

"What did you get up to last night anyway, until I got home?" I couldn't stop feeling at my head. It felt like a tennis ball. Around my neck was cold without the hair covering it. I'd kept my stubble though. No way was I going clean shaven.

"Here, give her this Hunger Games boxset when you see her. I no longer need it." Alyssa's swift subject change was not lost on me.

"Alyssa..."

"Calm down. I went to the cinema with Sophie. Now anyway." She walked over to me and smoothed down the grey chambray shirt she'd insisted I change into along with some denim jeans. "Now, are you ready to get up from the dump?"

"Yeah, I will be."

"Will is no good. Oh, and is Kim a brunette? Slim, tall?"

"Yeah, why?"

"Because there's a livid looking woman walking up to our front door, and that's what she looks like." Alyssa gathered her books up from the table. "I'll be upstairs, supposedly studying, but probably eavesdropping, so don't go at it in here, will you? Sterile food surfaces and all that."

I walked up to the door and opened it just as a fist was about to rain down on it heavily, so instead Kim punched my chest. Her hand lingered there a moment as if she was temporarily frozen. We looked at each other and that whole staring thing happened again. Eventually the staring competition broke.

"Your hair..."

"Yeah, I've had it cut."

"It looks..." She shook her head. "We need to talk, Darius Wild, and I'm not leaving until you've listened to me."

A smirk danced on my lips. "You'd better come in then."

Kim walked in and looked around. "Nice place. Yours?"

I shook my head. "My parents'. I'll get my own place when I marry. My wife gets to choose."

"Oh." Silence permeated the atmosphere. This shit was awkward.

The door flew open, and Alyssa stomped through. "Sorry, I didn't realise we had visitors." She held out a hand. "I'm Alyssa, Darius' younger sister, and you are?"

"Kim. Kim Fletcher."

"Oooh, you're the Kim he never shuts up about."

I was going to kill her.

Kim's eyes went wide. "Well, err."

Alyssa wrapped her in a hug. "Oh, no hand shaking for you when you're practically family. Now excuse me, let me just get a quick glass of water. I'm studying you see. Upstairs. Been there for hours and so got thirsty." She filled a glass with water. "Darius, you offered Kim anything yet? A drink. FOOD."

Kim's face went bright pink. Then Alyssa was gone as fast as she appeared.

"I must apologise about my sister. She's a teenager. I think that explains everything."

Kim smiled.

"Anyway, come through to the living room and take a seat. I'll make you a coffee, seeing as I know how you like it, and would you like something to go with it, like a pancake?"

"A pancake? Like you're going to cook one for me? Do you not have something easier like a biscuit?"

"I have, but I was just about to make pancakes," I lied.

"Erm, okay then, I'll have a pancake. Thank you."

She couldn't possibly know what me cooking this for her meant, could she? Or did she? If she did, she'd just accepted it.

WHOA.

"Right, I'll just be a couple of minutes."

"I'll wait with you in the kitchen, if that's okay? We can talk."

Oh God, now I was understanding why men trembled when women said they wanted to talk.

I started preparing the pancake mixture. Kim hovered nearby.

"Last night, Darius..."

My hand tightened around the whisk.

"I'd just gone for a drink with Seth. I thought it was as friends. He took me by surprise when he kissed me. It was one-sided. I don't feel that way about him. Actually, I popped into the coffee shop after work yesterday and made that clear."

I turned to her. "You did?"

"Yeah. My, erm, earth, erm, friend, suggested I come and speak to you. She says we keep dancing around each other and getting nowhere. I'm sorry, Darius. I'm sorry about arranging the date with Jett. I'm sorry about last night's misunderstanding. This is really hard for me..."

It was really hard for me too if you got what I was saying...

I dropped the whisk, grabbed Kim's shoulders and pushed her back against the kitchen wall. My mouth crashed down on hers hungrily. I'd imagined this moment for a long time and the reality was so much more than I could have anticipated. I pushed her thighs apart with my knee, grinding my erection against her heat. We devoured each other, moans and groans coming from both of us.

A loud banging noise came from upstairs and we sprung apart.

"Sister right above," Alyssa's voice yelled.

We both stared at each other and then collapsed into laughter.

"Bloody siblings," I told her. "Right, where were we...? Ah, yes, pancakes."

We sat opposite each other at the dining room table, and I watched as she tucked into her pancakes. Food... that I'd cooked for her. My indication I would care for her and our future offspring.

"I've been reading up on were shifter culture and traditions," Kim said slowly.

"Oh?" I swallowed.

"I'm aware that by asking Jett out I inadvertently put myself up as a potential mate for him. Although as a human I think that sucks. Surely if I don't know this stuff, it can't count?"

"We can't force you, but we can still fight amongst ourselves for the opportunity."

"I know who he is to you, Darius."

Time stood still. Of all the things I was waiting for her to say, that was not one of them.

"He is nothing to me."

"He's your half-brother and your enemy. I wouldn't call that nothing."

"Sounds like you really have done your homework. What else have you learned?"

"That I need to ask you out on a date to put you on an equal footing. I'm going to ask you again. Will you come out with me, tonight? I'd better say nine pm now I'm being filled with pancakes."

It wasn't the only thing I wanted to fill her with. Alyssa was a cockblocker.

"Do you know what the step after that is?" I asked her slowly and carefully.

Her cheeks flushed again. "Yes, I do. Darius, I don't do... well, I haven't done relationships. Now, I know it sounds cliché, but I had family shit and it messed with my head. I find it hard to trust people, to let myself go. But I want to try, Darius. I want to try, with you."

"Okay." I smiled. "Nine pm tonight it is."

She finished her pancakes and leaned closer. "Bring a toothbrush just in case," she whispered.

Then she got up and walked to the door. I wanted to pick her up, put her over my shoulder, and take her to bed. But I had to be patient. For all her bravado, it looked like actually, my mate-to-be scared easily.

She turned toward me at the door and reached up on her tiptoes, brushing her lips across mine.

"Oh, and Darius...?"

"Yeah?"

"Thanks for the pancakes. But I could already tell you were the sort of man who'd care and provide for his family." She smiled and walked down the path. "Nine pm, and if my annoying friend or her husband ring you, tell them you're the one tied up tonight." She winked.

I closed the door and leaned back against it. My head resting on the glass inset.

She knew.

Chapter 13

Kim

Gaaahhhhh. I had a date with Darius in a few hours and there was a pretty good chance we were going to get it on afterwards. Stripped of my clothes, I headed to the shower. I needed to make sure everything was shaved and moisturised. Just the thought of seeing him again had my stomach in knots. I wasn't sure I was actually going to be able to eat anything. Crikey, I'd better change the bedding and do a bit of housework. I looked around at the mess. I needed a miracle. Then I thought of one.

I dialled Frankie's number.

"Hello?"

"You know that problem I'm helping you with?"

"Yes...?"

"I'll make it super spectacular if you can zip over here right now to do me a favour. It won't take you long, but it's an emergency."

He sighed down the line. "Just a second."

The doorbell rang and sure enough Frankie was standing there, his hair a little mussed from the speed. "This had better be good. I had to make an excuse to Lucy because we had dinner reservations."

I handed him a bottle of furniture polish and a duster. "You know your super whizzy speed?" I said, and I displayed my best begging expression.

Fifteen minutes later, the house was immaculate thanks to my super slow vacuuming and Frankie's super-fast everything else.

Frankie stood in the doorway, ready to zap off again. He nodded at my towel turban and robe. "You might want to get dressed then for your date."

"On it now. Thank you so much, Frankie, you're a star." I kissed him on the cheek.

"Yes, well my proposal better be the more epic for all this," he told me.

"It will. I'll get my thinking cap on. Have a nice night with Lucy," I said.

"God, yes." As he looked at his watch, his cell phone rang out. He took it out of his pocket.

"I'll be right there," he said and then he was gone.

~

I kept it smart casual and wore jeans and a red silky V-neck. I walked into Hanif's to be greeted by Rav who worked there. Rav was a demon.

"Hey, Rav."

"Come in. Welcome to Hanif's. We are very happy to be assisting in this most auspicious occasion." He escorted me over to the man himself who stood up.

"Take your seat, Darius. I have it, my friend." Rav pulled my seat out and gestured for me to sit down.

"Rav, I've eaten in here loads of times and you've never pulled my seat out for me, what's got into you?"

"This is a special occasion, Kim. You are out on a date with one of my closest friends. Now, excuse me while I go and get you complimentary poppadoms and a pickle tray." He raced off.

I looked at my date. Darius had changed into a black t-shirt and jeans. I couldn't stop staring at his arms. They were muscled and defined. I'd bet he could pick me up with just one.

"I would have liked to have pulled the seat out for you myself, but it would seem my friend is determined to make our date special." A smirk flirted on Darius' lips.

"Thank you, but I'm perfectly capable of sitting down. It's one thing that has me a little uncomfortable about the whole wolf thing. You're like 'I will feed you, take care of you, pull out your chair'. I've been on my own a long time. I can take care of myself."

"You can but you shouldn't have to. Sometimes it's okay to let someone else take over for a while. Just imagine it. You get in from work and I have a bath running for you. You climb in and the heat soaks away the stresses of the day. Then while you do that, I'm cooking dinner. You come down, eat, and then I make love to you all night long. Are you telling me you have a problem with that?" He raised an eyebrow.

I'd lost my words. Lost them completely at 'make love to you all night long'. I'd felt that beast against me when we kissed. The thought of it inside me, well... NO. WORDS.

It was as well that Rav came over at that moment with the poppadoms and pickles because at least eating gave me an excuse for not talking for a while.

"I am delighted for you both, that you finally made it here on a date. My friend has been wanting to date you for a very long time." Rav stood beside us and smiled.

Darius' eyes flashed yellow, and it made me gasp. It was a reminder that not only was he a man, he was also a wolf. A goddamn animal.

"Thanks, Rav. If you could leave me and my date alone now for a while it would be appreciated."

"Oh, yes. Sorry. I will go make sure your starters are being prepared."

I laughed. "A long time, huh?"

"Well, I'd seen you around, but once Theo started to date Shelley, you were even more on my mind. But you were dating someone else, so that was that."

"Me and Frankie weren't dating. We were just..." *Fuck buddies*. I couldn't say that to Darius. "Friends."

"I know what you were. I have to accept that you have a past, that we both have a past. But let's concentrate on the future, shall we?"

"Yeah." I looked into Darius' eyes. I felt lost and found at the same time. Something was most definitely happening between us. I felt like I'd known him forever. It was hard to describe, but I just felt sure I'd found the one. What was happening to me? I'd been hit by the lovey-dovey express train.

"Erm, have you finished, only you've been sat staring at each other for seven minutes now?"

"Oh." I sat back. "Yes, thank you, Rav. I'm ready for my starter."

He rushed off with our plates and I looked at Darius and giggled. "We keep doing that."

He nodded. "It's because you were meant for me, Kim." He held out a hand towards mine.

"Kim!" a voice shouted out breaking our connection.

I turned around to find a certain barista standing behind me. *For the love of God. Not now!*

"Seth? What are you doing here?"

"I thought I'd grab a takeaway, but seeing as you're here, I might just stay and eat. I'm not interrupting anything am I?" He began to pull out a chair.

"Seth!" Lucy rushed towards us. Where the fuck had she come from? "You can eat with me and Frankie if you're feeling lonely. Over there." She pointed to a far corner of the restaurant while wearing a look that said don't even try to refuse me.

Seth's face fell. "Sure, that would be lovely, Lucy." He stared at us. "Well, have a nice evening."

He walked over to where Frankie was settling into a seat. I saw Frankie's brow crease, and he looked over at me with a confused look on his face. Staring back at him, I shrugged my shoulders.

"I'm only doing this because it's part of my earth angel duties. I'm watching you, Fletcher," Lucy spat out, before stalking off to her table.

Not knowing what the heck had just happened, I looked at Darius. His eyes were yellow, and he was growling.

"Oh, shit. You're not going to change here, are you? In the middle of the restaurant?"

Darius leapt from his seat and ran out of the door.

I got up to follow him.

Seth stood up. "Have you been ditched? I'd be more than happy to take over as your date," he yelled enthusiastically.

"Sit down!" Lucy commanded.

By this time, the other restaurant customers were watching the event like it was match point at Wimbledon.

I didn't know what was going off with Seth and Lucy, but right now all I could think about was Darius. I threw some money on the table and took off after my date.

Standing at the doorway, I couldn't see him anywhere. He must have changed and taken off. If I was him then I'd have headed for the pack's woodland. I ordered a taxi and headed for the caravan park.

I knocked on the door of his home and Alyssa answered.

"Oh God. You're supposed to be on a date and yet you're here and Darius isn't. What went wrong this time?"

"I think he changed into his wolf so I'm guessing he's out there." I gestured towards the woods.

"You see the woods?"

"Yeah, why?"

"They're glamoured."

I shrugged my shoulders. "Not to me."

"Huh. Well, come on." She grabbed her coat. "I'll take you. We need to make sure that he's there and that there are no other wolves out there. Don't want you eaten up, do we?"

I followed her into the woods, and she called for her brother. After a few minutes there was movement at the edge of the woods, though it was difficult to see what was happening as it was part shaded by trees.

Then my mouth fell open. There stood a huge wolf, with golden blonde fur and yellow eyes. That was Darius in wolf form?

"I got it from here," I told her.

"You sure?"

"Yeah."

Alyssa moved away as I moved forwards.

The wolf bowed its head as I moved nearer. "Darius, stay still. I want to see you." As I moved closer, my heart thudded in my chest because it was a fucking wolf. I hoped to God he wasn't about to eat me seeing as he'd only had a couple of poppadoms. I got closer. Now what did I do?

Carefully, I reached out and touched the wolf's fur. It was soft and felt lovely to my fingers. I began to stroke and pet the wolf, and he laid down on the grass. I sat next to him and snuggled close, carrying on stroking his fur. "You make a beautiful wolf, Darius Wild, but any chance of you changing back into a guy? Only it's getting cold out here and I'm really hungry."

The wolf shivered, and I watched as Darius appeared on the ground. A completely naked Darius. My eyes looked over every single inch of his body before resting on his now very erect cock.

"Oh my," I said.

"Still hungry?" he growled out.

"Only to be filled with meat," I replied, and he grabbed me and carried me further into the woodland.

He took me to an area where there was a yurt, and after checking that no one else was inside, he carried me in and laid me on a bed where he covered me in blankets. Then he headed towards the centre and lit a fire.

"I'm sorry our date got cut short. But I saw Seth, and then your ex, and it was too much. My wolf wanted to claim you. I had to get out and change."

"Your wolf is magnificent," I said. "Although you have to appreciate it's hard for me to get my head around the fact you are part-beast."

He sat beside me on the bed. "You would be too. You know that, don't you? If you decide to become my mate. I will bite you and you will change."

I sat quietly. It was a lot to take in. When thinking of the future and marriage and babies you thought about changing your second name, not your DNA.

"Well, first, before we worry about all that, don't we have to check we're compatible?" I stared at the handsome man sat beside me, and then I leaned over to him and raised my head next to his, so I was staring up into his eyes. I brushed my mouth against his. A growl erupted deep in his throat and then he claimed my lips with his and I forgot all about the cold.

There was no slow tease, this was a fast dance. Darius took off my shoes, discarding them on the floor, and then his hands were at the waistband of my jeans, where he opened the button and lowered the zipper before pulling them off my legs. I lifted my arms so he could lift my top up over my head and then I was left in only my mint-green lacy bra and matching panties—for about three seconds before they were also removed and thrown to the floor. Goose bumps rose on my skin with the nip in the air, but then I was covered by a well-muscled and warm body and all was okay in the world.

I could feel his cock, hard against my thigh, and my core went slick at the thought that soon he was going to be inside me. Darius nuzzled at my neck before grazing his teeth down over my breasts, capturing my nipples in turn and giving them a gentle nip.

I shivered, but it was with anticipation, not cold.

He pulled the covers up around us and whispered in my ear. "Next time, I'll take my time, but right now... I can't."

His cock teased at my entrance and then he pushed inside, and we both groaned with pleasure.

He filled me to the hilt and then drew back and pushed again. My hands gravitated to his buttocks, and I felt them clench with his movements. I wrapped my legs around him drawing him deeper inside.

"Fuck, you fit me perfectly," he whispered in my ear and then he took my mouth with his.

His kiss was almost brutal. He claimed my mouth as he claimed my body and I felt myself climbing the dizzy heights to orgasm. Then I exploded, taking Darius over with me. We were panting, it had been so, well, animalistic.

He gathered me in his arms. Darius was so broad that I felt like a waif in his arms. For a moment I tensed, feeling vulnerable, and then I thought fuck it. I was warm, cosy, and well fucked. Why was I trying to ruin this for myself? It was okay to give in to my feelings and they were telling me to lie in this man's arms feeling protected.

We had dozed, but then I awoke, feeling fingers teasing between my legs.

"This time I'm going to take my time with you. Until you're at my mercy and begging for more."

My heart rate quickened in excitement.

Sure enough, a few hours later one thing was for certain. We'd passed the compatibility test with flying colours.

Chapter 14

Lucy

Earlier that evening...

I didn't know what to say to my fiancé after overhearing his conversation with Andrew last night. He'd only just woken anyway, so I decided I'd save my questions for later. We were going out for a meal and I didn't want to ruin date night. Except the phone rang and his eyes got a shifty look about them. Information for those dating ex-demons—betrayal can be spotted a mile off.

"I've got to pop out," he told me.

"Oh yeah. Where?"

"Bloody Kim. Apparently, she's got some kind of emergency. There's always something with that lot: Kim, Theo, Shelley. Do you think we'll ever get a quiet night on our own?"

I folded my arms across my chest. "So don't go."

He tilted his head at me. "It's an emergency. I won't be long."

"I'll come with you."

He shook his head. "You get ready and go get our table at the restaurant. I'll meet you straight there."

Then he stood up, kissed my cheek and whizzed off.

I needed to follow him. Only my wings were so goddamn fluffy and enormous he'd spot me if I tried to fly, so I'd just have to get a taxi. Luckily the angel realm held an account with A1 Cabs. Angel 1 to those in the know.

I was just about to climb into the car when I felt something hard poking me in the back, something I'd not experienced for a day or two. I turned to see Andrew having premature wingulation.

"Put them away," I scolded.

He managed to get them to disappear.

"Look it's your fault, my angel bleep went off. Now I don't know what you are doing, but I have to strongly advise you against it."

"I'm only going to have a nosy at what my fiancé is doing." I gave Kim's address to the taxi driver.

"Can you hold on a minute?" Andrew said. The taxi driver shook his head in agreement. "Take as long as you like, my meter's ticking. Always drama with you angels. By the way, quick question. Any of you have a boss called Charlie?" He let his head roll back and cackled with mirth. It was times like this I wish I'd still got my pronged fork.

I turned to Andrew and tried to smile sweetly. "If you stop the taxi setting off again your mission will fail because I'm going to push you out of it, which evil doing will no doubt get me benched by Team Angel. Sit there, watch me, and I figure as long as you don't let me kill Frankie, we're good. I can't promise though."

He sat back and sighed. "I'd better get my job after this because they gave me the hardest gig ever."

We pulled up down the road from Kim's and I made the driver put us in invisible mode, one of the perks of Angel Cabs. We all watched as Kim's door opened and Frankie stood there on the step. She stood on the doorstep in only a robe and with a towel on her head, freshly showered, and then she leaned over and kissed him on the cheek.

My hand was on the door handle of the car, but Andrew leaned over and with strength I didn't know he possessed, he moved my hand back to my side and very bluntly said, "No."

I flashed him a look of hurt and anger.

"I'm your earth angel. You must be guided by me right now. No, Lucy. This is not the right path."

The fight left me, and I leaned back in the cab, my head against the back of the leather seat as I fought back tears. "Surely he wouldn't do this? And Kim, I thought she was wanting to date Darius. I can't believe them."

"Can you take us to Hanif's Indian Restaurant now?" Andrew asked the driver and once again we were on our way.

On route I got a text from Frankie telling me he now needed to go to see Theo again as he had a query about Ebony.

Was that the truth or had he turned back around for another round with Kim?

"Actually, I'd like to detour to The Marine," I told our driver. "I think I need a few mojitos."

∽

It was an hour later when I got a call from my fiancé saying he was at the restaurant and where was I? Andrew helped me walk from the bar to the restaurant entrance as I was a teeny bit wobbly on my feet due to a lack of food, and three cocktails. We were just about to cross the road toward Hanif's when I saw Seth dart into there. Then there was a bleep from my bag. My angel bleep had sounded. Seth was about to do something stupid.

Andrew recognised the sound. "Him?" He nodded toward the restaurant entrance.

"Yes."

He picked me up and ran with me across the road, through the entrance and down the stairs.

I ran over to my project. "Seth," I shouted, hearing him say he'd sit with Darius and Kim. On their date? Mind you, she did seem to be creating her own harem at the moment. Seth shot around facing me, his face masked with disappointment. "You can eat with me and Frankie if you're feeling lonely. Over there." I pointed to where Frankie was sitting, looking at me in confusion.

"Sure, that would be lovely, Lucy," he replied, though his face said anything but.

"I'm only doing this because it's part of my earth angel duties. I'm watching you, Fletcher," I spat out, before stalking off to my table.

"Lucy. Is this, or is this not date night? Only you've arrived with two other men," my boyfriend said.

"If I were you right now, I'd be quiet," I told him, my jaw clenching.

"Have you been drinking?" He sniffed near me. Stupid vampires and their enhanced senses. "Mojitos? You went for mojitos? With him?" His fangs descended. It was laughable. I'd just followed him to another woman's house, and he was acting like I'd done something wrong when he knew Andrew was my earth angel.

I was about to speak, but then I heard a growl from across the tables. Darius' eyes had turned yellow, and he looked like he was about to shift. He bolted out of the restaurant. Surely, she'd not confessed about her dalliance with Frankie, had she?

Seth stood up. "Have you been ditched? I'd be more than happy to take over as your date."

"Sit down!" I commanded.

Kim took one look at me, shrugged her shoulders and then throwing money from her bag onto the table she ran out of the restaurant.

"Are you ready to order?" Rav said.

"No," four people spat out at him at the same time.

Rav took a step back. "Whoa, you do know I'm the evil one, right?" he said. "I'll give you five minutes."

"Where have you been?" I said to Frankie.

Andrew's pager went off. Bleep. Bleep. Bleep. In other words, 'Shut up, Lucy'.

"I must go see that Kim is okay," Seth said. Bleep. Bleep. Bleep. My pager went off.

Rav came over. "Can you turn those off? They are the same bleeping noise as the ovens. We keep thinking food is ready when it is not."

"We can't. Sorry, Rav."

"Are you at least ready to order now?"

"No," we all said again.

Huh. I wasn't allowed to ask Frankie where he'd been. Great. Well, as it happened, Seth was looking like he was ready to bolt, so my mind was currently occupied as to what the heck was going off with him.

"Seth?"

"Yeah?"

"What's going on? You are acting very strangely."

He sat back in his seat. "I don't want her with that Darius guy. He's not for her."

Frankie turned to him. "I'm sorry, dude, but I really think he is. It was prophesied you know? Ebony, before she lost her visions, she saw it."

"I refuse to believe it. I believe in another outcome."

"Look, you have a crush. I understand. Kim's an attractive woman. I went there myself in the past."

Andrew shot up in his seat.

"You're making my job very difficult for me right now, Mr Love. Maybe you could please think before you speak, you know, in front of your fiancée."

Frankie looked perplexed. "But she knows my past. I know hers. I just saw her ex-boyfriend down at Shelley's. We all have a past."

"You saw Dylan?"

"Yes, everyone is trying to see what they can do to help Ebony."

"Is she in a bad way?" I asked.

"No. Quite the opposite. She's loving not having any visions and wants to go on a holiday. We're trying to explain that seers can't have breaks from their visions. That it's not normal. In the meantime, I'm trying to consult with Margret on whether we can think of a spell to help when they do return. Shelley is not well with the pregnancy tonight, hence Theo called me over to help."

Theo was calling my current boyfriend to help my ex-boyfriend's wife—the one who stole my previous boyfriend. I think I'd be having words with Theo at some point.

"Lucy, love?" He meant it as a term of endearment, but I heard it as my to-be-married name.

"Yeah?"

"Can we go home? I'll make you and Andrew an omelette. I've lost my appetite and I think this date night is a bust."

I had to agree.

Frankie whizzed home to make a start on supper while we got another angel cab. We dropped Seth off at his apartment. He exited the car without saying goodbye and walked up the street with his shoulders slumped. I guessed unrequited love could do that to a guy.

The taxi set back off and Andrew turned to me. "Thank you for listening to me. I cannot stop your actions. I can only advise as you know."

I searched his face for answers but there were none to be found.

"Yes, I do know, and that's the only reason my fiancé didn't find his face tandooried tonight. Because I finally have faith. It took me a long time to find it, but you are my earth angel and if you are advising me to not pursue this, despite what it looks like, then I'm listening. I want you to get your wings properly, Andrew, and I also want to believe that I'm not seeing what I appear to be seeing."

He nodded. "Thank you."

"But if I'm wrong and you've fucked up again, I'll skewer you and make you an angel kebab."

He shot a few feet away from me. You could lead an ex-demon to the good side, but you couldn't always make her drink—unless of course it was a mojito.

Chapter 15

Kim

I woke wrapped in blankets and Darius. It was heavenly until my stomach decided to let us both know that I hadn't eaten properly since the pancakes and the poppadoms.

Darius' head shot straight up. "Oh, that won't do at all. I can't have my woman hungry."

My woman. Those words should have scared me half to death and had me running out of here, but instead they made me break out into a big beaming smile. *What was happening to me?*

He leapt out of bed, and I let my eyes wander down over his muscled back, over those thick legs, and that taut ass, as he bent to pick up my clothing from the floor. Okay I could have done without that last visual. Next time avert thy gaze as he bends right over, Kim, but the rest of it *oh my*.

He insisted on dressing me, which took another hour, seeing as he insisted on kissing my skin over and over as he placed each clothing item on my body. Then he got a fresh robe from a cupboard in the yurt.

"We're well stocked because as I'm sure you can imagine, we tend to lose our clothes a lot."

"It's like you're the incredible hulk but not green." I laughed.

"I get green all right, especially when I think you're kissing other men."

"I'm not kissing any other men."

He walked over to the bed and scooped me up in his arms.

"Damn straight," he said. "Now I'm going to take you back to mine and get you some breakfast."

He held me in one arm as he used his other hand to push the door open. How strong was he? He put me down, and I turned around to see that on this occasion the kitchen was full.

"Meet the family," Darius said, completely unflustered by the fact that he was in a robe. Luckily there was an outbuilding behind the yurt that had a small bathroom, so I'd been able to wash myself a little and remove as much of yesterday's make-up as I could without my face wipes.

"Come take a seat," Alyssa said, a huge knowing grin on her face. "I bet both of you are starving. Big night?"

"We went out for an Indian," I said quickly. "And decided to stay in the yurt as not to disturb you as we were late back."

Darius laughed, a great hearty guffaw.

"Darlin', family of wolves. They can smell our coitus. No good being embarrassed around here. Now take a seat and let me get you a large breakfast, because yes." He looked at Alyssa and winked. "We have a huge appetite this morning. I'll let Alyssa introduce you to everyone because I can see she's dying to do so." He patted me on the butt before pulling out a chair for me at the table.

I sat down at the table with my head in my hands. I'd never been so embarrassed in all my life. Staring at the table, I daren't look up because I just knew there would be several sets of eyes looking at me.

Then the smell of coffee appeared under my nose, and I decided it was worth the stares to be able to drink this much needed nectar of the gods.

I clutched my hands around the mug and took a sip even though it burned my tongue.

Alyssa waved her hand around. "Okay, so, Kim. This is our mum Freya, dad Billy, and my older brother Rhett."

They all smiled at me.

"It's a pleasure to meet you at last, Kim," his mum said. "I know your journey here has been a little tricky." There was an underlying tension in her words. This mama was protecting her cub.

"Yeah. I'm sorry. I didn't understand pack rules and I know I've made a mistake that can have ramifications for the pack. If there's anything I can do to undo the mess, just let me know. In the meantime, I'm reading up on pack rules, so I don't do anything else that's stupid."

Darius served me a huge plateful of bacon and eggs before his mother spoke again.

"Well, if you mate with my son on the next full moon, there will be no war with Hogsthorpe as there would be no point. Darius could take on his true role as alpha of the pack and they would be of no threat."

"Mother," Darius scolded. "We've had one date. One. Please leave any further dating and mating stuff for me to discuss."

"You've slept with her, and Jett hasn't," his mother stated clearly. "Once that news reaches the mutt's ears, which it undoubtedly will, Kim will be in danger, as he'll want to even the score."

I dropped my fork. "You mean he might…"

"Attack you? He's not allowed via pack rules to do that, but he could just to spite Darius. However, he could use coercion, threaten other people to make you do his bidding. The full moon is next Friday, and I suggest we make an announcement as soon as possible."

I slammed my fist onto the table. "This is my life you're talking about. I get you have beef with Jett and his mother. What Darius' father did to you was unforgiveable, but I've been on one date with your son. You can't expect me to commit the rest of my life to him after one date." I leapt up from the table and then I did what I always do when faced with difficult situations. I ran.

Heading past the rows of caravans, I ran until I'd left the park. A bus was coming, and I jumped on it, letting it take me to Withernsea centre. I didn't feel like going home as I expected Darius would turn up there. I really did need to eat now. I was starting to feel faint with the lack of food because I had expended a LOT of energy the night before. It was my day off, and I'd thought after eating I would spend the rest of the day with Darius, getting to know him better—both his body and his mind—but no, here I was again all by myself.

I realised I'd walked up to work. Sod my day off, I needed to keep occupied. I unlocked and headed up the back stairs to find myself flung up against the stairwell wall tied in blue webs.

"Oh, it's you." My bestie let me back down gently, her eyes changing from a weird blue back to normal.

"What the fuck, Shelley?"

"Kim, when have you ever, EVER, come into work unless you were rostered? Forgive me if I thought we were being broken into."

"You have me there I suppose." I pouted.

"Anyway, what are you doing here?"

I climbed up the rest of the stairs. "Do you think I could actually get past the stairs and then I might tell you."

I followed her into her office and took a seat. "I'm sorry to disturb you at work, but I didn't want to go straight home."

"What's wrong?" Shelley walked up to me and placed a hand on my arm.

"It's Darius."

"God, what's happened now?"

"It's the pressure. I didn't know I'd set off this pack war thing. Then I find out Jett is Darius' half-brother, and now his mother wants me to mate him on the next full moon in a week's time!"

"Steady on there, rewind. Jett is what? Whose mother? Or is Jett's mother also Darius' mother? I'm lost."

I went through everything, bringing my best friend up to date.

"Flipping heck, Kim, you don't half know how to fuck up spectacularly."

"I know. Now what do I do about it?"

"As the current head of Withernsea, I'm going to ask for a meeting with Edon and Jett. They are the alphas of the pack. I need to discuss the situation, and ask for it to be taken into account that you are not pack, were not aware of pack rules, and therefore events should be excluded, unless you commit to them with full knowledge."

"You'd do that?"

"I would think it's part of my duties. Even though you are my best friend, you are also a Withernsea resident, and you are being held hostage to mate with a were shifter in order to avoid the repercussions from another shifter. I think in this day and age we should be able to choose our own partner, not be tricked into it or forced into it by arcane rules."

Shelley took out a bottle of blood, drank it down, and then followed it straight with another.

I sat there with my mouth agog.

She wiped her mouth. "As you can see, my thirst is getting worse. Theo and I are proposing that I go to the Caves soon to be turned. I have an appointment there tomorrow for assessment. That's one of the things I was doing here today, seeing if I could get through what I need to do in case I can't make it into work next week."

"Tell me what I can do to help," I said. "I could do with my mind taking off things."

We worked steadily all afternoon. Shelley had brought in a hamper full of food that Theo had supplied and insisted she take with her to satisfy any hunger she had, so I had had plenty to eat. I was ready for a coffee from Jax's though, so I decided that before I went home, I'd treat myself and get a coffee and a doughnut.

"Thanks for everything this afternoon, Kim. I'm hoping to be in this week, but it depends what they say at the Caves tomorrow."

"Keep me posted. I worry about you, you know? My best friend, the half-wyvern/half-witch, soon to be mixed with vampire. When I first met you at that dating event, I didn't realise what a weirdo I was getting involved with."

Shelley laughed. "There's a way to go before we get as weird as some of that lot! Anyway, you can talk. You might yet become part-wolf."

"I really do like Darius, you know?" I told her. "But I don't like being rushed into things. This is potentially my first serious relationship. I can't cope with the pressure. I just can't."

"There shouldn't be any pressure. Leave it with me. If I end up being turned, then my dad can step back in and help sort everything out. He'd probably love that, lording it over the wolves."

Me and my bestie hugged each other.

"Take care of you and that baby first and foremost. I'll manage to get myself out of the mess I'm in. It's not like I haven't had practice."

I said goodbye and made my way down to Jax's.

The best thing about a close friend running a coffee shop was that even if the sign outside said closed you could knock on the door and be let in, and if there was anything left in the baked goods section you got them for free.

Seth let me in.

"Hey, Seth. Where's Jax?"

"I'm in the back, babes. Knee deep in invoices," a voice shouted out.

"Can I get a coffee to go, Seth, please?"

"Sure thing."

"Pack her a selection of cookies and cake, Seth, if you don't mind."

"Has she been this bossy with you all day?" I asked.

"Worse." Seth winked. We both knew Jax was lovely. "Sit down, I'll bring everything over."

I waited until my coffee was prepared and a cardboard box filled with treats. Seth walked over to the table and hovered.

"Kim, I need to apologise for my behaviour last night. I'd had a bit to drink, and well, I got a little jealous seeing you with Darius. I'm really ashamed of myself now. Don't worry, I totally get you have me in the 'friend zone'."

"No worries, Seth."

"Look, on Monday, can you get me some dates organised? I need to get myself back out there. Truth is, you remind me of my ex-wife, and I guess I'm still not fully over her. Maybe if I have some dates with other people, I can finally move on."

"I'll get you all sorted. Thanks for apologising, but there's no need. We all do stupid things when we've had a few too many. Any idea why Lucy was being weird with me?"

"Lucy's weird with everyone isn't she? She keeps telling me she's my guardian angel and sometimes follows me around."

"That's true enough." I took a taste of my delicious coffee and then I stood and picked up that and my bag of goodies. "Ah, bliss. Tonight, it's just going to be me and my coffee and cake."

Seth stood up. "It's time for me to leave too. You not seeing Darius tonight then?"

"No." I didn't elaborate. It was none of his business.

"I'm off, Jax," Seth yelled.

Jax came out front. "Sorry, I'm being rude. I'll catch you Monday, Kim. First coffee on the house because of my lack of manners. Seth, thanks once again for everything. See you Monday too."

Seth saluted her then turned to me. "Right, seeing as I pass your house to get to mine, do you want a lift?"

"Yeah, that would be great. If you don't mind." I was tired after all my late-night shenanigans. Maybe the coffee would wake me enough to cook a pizza.

I sat in Seth's BMW and sunk into the seat. After having a nice big taste of it, I placed my coffee in the drink holder and put my bag of goodies on the back seat. God, this was much better than catching the bus. After a minute, I felt my bum becoming warm and felt at the seat beneath me.

"Heated seats." Seth laughed.

"Jesus, Seth, I thought my arse had gone into the menopause."

The heat soaked into my back too and as the events of the evening took their toll. I closed my eyes.

When I woke up, I did that 'where am I?' thing for a minute and then I remembered I was in Seth's car. I turned to him. "Shit, sorry. I didn't mean to fall asleep. How long was I out?"

While I asked the question, I was staring out of the window trying to get my groggy, confused mind to work out where I was because it wasn't at my house. I could feel sleep trying to pull me back under.

"What's happening? Where are we, Seth? Just take me home, will you?"

"Sorry, Kim. I'm afraid I owed a debt and delivering you was my payment. You'll wake up soon. I only put a small dose of sedative in your coffee."

"Wh-what are you talking about?"

My passenger car door opened, and I turned and looked into the face of Jett Conall.

"Well, hello there, Kim. You'll have to forgive the way I got you here, but I couldn't see you coming willingly. Now the sedative is going to have made you all kinds of weak, so me and Seth here are going to help you into the building."

My eyes went wide.

"I can promise you I've not brought you here to harm you. Just to talk to you. But please don't try anything silly because I'd hate to have to change my stance on violence towards women." Jett smiled, but rather than create warmth it chilled me to the bone.

"What do you want? Just take me home, Jett. This is stupid."

"I'm only taking you home once we've had a little chat. And as for stupid. Well the only one of us being stupid here was you when you slept with my *brother.*" He spat the word brother out like it pained him to say it. "Now he's in front and I don't like that, Kim. I don't like that in our current challenge he is winning."

"He's not winning. I'm not a chess piece, ready to knock over, you know? I'm a human being."

"Yes, you are," he said. "So utterly human, but not for long, hey, Kim? Because soon you will be my wife, and a wolf."

My mouth dropped open, but he held up a hand before I could speak.

"I suggest you keep that pretty mouth quiet for now, while we get you inside. Otherwise, just like that chess piece you spoke of, I will knock you over." He made a fist of his hand, leaving even a half-awake me under no illusion as to what he meant.

"Are you coming quietly?" he said.

I nodded and undid my seatbelt.

I was in so much trouble.

Chapter 16

Kim

As I tried to get out of the car, I looked at my surroundings. We were in an industrial estate. I tried to find the name of it, but all I saw from that moment on was Seth's butt as he carried me over his shoulder and into one of the buildings. Inside, I was taken into an office area where my bag and phone were taken away from me before I was lowered onto a ratty old sofa. I was starting to come around and did my best to glare at Seth and Jett. Seth sat at my side, obviously to stop me should I attempt to get up, and Jett carried a chair in front of me. I watched as he sat himself down, a smug smile on his face.

"Kidnap. Really, Jett? You can't get dates the old-fashioned way now, you have to have us bundled into cars?"

"Actually, you got in the car willingly," Seth said.

"To be given a lift home!" I yelled. "Now take me back."

"You're not going anywhere right now, Kim, so you might as well get comfy," Jett drawled.

I gave him the side-eye. "I'm telling you now, and you." I glared at Seth. "You came between me and my coffee. I don't know when, but at some point, you will both pay."

Jett guffawed. "You're going to make a brilliant wife. I'll need to hone that temper so it's only in the bedroom though. I shall look forward to our fireworks."

"If I get my way, I shall stick a roman candle right up your arse, and then I'll give away wolf kebabs to anyone passing."

Jett threw a scarf at Seth. "Tie her mouth with that will you? It's time for her to start listening."

I shot up from the sofa, but Seth was a lot stronger than me. Between him and Jett my hands were tied behind my back with one scarf and then another was fastened around my head and over my mouth.

I was pushed back onto the sofa. I could feel my wrists already going dead with the tightness of the scarf and I tried to move the one across my mouth by moving my lips, but it was no use.

Finally, I sat still and subdued. My heart thudded as I realised I was now powerless and in a warehouse with two strong burly men.

"Mmmm. I smell your fear. Good, maybe now we can get somewhere. Now I have you compliant in front of me, let me explain what is going to happen. Firstly, I am going to cook for you, and you will eat it and enjoy it. I have to demonstrate my ability to care for you and our cubs, and although my wife is the one who will be in the kitchen, barefoot and pregnant, I will follow the rules to be equal to my enemy."

I could still glare at him, so I did my best evil eye.

"And you will be pregnant. Continually. Because it is my intention to breed a whole new Conall clan. My sons will be strong and will rule Withernsea."

I wanted to say that Shelley would never stand for that, but I still had the stupid scarves on. It was becoming plainer to me that Jett was almost feral. Whereas Darius was a man with an element of wolf; with Jett it was almost the reverse. His wolf ruled him. He barely seemed human at all.

"Now, Seth very kindly let me know that he overheard that your dear best friend, Shelley, is pregnant. Pregnant with the forthcoming ruler of Withernsea, and well, I shall want to make sure my clan work very well alongside her child. To that end this is what is going to happen, Kim. You will be released from here, later, when I feel like letting you go and feel I can trust you, and you will tell everyone that you are rejecting Darius and that on the full moon this following Friday you shall become my wife. I shall prepare the announcement and the ceremony. If you fail to do this, I will make sure everyone knows about Shelley's secret pregnancy and I will raise a bounty on her head so that she's too busy fending off death threats to help you."

My eyes went wide.

"Oh good, it looks like this is being understood."

He was insane. I tried to stand up, but Seth just pushed me back down. Tears of frustration began to roll down my face.

"Look, she's so deliriously happy, she's crying." Jett laughed.

Jett was a stunning looking man with his hazel eyes and dark hair, and yet while he basked in his victory plans, he looked cruel. It gave an ugliness to his appearance.

"Here's what's going to happen. We will leave you here for a while to get used to the fact you're at my mercy, and then I'm going to make you something to eat, and I suggest you eat it all up like a good girl, because I don't think you'll like the consequences if you don't. Now I'm not into rape, I just want what is mine fair and square, and so even though I can smell that dog has had his hands all over you and sullied you with his seed, I will be the bigger person and let you go home, once you've accepted our engagement. After we mate at the full moon, you will become mine anyway once I've bitten you."

He stretched his arms above his head. "That's the plan, unless of course you start trying to play silly buggers, and I really suggest you don't." He tilted his head at me. "Because my bounty-on-Shelley's-head post is ready to be sent. I just have to press the button."

He laughed at me.

"Okay, Seth. Let's leave her in here." He looked at his watch. "It's eight pm now. I'll come back in the morning at eight am. See how amenable to my plan she is after twelve hours of no food or drink. You sit in the security office and watch her on the monitor from there. Don't go in. She's a clever lady. She'll try to get free."

And with that he walked out of the room, Seth following behind him. The door slammed, plunging me into total darkness and that was me stuck.

I laid back on the sofa for a moment trying not to let the panic seep into me. The last thing I needed to do was to have a panic attack, or for me to attempt something stupid and fall and hurt myself. As my eyes became accustomed to the darkness, I looked around the room, seeing if there was anything I could use to get my hands free. If Seth caught me, then of course I would have to face him, but I had to try. I got myself off the sofa and walked around to the edge of the desk and backed my wrists and the material against the corner and tried to rub through it, but it didn't work.

I guessed that Seth was watching me, probably laughing at my vain attempts to get free. Eventually, I gave up and went back to the sofa. I'd just have to try to sleep away the hours until they came to me again. I was cold, hungry, and knew at some point I would need to pee. The saddest thing of all was that I didn't know when anyone would actually realise I was missing. I mean, would they? Shelley had said see you Monday and her mind was on her appointment with the Caves. Same with Jax; she wouldn't know until Monday if I failed to turn up. Darius might try to contact me, I suppose, but it couldn't be taken for granted. My family certainly wouldn't care. That was one thing about a pack. A big group like that looked out for each other. I bet they'd notice if someone went missing.

And then I cried.

I cried for the family I didn't have.

The love I'd been too scared to embrace.

The predicament I was in because Jett had me held hostage and not only physically.

Until I knew Shelley and her baby could be safe, I would have no choice but to follow his instructions. I just had to hope to God that in the meantime I thought of something to help us both.

※

It was a long and uncomfortable night, spent with only my thoughts to keep me company. As the door opened and light came in, I winced while my eyes got accustomed to the brightness.

"Take the mask off her mouth. Leave the one on her wrists for now," Jett commanded Seth.

I stayed still while he undid it.

"Hmmm, you're not looking as feisty today, Kim. Have you thought about my proposal?"

"I have." It came out as a croak. I was so thirsty.

"Take her to the bathroom and get her some water while you're there," Jett ordered. Seth dragged me up and along the corridor to a bathroom. The odour of urine hit me as soon as I walked in. A typical men's urinal.

"Can you help me?" I asked. "I can't get my pants down with my hands being tied."

It was the utmost in humiliation, and I would never forgive them for this. I'd had the devil himself try to kill me and it hadn't hurt me this bad.

As Seth helped me pull my pants back up, I brought my knee up and kneed him in the mouth with it. He backed away wincing with pain. My knee was in agony, but it had felt good to inflict pain on him.

He wiped his mouth, a touch of blood coming away from a cut on his lip. "I guess I deserve that. I'm sorry. You're not the only person he's blackmailing. If I could help you, I would."

I wondered what he'd done to Seth, that would make him assist in a kidnapping. It must be pretty bad. But regardless, I was here directly because Seth had brought me, so there was no sympathy coming from me whatsoever. I despised him.

Lowering my head under the tap that Seth put on, I took several large gulps of the water. I'd never take simple things like that for granted again.

Then I was taken back to the office.

"Oh, Kim. I hope you didn't try to escape."

"No. Just an accident," Seth said. "While I tried to assist her in the bathroom."

"You can untie her hands now. They'll take a while to get the strength back in them anyway."

When the scarf was untied, I rubbed my wrists against my body frantically. I was in so much pain from how long they'd been tied.

"Okay here's a slice of toast I've made you. Eat that and then I've fulfilled my feeding part of things."

He thrust the toast into my hands, and I was so hungry I ate it too fast. The bread felt like it was stuck in my throat.

"Right, let's conclude our business, shall we? All I need from you now is your signature on this piece of paper that says you agree to marry me on Friday night and mate with me under the full moon. As soon as I have that signature, I can send out the engagement notice and the invitations. The woods at the back of this industrial estate are lovely for the ceremony and then for the evening reception I think we'll go take over our rightful land in Withernsea."

He placed a pen on the desk. "Soon as you sign that, you're free to go." He laughed. "Well, obviously you're not free. I mean you've a wedding outfit to sort out. Make sure the undies are nice, won't you? Oh, and do you like home movies, only I was thinking of filming us and sending my brother a copy. Then again, he'll probably be dead and unable to watch it."

"Please don't kill him," I choked out. "I want to save my friend and please leave Darius. If you take the pack and me, is that not enough? If he's alive he'll suffer more watching us, won't he?"

Jett scratched his chin. "You have a point. I can't let him live long because he'll try to find a way to retaliate, but maybe just for a little while I could let him watch me gloat."

I walked over to the table and signed the paper. It was official. I was engaged to Jett Conall. Our wedding set for Friday evening. I had just over five days to pray for a miracle.

Seth dropped me at home. Come Monday morning, he would be back at the coffee shop as usual, and I wasn't allowed to say a word. The minute he suspected anything, Shelley and her baby's life was in danger.

I had to go back to being Kim, the selfish bitch, and I didn't like it one bit as it had taken me until now to realise I'd finally lost her.

Chapter 17

Lucy

I sat in the office typing up Frankie's latest findings on supernaturals. My angel bleeps had developed malfunctions, going off over and over again, driving me mad. When I'd called Seth to check he was okay and asked him if he'd seen Kim, he'd told me that they were out together having dinner and her phone battery had gone flat. Everything was okay, so why did I have a feeling in the pit of my stomach that things weren't okay at all?

Frankie had been his sweet usual self. I didn't know what his secret was and how Kim was involved but I was 90% convinced now that they weren't having an affair. Not completely, because he had left her house while she was wrapped in a bathrobe, but she'd not snogged him on the doorstep which I would have done if someone had just boned me good and proper. I was doing as advised by Andrew and waiting it out.

Theo had called first thing saying that the Caves had decided to admit Shelley for turning after she'd bitten him again last night. I'd assured him that Kim and I could cover. All we needed now was for the lady herself to turn up.

The door to her office banged. Talk of the devil. I went in to tell her about Shelley.

"Fuck, you been on the lash all weekend?" I said as I took in her haggard appearance. She had dark bags under her eyes, like she'd not slept for a month.

"Yeah, I've been celebrating," she said.

"Celebrating?"

"Yeah. I'm engaged, just like you. No ring yet though, we're going to get that later."

"You, and... Darius?"

She shook her head.

"Seth?"

Her head shook again.

"Not my Frankie!" I screamed.

She cut me a look. "Don't be ridiculous. I'm engaged to Jett. Jett Conall."

"Who?"

She actually eye-rolled me. "Jett. He's a were from the Hogsthorpe Pack. I was on a date with him the night you first got together with Frankie."

"Oh, him. And you're engaged. Already? How long have you been dating?"

"Three days. I mean when you know, you know, right?"

"When's the wedding?"

"Friday."

"Friday?" I yelled. "This coming Friday?"

"Yeah, so as you can imagine I have lots to do to prepare for married life. Sorry that I'm taking the edge off your proposal a little by getting married first."

"Does Darius know about this?"

"No. What business of his is it?"

I held my hands up outstretched. "None, unless you consider that four days ago you were out on a date with him."

She waved a hand at me. "He's of no consequence. Now I'd better go see Shelley and see if she can help me shop."

"Oh, Shelley's at the Caves. We've to cover for her. She'll not be out until Thursday morning apparently. She bit Theo again and so she's being turned."

"That's good. Until Thursday you say?"

I furrowed my brow. "It's good? That your friend is being turned into a vampire?"

"She's married to one and having a baby one, well a mix up with vamp in it, so it makes sense for her to be one. I'll be part-wolf on Friday."

I smacked myself in the forehead. "Have you taken some hallucinogens? Actually, have I taken some hallucinogens?"

"I don't know. Have you?"

"Well, you tell me, because I'm sure you've told me that you're marrying a werewolf on Friday, one that I wasn't aware you were dating. Plus, you're happy, rather than worried that your friend is in the process of being changed into a vampire."

"Just a regular Monday morning really working here," Kim said nonchalantly. "Anyway, I'm hungry and thirsty, so why don't you pop down to Jax's and get us both a coffee and some cake? Seeing as Shelley is off, I reckon that makes me your boss, right?"

The old me would have singed her hair off. The new me smiled and agreed. Mainly because something was wrong—very, very wrong. I'd get our drinks and question Seth, see if he could shed any light on the problem.

I'd returned to my office to get my bag and purse when an almighty white light almost blinded me. I turned around to find my boss, Angel Sophia, standing in front of me, looking all celestial in a long white dress covered in diamante.

"Thank goodness you're here. My pagers aren't working properly," I told her.

She walked over and gazed down into my eyes. "Lucy. Your pagers are working perfectly. That's the amount of trouble both your charges were in, and you ignored them."

I gaped at her. "But..."

"It's not your fault. We're looking at an alternative communication system. This one was poorly thought out. It's really hard to get everyone on board with technological advances though when most of us are thousands of years old." She sighed. "Anyway, Lucy, your main challenges have arrived. Both of your charges have made, or are going to make, mistakes that could have repercussions for the whole of Withernsea. It's time for you to step up, Lucy. You're needed. The angels above need you to take care of the potential hell about to be wreaked down here.

"I knew it. I knew there was something off about Kim's wedding. Leave it with me, Sophia," I said. "I got this. I promise."

"I hope so," she said and then with a kindly stroke of my shoulder she disappeared in a blast of white light leaving only a trail of white feathers behind her.

Definitely the first thing I needed to do was talk to Seth. I needed some help though to get to the bottom of things. I could no longer be evil... but that didn't mean someone else couldn't.

The coffee shop was packed with people once again. This was getting on my nerves now. Damn, I didn't want to wait in a long queue, and I needed to talk to Seth. I decided that seeing as it was being done with good intentions it would be okay and so I shouted, "Fire," at the top of my voice until everyone had run out screaming.

I'd run through to the back just in time to stop Jax from actually calling the Fire Brigade. "Sorry, Jax. I needed to talk to Seth urgently."

"So you created panic in my customers and cleared them all from the shop? It had better be life or death, Lucy. Life or death."

I'd never seen little Jax with attitude before. It was actually kind of amusing, though inappropriate, you know, on the lines of a circus freak show. *Let's watch the angry pixie squeak.* Yeah, I knew she wasn't a pixie. I'd already had an encounter with a real one of those, but she was short, okay?

"I'll get them all back in afterwards. They'll just be admiring all the little doggies in the grooming parlour. It's all bitches on heat around here these days."

Jax rolled her eyes and went out the back. "Shout me if you need me, Seth."

"What can I get you, Lucy?" he asked me.

"Just need a coffee for me and my friend, Kim. And two chocolate doughnuts. Only we're busy today. Shelley's off."

"Oh? Everything okay?"

"Yeah, fine. Well, it is with Shelley. Listen, you were out with Kim on Friday night, right? That's what you said when I called you. Only she's in a mood today. Not talking much."

"Yeah, we had dinner."

I nodded my head. "Thought so."

"What?"

"Well, she was with Darius Thursday night, and you Friday night, but after that she was with yet another man, and well, I hope I don't upset you telling you this, but... she's marrying him."

"She is? She's getting married after having been out with me Friday night? That's disgusting." Seth pulled a face. "Well, that's just charming that is."

"I knew she wouldn't have told you. She's so blasé. She used to date my fiancé you know. I'm surprised she's not in the tabloids with her exploits—the *I have a different guy every day of the week* stories. I think I should find this Jett dude and have a word with him. Let him know what she's like. It's not fair. She's probably given him a disease." I stared. "You didn't sleep with her, did you? She's probably riddled."

"No. No. Listen, I would just leave her to it. She must love the guy if she agreed to marry him."

"Huh, she loved him yesterday, but today's Monday, maybe today it's the postman's turn or something. I think he deserves to know what he's getting himself into."

"Seriously, I wouldn't. I once tried interfering in someone's business and it didn't end well for me," Seth said, his head dipping down.

"Look at that. I'm letting our coffees go cold," I said. "Okay, I'll keep my mouth shut. It's her life after all. I'll just concentrate on my own wedding."

He nodded.

"Right, I'll just go apologise to Jax again, and then I'll go out the back entrance and up to ours, so thanks, Seth, and I'll see you again soon."

"Yeah, see you, Lucy."

I walked into Jax's.

"Sorry about that, Jax. Listen, you know how busy you are? Did that start the same day Seth started?"

"Yeah. Aren't women fickle? Get some man candy and they're here like a shot."

That word hit me like the cold jet from a water pistol. Shot! Could that be it? Was there something in the drinks? Things weren't adding up where Seth was concerned.

"Yes, unfortunately we are. Yet if a guy did that to us, we'd call them a sexist pig. Good to be a woman, hey? See you soon."

I went back out to the cafe. "Sorry, Seth. I can't find my mobile. Just seeing if I left it out here. Oh there it is," I said, lifting it out from behind the napkin dispenser. "I don't suppose you have a tray I can borrow for carrying this stuff? It's burning my hand a little."

As he bent down to get a tray, I switched my drink with one left by a human customer.

"Thanks, Seth. I'll stop being a pain now and get out of your hair."

The moment I returned to my office, I quickly dropped a coffee and bun off with Kim and then I sat at my desk and pressed play on the phone. I'd left the voice recorder going while I'd gone into Jax's.

"Jett. It's Seth. Listen, if you get contacted by a woman called Lucy, as far as she's concerned Kim was with me all Friday night, all right? No. No, she's not suspicious. She's fine. No. There's no problem here. I've got it covered. Just promise me please that when you're in charge of the pack, you'll get her back for me. That was what we agreed. You'd get the pack, and I'd get my wife back. Yeah, man. Just tell me when to drop the news and I'll do it. Withernsea Gazette. On it. Okay, boss. Yeah, jobs secure, can keep a close eye on her from here. That love spell is working like a charm. A charm, get it? Oh yeah, bye then."

I listened to it one more time and then I knew I had a wait ahead of me. Until my vampire fiancé would be out of bed and could help me make sense of all this and what could be happening. I carefully picked up the drink I'd took from the coffee shop and put it in the small space behind the filing cabinet. I couldn't afford for it to get tidied away.

Chapter 18

Darius

We'd been called into an urgent pack meeting, so I made my way quickly to the hall. I walked in to find everyone being handed a sheet of paper. The way they looked at me when they read it filled me with dread. Edon passed me a copy. It was a printout of an email sent to the pack.

To:Withernseashifters@btinternet.co.uk
From: Hogsthorpeshifters@btinternet.co.uk
Date: Monday 5 February 2018
Time: 07:00

ANNOUNCEMENT

The Hogsthorpe Shifters are delighted to announce the engagement of alpha Jett Conall to Kimberly Louise Fletcher on Friday 9 February 2018 at nine pm.
The ceremony will take place in Hogsthorpe Hall before the newlyweds consummate the wedding under the full moon in Hogsthorpe Woods.
Hogsthorpe pack only in attendance.

End of message.

I fell onto the nearest seat. "What? This can't possibly be right.

She wouldn't do this, so he's forcing her somehow. What do we do? What can we do?"

Edon looked at me in a kindly, fatherly way. "That is why I have called the meeting, Darius. I know how I would proceed, but on this occasion I feel you should direct the pack.

I sat for a moment with my hands steepled, my elbows resting on my knees. Trying my best to breathe slowly through my nose and quiet the wolf threatening to erupt from me to rip out Jett Conall's throat.

"Okay. I feel I need to see if Kim is with Jett or at home. If she is at work, I shall attempt to talk to her as a first course of action. We shall reconvene at midday once I have more information.

Edon nodded and the rest of the pack murmured their agreement. With the next meeting set, the others left, leaving me with Edon.

"Spoken like a true alpha." Edon smiled. "It would seem when it comes to discussions about your mate, you find your confidence."

I considered what he was saying.

"She makes me feel whole. If she marries that mutt, I don't know how I'll survive."

Mates were our everything, and I had no doubt in my mind that she was mine.

He nodded, and I left, grabbed my things and set off on my bike to drive to Kim's office.

Once there, I walked to the back door and knocked with such force that I put several dints in the door. A buzzer sounded and Lucy's voice came out.

"Darius. Pack it in, or I'm not letting you in. And straight to my office, not Kim's. We need to talk first. You got me?"

"I need to see her," I growled.

"Won't do you any good, and I have intel, so you need to speak to me first. Comprendez?"

I sighed. "Yes, okay. You first."

She sounded the buzzer and ignoring her instructions I stomped straight into Kim's office.

Kim startled when I walked in.

I held up the piece of paper. "What's this shit about you marrying Jett?"

She looked me straight in the eye, no smile on her face, just a dead-eyed look. "What about it?"

"Don't give me that," I roared. "What's he doing? It's got to be blackmail because no way would you marry him voluntarily."

She stood up. "Not true. I intended to marry him all along."

"Then what was all the other night? Sleeping with me, meeting my family? I know you felt what I did."

At this point the door flew open and Lucy stood there. "God, you stubborn arsed manbeast."

"I didn't feel that, Darius. I just pretended, so as to crush you further. That was my plan all along and well, look at you, it would appear I'm succeeding."

"This is bullshit." I punched the wall with my fist. The plaster broke off in chunks and dust rained down on the floor.

I turned to Lucy. "Sorry, I will have that made good." I moved back around to face Kim. "Stop your lying and tell me the truth. I can help you. The pack will help you."

"The truth is, Darius, that I love him. He's my true mate and I'll be marrying him on Friday. You need to deal with it."

She sat back down on her chair and started tapping on her keyboard.

"That's all you're saying?"

"Yes. To be honest I'm bored now, and as I'm sure you can imagine, with my wedding being on Friday, I have a lot to do. So if that's all... unless you want me to put you back on the dating agency books now with you being a free agent?"

I stomped out of the office, Lucy moving ahead of me, and then I swung the door shut with such force that I ripped it off its hinges.

"I'll be back, shortly," I said to Lucy and then I ran down the stairs and behind some storage sheds where I sat down and calmed my breathing so I wouldn't change, because if I did, I was going to be out of control.

I'd smelled her when I'd walked in. My mate. MINE.

The words she'd said. I couldn't believe that they were true because if they were... well it didn't bear thinking about. I needed to throw down against Jett.

"What are you thinking there, while looking all Beast?"

I looked at my hands and felt around my chin. Fur. Oh shit.

"Lucy, I'm sorry."

"Sorry for not coming to my office and listening to me? It's probably better we get to talk here actually. Out in the fresh air and away from Kim." She took a seat on a concrete step at the side of me.

"I think she's being blackmailed by Jett, and Seth is involved somehow. I overheard him on the phone. He said something about Jett getting him his wife back.

I stood up, flexing and stretching my arms. "I need to talk to Seth."

"No. And I insist this time, Darius. No bull in a china shop. I'm waiting for Frankie to wake up because there's something else going on. The coffee is being spiked. That's why there are so many customers. I want Frankie's expertise on everything before we decided on a course of action."

"What's Shelley said about this? Surely she thinks it's crazy what her friend is doing?"

"Shelley's in hospital being turned right now. Theo's with her. So she can't help."

I thrust out my chest. "Right, I need to get back to my pack for midday to make plans. I think I shall make a challenge for supremacy."

"Look, could you change your meeting time to say, five pm? Then I can attend and bring Frankie. Only I know you have pack business, but like I said this goes deeper than that. I've been given a job to protect Kim, Seth, and Shelley, so I need to know what your plans are. Seriously. Don't take on the angelic realm."

A white feather floated down in front of my eyes at that point.

"See, there's your message. Don't piss us about."

"Okay." I exhaled. "Five pm at the caravan park. Ask for the meeting with Edon at reception and they'll show you through."

"Thank you. Please in the meantime don't do anything stupid. Not until I'm up to date with everything. I need Frankie's files on the packs so that I'm up to speed."

"Lucy, I can tell you anything you want to know right now. I suppose we should start with the fact that Jett is my half-brother."

Lucy groaned. "Oh this just gets better and better."

~

"The meeting has been re-convened to five pm. In attendance today it is our honour to host Lucy Fir and Frankie Love. To those who are unaware: Lucy is an ex-demon and is now an earth angel with the current responsibilities of caring for the futures of Kim Fletcher; Shelley Landry; and a Seth Whittaker, a barista from Jax's whom we shall discuss in due course. Frankie is an ex-wizard, now vampire, who is researching supernatural history." Edon stopped speaking for a moment and the pack welcomed Lucy and Frankie. "I would now like to invite Lucy to speak."

"Thank you, Edon," Lucy said, extremely respectfully and politely. "I have known Kim Fletcher for quite some time now, and it is my opinion that she very much cares for Darius here, even if she's too stupid to admit it. There is obviously something else going on, blackmail or whatever, that is forcing her to carry on with this wedding charade. Since she first met Jett at the restaurant, she has made no effort to see him since, and only called him to apologise for involving him in a bid to make Darius jealous. However, she was only able to leave an answering machine message."

"She recorded this information on her non-interest in Mr Conall?" Edon clarified.

"Yes, your honour. I mean, Edon."

A few shifters laughed only to be silenced by a glare so evil it could only come from someone who'd spent time in Hell.

"Darius, as a police officer in special investigations, could you manage to trace this message?"

"Possibly. I'm sure I could get someone to look into it."

Edon nodded. "It is evidence that can help us."

Lucy continued. "Now, the barista, Seth. He has for some reason been placing a love potion in certain coffees. Not all, but enough that Jax's has had a steady stream of customers over the last few weeks. I'm not sure in what way this ties in with everything, but I need to find out. Also, Ebony, Withernsea's seer, has been without her visions for the last few days. This also needs investigation."

Edon looked over to me. "Would you like to direct the pack, or shall I?"

I cleared my throat. "Alpha Edon, I would like to suggest the following as a possible course of action. Firstly, we reply to the Hogsthorpe email with our protest and challenge."

"What does that mean?" Lucy interrupted.

"That we do not accept the engagement notice, as one of our pack wishes to challenge for the position of mate. This in pack law is a declaration of war as Darius would be directly challenging Hogsthorpe's alpha. Something I suspect is exactly what young Master Conall wanted, as if he wins Darius, he can then directly challenge me as alpha, and potentially take over the whole pack."

"That's what Ebony saw," Lucy said. "It's coming true."

"After this, I propose we capture Seth Whittaker and bring him here for questioning. Holding him here until after our business with Hogsthorpe is concluded, or until the marriage of Jett and Kim has taken place should it still proceed."

"I agree," Lucy said. "We need to find out what's going on. Although if he goes out of contact it will tip Jett off that something's not quite right."

"Jett knows exactly what's happening," I told her. "We've no time to lose." I turned to our secretary. "Please prepare the protest."

To:Hogsthorpeshifters@btinternet.co.uk
From: Withernseashifters@btinternet.co.uk
Date: Monday 5 February 2018
Time: 18:00

STATEMENT OF PROTEST

In accordance with the Shifter Handbook please take note of Chapter 4, Section 2a.

We hereby declare a protest with regards to the forthcoming marriage of:

JETT CONALL and KIMBERLY LOUISE FLETCHER

Please note receipt of this statement and choose a time and place for this matter to be debated.

ALPHA EDON WOODLAND

End of message.

With the protest sent, it was time to bring Seth in for questioning. We agreed that we would await the response from Jett and that nothing more should be done today. Lucy and Frankie went home, and I went back to my family where I had the great task of letting my mum and my sister know that we were about to go to war.

To:Withernseashifters@btinternet.co.uk
From: Hogsthorpeshifters@btinternet.co.uk
Date: Tuesday 6 February 2018
Time: 07:00

ACKNOWLEDGEMENT OF PROTEST

In accordance with the Shifter Handbook, Chapter 4, Section 2b, a meeting has been arranged for:

Thursday 8 February 2018, 7pm
Building One, Henry Smith Retail Park
Herring Road, Hogsthorpe.

End of message.

Chapter 19

Kim

I could barely motivate myself to get dressed. In fact, it was only the fact I was covering for Shelley that made me get out of bed to shower and get ready for work. Seeing Darius yesterday had almost killed me. Since we'd slept together there was a pull drawing me to him. Keeping my distance was physically and mentally hurting me. I couldn't explain it beyond it being some kind of physiological or biological response.

I was also worrying about Shelley. Was the turning going okay? Was the baby alright? There had been no word and no response to texts although reception at the Caves could be funky.

The truth was, I had nothing to do for the wedding now. Jett was arranging everything. Obviously, he didn't trust me. He'd called last night reiterating his threats and telling me to spend the next couple of nights packing my things because Thursday evening I was to gather my essentials and move to Hogsthorpe. My other belongings would be collected after the wedding. I hated what was happening to me, to my life. Maybe I only had to stay married to him until Shelley had the baby? It was going to rule Withernsea. Surely, she could take it from there? Yeah, I just had to wait out the birth. But by then what would have happened to me? What would Jett have done to me? Would the mating itself make me like him? Love him even? Would he have killed Darius or at least reduced his pack to such a position that he would hate me? Passing my hall mirror, I stared at myself. Where was the girl with the attitude who stood up to her father and didn't stand for this crap? She just wasn't here today. Too many bad memories flooding my mind.

There was a knock at the door. Sighing, I walked over and looked through the spyhole.

Alyssa. Darius' sister.

Fuck.

"I know you're there. I can smell you. Open the fucking door. We need to talk."

I walked away and wandered back into the living room to sit on the sofa. I couldn't risk being seen letting Alyssa in. Hopefully she'd go away.

There was an almighty cracking noise, and I cowered behind the sofa. The next thing I knew I was being pulled out by the roots of my hair.

I whimpered in pain, following her where she walked to keep my hair in my scalp. "I've come to see what the hell you're playing at. My brother just declared war. War. For you." She pushed me onto the sofa.

"Wh-what?" I gasped.

"News of your engagement was sent by email. He, well, the pack on his behalf, replied. They refuse to accept the ceremony as official and so a meeting has been arranged for Thursday evening. He's keeping it close to the wire is Jett. Now, what I want to know is do you love Jett or Darius? And don't give me any shit because as you can see, I deal it, I don't take it."

I stared at the growing woman in front of me. No fear, and full of sass, she was everything I was a few weeks and months ago. I burst into tears.

"Such a mess. Such a mess." I shook my head.

Alyssa looked around. "Ah. Just a sec." She went out of the room and came back with some toilet tissue and a paper and pen. On the paper she wrote:

In case you're being bugged.

I scrawled on the pad.

. . .

Hate, Date, Or Mate?

He threatened to kill Shelley and the baby. I can't risk that. Not even for your family. Shelley's baby is the future ruler of Withernsea. She has to come first, above us all.

I gave her the pen back. She nodded and wrote on the paper.

Do you love my brother? If you had a choice, would you choose him?

I took the pen back.

With all my heart.

I'm sorry for pulling your hair and shouting.

It's okay. I guess if I had a sibling, I'd do the same.

Sorry about your door. I'll get it fixed.

God, what was it with these wolves and doors?

In case we're being recorded, I need to say some more shit and then stomp out. Carry on as normal and know that we have your back. We will sort this, and we will make sure your friend and baby are okay.

Listen, if it comes to Shelley and the baby, or me. You choose them, you promise? I'm expendable. They aren't.

. . .

My brother wouldn't agree, but I promise.

Alyssa stood up. "Right, now you're a little more subdued, stay away from my brother, you hear me? He deserves better than you. You're a tramp, going after all those men at once. Jett deserves you. Come near us again and I'll hand you your arse." She winked at me and then left.

Her words, although a joke, should have stung, coming as they did on the anniversary of my father's death. It was a reminder of all the things he used to say to me. But I wasn't a tramp. I had to remember that. Blowing my nose again, I went into the bathroom and splashed my face with cold water and then I brushed my teeth.

Where are you, Kim? I said in my mind to my reflection in the mirror.

I'd said myself in my writing that I was expendable at the side of Shelley, and without a life with her and Darius in it, what was the point? There was no point in anything if my future was a life with Jett.

What did I have to lose? I may as well come out fighting. I'd look for the cues coming from the Withernsea pack, and I'd look for a weapon. Anything I could use to take Jett out.

It had taken a young girl to show me the way. Her attitude reminded me a lot of myself at that age. Standing up for myself against my father. He hadn't changed me, and neither would Jett.

I was ready to fight.

Chapter 20

I looked at the paper my sister gave me, and I couldn't believe my eyes.

"I don't know whether to kill you for going to see her alone or hug you for what's written here."

"Can you do neither, cos I like my life and then there's my personal space."

"That's why she's marrying him. Can you see, she would give up her life for the ruler of Withernsea. She is such a suitable mate."

"Yeah, whatever, bro. Maybe instead of dreaming, you could formulate a plan that takes care of the heir, ya know."

"Seth is being picked up as we speak. He frequents a gym that has a handy back entrance."

"Yeah, well any trouble and I'd go for *his* handy back entrance, with a sharp stick. Now, it's been swell chatting with you, but I have things to do."

"Please take extra care, Lys. Especially right now. I don't want a Hogsthorpe mutt near you."

But she just waved me off as she headed out of the door.

No one put my baby sister in the corner.

~

Seth's eyes were wide as he sat on a chair in front of the pack; some of whom had turned into their animals for added effect. His hands were bound behind him, and his feet were tied to the chair.

Once again Edon had stood back to let me proceed.

I paced in front of Seth. "I'll just let you listen to this." I played the message Lucy had recorded and his face fell. He couldn't deny what was so blatantly there. His head hung.

"My ex. She went off with one of his pack. I went to see them. He promised me he'd get her to come back if I helped him. All I did was watch Kim, man. I didn't harm her. I just had to try to disrupt the two of you getting together. Try to get her to date me instead until nearer the full moon."

"What was the deal with the love potion in the coffee, and how did you choose who got it?"

"Everyone got it. It just works on some people and not others. I needed to make sure we had plenty of customers so I could keep my job. I needed to be in that shop near to Kim. That was the easiest way."

"Where did you get the spell? Only it was pretty powerful. Even Margret, Shelley's mother didn't detect it."

"Jett acquired them. I don't know where from."

"Them? There was more than one?"

"I meant one. The love potion."

Lucy looked at me. Seth was clearly a terrible liar, and I felt he was owed for the shit he'd put us through, blackmailed or not. I hit him with a powerful right hook, opening up a cut on his cheek.

"Okay, man. Okay. Not the face."

God he was vain.

He looked at Lucy. "There was a spell on that fortune teller too. To block her visions. I distracted her in her shop and put something in her vodka. It lasts one to two weeks."

"Rav. Smack him for that," Lucy yelled. The demon she had brought with her backhanded him. It must have stung like a bitch.

"That felt wonderful. Thank you for inviting me."

"You're welcome. I can't do bad stuff now, so I needed an old colleague, and I thought of you."

"I'm honoured."

"Okay." I lifted my hand to quieten them all down. "Seth. You will be placed in a room here and put on constant guard until you can be released safely. We have your phone. Should you find some way to contact and warn Jett and endanger the pack then I will literally have you thrown to the wolves." Drool and growls came from the animals and the smell of urine filled the air as a wet patch seeped onto the chair. "Take him away and get him cleaned up please."

"Right, what now?" Lucy asked. "If you don't need me, I'm going to collect Ebony from Theo's. She's been trialling the B&B, said it's been even better without the owners there, like a retreat. There's only been Mary around. I need to get Frankie on the case and then we'll get in touch with Theo and make sure Shelley has extra protection."

"When needed I will send you two of my wolves to help protect Shelley and her baby."

"No, you'll need them all to fight Jett."

He shook his head.

"Like, my mate said on her note, I am expendable when it comes to the future ruler of Withernsea."

"You're both crazy, there's no wonder you get along." Lucy sighed and left taking her demon friend with her.

Left with the pack, Edon asked for us to be excused for a moment and we stood to one end of the room.

"You are handling this beautifully, Darius. I would like to take this opportunity to propose you now take over from me as alpha of the Withernsea pack."

I shook my head. "My father was scum."

"Yes, he was, but you are not. You have his blood running through your veins. I have been watching you, Darius. You command with ease and your wolf; he is growing ever stronger. You were born to be alpha."

"I would not take your place. You have my utmost respect."

"I know. But to be honest I'm fancying a few holidays abroad. I'm not getting any younger."

"But what about Reid and Sonny? Do they not want to succeed you?"

"No. They don't have the slightest interest, and I believe it's because we weren't born to the position. You were. Meet Jett alpha to alpha on Thursday, Darius. We can have the coronation ceremony tomorrow evening."

I looked at Edon. Could I do this? Be alpha? Lead the pack?

I imagined myself with Kim at my side. Yes, I could do this. For the pack, and for us. I would meet Jett on an equal footing. The ceremony would strengthen my wolf. It was time.

"Make the arrangements," I told Edon.

The ceremony took place the following evening. There was a procedure to follow from the Handbook. Edon spoke first, retiring from his role and then he crowned me with a crown made of twigs and I said my own speech and commitment to my pack.

> "I vow to protect you with my very last breath.
> To my family.
> WITHERNSEA."

Everyone raised a glass filled with either water or whiskey. "Alpha Darius. WITHERNSEA." My mum was crying, the rest of my family whooped and cheered. Then all changed into their animals and we ran through the woods and chased each other. My wolf was joyous, exultant. For the first time in my life, I felt completely comfortable in my own skin and fur.

This was who I was born to be.

The alpha.

Chapter 21

Lucy

I went to the farm to pick up Ebony.

She came to the door looking very relaxed. "Lucy? What are you doing here? They aren't here, you know? Shelley has been turned."

"I know. I also know why you aren't having visions. Can I come in?"

Mary appeared in the doorway. "Course you can, love."

I walked inside and took a seat.

"It would appear that a very clever spell was placed inside your vodka. Your visions won't return for up to two weeks, but then they should be back."

Ebony looked relieved.

"I thought you'd be devastated that they were coming back."

She shook her head, her eyes glassy. "I know they cause me a lot of upset, but they are my legacy, my life. Without them I feel I am nothing."

I placed a hand on her arm. "I understand." Before we set off, I filled her in on recent events. "Frankie is going to try to investigate who this wizard could be who is supplying Hogsthorpe with these potions. If he can find what was used to block your visions, he's hopeful that he could maybe work out a diluted potion that can give you some relief, and not wreck your liver."

"That would be ideal," Ebony said.

"Anyway, I've come to take you home. Now we know your visions will come back in time there's no reason for you to stay any longer, and I presume Theo and Shelley will want to be alone when she returns. We don't want her taking a chunk out of you."

"I suppose..." Ebony sighed. "All good things must come to an end, hey, Mary, my darling?"

"Yes, love. I will miss you, but Lucy's correct. Right now, I need to focus on getting things shipshape for my son and daughter-in-law's return."

"I will go pack my things," Ebony said and left the room.

The minute she was gone Mary let out a massive sigh of relief. "Thank God. I thought she'd never go. Bloody pampered princess wanting me to cater to her every whim. It's a B&B, not a five-star hotel."

I laughed. "Mary, I'll leave you to get some rest. However." I stared at her. "If you are ever ready to leave and to go to Heaven and to your husband just let me know. I'm sure I can arrange it for you. Help you."

"Oh wow. Gosh, I'd be reunited with Edward, but then I'd miss seeing my grandbaby..." Mary looked agitated.

"Mary, you don't have to make a decision now, and I don't know for definite that I could help you. I just have a feeling inside that I would be able to. I agree, for now your place is here, to care for Theo and Shelley and to meet that grandchild when she comes."

Mary nodded, but then stepped back a little, as if it had just dawned on her I worked for Heaven. The place she was eventually destined for.

I dropped Ebony off home and then made my way home to Frankie. It was then I realised that Andrew hadn't been around... at all.

"I'll not be too offended that it took you so long to notice my presence was missing." He appeared behind me with his arms folded.

"Sorry, things have been a bit hectic." I shrugged.

"The reason I haven't been around is you no longer need me. My mission is accomplished, and I've been given my job. I'm back as an earth angel, but I'm off to work in Hull, so you'll not be seeing me around."

"Why do I no longer need you? What did I do?"

"Without too many spoilers, Seth will return home to Hull, where I shall keep an eye on him. Also, despite your feelings for Kim with regard to her spending time with your fiancé, you have put her needs above your own, and in doing so have done all you have the power to do with regards to keeping Shelley and the baby safe. In addition, you just offered to help a ghost move to Heaven if she wished. Your current jobs are done, and Sophia is giving you a sabbatical for now as there is much change coming to Withernsea."

"Really? I have time off? I can help Frankie with his project."

"You can also arrange your wedding."

I beamed. "I can, can't I?" I flung my arms around Andrew causing his wings to pop out. "Ooops." I laughed. "Thank you, Andrew. I'm so glad you finally passed your angel exams."

"Me too," he said and then he disappeared leaving only a feather in his wake.

Chapter 22

Shelley

Dear God. I would never moan about period pains again. Literally I wouldn't either because now I was part-vampire I wouldn't have any more.

The first pains had come from the flu-like symptoms associated with me getting accustomed to my new blood type. Then my body had adjusted itself, becoming stronger. The baby had been kept on foetal monitoring throughout with no concerns at first until my stomach had swollen. Panic filled me and I screamed for my mum and for Theo, only to find on ultrasound that my turning had accelerated my pregnancy. I was now the equivalent of eight months pregnant in human terms.

I think my husband was close to a nervous breakdown.

"But we still should have months to prepare. The B&B isn't operational. We have no nursery done yet. What about childbirth classes? Names? We are completely unprepared."

Yeah. I'd just become part-vampire, and he was worrying about childbirth. Meanwhile, I'd spent two days resisting the urge to try to drain him of all his blood.

It was Thursday morning, and I was being discharged. Theo had gone home just before dawn to get the house ready. I had checked with him that he meant to ensure I had clean bedding and not to start painting the nursery.

And yes, I was leaving in a morning. Being vampire mixed with wyvern and witch, had produced a handy side-effect. I could still go out in daylight, and we had found that I only needed a few hours sleep a day to reboot. I was super-charged. Food wise, I required blood and a human diet in a mix. My cravings had subsided. It was just my strength I needed to get used to now.

On that side my husband couldn't wait, saying we'd be able to go for it all night long.

When the baby came, he was going to have a huge shock.

"Okay. Have you got all your things?" Mum asked.

"Yes. Please take me home. I want my own bed, and then after I'm rested, I need to get caught up on the business and on anything else that's been happening in Withernsea."

While I'd been changing, everyone had left us alone. It had been strange, not being in the thick of Withernsea goings on.

"I wonder if Ebony has her visions back yet?"

"Let's get home and find out, shall we?"

Mum helped me pick up my belongings, and we left.

~

I let myself into the house, mum following behind me and was greeted with utter silence. No Mary, no Ebony. Nothing.

"Theo must have asked them to keep out of the way." I shrugged.

"Is there anything you need me to do while I'm here?" Mum asked.

"No. I'm just going to go straight to bed and set my alarm to get up with Theo, unless I wake earlier. I know I only need a minimum amount of sleep now, but my bed is warm, cosy, and has my husband in it."

"It's not cosy on his side, I'll bet."

"No, he's a tad on the cold side. Great in summer though." I'd remained the same temperature as before.

Mum kissed my cheek. "Right, you know where I am if you need me. I'll leave you to rest." She touched the bump. "Grandma's leaving, bye bump." My stomach lurched as the baby tried to move.

"It's getting tight in there now, isn't it bump?" I spoke to my belly, putting my hand on it.

Mum left and then I went to bed.

I managed to sleep until two in the afternoon. After lounging a little more, I got up, dressed, and went down into the kitchen to get a drink of O-neg. Mary appeared through the doorway.

"I wondered where you were," I said to her.

"Your friend wore me out, so I've been away resting."

"I know the feeling."

Mary's eyes went wide looking at my heavily pregnant stomach. "What has happened here? Is everything okay?"

"Everything's peachy. The turning brought my pregnancy on faster. I'm the equivalent of eight months now. Where's Ebony?" I asked.

"Lucy came and took her home. She said Ebony's visions were down to a potion in her vodka and that they would come back within two weeks and Frankie would try to find the wizard who made the potion for Hogsthorpe and see if he could make a dilute version for her."

"Oh that's good news. I'd better put my phone on and see what else I've missed. Or I could just ring Kim, that'd probably be quicker. She'll know everything." Then I paused. "Hang on, did you say potion for Hogsthorpe?"

"That's what Lucy said."

"On second thoughts I think I'll call Lucy first."

"I'll be making you a drink. Welcome home," Mary said and then she began busying herself with cups and bottles of blood.

∽

"Shelley! How are you? Did everything go okay?"

"It went fine. Thanks for sorting Ebony out. What's this about some potion for Hogsthorpe?"

"Ah, okay. Are you sitting down? There's a lot to tell you."

"I wasn't but hold on." I plonked myself on the sofa. "Spill."

"Let me say everything and then ask me questions or we'll be here all day."

"Lucy..."

"Fine. Seth has been putting love potions in people's coffees to get them to return to the coffee shop to see him. Just so he can keep his job there and keep an eye on Kim. He's been blackmailed by Jett to do so. Jett also arranged for Seth to place a different potion in Ebony's vodka so that she wouldn't see his plans."

"And his plans are...?"

"To marry Kim and to take over the Withernsea pack."

"Huh, I bet Kim laughed him out of the building."

"They're getting married tomorrow evening."

"Whaaat?"

"He threatened to publicise your pregnancy and place a bounty on you and the baby. She put you first."

"Oh my god."

"Anyway, Darius did not accept this plan. He's taken over as alpha of his pack and has a meeting with Jett tonight. It was basically a declaration of war and so this evening it is likely that either Jett or Darius may not survive."

"And what's the plan? What do we do?"

"The plan is that Darius and his pack go take down the Hogsthorpe pack."

I sat with my head in my hands. "And that's it? Does he not think Jett will no doubt have some spells or potions ready for this if he has a wizard in his pocket?"

There was silence at the other end.

"We'd not thought of that."

"Well, I'm thinking about it. What time is this meeting?"

"Nine pm."

"Right, I'll be there and so will Theo."

"No, Shelley. Kim would never forgive you, or me, if something happened to the baby."

"And I'd never forgive myself if something happened to Kim or Darius. Anyway, when you see me, you'll realise trying to keep my pregnancy secret is no longer an option. Now, I'm going to call Darius, then my mother. We need to get our battle plans together. How's my best friend doing?"

"Not good. She's in the office and staring at the walls a lot. Apparently, Jett has commanded that she move in with him. She spent last night in his room. He told her he wouldn't touch her until the mating, but she still was made to share his bed. He's told her she will be there tonight at the meeting."

"In order to show Darius she belongs to Jett. He no doubt intends to parade her like a trophy."

"It would appear so."

"Yes, well it's about time Jett found out who rules things around here and it's not some jumped up mutt from Hogsthorpe."

"It's good to have you back, Shelley."

"Well, I'd like to say it's good to be back but once again someone is causing shit around the place. Time to clean up."

We said our goodbyes with an agreement that we would meet up with Darius later.

Now it was time to talk to the man himself and get our battle plans drawn up.

Chapter 23

Kim

It was time. We were sitting in the middle of one of the warehouses on the industrial estate. The room was vast. There were seats in a circle in the centre and Jett had a larger seat at the top of the room with a smaller one for me at his side. Like we were King and Queen.

Jett's mother had been on holiday and had returned this morning. She'd taken me to one side to let me know that although I would be an alpha wife in name, she was the top woman of the pack, and I would need to learn my place. She wasn't impressed therefore at having been relegated to one of the circle seats for the meeting.

The Hogsthorpe pack walked in—every one of them—around twenty in total. They took seats at the left-hand side of the circle. A tall man joined them. He was dressed in a suit. There was a knock on the door and Jett shouted, "Enter."

In walked Darius and some of the Withernsea pack. I felt my heart might stop with shock.

But he didn't look at me. Not at all. His eyes were fixed on Jett's.

"Brother, so good to see you again," he said to Jett, and then he laughed. "I have brought some interested parties with me." He turned to look at the suited man. "I note you have the same, so I presume you have no objections?"

"Not at all," Jett replied.

"Come," commanded Darius.

In walked Lucy, Frankie, Theo, and Shelley. My eyes were almost out on stalks at seeing Shelley's pregnant belly. What the fuck? Had I been in a coma for a few months? Time travel? Had my dreams about flying around the world with David Tennant in the Tardis come true and then I'd been struck by a cruel form of amnesia?

I saw Jett's calm demeanour shake a little when he saw Shelley.

"Where is your alpha, brother? We cannot start the meeting without your pack's alpha present."

"Didn't you get the memo?" Darius smirked, taking a sheet of paper from his pocket and handing it to Jett. "I'm the alpha of the Withernsea pack now."

"You are?" I said loudly, forgetting myself.

"SILENCE," Jett roared.

Then all hell broke loose.

"DO NOT TELL MY MATE TO BE QUIET," Darius snarled.

"She is not your mate!"

I nodded at Darius behind Jett's back and mouthed, "I am."

One by one the pack turned into their wolves and then the suited man said an incantation and the Hogsthorpe wolves grew to twice their normal height and took on an eerie yellow glow.

Shelley rose. "Jett Conall, I command that you refrain from this course of action."

Jett looked at her. "Which would be great if we were on Withernsea turf, but we aren't. We're in Hogsthorpe, and you don't rule here."

Shelley looked shocked. The suited man smirked.

The wolves got up until one wolf flanked every one of the other pack, and each of my friends. I had a wolf from both packs appear either side of me and Jett stalked over to Darius.

We had no chance. I knew Shelley was a powerful witch and I could see her calculating moves, but how could she possibly do anything without the loss of life here? I just didn't see a way out.

There was a stalemate, and I knew that as they had made the protest it was down to Darius and his pack to make the first move, or withdraw and give in.

I watched as Darius bowed his head.

I wanted to cry. I wanted to yell for him to fight for me, but I knew to do so would be to put his pack and my friends at risk and I couldn't do that. But there was one thing I could do.

"Whether you win against Darius or not, I will not marry you. You might be the leader of Hogsthorpe but you are not the boss of me."

"Or me." A familiar voice came from the ceiling. As she dropped down, she changed into wolf form, and she landed directly on Jett's body. He had the room surrounded, but he'd not had the ceiling watched, and Alyssa had decided to join the party. I'd never seen a wolf like it. She was lithe, her muscles rippled, and her teeth when she roared were pincer sharp. Jett swung out with a claw knocking her to the floor and Darius roared, moving to his sister's side. I looked over at Shelley who smiled at me as her eyes turned blue. Then she lifted her hands and her blue webs wrapped around the suited man. He'd been so distracted by Alyssa that he'd dropped his guard. The minute Shelley wrapped him in her webs, the spell on the Hogsthorpe pack broke and they returned to their normal size. But where I expected Hogsthorpe to launch into an attack on Withernsea for attacking their alpha, they stood still and watched as Alyssa leaped back up from the ground and bit down on Jett's neck, tearing at his jugular. Blood spurted across the room and Jett's body slumped across the floor, remaining in wolf form. Red blood pooled around his black fur.

His mother let out a howl of anguish and then leapt for Alyssa, but she was no match either and succumbed to the same fate as her son.

There was silence and then Alyssa returned back into her human form. Blood dripped from her mouth.

One by one the wolves also returned to their human forms. Whoa. That was a whole lot of naked.

"And the lesson is don't threaten the family of a female wolf with pre-menstrual tension," Alyssa spat out.

"How the hell did you do that?" I asked.

Darius turned to me. "It would appear that while I thought my sister had been up to no good with teenage boys, she'd actually been training in an aerial circus appearing in town. She's been making pocket money appearing at eight pm every night."

He shook his head. "Sisters."

"Just got your ass out of trouble," she said, and then she turned to the other pack. "What's going on anyway? Why didn't you fight?"

One of the men, an older one, stepped forward. "Our alpha had become dangerous of late. Unpredictable. And it is not of our ways to war using magic. It is against the rules of the shifter handbook."

Darius spoke, though to be honest I was having trouble keeping my eyes on his mouth.

"You can elect a new leader now, or you can pledge allegiance and join Withernsea. It is up to you."

"May we have a few moments?"

"Of course."

They went over to one corner of the warehouse. I ran to Darius. He flung me around in his arms and I wrapped my legs around his waist. We kissed each other over and over. Then he put me down.

"What happens now? With Jett and his mother, I mean?"

"The Hogsthorpe pack shall bury their bodies somewhere undetectable."

"He would have killed you, wouldn't he?" I said.

"Yes. We are not like humans. In animal form sometimes we have to fight to the death. Jett would have had us all slaughtered."

I nodded as I knew he spoke the truth.

"I must go to see Shelley."

"And I need to talk to Alyssa and speak to the pack."

I walked away and went up to my best friend. Frankie was currently sat next to Mr Suited and Booted.

"Who's the dude?" I asked her.

"He's shy and doesn't want to give his name. He's being taken to the Caves where he'll be imprisoned until he wants to speak. I've disabled his powers, so he's no threat to anyone."

"How come you didn't detect the potions though? Does that mean his powers were stronger?"

"No. I believe mine were weaker. My pregnancy was taking it out of me, making my human body weaker. My wyvern and witch side were supporting my humanity and therefore weren't operating at one hundred percent efficiency. Now I've been turned and have no human part, I'm stronger than ever. And my mum was distracted that day. I was having a good old whine about life."

"You appear to be ready to give birth. I'm guessing that's due to the vamp mojo?"

"Indeed." Theo joined us. "And has thus given me quite the dilemma. It would appear the B&B shall be delayed once more as now all my attention needs to be given to the nursery and to organise things for our daughter seeing as she'll be making an appearance a lot sooner than we thought."

"Hey, what's happening?" Shelley looked over my shoulder.

The Hogsthorpe pack one by one stood in front of Darius, went to their knees, dipped their heads and murmured something. We moved closer to hear the words.

"I pledge my allegiance to the Withernsea pack and to you Alpha Darius…"

"I pledge…"

Every wolf there did the same and then Darius spoke to all of the assembled wolves.

"I thank you for your pledges. After speaking to my younger brother just now, I would like to note our future plans. I will happily rule you all until such time as my sister, Alyssa, becomes eighteen years of age. At which time, in the interests of modern times and with my pride at her courageous actions today, I shall offer the alpha position to her. The first time a woman will have been offered the post."

A joyous roar came from the rest of the pack which surprised me given how a lot of men still thought women belonged in the kitchen. Then again, she did still have blood stains around her mouth and had killed an alpha and his mother like swatting pesky flies, so I guess they might just be shit scared of arguing the point.

Alyssa's mouth dropped open. "Thanks, bro, but I'm planning on going away with the circus. No one else has an aerial artist who turns into a wolf by 'magic'."

"Please tell me you have not been revealing yourself."

"Calm down. I shall behave, but only until I'm eighteen, and then you'll just have to put up with it."

"Not as alpha, I won't."

"As a *brother*, you will."

"Okay, okay," I said stepping between them. "If all business is concluded then can we get out of here? I'd quite like to go home now."

"Could you kindly get us some robes, or spare clothes?" Darius asked one of the ex-Hogsthorpe shifters.

Once dressed he took my hand. "Come on, I'll take you back to your place."

I stared at him. "I said I wanted to go home, Darius."

His forehead bunched in confusion.

"To my future pack. To my future family. I belong with you, Darius, and I don't want to waste another minute."

Chapter 24

Kim

I looked at the quickly printed invitations. With the short notice I think I'd done an excellent job.

You are invited to the wedding of:

Kimberly Louise Fletcher and Darius Wild
Friday 9 February 2018
10pm
**The Main Hall
Withernsea Caravan Park**

A celebration party will take place straight after the ceremony.

Please be aware that guests at the wedding MAY see naked bodies during the celebrations due to wolf/human transition

It was so good when your boutique owning friend had contacts. Ebony had managed to get me the most beautiful dress. It wasn't a full proper wedding dress. A sleek dress with white lacy sleeves, it came to just below my knee and looked elegant. She'd curled my hair into ringlets and done my make-up.

I looked in the mirror. I looked happy. Something I'd not seen in my reflection in quite a while.

"Thank you, Ebony," I said.

"I told you so. Told you, you were meant for him."

"Yes, alright, Mrs Clever Clogs. You were right. There, I said it. Are you happy now?"

"Yes, darling, I just needed to hear you say the words."

Shelley was walking around whining. "Look at me. I'm a walking marquee." She'd had to be changed into a larger dress due to her ever-expanding stomach.

"Excuse me. Today is all about me," I reminded her.

She burst into a peal of laughter and clutched her tummy. "Oh, it is good to have my best friend back."

Freya stood in the doorway. "He's here. It's time to go."

I turned to her and smiled. My own mum wasn't here, but I didn't need her. I had Freya now.

∽

Frankie walked me down the aisle taking the place of my father. I'd thought about who could accompany me and had decided that Frankie was kind of my male best friend. He'd been honoured, and Lucy had looked really happy when she'd found out, although for some reason she thought I'd asked him ages ago.

And then I was at the front and everyone else faded from my attention. It was just me and Darius.

The registrar spoke. Before I knew it, he said the words I'd been waiting for.

"I now declare you alpha and wife."

And the celebrations began.

∽

At midnight, Darius and I walked down to the yurt together. The whole inner woodland had been decorated in fairy lights.

"Finally, I've got you alone," Darius said, his voice low and husky. Last night, his mum had insisted we sleep in separate beds and that he didn't see me today as it was bad luck. You'd think she'd have let tradition ride after we'd all just survived a pack war, but no.

"You have." I looked up at him. His eyes flashed his wolf look for a moment. Desire pooled low in my belly.

"Wife. I have needs and I command you come into this yurt and attend to them."

I bellowed with laughter. "If you're going to start talking to me like that, we'll be divorced before sunrise."

"Never," he growled. "You're my mate for life."

With that, he picked me up and carried me through the yurt's opening and put me on my feet next to the bed. He turned me so that my back was to him and he unzipped my dress. I let it shimmy to my feet and he picked it up and placed it over the back of a chair. I was now standing in front of him in my bridal undies. White, lacy, and oh... already off.

He in fact had peeled my thong off with his teeth, eliciting shivers down my spine. Goose bumps rose on my arms. He stood behind me, his erection against my ass and he cupped my breast in his hand.

"All mine," he said.

I turned around in his arms and cupped his pec.

"All mine," I repeated.

He threw me on the bed. "You leave me no choice but to shag this insolence out of you."

"Ooh if you insist," I replied, and then I couldn't speak anymore because his mouth was on mine.

He trailed his mouth down the side of my neck and all the way down to my thighs, and then he nestled between them and his mouth fastened on my core.

"Oh God," I screamed as his tongue flicked over my nub and then dove inside me. He drove me wild which was ironic given that was now my last name. I was Mrs Kimberly Wild. Oh. My. God. My name was Kim Wild—with the exception of a missing 'e' on my surname, I now sounded like a 1980's pop star. I felt like bursting into a chorus of 'You came' but given we were having sex right now I felt it might be a tad Freudian.

I exploded on his mouth. While I got my breath back, Darius moved up and over my body. "Babe, I saw stars. It was that good," I told him. He shook his head at me. "Kim, you can see stars. There's a space in the yurt roof, where the smoke from the fire exits."

"Oh yeah."

"But maybe I caused some extra ones," he said, lining himself up at my entrance.

"Are you ready to properly become my mate?" he asked.

"Yes." I nodded. "Now get inside me already."

He pushed deep, and I moaned in lust. He took his time

building us up to our climaxes and then just as I started to lose it, I felt the graze of sharpened teeth and he bit my neck.

"Oooooohhhhh."

We both came hard and then I felt a fizzing sensation throughout my body. I saw Darius change into his wolf, before my eyesight went blurry and then a weird rippling sensation took over. It wasn't painful; it was just very, very, strange.

My eyesight cleared, and I stared at my arm. It had fur, and I had claws. I was a wolf! My fur was dark brown. Was there a mirror here? Oh, yes, in the corner of the yurt. I padded over to it.

God, I even looked good as a wolf.

Yes, you do. My husband's voice echoed in my mind.

You can read my thoughts?

Yes, and you can read mine. You can control it, but yes, we can communicate in this way as pack.

HMMMM, can you read this thought?

The wolf bounded over and confirmed he could indeed.

After we'd made love in our wolf forms, we ran through the woods together. It was an amazing experience, so freeing. I didn't realise however that I'd run right up to the hall entrance where some guests including Frankie, Lucy, Shelley, and Theo, still stood. In my surprise I lost my wolf fur.

Yes, the bride stood in front of her guests in her birthday suit.

Lucy dived to cover Frankie's eyes.

"What are you doing, woman? It's nothing I haven't seen before."

"Yes, I'm well aware of the fact she's your ex."

"I meant as a physician, you daft bat."

Theo took off his suit jacket and walked over to me. "Here you go, Mrs Wild. We don't want you catching a chill."

Meanwhile my best friend stood there laughing. Pointing... and laughing.

"I laughed so much I weed myself." She giggled.

"Not wee, bestie," I told her. "Not wee."

Suddenly she wasn't laughing anymore.

Theo started shouting. "We need an ambulance. My wife's having a baby. Help please."

I left them to it as my mother-in-law took over.

I walked over to Frankie. "I have you covered. Walk into the centre of the woods, then yurt number one is free if you want it. It's just been readied for guests. I'll ask them to re-launder afterwards."

"Thank you. I need to do something, she's looking murderous."

Frankie spoke to Lucy and rolling her eyes at him she set off into the woods mumbling that he 'Would owe her big time for looking for rare insects'."

"What are you up to, Mrs Wild?"

"Come to the woods with me and see."

"We just got back from there."

"So?"

He followed me having been told to be extremely quiet. We watched from a distance as Frankie got down on bended knee in the woodland, surrounded by fairy lights. And then dozens upon dozens of white feathers fell from nowhere and covered the floor in a blanket of softness. It was beautiful.

Lucy nodded and said, "Yes," and he placed a ring on her finger.

I'd offered the yurt, but they clung to each other, kissed, and then walked back towards the party. I would bet they were going home.

"Well, it's just you and me again, and a yurt. What shall we do, hubby?" I asked.

Then a voice shouted out behind me.

"They're back. Kim, the voices are back."

I sighed. "Ebony, that's great and all, but you didn't need to rush to tell me."

"But you were in my vision..."

Oh no. What had she seen now? Was I about to cause an apocalypse?

Darius looked worried. "What did you see Ebony?"

"I saw a wedding dress. I was wearing it, and I was standing in a church. Kim was my bridesmaid."

"I thought you weren't supposed to see your own future?" I queried.

"That's just it, Kim. I could see I was getting married, but I couldn't see the groom! I don't even have a boyfriend, so who the hell am I marrying?" she screamed out.

"I don't know, but I do know who I just married, Chica, so you go get a vodka and I'll go get my man." I winked. "We'll sort it, Ebs."

Then I dragged my husband back into our yurt. It was time to get... WILD.

THE END

About Andie

Andie M. Long lives in Sheffield, UK, with her long-suffering partner, her son, and a gorgeous Whippet furbaby. She's addicted to coffee and Toblerone.

When not being partner, mother, or writer, she can usually be found wasting far too much time watching TikTok.

Andie's Reader Group on Facebook
www.facebook.com/groups/haloandhornshangout

TikTok and Instagram
@andieandangelbooks

Also by Andie M. Long

PARANORMAL ROMANCE BY ANDIE M. LONG

Supernatural Dating Agency

The Vampire wants a Wife

A Devil of a Date

Hate, Date, or Mate

Here for the Seer

Didn't Sea it Coming

Phwoar and Peace

Acting Cupid*

Cupid Fool*

Books one to six also on audio.

Series available in paperback.

Series bundles of books 1-3, and 4-6 available.

Acting Cupid and Cupid Fool were previously released as Cupid Inc, but have been extensively rewritten and now form part of Supernatural Dating Agency and...

the series will continue... in 2023.

The Paranormals

Hex Factor

Heavy Souls

We Wolf Rock You

Satyrday Night Fever

Also in paperback. Complete series ebook available.

Sucking Dead

Suck My Life – available on audio.

My Vampire Boyfriend Sucks

Sucking Hell

Suck it Up

Hot as Suck

Sip and Suck

Also available in paperback and bundle of books 1-3 available.

Filthy Rich Vampires – Reverse Harem

Royal Rebellion (Last Rites/First Rules duet) – Time Travel Young Adult Fantasy

Immortal Bite – Gothic romance